HUSBANDS AND MARRIAGE

"I believed in the power of love to eclipse any hardship life could deal out. I don't anymore." She stated the last part with such finality that deep foreboding filled him.

"Would you, ah, ever consider marrying again?"

A sudden smile lightened her features. "Are you proposing?"

"No, not me..." he hurried to say, then realized she was teasing him. "But perhaps someday, here on Blackfell, you might find marriage convenient—"

"Oh, that's right. I remember now. You and your older friend brought me here as a bride. You want me to marry someone. You're quite the matchmaker, aren't you? All this talk about husbands and marriage. Thinking about trying it out yourself?"

Her husky voice sounded soft to his ears. His gaze flicked to her full breasts before he even realized where he was looking. Quickly he glanced away and angrily berated himself for ogling his father's future wife. But then, a moment later, he suddenly found himself wondering what it would be like to take her to bed with him every night. God knew his bed was cold now. She would warm it up pretty damned quickly.

Portrait of a Bride

TRACY FOBES

LOVE SPELL NEW YORK CITY

For Raymond Stevenson, my grandfather.

A LOVE SPELL BOOK ®

January 2005

Published by

Dorchester Publishing Co., Inc.
200 Madison Avenue
New York, NY 10016

ISBN 0-505-52577-1

Visit us on the web at www.dorchesterpub.com.

Portrait of a Bride

Chapter One

A whisper of ultra-pure air flowed down from the ceiling to spread out across the laboratory. It swirled around Jordan before finding an outlet through the vents in the walls, its passage marked only by the whirring sound of the fans that had produced it. Her eyes burning, she blinked and shifted against the back of her chair as she stared at the monitor in front of her.

She'd been sitting here for at least twenty-four hours and her back felt every minute of it. The continuous flow of cold air had worked its way through her sterile gown and street clothes, making her shiver. Even her stomach, which had missed three meals in a row, grumbled in complaint. But the chill seeping through her bones and the hunger gnawing at her couldn't compare with the despair that had invaded her insides as she stared at the image presented by the electron microscope.

She narrowed her eyes and leaned closer toward the monitor, looking for some detail that she might have missed, some sign of improvement in the sperm's motility. A slide of tubules, sertoli cells and sperm with dubious stability, immature formation, and lackluster movement stared back at her. She swallowed, her gaze locked on the image. She could detect no difference between this sample and the one they'd taken prior to genetic splicing. As before, the sperm blundered around with a peculiar jerking motion. Essentially, it hadn't a snowball's chance in Hell of ever fertilizing an egg, despite the therapy she and Dr. Rinehart had labored over for weeks.

She had a pencil in her hand, poised on a pad and ready to record their success, but she didn't realize how hard she was pressing it against the paper until the tip broke off with a jarring *snap*.

Damn.

She threw the pencil away and stood abruptly. The concept behind their latest attempt at genetic manipulation had been her idea. She'd suggested it out of desperation, when all of Dr. Rinehart's efforts had failed. Dr. Rinehart had pursued her idea with enthusiasm, and all of their preliminary experimentation had shown such promise.

So why wasn't it working?

There *had* to be something she was missing. They needed much better results than this or they wouldn't receive approval for extending their grant. Another laboratory out in Michigan had already demonstrated a successful preclinical run at gene therapy for male infertility, and unless she and the rest of the team could demonstrate equal or better success very soon, the money would go elsewhere and the Rinehart Project would be shut down.

Her hand trembling, she chose different settings for the microscope and zeroed in on another portion of the specimen. Then she turned back to the monitor and stared.

Another uninspiring specimen slowly filled the screen.

Lower lip caught between her teeth, she looked for evidence that the method they'd used had failed them somehow . . . created some sort of toxicity, perhaps. She turned the knobs again and again, chose new settings. But each aspect of the specimen she'd prepared told the same story. They'd failed to produce any positive results at all.

Defeated, she took a few steps back from the microscope and gazed at it. An absurd impulse to beg came over her. Would the microscope respond to pleading and show her what she wanted to see? A smile that had nothing to do with humor twisted her lips before becoming a grimace.

Damn, damn. She was going to have to call Dr. Rinehart and give him the bad news.

Her heart sinking, she turned off the power switch to the microscope. It shut down with a dying hum that seemed both terrible and prophetic. They'd been working so hard on the Rinehart Project, and then that laboratory in Michigan had published findings similar to theirs. The other lab had begun to compete with the

Rinehart Project for the available funding, and now it seemed that they'd won the race to test infertility cures in clinical trials.

Frowning, she plopped down into the chair in front of her desk. Her gaze wandered to the metal stand directly to her left, the one holding the dyes used for cellular analysis. The desk lamp, now shining brightly over the disorganized mess that was her desk, also illuminated the glass beakers holding the dyes, making them glow like precious jewels. Red, silver, violet, magenta, yellow, green, blue—these were the colors she used to open a window on the processes behind health and sickness.

It all seemed so useless, so . . . irrelevant now.

A soft whoosh of air escaping into the gowning room drew her from her thoughts. When she looked up to see who had opened the door, her throat tightened. Dr. Rinehart, his eyes bloodshot, strode into the room. He held a digital camera in one hand. She could see square impressions on his left cheek, as though he'd just woken up from sleeping on a checkered-knit blanket. He must have rushed down here as soon as he'd gotten out of bed.

She pushed back her chair and stood, dreading what she had to tell him. Having to relay the bad news in person was much harder than a simple phone call. She gripped the back of the chair and swallowed.

"You didn't sleep," she murmured as he reached her side.

"Sleep? How could I sleep?" He shrugged. "I managed about five hours before I gave in and came back to celebrate. Here's to success! Give me a smile."

4

Without warning, he took a picture of her with his digital camera.

The flash momentarily blinded her. She blinked and cast around for an easy way to tell him to put the camera away, that the technique she'd developed was just as much a failure as all of their other attempts.

Dr. Rinehart's brown eyes became penetrating. "So, where is your smile?"

Like a fish caught on a hook, she returned his gaze, seeing the purplish shadows beneath his eyes and the shadow of a beard on his cheeks. He looked so tired, so beaten. Unable to answer him, she motioned him toward the electron microscope.

"Oh, lord." He rubbed his eyes and put the camera on her desk, then moved toward the microscope, which she turned on with a snap of the power switch. "The sperm didn't improve as much as we'd thought they would, did they?"

She shook her head. "No, they didn't."

"How bad is it?"

Rather than answer, she stared at the microscope's monitor and waited for the image to assemble itself. The seconds ticked by, each one seeming to last an hour. But the image had formed only partially when Dr. Rinehart cursed beneath his breath and looked away. "My God. They haven't improved at all."

"Not that I can see," Jordan confirmed, her voice trembling. She braced herself for a major show of temper. Lately, Jordan had been seeing a lot of his temper as each of their various attempts failed.

He turned and sat heavily in her desk chair. "They

didn't improve. Why not? What did we do wrong?" His voice rose on the last syllable when, suddenly, he slammed his fist down on the desk. "There must have been something wrong with the transfer method. Did you check for toxicity?"

She nodded miserably.

"Are you sure?"

"I checked, Dr. Rinehart."

"We need to try a different transfer method," he said, his voice almost feverish with intensity. "What about a lentivirus?"

"Last month . . . we tried a lentivirus," she reminded him hesitantly.

"Did we?" His face had become ashen. "There are nonviral methods of transfer. Naked DNA, liposomes, molecular conjugates . . ."

Jordan said nothing. He was really reaching now. These methods were unproven and, by their very nature, had little chance of success. Still, he was desperate. And she understood desperation very well.

He glared at her. "All of this expensive equipment, all of the time we've spent, all of the ideas, the effort . . . and we're going to allow ourselves to be upstaged by some lab out in Podunk, Michigan?"

Mute, she looked at the rubber-tiled floor.

"Damn it, it just isn't fair," he barked, standing so abruptly that he sent the chair crashing against one leg of the staining station. The shelf that held the beakers of stain, propelled by the table's jostling, surged backward and dumped its jewel-like contents onto the floor.

The sound of the beakers breaking rang out like a gunshot.

Shocked, she stared at the liquid spreading out across the tiles. Rivulets of blue, yellow, red, green, violet, and silver ran together to form one big puddle of dirty gray.

"I'm sorry, Jordan." Shoulders slumped, Dr. Rinehart toed the larger pieces of glass toward the center of the mess.

Jordan passed a shaky hand across her brow. "You're right. We need to try another transfer method. Molecular conjugates might work—"

"But we don't have the time, do we?" Quiet surrender muted his voice. "The lab in Michigan has beaten us to the punch. We might as well accept it."

"There are other projects. Other ways to combat infertility. We can try something else, some new technique. I know you can win more grant money. A man with your stature can't help but do so."

"The Rinehart Center is going to have to close," he went on, as if he hadn't heard her. "A government consultant visited here a few days ago. He asked me to join a project team studying specialized viruses. I could re-hire you as my assistant once I'm there, Jordan."

She stared at him in shock. "Specialized viruses? Do you mean biological weapons?"

"He didn't say. What difference does it make?"

"It makes a lot of difference. Do you want to help people or hurt them?" Panic made her voice shaky. "Please, Dr. Rinehart, don't give up the fight on infertility."

He looked at her for a moment with an expression very close to annoyance. "You have a habit of seeing everything in a positive light, Jordan. You wear the proverbial rose-colored glasses and refuse to see the truth. Sometimes I think you wouldn't recognize misfortune even if it bit you on the ass. There comes a time when you have to admit you've failed, otherwise you're going to keep spinning your wheels and going nowhere . . . forever."

Jordan frowned. This assessment hurt deeply. Hadn't her ex-husband said the same damned thing to her, after putting up with two years of unsuccessful attempts at in vitro fertilization? Acknowledging such a major failure for the second time in her life was just too much to bear.

He seemed to sense her pain, for suddenly he was patting her on the arm. "Ah, Jordan, I think I may be apologizing to you all night. I'm sorry. God knows you have a reason to be so stubborn." Like a broken man, he shuffled away from the shattered glass and moved toward the door. "I'm going to go home now and sleep."

Fighting the feeling that she had nothing left inside that anyone would want, she nodded. "I think I'll do the same." Then, silently, she watched him go.

Once the door had closed behind him, she began to clean up the mess on the floor. Her chest felt tight with grief. Tears pricked at the back of her eyes and she knew she was in danger of losing it completely. Sleep, she decided, was the best thing for her. She couldn't discount the possibility that the situation might appear better after a nap.

Her gut, however, told her otherwise.

Chapter Two

The Province of Blackfell

From the road, the Patriarchal Manor House was invisible. Hidden by tall grass, which the manor house gardeners had woven together to form a hedge, it blended into the landscape as though it had arisen from the ground rather than having been built by imperial craftsmen. Even the road leading to the manor, made of stones embedded in moss, seemed a haphazard creation of nature instead of a deliberate path. But Conlean, a descendant of the Royal House of Arador, didn't need to see the manor house to know intimately of its existence. He'd spent most of his youth there and, as he knocked softly on the panel leading to the Receiving Pavilion, he knew that no other building in the province so accurately reflected his father's love of tradition and reverence for nature.

The shadow of a figure on the other side of the partition danced briefly on its opalescent surface before the panel slid to one side and the dignified countenance of his father's most trusted retainer presented itself.

"Hello, Willmen. I'm here to see the Patriarch."

Willmen inclined his head, the points of his starched white collar high against his throat. Over his shirt, he wore a flowing navy blue sash, while loose-fitting navy pants tied at the waist with a bright red sash concealed his spindly legs. This, of course, was the uniform of all the patriarchal servants, but on Willmen it didn't look like a uniform at all. Rather, it gave him the aspect of a man who had grown used to giving orders and having them obeyed. "Please come in, Son of Arador . . . that is, Artisan Conlean. He'll receive you in the garden viewing room."

Conlean smiled slightly, amused by Willmen's calling him Son of Arador. He used to be one of the extended royal house before the Guild of Artisans had discovered his talents and drafted him into their service.

Willmen moved aside, allowing Conlean to enter the manor house. His soft leather boots soundless on the woven mat flooring, Conlean walked through the Receiving Pavilion, a room without walls and empty but for a few chairs. Ahead, the garden viewing room opened to an inspired view that the artisan in him couldn't help admiring.

The sun, which had come up several hours before, had heated up the surrounding woodlands. In the distance, through a stand of trees whose leaves hung limply in the gathering warmth, a hot mineral spring of aqua blue water gurgled pleasantly, drawing the attention of a dragonfly whose iridescent wings glittered in

the sunlight. As he walked into the viewing room, Conlean glanced toward the imperial pond and saw a
woman in a silken gown skimming pine needles from
its surface.

Troubled by the sight of her, he frowned.

For as long as anyone could remember, Blackfell
had been in one hell of a bind. A plague had swept
through the land in ancient times and rendered most
women incapable of conceiving a female child. The
birth of a girl became an extremely rare event, and
eventually the population had dwindled to nearly nothing. If it hadn't been for the discovery of Nicholas
Flamel's diary and his cache of Prima Materia, which
led to the ability to retrieve women from the past to
Blackfell, mankind would have long since died out.

Unfortunately, though, the women they retrieved had
no more luck at bearing females than their own
women, because as soon as they arrived, they contracted the same ancient and incurable plague. And so,
artisans had to keep painting portraits of brides and retrieving them from the past.

Women, in fact, had become Blackfell's most valu-
able commodity. Far too precious to perform menial
tasks, they became wives with numerous servants to
see to their needs. Only men with influence and wealth
could afford a wife and family, though occasionally the
patriarchy awarded women to those who accomplished
some great deed. And those men who weren't rich and
powerful simply had to strive for a notable achieve-
ment and hope they won a bride, or accept the fact that
they'd never know the love of their own children.

Conlean knew that resentment was growing among

the men who hadn't the means to afford a family, like a festering wound that couldn't be healed. He wondered how much more time they had before the wound destroyed Blackfell utterly.

Worry weighing heavily on him as it seemed to do so often now, he glanced around, looking for his father. The groupings of chairs were empty, and so he gave himself over to memories of the years he'd lived here. He'd climbed those trees in the garden, and he'd swum in that spring, making a muddle of the imperial gardeners' artistry and enjoying every minute of it. He'd gone exploring overnight, sending the household into an uproar and bringing on day-long lectures from the Patriarch about his wildness and lack of discipline. There wasn't a single place in the manor house that he hadn't explored, or a single square of ground that he hadn't trod, and he'd surveyed his land with the cool confidence of a boy who knew that someday the estate would be his.

But then, by chance, he'd sketched a portrait of a woman, and his fate had been sealed like the other youths who displayed similar abilities. At the age of twelve he'd gone to live inside the cold stone walls of the Gallery and had learned how to enhance his artistic talent with both meditation and alchemy. His father had fiercely resented the idea that he was going to lose his only son and heir to a community of long-haired, grouchy men with paints and brushes, but despite his exalted status, he'd had no more choice in the matter than Conlean. The law stated that those who displayed artistic talent had to live and train at the Gallery.

"Hello, son."

The masculine voice, once so deep and rich but now sounding weary, broke into Conlean's thoughts. He schooled his face back into a smile and faced the Patriarch of the Royal House of Arador: Blackfell's sovereign ruler. "How have you been, Father?"

"I'm feeling old. Sit down, Conlean," the older man said with a wave toward one of the chairs, a petulant quality entering his voice. He sat in a chair himself and regarded Conlean with tired eyes. "There's no need for us to be standing about as though we were attending an imperial function."

With a sleek flash of white fur, Baudrons chose that moment to jump into the room through an open panel. She skulked across the floor before settling down on a cushion that matched her amber eyes exactly. Conlean barely hid a smile. Baudrons had always had a flair for drama. Evidently she'd followed him from the Gallery. He hadn't noticed her, though. She also had a gift for stealth.

"Hello, Baudrons," the Patriarch said to the cat. "I see you're doing well."

Baudrons didn't bother to look at the older man. Rather, she licked her white fur with languid motions. Conlean didn't think she liked his father all that much, judging by the distance she kept between herself and the older man. He wished the cat could tell him why.

Conlean seated himself as the Patriarch had indicated and took a moment to study his father. The older man wore a rich burgundy robe edged in gold that seemed to accentuate the sallowness of his skin and the blue circles beneath his eyes, circles Conlean didn't remember from his last visit. He glanced at his father's

13

hands and saw a slight tremor shake them, and noticed that his hair had gone almost completely white. The Patriarch, Conlean decided, suddenly looked every one of his sixty-odd years. A rush of affection for the old man surprised him with its intensity. "You look like you need a few days off."

The Patriarch sighed. "Believe me, Conlean, if I knew of a place to hide, one where my advisers couldn't find me, I'd take more than a few days off. Unfortunately, there doesn't seem to be such a place."

Conlean shook his head. "Come to the Gallery. I'll hide you in my closet."

"The Gallery? Hmmph. The Gallery swallowed up my only son. I'd sooner go to Hades than step within its walls."

"The Gallery isn't so terrible," Conlean replied. "The food is good. And we both know it's my duty to live as an artisan."

For nearly fifteen years now, he'd studied artistry. His special talent allowed him to take likenesses of women from the past and reproduce them on canvas. Through the use of Prima Materia and meditation, he turned the canvases into time-dimensional portals to the past, which he then traveled through to retrieve the desired brides. All in all, he took great pride in his portraits and took every retrieval from the past very seriously. He knew that without his work and the work of others like him, Blackfell would become a barren world with no hope of survival.

And yet, he knew that for every woman he delivered to some rich and powerful patron, he alienated another man who desperately wanted his own family but couldn't afford one. Ironically enough, the more troubled he became, the more passionately he painted, and now he was one of the most prolific artisans in the Gallery.

"Don't talk to me about duty. I've lost far too much in the service of it." His father rolled his shoulders, as though squaring off for battle. "How are you, Conlean? Are you happy?"

"Of course I'm happy. I love what I do," Conlean said quickly, though he knew that wasn't quite true. He did love what he did, but it wasn't making him happy. He'd been lonely most of his life and, lately, that loneliness had become a void in him, one that bothered him like a rotten tooth. Without meaning to, he glanced at Baudrons. The cat had a knack for sensing emotions, and he wondered if she knew how torn he felt about artistry. Baudrons gazed back, the expression in her eyes inscrutable.

"I've been learning a new technique from Grand Artisan Hawkwood," he offered, turning back to his father. For the next several moments, he described the latest techniques he'd been studying under the Grand Artisan. But when his father's attention wandered to the portrait that hung on the wall behind Conlean, he slowed; he stopped altogether when the Patriarch's eyes grew moist and unfocused. Following the direction of his father's gaze, he turned and studied an exquisite portrait of a woman.

Carefully balanced and structured, the composition depicted her sitting on a velvet-upholstered settee. Her sitting room, which formed the background, was sketchy and simple, with loosely brushed strokes of garnet, giving the impression of luxury. At the center of the portrait, the woman's intense amber eyes regarded the viewer with something close to amusement, and her soft blond hairstyle rose in beribboned splendor above her eyes.

This portrait was one of the few existing in Blackfell that hadn't been used to retrieve a bride. It hadn't been necessary to retrieve this woman, because she was one of the very few born naturally into the world. His mother, he mused, had been an extraordinary woman.

Eyes narrowed, Conlean studied his mother more closely and swallowed against the grief he still felt at the memory of her disappearance some five years before, grief that had gathered like a knot in his throat. The artist had used pastel colors he'd mixed directly on the canvas with loose, sketchy brushstrokes. Her face was blurry, the edges soft where the painter had blended the colors of her features with the velvet behind her, and the painting had not the slightest hint of darkness. She'd been that way, too, laughing at boyish antics and untouched by dishonorable thoughts.

The Patriarch cleared his throat. "She was so beautiful. Every morning when I wake up, I expect to see her by my side."

Conlean had no reply to offer. He knew well how much his father missed his first wife. The care that he took with Marni's portrait—the regular touch-ups he ordered—were ample evidence of his devotion.

After a time, Conlean murmured, "Have you heard anything?"

"Nothing. Nothing at all."

Conlean frowned. His mother's disappearance had

shocked them all. No bigger scandal had ever rocked Blackfell. At first they'd hoped that she'd been abducted, and that her kidnappers would demand a ransom. When that demand never arrived, however, they began to think the worst. Now, everyone was certain that she'd been the victim of a fatal attack. But he kept hoping against hope that someday she would come home and tell them what an amazing adventure she'd had.

"She's the reason you're here today, son," his father continued. "Five years now she's been gone, and since the Gallery has its claws into you, I'm going to need another heir. Soon, because I'm feeling terribly old."

Conlean frowned. Sooner or later, he'd known that his father would need to replace his absent mother, and he'd been dreading this moment. Could his father even sire a new heir at his age? He walked to the edge of the viewing room and stared out at the garden, trying to swallow his dismay.

Stepping stones offered an uneven pathway around the pond; fish created orange and yellow shadows as they darted beneath the ripples; and a showy display of purple flowers drew the attention to the opposite shore. A wooden boat rocked gently on its surface and white blossoms on a nearby grove tree perfumed the air with a spicy fragrance. Even the birds singing in the treetops added to the experience.

Everything seemed quite natural. Conlean, though, detected the artifice throughout the design, having studied under the imperial gardeners for some time. He knew that the boat had been placed there deliberately, that the woman was collecting pine needles in order to create ripples to rock the boat, and the birds were tame and had been trained to sing those particular melodies. And while he acknowledged the beauty of the garden and the mastery of the imperial gardeners, a sense of doomed artificial harmony ruined the scene for him.

Swallowing, Conlean turned back toward his father. "So you think she's dead?"

His father looked away. "I don't know. I pray she isn't. But I can't wait any longer for her. The stability of Blackfell depends on my producing an heir to take over the Patriarchy once I'm gone."

"Why am I here, then? You know I can't leave the Gallery."

"I want you to paint a new bride for me."

Conlean stiffened. He stared at his father. "Me? I'm simply an artisan. You need a grand artisan. Hawk-wood is your man."

"I need *you,* Conlean. No one paints faster or with more accuracy than you. What you can do in a week, other artisans need years, and I don't have years, son. I want you to retrieve my next bride."

A beat of silence passed between them, during which Conlean's gut twisted with betrayal. He'd be damned if he'd be the one to replace his mother with someone else. He abruptly rose from his chair to face his father head-on. "I won't do it."

"You're the only one who *can* do it. Don't you see, Conlean? Marni was well loved by everyone. They'll find her replacement unsettling. But if *you* retrieve my new bride, people will know that you accept the necessity of my having an heir. How can they do any less?"

"You think they'll find her replacement unsettling? I think envy is a better word for the way people will feel.

Not many men get two chances at a family," Conlean told him, his voice low. "Regardless, I'm not sure I *want* to do it."

"Conlean, son, please think about it before you say no. I must have an heir, and I will have a bride painted. You must see the advantages of your accepting my commission. I hope you'll do your duty by your family and by Blackfell, and retrieve my new bride as I've requested."

Conlean turned away from his father's needy stare and walked toward the door leading to the Receiving Pavilion. "I have to go. Thank you for inviting me to visit."

"Will you at least consider what I've asked?"

His father's request churned in his gut like acid. And yet, he couldn't deny the legitimacy of that request. Hating himself and yet feeling bound by duty, he muttered, "I'll consider it."

Baudrons stood abruptly and stretched, as though the conversation no longer held her interest. Without a single backward look, she climbed off the cushion, walked across the room, and jumped through the open panel into the gardens beyond.

Chapter Three

Conlean pressed his hands against the small of his back and leaned backward in an effort to get the kinks out. He'd been working in the studio for almost forty-eight hours now without rest, preparing the paints for his father's commissioned bride. And yet, though he craved a few hours' sleep, he stayed nevertheless, because the work that went into preparing the paints for the portrait was even more important and required more skill than the painting itself.

He glanced around to make certain everything was as it should be. All of the lanterns, he saw, had ample supplies of oil and were still burning brightly from their posts on the walls, and the smoke that billowed up from the furnace and hovered near the ceiling nearly smothered the room with the stench of metal newly transmuted. The canvas, which he'd already washed with a preliminary coating of Prima Materia, stood bright white and ready for the portrait he planned to paint. Nodding with satisfaction, he walked over to the furnace and checked inside the crucible that hung suspended from metal supports atop the furnace.

Jet black fluid—Prima Materia in a liquid state mixed with metals—boiled sullenly inside the pot. He surveyed the material with both reverence and uneasiness. The artisans at the Gallery had already used up more than half the Prima Materia in their storerooms and, though it wasn't likely to happen in his lifetime, they would eventually run out of the substance . . . if the men who weren't fortunate enough to have families of their own didn't steal it or destroy it first. A team of the most talented alchemists was studying the recipe for Prima Materia, as given by Nicholas Flamel, but so far they hadn't managed to reproduce it. And yet, no one seemed terribly worried about the possibility of using up Blackfell's reserves of Prima Materia.

No one, it seemed, except him.

He glanced at his copy of Nicholas Flamel's journal, *The Fundamentals of the Grand Artisan.* Flamel, a painter and alchemist, had lived many thousands of years in the past. The ancient alchemist's journal had become the basis for Blackfell's society, and his Prima Materia had saved them all from ruin. He'd been the first and only person to create Prima Materia, and had found many uses for it, the least of which was turning ordinary metal into gold. Apparently he'd become a target for the greediest and most influential rulers in his time, and had gone into hiding to save himself.

Before his death, Flamel had buried his journal along with a cache of Prima Materia. When the plague had taken hold, and no stone had been left unturned in an effort to ensure the human race's survival, a scholar had discovered both the journal and the mysterious substance. The scholar experimented with them and eventually stumbled upon Prima Materia's strange properties, including its ability to bend time and space. From that time on, the men of Blackfell and the other kingdoms dotting the globe had been clinging to life, retrieving brides from the past to bear sons in the present.

"What do you think?" he said to the cat, who sprawled on her customary chair. "Is this batch of tincture a good one?" Sometimes, if he made a bad batch, the portal didn't open; the result was days of wasted time.

Baudrons stretched and purred. Conlean took that as a *yes*.

Nodding with satisfaction, he moved to his worktable and examined the other ongoing processes. The tincture he'd collected earlier and mixed with oil now bubbled in a glass alembic, its more volatile constituents evaporating and collecting in the spout. A greenish-blue residue coated the bottom of the container, and he noted that the color was just as he'd hoped. He'd already finished with all of the other colors he'd need; this aquamarine was the last one. Now he just had to combine the appropriate amounts of tint with the Prima Materia mixture, and then he could fetch the likeness of the woman he was to paint. Since the woman his father had chosen lived in the twentieth century, he'd be using a photograph as a likeness, which was much more accurate and easier to work with than the paintings he used for women who'd lived before the camera was invented.

With this in mind, he began to clean the mortar and pestle, which he would use to grind the residue produced by the alembic. He made a mental note to adjust the scale so it would perfectly weigh the Prima Materia mix before he added it to the tint.

Grand Artisan Hawkwood chose just that moment to come into the studio. "Good evening, Conlean, Baudrons," he murmured, walking over to the furnace to stare at the jet black substance bubbling away in the crucible.

"Grand Artisan Hawkwood," Conlean acknowledged, nodding pleasantly, though inside he wished that the Grand Artisan had chosen another time to visit. He needed to focus on the creation of the paints. He hoped the other man had simply come to observe rather than to gabble.

"I see you're deep into the preparations for your next portrait. It's for your father, I understand."

Conlean laid down the rag he'd been using to clean the mortar and resigned himself to some gabbling. "The Patriarch has commissioned me to paint him a new wife."

"So I've heard. You agreed without reservation?"

"Of course not. This commission bothered me on several levels."

"But you accepted it anyway." Lips pressed together, the Grand Artisan studied Conlean. Tall and spare, with a gaunt face and long white hair held back with a black ribbon, he appeared very imposing to the uninitiated. Even the artisan's icon etched on his cheek seemed to glow with authority. But Conlean knew that Hawkwood had a soft heart and a fondness for cookies; more than once Conlean had come to his quarters for advice on some issue or another, only to discover the Grand Artisan wearing bakers' mitts and holding a wooden spoon coated with batter.

"I did accept it, despite my worries," Conlean admitted. "I thought about it for a long time. I wondered how I could replace my own mother. She *can't* be replaced, though my father doesn't seem to see that. He gave me several reasons why he'd chosen me to retrieve his new bride. It's my duty, he said, both to him and to the citizens of Blackfell."

Grand Artisan Hawkwood raised an eyebrow. "So you're doing your duty by painting the portrait and retrieving the bride?"

He nodded reluctantly. "I'm my father's first-born son. I would have been his heir had I not come to study and live at the Gallery. Although it galls me, I've agreed to do this one thing for him, because there are so many things I should be doing for him but can't."

"Because you're an artisan."

"That's right. Since I left to live at the Gallery, he's asked nothing of me until now. How can I deny him this one request?"

Grand Artisan Hawkwood moved away from the crucible of bubbling Prima Materia and wandered over to the shelf where Conlean stored his jars of tint. With his back to Conlean, he studied each of the colors as he said, "You're right. You can't deny him. And I admire you for your integrity and loyalty to your father."

"It's my lack of loyalty toward my mother that bothers me," Conlean admitted. "I'll have no problem retrieving a new bride for my father, but how will that affect my mother? She'll have nothing to return to. If she returns."

Hawkwood swung around to stare at Conlean, a thoughtful look in his eyes. "What if I were to tell you that both your mother and I insist that you retrieve a bride for your father?"

Conlean stilled. "What does my mother have to do with this?"

His attitude one of studied nonchalance, the grand artisan withdrew a folded, crumbling piece of paper from his pocket and handed it to Conlean. "Study this photograph."

Confused, Conlean accepted the photograph. It felt dry and ancient, similar to the other photos he'd used for retrievals. Baudrons went from sprawling to sitting, as though she, too, was interested in looking at it. He moved closer to Baudron's chair, so she might see it if she chose to.

Having retrieved other brides from this time period, he recognized the style of the woman's dress and the furniture behind her, and knew the photograph had been taken early in the twenty-first century. The woman was staring into the camera with a candid, open expression. He studied the caption below the photo and understood he was looking at a page from a book that had been written just before the plague had appeared.

"She is beautiful, no?" the older man pressed.

"This is a page from one of the ancient books," Conlean stated. "Did a seeker leave it for us in the vault?"

"A seeker did indeed retrieve this picture for me."

"Which seeker?" Conlean's confusion grew. Hawkwood was refusing to meet his gaze. He began to think that the older man was withholding information from him.

"This Seeker hasn't been sanctioned by the Guild of Artisans."

Shocked, Conlean stared at the older man. "A rogue Seeker? Are you joking?"

"No, I'm not."

"Good God."

Seekers were men and women with artistic talent who traveled through a portrait and then stayed in the past to find women who might be interested in becoming brides to the men of Blackfell. When the Seeker found a likely candidate, he or she placed a likeness—either a photograph or a painting—of the bride in a specialized vault. Thousands of years later, artisans retrieved those same photographs from the vault, painted portals, and then retrieved the brides themselves.

All of the seekers had to be trained and sanctioned by the Guild of Artisans before going into the past. And once they went into the past, they couldn't return. The portal they painted only remained open for a specific period of time and, once closed, it remained closed forever. Therefore every seeker was revered for his or her sacrifice and their names were well known among all. Conlean had never heard of a rogue Seeker before. But he had heard of the punishment for those who went into the past without the guild's consent: execution.

For all involved.

Conlean looked warily at the older man. "I don't know what you've gotten yourself into, but I have a feeling you're going to tell me all about it, and I don't think I'm going to like it."

"Just look at the photograph."

His pulse beating harder, Conlean stepped away from the Grand Artisan and examined the paper more closely. He noted the perfect ratios between her lips and nose, her eyes and forehead, and indeed in the entire shape of her face.

She *was* beautiful, in a primitive way, with unbound hair curling softly around her shoulders and chunky metal decorations dangling from her ears. And yet, there were enough incongruities in her features—freckles and dimples and a somewhat lopsided smile—to give her character. He tried to picture in his mind what this woman's life had been like, living so very long ago, before the plague had come. Had she given birth to a female child?

"Read the biography on the back of the photograph," Hawkwood urged.

Conlean flipped the photograph over. The rogue Seeker had indeed written a biography. The handwriting looked strangely familiar. A fresh wave of uneasiness stirring in his gut, he skimmed through the biography. The words *And Baby Makes Three: Fertility and Gene Therapy* jumped out at him. "This seems to be describing a scholarly treatise of some sort."

The Grand Artisan steepled his fingers. "It's a description of a book that details the mechanisms behind the plague."

"The plague?" Conlean dropped the photograph as though it had burned him. "The woman in the photograph . . ."

"Has intimate knowledge of the plague," Hawkwood finished for him, retrieving the photograph from the floor. "My Seeker informed me that she had been researching infertility and viruses, and that the use of her research by others created the plague."

Both men grew silent. Conlean understood instantly the significance of finding a woman who had knowledge of the plague. If she understood how it worked, she might be able to cure it. And if they could bring her to Blackfell, and she managed to cure the plague, they wouldn't have to worry any more about retrieving brides. All men would be able to have families of their own.

At the same time, he knew the system that had evolved around retrieval of brides pervaded every aspect of Blackfell's existence. It had become so rewarding that those in power would never willingly relinquish it. He suspected that their entire society would collapse if Prima Materia and brides were no longer precious commodities.

Conlean measured the older man with a stare. They were skirting the idea of revolution, treason against the Patriarchy. And though Conlean understood the foibles of the current system, the Patriarch was his *father*. "You want to bring her here, don't you? So she can try to cure the plague."

Hawkwood wandered over to the furnace and glanced at the crucible. "That is my hope."

A beat of silence passed between them, during which Conlean tried to get his mind around the fact that Hawkwood, one of the most revered and respected members of the Guild of Artisans, was plotting to bring about an end to the bride retrieval system forever.

"But you can't just smuggle her into the present from

the past," Conlean finally said. "Everyone in the Guild of Artisans is aware of a retrieval when it takes place. The time displacement wave can be felt for leagues."

"That's right. Obviously I need to bring her here under a legitimate guise."

A legitimate guise . . . Conlean took a deep breath and let it out slowly. He suspected what Hawkwood wanted, and yet he couldn't believe the older man would have the nerve to suggest it. "You want me to retrieve this woman as my father's bride."

"It's the only way to bring her to Blackfell without arousing suspicion."

"Good God, Hawkwood!" Conlean strode away, muttered a few oaths, and then turned to face the grand artisan again. "You're suggesting treason! Treason is punishable by death. And you're demanding I betray my own father!"

"I'm not in this alone, Conlean," Hawkwood said.

"What do you mean?"

"Your mother, Marni, is my Seeker. She deliberately went into the past, knowing she could never come back, just to find this woman."

Conlean felt his gut tighten. He couldn't believe his ears. "No. My mother would never do that. She loved my father too much."

"She loves you and your father both, but she also knows that if we don't find a cure for the plague, humankind will die out, just as the dinosaurs became extinct."

"She was *kidnapped*," Conlean insisted, although in his gut, he knew that the handwriting on the back of the photograph Hawkwood had shown him was Marni's.

He'd recognized it on some visceral level. The Grand Artisan wasn't spinning a wild tale. He was speaking the truth.

Hawkwood looked at him with sympathy. "She took no pleasure in pretending to be kidnapped so she could secretly go into the past. She knew how much she would hurt both you and your father. And she knew how much she'd miss you both. Still, she was successful in her mission. She found the woman we need. Now it's up to us to retrieve this woman to Blackfell."

Conlean sat heavily in the nearest chair. A storm of emotion whirled through him—disbelief, elation, confusion—but most of all anger. The tumult made him dizzy. He barely noticed Baudrons jump to the floor and brush against his legs.

Steeling himself with the arms of his chair, he asked, "If she went into the past, then she learned the skills of an artisan. Who taught her?"

"She discovered her artistic skill by accident and came to me. That was five years ago. Together we decided we could put her skill to use, and I helped her learn how to pass through a portal."

"How did she pass through the portal without alerting the Guild of Artisans? You know that the time displacement wave can be felt by every artisan during a retrieval."

"Do you remember that accident I had in my laboratory five years ago? When my experiment with Prima Materia accidentally created a time displacement wave? That was no accident. That was your mother going into the past."

"And the Gallery didn't question it because you're

one of its most trusted and revered members," Conlean added bitterly.

"I'm not proud of betraying the people who trust me. But I felt that I had no choice. Our supply of Prima Materia is dwindling and we can't manage to manufacture any more. Blackfell teeters on the edge of total extinction. We had to find someone to help us."

Conlean fought down the pain of knowing that he'd never see his mother again. He thought of all those years of wondering what had happened to her and wanted to slam his fist into a wall. "Why didn't she contact me, just to let me know she's safe? I wouldn't have betrayed her. She should have known that."

"She was protecting both you and herself, Conlean. Secrecy's necessary to insure that no one is compromised. You must realize that the elimination of the plague will topple some very old and profitable establishments in Blackfell—including the Gallery. Revolution of that sort won't be tolerated. And if the Gallery finds out that she went into the past, they'll send someone back to assassinate her."

Rocked to the core, Conlean shook his head. A secret resistance movement against the Patriarchy, rooted in the very foundation of the Guild of Artisans and led, in part, by his own mother!

The older man sat down close to Conlean. "I'm taking a risk in enlisting your aid, of course. I have no guarantee that you won't report my activities to the Patriarch and have me executed for treason."

"How can I report you? Do you really think I'd risk my mother?"

"No, I don't. Besides, I think you're on my side,

Conlean. You understand the importance of curing the plague."

Conlean's frown deepened. Hawkwood knew him very well. Lately he *had* been questioning the bride retrieval system, and worrying about their dwindling supply of Prima Materia. "Let's just assume, for a moment, that I decide to go along with your plan. How are we going to convince my father that the woman in this photograph is the same one he picked for a bride?"

"There are some resemblances between the two," Hawkwood insisted. "How much does your father know about the bride he picked? Did he read her biography?"

"He didn't look at her biography," Conlean said, recalling the brief discussion he'd had with his father on the subject. "I don't think he even knows her name. He assumes that the Seekers would not have recommended someone unsuitable."

"What about his advisers? Would they remember her biography?"

He shrugged. "I don't believe he consulted with them on his choice. You know my father. When it comes to personal matters, he won't take any advice."

"Not after losing you to the Gallery," Hawkwood said. "I don't think he trusts any of us."

"With good reason," Conlean added, thinking of the conspiracy they were plotting at that very moment.

"Yes, it's unfortunately so. Give me the photograph that your father provided for your retrieval. I'll take it and rewrite a biography that's more suited to our plans."

"What kind of biography are you talking about?"

"Our girl is a scientist. She's going to know a lot of

things related to the plague. I thought her biography should include a past as a librarian, with a love of books and a specialization in the sciences. That would explain any scholarly knowledge she might reveal."

"Why not just say she is a scientist?"

"You know the Guild has a particular interest in scientists from the past. They'll question her thoroughly about her scientific work, forcing us to invent a whole new set of lies. We'd eventually lose track of the story and slip ourselves up."

Conlean had to acknowledge that Hawkwood made sense. "So you'll rewrite her biography, and I'll retrieve her from the past. With luck, we could have her installed as Matriarch in a few months. But I don't know if I can do that to my father," he said, his gut churning over the depths of the betrayal he was considering.

"The idea pains me as well. I may not like the patriarchal system, but your father is my friend."

Conlean wiped a thin film of perspiration from his brow. He discovered that his hand was shaking. The information that the Grand Artisan had revealed had changed his life forever . . . perhaps for the worse. Now he'd be forced to decide between helping his mother and taking a chance on curing the plague, or remaining true to his father, which would do nothing to stop Blackfell's eventual slide into extinction.

His thoughts zeroed in on the woman Hawkwood had found, the one whose mere existence had put this choice before him. "Has this woman Jordan agreed to come to Blackfell, then, and help us?"

"She doesn't know about us. Your mother hasn't approached her. This isn't a matter of choice, you know.

She must come with us, and your mother and I decided not to give her a chance to refuse."

"But the Guild of Artisans will expect her to have signed a contract, agreeing to marry the Patriarch and place the highest priority on having children."

"We'll put together a fake contract that shows exactly what they expect to see."

Conlean let out a deep breath. "So we have the woman, but not the woman's consent. What do you expect me to do, just appear in her time and take her home with me? What if she doesn't want to go?"

"She must go. Do what you must to secure her cooperation."

"I'm an artisan. Women aren't a part of my life. I know nothing about them . . . what they want, what they need, and what might induce one to come along with me."

"Then don't ask her permission. Just bring her along."

"You want me to *steal* her from her time?"

"Yes, if necessary."

"And once she's here? What happens next?"

"She'll assume her role as your father's wife."

"You're expecting a lot. Many things could go wrong. What if she refuses to help us, even after we explain our situation to her?"

"It may take time to convince her," the grand artisan agreed. "Still, we have to try. You'll have to get close to her and gain her trust. Will you help us, Artisan Conlean? Will you help your mother?"

Conlean glanced down at Baudrons. She was looking at him with her fathomless amber eyes, eyes that reminded him of his mother's. Drawing in a long, ragged breath, he returned his attention to Hawkwood. "The choice you've given me is damned difficult. You're asking me to betray either my mother or my father."

"I'm asking you to help me cure the plague."

"And that's why I'm going to help you, Hawkwood," Conlean said. "Because, like you, I can no longer stand by and do nothing. I'll get started on the painting right away."

Chapter Four

A quick tour through Jordan's apartment might have convinced a casual observer that she was a bohemian minimalist, an interior designer with a love for wide-open spaces and sleek silver furniture that had seen its heyday in the disco era. But the sad truth of the matter was simply that she hadn't bothered to shop for the reds and oranges and yellows that would have brought some color to her life. She'd been too focused on infertility to do anything more than hang a coatrack near the front door. All of her furniture had come from her father's house after he'd died.

And yet, her apartment was not entirely without color. Her furniture might have been spare and cold, and the walls white, but she had a vivid print on one wall. A copy of an old English illustration by Louisa Twamley, called *Earth Stars*, the print had all the color that her apartment lacked, in the form of a bouquet containing white lilies, fuchsia, river roses, and butterflies. It was upon these vibrant flowers and insects that Jordan focused as she emerged from her bedroom after managing only a few hours of sleep. In her old fuzzy slippers, she walked past the print and into the kitchen for a cup of java, pausing only long enough to glare at a few scientific periodicals scattered near the sofa.

With no room for a table, chairs, or countertop stools, the kitchen had a claustrophobic feeling that kept her from lingering too long within its narrow confines. She set the kettle of hot water on to boil, poured herself a cup of coffee, and walked back into the living room.

Coffee in hand, she sat down glumly on one of her silver cafeteria-style chairs and contemplated the floral print. She wondered what the hell she was going to do with her life, now that the Rinehart Project was ending. Dr. Rinehart had indicated that he could rehire her as his assistant in a government facility, but she wasn't certain if she wanted to work on a project that could potentially be used as a weapon. At the same time, she couldn't imagine a day without the excitement their scientific collaborations had brought.

He'd been more than just a colleague; he'd actually cared what happened to her. He'd given her a sympathetic shoulder when Dennis had announced that divorce was the only option left for them. He'd been the one to convince her that she wasn't alone, and lonely, and useless and extraneous, even if she was infertile. He'd made her realize that she *could* have purpose in her life and *could* look forward to the future, even if that future didn't include children. Ultimately, the Rinehart Project had eased the emptiness inside her.

But now that the project had failed, the emptiness

had come back, and it felt even more bottomless than before.

Her grip on the coffee cup relaxing, she allowed her gaze to become unfocused as in her mind a scene emerged: herself on the phone with her sister, spilling out her problems, easing her loneliness, and getting some advice that might or might not be good. She imagined sitting on a park bench with her father, telling him how she'd failed and feeling better when he told her that it didn't matter, that he still loved her no matter what she did. The problem was, her father was dead, she and her sister Alexis had drifted apart, and she had no friends, no lovers to confide in. Other than Dr. Rinehart, she was alone and, regardless of the reasons behind her loneliness, she had no one to blame for her condition but herself.

Her stomach tightened with misery.

Outside, an unusually strong wind swept past her windows and through the eaves, moaning as it skimmed downward toward the river. The digital clock on a side table flickered in protest, and then reset itself to midnight. She wondered if she was going to lose power. The idea seemed fitting, somehow. She'd lost everything else.

Moments later, an odd warmth drifted across her face. With it came the sense that something was going to happen, something unusual and perhaps not pleasant. Jarred from her thoughts, she glanced at the radiator. Had it belched out a stray eddy of hot air?

No, the radiator hadn't turned on this morning. Her apartment hadn't been cold enough to require it, although that howling wind outside might change things.

Another warm draft wrapped itself around her. Eyes widening, Jordan looked around. While the sensation wasn't unpleasant, she wanted to know what had caused it. She didn't like things that science couldn't explain or quantify, things that couldn't be taken apart and understood. She didn't believe in anything that couldn't be proven or rationalized in some manner. Her long love affair with science, and the ineffectiveness of her prayers to become pregnant—and she'd prayed to just about everyone: God, Shiva, Buddha, Confucius—had confirmed her dependence on reason.

And yet, she couldn't seem to find the source of the warmth.

Frowning, she put her coffee cup down on the scarred butcher block that served as her coffee table and stood up. She looked around. Sniffed the air. A very faint yet unmistakable burning odor filled her nostrils. Her heart began to beat a little faster. Could a fire have started on one of the lower levels and even now be eating through the floors and walls of her apartment?

No, she would have heard sirens, whistles, other people leaving their apartments by now. This was something different.

Muted flickering caught her attention. She turned very quickly in its direction, expecting to see the first fingers of flame licking through her walls, and instead found her gaze locked on the only bright spot in her apartment: *Earth Stars*.

Only she wasn't looking at *Earth Stars* anymore.

Instead, a painting of a medieval workshop filled the frame, with a fire blazing wildly in a stone hearth. The fire cast a lambent glow on glass alembics, crucibles, and other ancient pieces of laboratory equipment.

She furrowed her brow and tried to remember whether *Earth Stars* had been hanging on the wall when she'd passed through to the kitchen earlier. She thought maybe it had, but obviously her memory was faulty, because *Earth Stars* wasn't there now. Then she wondered how in *hell* a painting she'd never seen before had found its way into her living room. Who had a key to her apartment? No one but the landlady.

A few years ago, her sister Alexis had given her a print for her birthday. The print was one of those line drawings that looked like a collection of random dots until you stared at it with your eyes unfocused, at which point it became a three-dimensional object. After Jordan had stared at it for minutes, the dots became the words "Sisters Always" entwined with roses, reminding her that she and Alexis would always be linked even though they'd fallen out of touch. Maybe she was now seeing the *Earth Stars* painting in a different way, just as she'd once seen Alexis's print morph into "Sisters Always."

Coffee mug in hand and her gaze fixed on the painting, she walked over to it.

As she approached, it became brighter somehow, even if a little more blurry; and the fire in the hearth now looked so real, and so hungry for wood, that she almost stretched out her hand to touch it to see if it scorched her. Another eddy of warmth curled around her and, for one split second, she could have sworn that the flames moved.

This, she thought, was no dot print hiding a three-dimensional object.

It was something much, much stranger.

The painting became even more blurred. A gray haze was washing over it. Seconds later, the blurriness cleared enough to reveal a scene that left her thinking she had a serious need for glasses. Squinting, she leaned forward.

Everything in the painting seemed to be glowing and alive in a way that her eyes registered but her mind just couldn't accept. Smoky lanterns flickered near the ceiling, bringing murky light to the workshop. The fire in the hearth licked at a crucible suspended above it. A jet black substance in the crucible was bubbling. She could hear the noise of the wood burning, smell an acrid odor she couldn't identify, feel the warmth of the workshop . . .

Suddenly the painting didn't seem to be a painting at all, but instead a rain-washed window that gave a view of another place. Jordan sucked in a quick, frightened breath. This went far beyond a vision problem. She swallowed. Closed her eyes. When she opened them again and gazed at the print, it looked less vital, two-dimensional, and without any blurriness. She couldn't immediately recapture her perception of the painting being more than just a painting.

Clearly her mind was playing tricks on her. The stress she was under, she decided, must be giving her hallucinations. But the last thing she needed right now was to go batty.

The teakettle's shrill whistle blasted through her

apartment, making her jump. She gasped aloud, pressed a hand against her chest . . . and then shook her head as the implication hit her. The warm draft had come from water boiling in the teakettle, and her stressed-out imagination had taken it from there. What an idiot she was, thinking that a painting had come to life! Damn, she'd slipped into the danger zone. A visit to a therapist might even be in order. At least then she'd have someone to talk to.

Her frown growing deeper, she returned to the kitchen and turned off the gas on the stove. The kettle immediately stopped its screaming. She no longer felt like having breakfast, though. Instead, she poured more java into the mug, knowing she was going to jack her pulse rate up even more with the caffeine but needing the comfort of another cup of coffee.

The wind blew around the corners of the building again, rattling her windows she went back into the living room. She shivered and held the mug close, as though it could banish the coldness that had crept into her bones and refused to let go.

A crackling noise, all the louder for the quiet in the apartment, caught her attention. Again, a very faint scent of burning wood drifted toward her, along with an acrid undertone, the kind that comes from melting metal. Convulsively she gripped her coffee mug and swiveled to stare at the painting on the wall.

Chapter Five

Jordan stared with something close to wonder at the print that hung on her wall. She blinked once, twice, certain that her eyes were deceiving her, and then took a few hesitant steps toward the strange painting.

The flames in that ancient hearth *were* flickering.

Lips parted, she raised her hand to the level of the print. Warmth engulfed it. Warmth from the *fire*.

"Oh, my good God."

Eyes narrowed, she allowed her hand to drop to her side and moved closer.

Immediately she noticed the same blurry details she'd seen before: lanterns flickering, the jet black substance in the crucible bubbling. She could also hear a hissing noise, as though steam was escaping, and smell an odor that reminded her of copper pennies warmed in the palm.

She had to be dreaming this . . . hallucinating . . .

Eyes wide, she fixed her gaze on the print. The black

material in the crucible, she saw, was becoming lighter by the minute and turning a greenish-blue color. Seconds later, it flashed with an astonishing iridescence, as if it had captured a rainbow at its source. When the rainbow faded away a few seconds later, the material in the crucible had the appearance of an aqua-colored paint.

Her breath caught in her throat. She now stood maybe two feet away from the canvas. Mesmerized by the print, she lifted her hand and very slowly, very gently, placed the tip of her forefinger on the glass covering it.

It felt hot.

She recoiled and stumbled away, her fuzzy slippers tripping her as they came off her feet. She landed on her worn leather sofa.

Goose bumps rose on her arms. She gripped the side of the sofa, her gaze locked on the print.

What in *hell* was going on?

A soft groan escaped her.

"Did I remember dust of electrum?" a male voice asked without warning, just seconds before a new figure appeared in the painting.

Jordan stiffened and dug her fingers into the couch's leather arm.

A man in dark track pants and a loose, flowing cotton shirt walked into the frame. He was *moving*, as though she was watching a television screen rather than staring at a painting. He held a snowy white cat in his arms.

As she gaped in disbelief, he strode over to the two dimensional but flickering fire, his attention focused on the substance inside the crucible. An apron of the sort she imagined a blacksmith would have worn covered the front of his body. As she watched, the cat jumped from his arms to an embroidered chair. He rolled up his sleeves and said to the cat, "I thought I'd forgotten it."

He dipped his fingers into a small earthenware container and grasped a pinch of glittery powder that appeared to be made of gold and silver. This he tossed into the crucible, making the aqua substance sparkle before it settled down with a soft glow.

"Perfect," the man announced, after examining the substance. "I couldn't have matched her eyes more closely."

Jordan passed a shaky hand across her brow.

Nodding, clearly satisfied, the man lifted the crucible from the fire with a long iron hook and set it on top of a mat, presumably to cool. Then he began to gather other supplies, including a palette, brushes, and containers. These he placed near the edge of the print frame. To Jordan, they appeared larger than everything else in the print, as though she, too, were sitting in the laboratory and they were right in front of her.

She watched with reluctant fascination. She might have been completely crazy, but she had to admit that her craziness was damned interesting. She couldn't wait to see what the man would do next, to hear him speak again. The cat, she thought, seemed equally entranced. It kept its gaze trained on him.

Without warning, he turned to face her. She recoiled against the back of her sofa. He seemed to be looking right at her. But no, he was peering at something in the print that she couldn't see. Her viewpoint of the laboratory apparently coincided with the object he was now studying.

Her heart pounding, she studied him, too.

His eyes, a jade color, reminded her of cat's eyes—predatory, hypnotic, so very strange. He had a strong chin and a straight nose that suggested he wouldn't compromise very easily. At the moment, he was frowning thoughtfully, his brows drawn, as if he were confronted by some momentous problem. Bluish shadows beneath his eyes and lines around his mouth testified that he'd been working on this problem for some time. Still, it was the tattoo on his cheek, an arcane-looking symbol traced in some sort of blue phosphorescent paint, that made her catch her breath.

The man stretched mightily, displaying a trim and well-muscled form, before sitting down on a stool directly in front of her. Then he picked up what looked like a pencil and began to sketch on the glass covering the print in *her* living room. The idea that the painting was also a window made her tremble.

She seemed to be sitting on one side of the window.

And he was sitting on the other side, using the window as some sort of artistic canvas.

Conlean paused to study the portrait he'd been sketching. He'd faithfully copied the photograph of Hawkwood's woman, but his sketch lacked the depth, the sparkle he imagined in her eyes. Dissatisfaction filled him. If his painting didn't capture a close enough likeness of his subject, the portal wouldn't open and the bride retrieval would fail. Some of the less talented artisans needed years to create a painting that would open a portal to the bride. Even he, a master artisan, couldn't guarantee a faultless painting. Sometimes he wondered if he'd ever manage to create a perfect likeness, or if anyone else had. Could something completely perfect ever exist in this imperfect world?

He suspected not.

It was also very possible, he mused, that he'd managed to compromise his ability in this instance by worrying over the ramifications of bringing this particular woman to Blackfell. Most likely, though, his problem went deeper than mere uncertainty over the future. His talent at artistry was not something he possessed, or a skill he had cleverly formulated; rather, it came to him like a gift. Every time he faced a blank canvas it was the same: What if the channel of inspiration remained closed this time? What if the gift was not given? This retrieval was so much more important than any other that his fear seemed doubled.

Still, he'd learned both through observation and experience that the process would become more difficult the longer he lingered and dawdled. Fear grew stronger when it wasn't confronted immediately and directly. The stronger it became, the harder time he'd have conquering it. He'd known a few artisans who had waited too long before facing their fear; they'd never painted again. He didn't want to join their number.

He *had* to begin painting soon.

Silently, irritably, Conlean recited the rules for painting women to himself, as stated in the *Fundamentals of the Grand Artisan*. Sometimes he fell back on these rules when things weren't going the way he wanted them to. They extolled the virtues of a woman's humility and submissiveness; and yet, he saw little he could characterize as humble or passive about her face. Nor was her body the lush composition of curves all women on Blackfell possessed. She looked leaner than usual, stronger than any of the women in the portraits he'd created previously.

With the knowledge that he was all but throwing *Fundamentals* out the window, he drew her not as conventional wisdom dictated but as his gut said to draw her. At some point during his twenty-eight years of life, Conlean had decided that the exceptions to the rule were far more interesting than the rules themselves, and he had the feeling that she was going to be very interesting indeed.

When he finished, he stepped back. Arms crossed over his chest, he studied first the photograph and then his sketch. She was not round and delicate but angular. Silently he admitted to himself that other men might judge her plain beyond imagining—far outside the standards for beauty. Nevertheless, he thought she was the loveliest woman he'd ever had the good fortune to work with.

"What do you think, Baudrons?" he murmured, his gaze staying on the sketch.

The cat purred in reply.

"It's very strange," he continued softly. "She has some elusive quality that I can't describe. But it's there. In the photograph. I think I managed to capture it in my sketch, too."

Baudrons conveyed her agreement with continued throaty purring.

Emboldened by his perception, he put his pencil to canvas and added more detail. Still, the oil in the lanterns had burned very low before he decided he had a pretty good sketch of the way he thought she would look in real life.

When, at last, he stepped back for the final time to view the canvas, his eyes scratchy and his back aching with effort, he knew he had done her justice. There was something delicate yet resilient about her. Her body flowed in a feminine way but had a leanness that promised a strong will, while her face possessed an intriguing mixture of sensuality and innocence. He'd never drawn a woman more in conflict than she, a more interesting paradox. Sighing, yet fulfilled, he slumped into a chair and pulled on the bell cord that would summon his assistant.

Baudrons slunk off her chair and jumped out the window. Either she'd had enough of sitting around in his smoky studio or she was satisfied with his sketch. He smiled and silently wished her good hunting.

A minute or so later, his assistant arrived with a dinner tray. He took the tray and made quick work of the herbed bread, cheese, and mead before jumping to his feet again and examining his sketch with an eye for color. Because the photograph he'd been working from was colored in shades of gray, he had to approximate the shades of her eyes, hair, and skin. Again, he had only a gut feeling to rely on when making his color choices. Still, he understood on some level that he had to use deep, vivid colors rather than the pastels most artisans preferred. The very contradictions in her nature and the challenge he saw in her eyes demanded that he do so, or he might not be successful in retrieving her.

Excitement and anticipation allowed him to work very quickly and efficiently. A strange sort of creative genius had seized him, and he took advantage of it by furiously capturing the essence of the woman while he still had the energy to do so. He locked the studio door, pausing long enough to glance in a looking glass on his way back to his easel. The knowledge that he looked like a wild-eyed heretic with dark circles under his eyes and lines of weariness around his mouth bothering him not the slightest, he picked up his palette and started to bring the portal to life.

Jordan shifted on the couch. Her butt was going numb. She'd been sitting here for a long time—a couple of hours or so—watching him paint the glass that stood between them. Sheer fascination with his movements and the intense concentration he was putting into the effort had kept her on the sofa.

At first, when the fire in the print had started to flicker and she'd been gripping her coffee mug for dear life, she'd suspected that someone had accidentally picked a few peyote mushrooms along with the beans that had gone into her coffee. That conviction had faded with the hours. Everything else about her apartment seemed normal, and she felt normal. In fact, as she'd sat there on the sofa and gradually calmed down, she'd become even more certain that something inexplicable, yet very real, was occurring in her apartment. She'd even tried to call Dr. Rinehart and tell him about the situation, but he hadn't answered his phone. Having no one else to call besides perhaps the police, who would think she'd gone nuts, she'd decided to wait this one out by herself and see what happened.

At that moment, the alchemist picked up a container

of pale, flesh-colored paint and selected a thin brush. Earlier he had put a black jacket on over his shirt, leaving a little square of white visible above the collar. Suddenly he reminded her of a priest . . . or some sort of dark angel. His lips compressed in what she interpreted as a contemplative frown, he began to fill in portions of the glass that he'd passed over earlier. The phosphorescent tattoo glowed on his cheek, and the cat she'd noticed near his side earlier had vanished.

She couldn't see what he was painting. She could only see him stroking the glass between them with a brush, and then stepping back to review what he'd done before continuing. Still, the blurriness that had obscured the print from the moment it had come to life faded with every stroke of paint. The laboratory on his side of the glass was slowly becoming clearer to her.

She had no idea how much time had elapsed. Outside, the sunlight had gained strength. Noon was obviously fast approaching. Her stomach rumbled a protest. But it wasn't as easy to tell if the same amount of time had passed in the place where the alchemist painted. In fact, she had the impression that time passed more quickly there than here. Every now and then, the print would become hazy with gray mist, and when it cleared, he'd have a lot more paint splashed on his pants than a few moments of work could explain.

She dragged her gaze away from the print and glanced down at herself.

She still hadn't changed out of her silk pajamas. Suddenly she felt naked, exposed, as if the alchemist could actually see her. After casting one swift glance at the print to ensure that the alchemist was still busy painting, she hurried into her bedroom and dragged on an old pair of jeans and a sweatshirt, and piled her hair into a hair clip before surrendering to her curiosity and speeding back into the living room.

The print drew her attention like a lodestone; eagerly she fixed her gaze upon it.

It was gray, swirling with mist, preparing to reveal yet another moment in the alchemist's day.

Heart pounding, she plopped back onto the sofa.

Slowly, as it had before, the mist cleared. Again she observed the alchemist's laboratory, only this time *two* men stood within the print's frame: the alchemist and an older man with a flowing gray beard. They were both standing there, contemplating her with serious expressions. And though she knew they weren't exactly looking at *her*, but rather at the painting the alchemist had been working on, their stares nevertheless unnerved her.

"Well, what do you think?" the alchemist asked.

The bearded man stroked his chin. Several moments passed before he finally nodded. "A wonderful likeness of the photograph I gave you. She's your best work to date, Artisan Conlean. Well done."

Artisan Conlean. Jordan rolled the name around in her mind. Was Artisan the younger man's first name, or simply a title? And Conlean sounded rather . . . Celtic. Before today she hadn't placed much faith in witchcraft, but if witchcraft capable of performing this miracle existed anywhere in the world, she would find it in the British Isles.

"Thank you," Conlean murmured. "I'm ready to open the portal."

"Then I came at exactly the right time." The older man stepped away, toward the back of the laboratory and almost out of the print's frame.

"Have you brought the final Prima Materia glaze?" Conlean asked.

The older man withdrew a vial from his cloak. He swirled its contents—a jet black material similar to what she'd seen inside the crucible earlier—and then held it up to a lantern to study it before handing it to Conlean.

With the older man watching closely, Conlean poured the contents of the vial into a wide-mouthed jar. He set the jar close to his painting and plucked a large, soft-looking paintbrush from a drawer. Excitement tightening his features, he dipped the brush into the wide-mouthed jar and then began to lay the glaze across the painting.

An odd sense of expectancy gripped Jordan. Something was going to happen, something strange. She could feel it gathering in the air around her. Lips parted, she watched as he dragged his brush back and forth, erasing the blurriness in the print. If she hadn't known better, she might have guessed that he wasn't painting at all, but instead putting some cleaning touches on a hazy window between them.

After a minute or so, he finished and set down the brush. His eyes glowed luminously in the shadowy workshop. He turned to exchange a glance with the older man before facing her once again, sitting down in a cross-legged position at the bottom of the frame and closing his eyes.

He rested his hands lightly on his knees, palms up,

like a Tibetan yogi. His lips began to move but issued no sound. At the same time, the last bit of haze on the window between them began to clear.

Several minutes passed. Still, the artisan continued to chant. Jordan blinked once, then twice, when she noticed an unexplainable glow forming around him, like a halo around an angel. The bearded man had at this point taken several steps away and had also assumed the yogi position. Though his lips moved in a silent chant, he hadn't the same glow that his younger companion possessed.

The hairs on the back of her neck and her arms rose. She could almost feel the power emanating from the man in the painting. It arched across the space separating them like electricity, a surge that grew even as the painting sharpened and became even more realistic. Anticipation and fear built inside her. How would all this end? With a giant thunderclap? An earthquake? She wished she could hear what he was mumbling. Despite the sensation of danger, though, she couldn't seem to move. Fascination held her captive.

Just when the hair on top of her head began to waver softly upward, the painting cleared completely and the man opened his eyes. She had a sense of letdown, of power levels suddenly cut off. Her hair dropped without warning, and both the men stood. The younger man glanced at his companion before placing a hand against the window that separated him from her apartment.

The glass covering the print in her living room suddenly depicted a large male palm.

Everything in her apartment, she realized, had gone

completely quiet. The air seemed without odor, the light coming from behind the drapes, muted. She imagined that the entire world had stopped in awe of this strange magic she was experiencing. Without quite knowing why, she stretched out her arm and touched the glass covering the alchemist's workshop, so that her palm covered his.

Instead of feeling smooth glass, she felt skin.

Gasping, she recoiled.

He didn't appear to notice their contact. Rather, he pushed his hand *through* the glass, as if the glass wasn't even there.

A low moan escaped her as his other hand and both arms followed his hand. He braced himself on the bottom of the print's frame, and then his feet were coming through. Within seconds, he had slipped his entire body through the print's frame and landed on her living room floor with a slight exhalation of air. Straightening his back, he offered her a welcoming smile that she would have found charming had the circumstances been different.

But Jordan, unused to seeing grown men pop out of prints that had come to life, staggered backward with one hand pressed against her breasts and the other against her lips—to stifle the scream that threatened to erupt. Her calves banged against the sofa and, losing her balance, she fell back against its worn cushions.

"Oh, this is too much . . ." Her voice failing, Jordan trailed off and sat there helplessly, gaping at him. "Who—what—"

A smile lighting his features, he stepped toward her

until he stood only a few paces away, and then offered her a courtly bow. "I'm Artisan Conlean. I've come to take you back to Blackfell with me."

Her heart beating wildly in her chest, she shrank back against the cushions. "How . . . did you get here? Where is Blackfell? Is it in the British Isles?"

"The painting allowed me to come here," he said, his voice patient. "It's a portal between our worlds. I don't know of this place called the British Isles. Blackfell is my world and I've come for you."

Painting. Portal. Normal words, but in this context, the words of a madman. Or maybe she was the one who'd gone crazy. "You've come for me?"

"I know how strange this must seem. Nevertheless, you're needed on Blackfell. I'm here to fetch you."

"I won't go anywhere with you," she announced breathlessly, thinking that he *had* to be a hallucination. That sushi she'd eaten for lunch yesterday must have gone bad. "Are you some sort of witch? Or warlock?"

His brows knitted. He didn't appear to understand her. "Do you have a husband who will miss you?"

A bark of laughter that sounded disturbingly high erupted from her. He was asking about her love life, for God's sake. "Me? Have a husband? No, I've learned my lesson."

Relief washed over his features. "I'm very glad to hear it."

She frowned. "I don't know who you are or how you got here, but if you try to kidnap me, I'll call the police." To make good on her threat, she grabbed the phone's handset and lifted it to her ear, only to realize that it had no dial tone. Frantically she punched the buttons on the receiver, dialing nine-one-one several times over.

Nothing happened.

His eyebrows drew together. "Don't be frightened. I won't hurt you."

As strange as it seemed, his gentle manner tempted her to believe him. Slowly she replaced the handset on the receiver. "What did you do, cut the phone lines?" Looking around, she suddenly realized that all of the power had gone out. The digital clock wasn't blinking; it simply appeared dead. The refrigerator wasn't humming, either.

"You cut the power, too, didn't you?" she accused.

Taking a step closer to her, he asked, "What's your name?"

"Jordan," she whispered, her attention captured by another little fact: even the street noises had stopped. Oh yeah, that sushi had definitely been way past the expiration date.

Keeping her gaze locked on him, she stood and backed away until she'd moved near the windows. Then, her hand trembling, she pushed the drape aside and risked a glance outside. A gray mist—the same kind she'd seen in the painting—blanketed everything. She saw no evidence of life: no people, no cars, no dogs barking, no airplanes, nothing.

Her head beginning to throb, she released the drape and pressed her palms against her temples. "I don't understand what's happening."

"The portal between our worlds is open," he murmured, small lines of concern appearing around his mouth. "We're between time."

"*Between* time?" A rising note of panic tinged her voice. "You're some kind of psycho, aren't you? Or maybe *I'm* the psycho."

"Shh. It'll be all right, Jordan." He drew her close enough to put an arm around her shoulders.

The moment he touched her, she felt the heat of his skin through his shirt and her own. Either she was hyperaware of him or his body temperature ran very high, for he felt far warmer than he should have. *Magic,* she thought wildly. She'd never believed in magic in the past. Science was her thing. But suddenly the idea of magic didn't seem so farfetched.

"What do you want from me?" she asked, trying to pull away from him.

He maneuvered around her, holding her tightly; and before she knew what he was about, he'd lifted her into his arms. "I'll tell you once we've returned to Blackfell."

Openmouthed, she stared at him for a split second before an instinct for self-preservation kicked in. She twisted wildly in his grasp and tried to get her arm free so she could punch him in the ear. "You lunatic! Put me down!"

He evidently sensed her intention and shifted her body to tighten his grip on her. "Don't fight me, Jordan. Please. We have to go."

"Bastard!" Her heart pounding, she struggled against him. She needed some room so she could land a punch somewhere. Anywhere. He had her squashed against his own body, though. She couldn't break free. With growing alarm she realized they were lurching toward the strange painting.

"Hey, just a minute," she said with a hitch in her breathing. "Let's talk this over. We have some time, don't we? I'm not ready to go to Blackfell just yet."

"The portal will close soon and I don't want to be stuck in your world," he told her, a grim look replacing his earlier smile. "We have to go. If you stop struggling, it'll be easier on both of us."

Stop struggling? Was he insane? She fought to kick her legs and make him lose his balance. "If you put me down now and leave my apartment, it'll be easier on both of us."

The alchemist said nothing in reply. He was too busy trying to keep his hold on her, she thought, as she managed to free one arm and deal him a solid blow to the cheek.

"Damn it," he growled. "Stay still, Jordan, and let me get you to Blackfell in one piece!"

"Screw you," she told him, as he paused in front of the painting, shifted her weight in his arms, and then stepped through the frame.

Chapter Six

Reflexively, Jordan stiffened as Conlean extended one leg through the portal. She expected to find herself jammed against the glass covering the print. And yet, instead of feeling a solid barrier, she suddenly found herself in complete and unrelieved blackness, a nothingness that brought with it a sensation of intense cold that penetrated to her very bones.

The cold had a peculiar quality about it. It wasn't the kind of chill that a bitter winter evening brought, but rather an iciness that reflected the complete absence of everything—sight, sound, touch, taste, smell. Only her thoughts seemed to exist, and they were growing more terrified by the moment. Where had he taken her? What sort of place possessed no sensation at all? The chill around her settled into the pit of her stomach.

She tried to flail her arms, to shout, to prove to herself that she was still living, breathing, her heart still beating. Nothing changed. She couldn't even feel the arms of the alchemist holding her anymore. The emptiness was all around her, a timeless, featureless netherworld from which she thought she might never escape. Her shout disappeared into the silence as though she'd never uttered it.

Then, just when the darkness seemed as if it would never end, a surge of warmth shot through her. A rush of sensations took over: two voices talking over a loud, crackling noise, jarring her thoughts, making her head ache; her body painfully tingling all over; her tongue dry like cotton; a thousand-watt bulb shining somewhere in front of her closed eyelids. The abrupt change was too much for her and she trembled.

Suddenly she could feel the alchemist's arms around her, steadying her. She was holding him even more tightly and reluctantly let go only when he set her down on something very soft. Then she opened her eyes slowly, afraid of what she might find.

The alchemist was looking down at her with a fathomless jade green gaze. The older man stood next to him, and the white cat was back on its chair.

"Breathe deeply," the alchemist counseled her. "It'll help to lessen the effects of transmutation. It's always hard traveling between time."

Between time? The words circled in her head. She was too rattled to pursue them aloud. She didn't think she'd ever been this damned scared . . . or this godawful confused. Rather than try to speak, she did as he'd said, drawing air into her lungs and letting it out. Moments passed, and the explosion of sensation became more bearable. The thousand-watt bulb, she discovered, was just a lantern affixed to a stone wall nearby, and the crackling noise was coming from a fire in a massive furnace. Her body stopped tingling as she warmed up, and slowly her vision cleared.

She realized she was sitting in a soft, velvet-upholstered chair.

Between time. What in hell was that?

She risked a glance at her captors first. They were studying her closely. The older one had a flowing gray beard and bright blue eyes, reminding her of a Tolkien mystic. The expression in his eyes could only be classified as kind. The younger one—the alchemist—looked more worried, his dark features brooding with some indecipherable emotion.

A few choice curses formed on her lips, but she hadn't the strength to say them. That trip *between time* had stolen all her energy.

She dragged her gaze from the alchemist and his bearded friend and looked around. The furnace, she saw, had been constructed of simple brick and mortar. An iron crucible was suspended over the fire. Heat from the furnace washed over her, and the acrid smell of melting ore tickled her nose. Slitlike windows revealed darkness beyond. Night had fallen here.

Her immediate impression was one of general weirdness. Twilight Zone–weirdness. Travel-back-in-time weirdness. She didn't know what *between time* meant. Still, she couldn't argue with the fact that she was no longer in her apartment. Somehow, these two men had instantaneously moved her from one place to another, through this space they termed *between time*. The last she'd heard, going from one place to another without actually moving was considered teleportation, a concept previously relegated to *Star Trek* and *The Fly*. Evidently these two rejects who looked as if they belonged on a Harry Potter movie set had discovered the secrets behind teleportation.

Her eyes wide with the implications of their discovery, she returned her attention to the men. They appeared harmless enough, their faces creased with what looked like worry . . . for her.

Assaulted by a sense of unreality, she glanced at the jars of paint that were grouped on a nearby table. There had to be at least a hundred colors represented, and they all had an iridescent quality, as if imbued with magic. Brushes and crude-looking pipettes stuck out of an earthenware container, and glass alembics sat on a shelf next to an array of sponges, giving her the overall impression that the laboratory was an unusual mix of science and artistry.

At the same time, she saw no electric lights, outlets, microscopes, or any sort of modern accoutrements at all. She'd expect all sorts of high-tech whiz gear from a pair of geniuses who'd discovered teleportation; and yet, with its damp stone walls, primitive furnace, and lanterns, this laboratory had more in common with a medieval dungeon. In fact, it looked a lot like the ancient room depicted in the mysterious painting that had replaced *Earth Stars*.

She shook her head. Hallucinations aside, the situation was getting more bizarre, more shocking with each minute. She had to assume that these two had teleported her somewhere, and clearly the painting was an integral part of their teleportation device. But where were the supercomputers that disassembled and re-assembled people molecule by molecule? Where were the teleportation pads? The control panels?

"How did I get here?" she croaked.

"Shh," the alchemist said. "Wait a few more moments before you try to talk. The effects of between time will pass soon."

He was right, she thought. She felt as though she'd been run over by a herd of elephants, but the bruised sensation was quickly dissipating. Quietly she studied them, wondering how two scientists who looked like complete crackpots had discovered and made feasible such a revolutionary concept as teleportation. How sound was the technology? Was she going to grow wings and throw up on her food to digest it, like that poor sucker in the movie *The Fly?* Surreptitiously, she wiggled her fingers and toes, and then tensed her muscles. Everything seemed to be in working order.

Both the men were now looking at something behind her, she realized. She turned around to see what had attracted their attention. There, on an easel, was a painting of her living room. It appeared large enough for just about anyone to step through.

She drew in a quick breath. That was the painting they'd brought her through. A wormhole, according to quantum physics. A portal connecting one place to another. A folding of space. Presumably this wormhole led back to her living room.

Her living room!

She grew very still. The wonders of teleportation aside, she would very much like to be back in her own living room. Being careful not to broadcast her intention to rush the painting and get the hell out of there, she tensed to heave herself out of the chair and make a break for it.

An unexpected movement caught her attention. The cat had hopped from its chair to the table next to her. Jordan looked into its amber eyes and saw that it knew what she planned to do.

A second later, the alchemist's hand settled heavily onto her shoulder and pushed her harder into the chair. She yelped and twisted away from him.

Movement on canvas caught her attention. She focused on the painting of her living room. It was rippling like a pond skimmed by a high wind; then it quickly smoothed out. As it stilled, the painting lost some indefinable quality that had made it seem alive. No longer was it a three dimensional view into her world, but rather a mundane, two dimensional portrait of her face.

The wormhole had closed.

"I'm sorry," the alchemist said matter-of-factly. "We can't allow you to leave."

On the heels of the alchemist's statement, the mystic asked, "Are you feeling any better now?"

She turned to stare at them. "You two have a teleportation device."

"A what?" The two men looked at each other and then back at her. "Oh, yes. We do have a teleportation device," the younger one said with a shrug. "That's how I brought you here."

A thousand questions threatened to erupt from her: How long had they had it? Who had funded the research? When did they plan to break the news to the public? But she only managed to stare at them and marvel at their mundane tones regarding such a fantastic breakthrough in technology.

"Are you feeling better?" the older man pressed, evidently trying to change the subject. Clearly he didn't want to talk about the teleportation device. Well, that was fine with her. She could play it cool, too.

"How dare you ask about my health after kidnapping me?" She spoke in the iciest tones she could muster. "In case you didn't know, the law considers kidnapping a felony. You could go to jail for bringing me here."

"I think she's feeling better," the younger man muttered.

She fixed her glare on him, her gaze raking across his medieval-looking tunic. He certainly was good-looking, in a dark way. "Who are you two, anyway? Stand-ins from some science fiction movie set?"

"I'm Artisan Conlean," he said, repeating what he'd told her earlier.

"And I am Grand Artisan Hawkwood," the graying mystic added. "As for what's going on . . . well, we'll need some time to discuss it fully."

She lifted an eyebrow. *Hawkwood?* What a name. It sounded like the kind of name the leader of a Druidic coven might have. Her attention slid over to the cat sitting nearby and decided that the creature was the perfect companion for a Druidic coven leader. She remembered the intelligence in its eyes and felt a superstitious chill creep through her. Was it more than just a cat?

The alchemist—Conlean, she silently amended—pulled a blanket off the back of a seat and handed it to her. "You're trembling. Wrap this around yourself. You'll feel better in a moment."

"Gee, thanks. I hadn't realized you cared." She snatched the blanket from him and slung it around her shoulders. "So, why did you kidnap me?" She paused to glance at the cat, who blinked a few times, as if trying to send out Morse code. "And what's with the cat?"

Conlean's eyebrows rose. "Nothing's 'with' the cat. Her name is Baudrons."

"She looks strange. Like she knows what we're saying. Does she talk or something?"

"A cat, talk? As you and I are talking? I'm afraid not."

She frowned. "I just stepped through a picture, buddy. So don't go looking at me like I'm an idiot for asking if a cat can talk."

"My apologies, Jordan," Conlean said, a touch of amusement in his tone.

She narrowed her eyes. "On second thought, I don't care what you're doing or why you brought me here. I need you to take me back to my apartment. Now."

"I can't," Conlean said. "You're needed here."

"Needed here? What are you, nuts? How do you even know me?"

Though both men gazed at her neither offered an answer.

"I'm needed back home, too," she insisted, knowing the claim to be as false as the teeth in George Washington's mouth, but preferring to be useless and lonely over being completely out of control of her own destiny. "Take me back to my home."

"First, hear us out," the older man said.

She wasn't hearing *anyone* out. She wanted one thing: her apartment. "I don't know why you think you need me, but I can't help you. And even if I could, I won't help. I refuse. I don't like being pushed around."

"Pushed around?" Conlean's eyebrows drew together.

"Kidnapped, then," she clarified angrily, and pointed to the painting that had teleported her from her apartment to their lair. "Make the painting of my apartment ripple. If you don't want to go, I'll take myself back."

The lines on Hawkwood's face grew deeper. He exchanged a glance with Conlean.

"If you send me back, I swear I'll keep quiet," she said, knowing it was one of the biggest lies she'd told in her twenty-odd years. "I won't tell the police. We can all forget this ever happened."

"We aren't worried about the police," Hawkwood replied. "I'm sorry, but we simply cannot send you back. We have to talk."

Talk? *Talk?* Carefully she swallowed back the hot words that threatened to erupt. It wouldn't do her any good to antagonize her captors. She would have to try another tactic, maybe try to gain some useful information. "Where am I?"

"In Blackfell," the older man replied.

"Is Blackfell a place or some sort of castle?"

"Blackfell is a province," Hawkwood replied. He walked to a side table and began pouring three glasses of an amber-colored fluid. "Artisan Conlean, would you please take over the explanation from here?"

Conlean sighed, as if the assignment he'd been given was the most unpleasant imaginable. He took a seat near hers and stretched mightily, then rubbed his forehead in a weary manner. As she waited impatiently for him to start clarifying things, he accepted a glass of liquid from Hawkwood and tossed down its contents in one gulp.

"Would you like some?" Hawkwood asked her, two more glasses in hand.

She shrugged. "Why not?" If this stuff bore any resemblance to the alcohol she was familiar with, she'd be very happy to have a sip. Or two. Or three. Accepting the proffered glass, she took a moment to swirl the glass's contents. It sure looked like whiskey. She brought the glass to her lips and took a hesitant taste.

Whiskey, all right. Or something very much like it.

She gulped down a mouthful.

Immediately her eyes watered. She coughed. Fire slipped down her throat.

The two men exchanged glances.

Squaring her shoulders, she eyed Conlean closely and noted with some satisfaction that he had a bruise on his cheek, where she'd clocked him earlier. "So, Artisan Conlean, do what the man said. Explain."

The alchemist viewed her warily. "You have a right to be angry, Jordan—"

"You're damn right," she cut in.

"Still, I want you to try to listen with an open mind."

"You're asking a lot," she informed them evenly.

Another furtive look passed between the two men. "The Patriarch won't be able to push her around too easily," Hawkwood murmured.

A glimmer entered Conlean's eye. "Thank God for that."

She cleared her throat. What sort of kidnapping was this? When were they going to get down to business? "Hello? You're talking like I'm not in the room. Well, I'm here and I'm waiting for the explanation you promised me."

Hawkwood's lips twitched, as if he was holding back a smile.

Conlean gave her an earnest look. "Basically, Jordan, we brought you here because we need your scientific expertise. We need your help regarding a certain problem we're facing."

"My scientific expertise?" Confused, she shook her head. This was the last thing she'd been expecting. Rape, torture, murder—maybe. But two wacko geniuses needing *her* scientific expertise? Never. "What kind of expertise do I have that you need?"

"Your research into the field of infertility interests us particularly."

"Oh, let me guess. Someone wants to have a baby. And you guys can only teleport human life, not create it."

The older man gave her a sickly smile. "Not exactly."

"Then what kind of problem are you talking about? And why me? Why not one of the world's leading infertility experts? I'm just a worker bee in a big scientific hive."

"We chose you because we need a woman, among other reasons," Hawkwood said.

She raised her eyebrows. "Why do you need, specifically, a woman?"

"Because we also need a bride, and only a woman can be a bride."

"A bride?" Shaking her head, she looked at Conlean. "You know what? I don't want any explanations. Because your explanations make absolutely no sense."

"Just a minute—"

"Minute, nothing. I'd need a whole year to figure out what a bride, scientific expertise, and infertility have in common."

"Can we try, at least, to sort through this?" Conlean asked softly.

She sighed. Did she really have any choice? "Let's just focus on the bride part for a moment. Why do you need a bride, for God's sake?"

"Artisan Conlean and I are in the business of retrieving—teleporting—brides to Blackfell," Hawkwood said. "We *only* retrieve brides. We don't usually, ah, kidnap them, though. They agree in advance to come here."

She looked at them with something close to amazement. "So, you two run a mail-order bride service, like they used to have in the Klondike back in the eighteen hundreds. And the brides, they agree to this?"

"They all sign contracts before they come here," Conlean asserted.

"But I wasn't offered a contract," she pointed out.

"I wish we could have given you the luxury of choosing. This would have gone much more smoothly," Conlean said with a sharp look at the older man.

"Just in case you were wondering, I *refuse* to be one of your *brides*," she told them. "You kidnapped me, guys. That puts me in a bad mood. And people in bad moods generally don't cooperate. Besides, marriage is for idiots."

"Jordan," Conlean said, "you have a right to consider me a kidnapper, but in my defense, I tell you that I wouldn't have bothered you if we could have thought of any other way."

"You know what would make me feel better? I'd feel better hearing that you don't expect me to be one of your brides. Tell me that you don't actually expect me to marry someone."

Conlean hesitated. "There are mitigating circumstances at work here—"

"Just a *yes* or a *no* would do," she cut in.

"Yes," Hawkwood said. "We want you to marry someone."

She laughed without any amusement. "Well, scratch that plan."

"We'll give you some time to think about it," Hawkwood said in soothing tones.

"You guys don't listen, do you?"

Hawkwood lifted his glass and drank. "I believe we're going to need more fortification."

Nodding, Conlean emptied his glass.

Thinking Hawkwood's advice some of the best she'd had all year, she lifted the glass to her lips and tossed its entire contents down her throat before setting the glass down, hard. Normally she preferred to taste what she was drinking, but today she was more interested in the alcohol's anesthetic effects.

Motionless, the two men watched her with parted lips.

She lifted an eyebrow. "What's the problem? Never seen a woman down a shot before?"

Conlean set his glass on the table. "The women here

tend to be more . . . reserved in their drinking, particularly with strong brews."

She frowned. "Your brides must be very dainty, very ladylike. How nice for them. Obviously I'm not cut out to be a bride. You should just send me back home and find a more willing woman with scientific expertise. It would save us all a lot of aggravation."

"We can't send you home. The portal is closed," Conlean murmured, directing her attention to the painting that had at one time pictured her apartment.

"Ah, yes, the portal," Jordan agreed. "An interesting thing, that portal of yours. I'd love to know how you created it. And where you're hiding the supercomputers. You must have supercomputers somewhere, or how could you disassemble and reassemble the objects and people you're teleporting?"

"Supercomputers?" Conlean shook his head. "We don't have any of those."

"No supercomputers. Of course. How foolish of me to expect them. Nowadays, teleportation technology is so advanced that there's no need for supercomputers. I wish I were smart, like you guys. But I'm just a poor dumb scientist-bride with infertility expertise, right? So you'll have to go step-by-step and explain this technology to me in detail, so I can understand it."

"You want to know how I created the painting that brought you here?"

"Yes, if you wouldn't mind explaining it."

"Well, I used a canvas and specially prepared paints. After a week or so of sketching, a glaze of Prima Materia, and meditation, I was ready to open the portal—"

73

"Canvas? Paint? Sketching?" she interrupted. "I don't want to know about your painting techniques. I want to know how you tapped into the wormhole that brought me here."

"I'm not certain what you mean by the term *wormhole*," he said carefully, "but I created the portal that brought you here by painting your portrait," he said. "I'm an artisan. This is what I do."

"Okay, so you're an artist . . . or an artisan. Artisans paint, I understand that. What I don't understand is how you generate *portals*. Don't you have a machine of some sort that makes use of the principles of quantum physics? How are people reassembled and disassembled?" At his look of incomprehension, she added, "I'm used to artists painting on canvases that are flat. Two dimensional. You can't step through them. Instead you look at them. They brighten up a room. But your paintings could be the subject of a *Twilight Zone* episode."

"I'm not certain how to explain it to you. We simply paint them," the Artisan said with a shrug. "It is an artistic rather than a scientific endeavor."

"Okay." She fought for a moment to get her mind around that one but couldn't quite succeed. "Let's talk about the business you're in for a second. You said you're a mail-order bride service. Where do these brides come from?"

"We have agents in many different time periods who scout out potentials, women who we think might enjoy a life in Blackfell. Usually the potentials' circumstances in their own times are pretty desperate. Most of them jump at the chance to live a comfortable life in Blackfell, where they are well loved."

She drew in a quick breath. "Did you say *time periods?*"

"Yes, time periods."

"So, you're saying that this portal you create doesn't just teleport brides instantly across long distances. It also transports them through time."

"Of course," he said. "What use would we have for a portal that doesn't open into the past?"

Jordan was caught between an urge to strategically pass out and hope she awoke in her apartment, and a need to try to figure this situation out. Being of a practical nature, she ended up choosing the second option. "So, you collect your brides from various times in the past and bring them here, to this time. When is 'this time,' in comparison to my own? Am I in the future or the past?"

"You're in the future."

She glanced around at the primitive workshop they were sitting in, with its complete lack of any modern convenience at all, and nodded, her eyes wide. "The future. I should have guessed. How far in the future?"

"Many thousands of years."

"And I have some kind of scientific expertise you need?" she asked, feeling dizzy all over again.

"Look at this." Conlean stood to retrieve a slip of paper from a workbench, then handed it to her as he sat down again. It felt crisp in her fingers, like antique parchment, and had water and mold stains on one side. Holding the paper carefully, she turned it over.

A book title, *And Baby Makes Three: Fertility and Gene Therapy,* scrolled across one half of the paper in block letters. It was the remnants of a book jacket.

On the other side a black-and-white photograph of the author stared out at her. Stains and cracks due to the paper's age distorted the photograph. Even so, there was something familiar about that partially obscured face.

She squinted and brought the paper closer, until it was just in front of her nose.

Freckles. Dimples. A lopsided smile, tinged with sadness.

She drew in a quick breath. She was looking at herself!

Intently, she scanned the portrait, searching for confirmation of the idea. Discolorations covered most of the eyes and forehead, but the hair . . . softly waving, with blond streaks that betrayed an unfortunate obsession with Clairol Brush-on Highlights . . . the hair could have been hers. And behind her, she could see her desk at the Rinehart Center, and an electron microscope. When had the picture been taken? She couldn't remember ever having posed for a photograph there.

Suddenly, she remembered Dr. Rinehart coming into the laboratory yesterday with that digital camera, and taking her "victory" picture.

Yes, this could be her. Still, her picture was on a book cover, and she'd never written a book.

She turned the paper over, and then back to the front, then over again. She must have missed something, some little detail that would explain the situation, because she was so completely mystified at the moment, her brains so completely boggled, that a duck could come quacking through the studio and she wouldn't even notice. "What is this?" she finally managed.

"It's the cover for a book on the plague," Hawkwood said. He was watching her very carefully.

"A book on the plague?" She turned the paper over, her confusion growing. "What plague?"

"All babies born in Blackfell are male. They become sick shortly after their birth. It's a terrible illness with a fever that nearly burns them up. But most survive. Still, the plague leaves the male babies unable to conceive female children once they become adults."

"Oh, that plague." She shook her head. "I've never heard of such a plague!"

The two men watched her closely.

After a few moments, she shook her head again. "All right. I'll play along. So, what you're saying is, the entire world is fighting a plague that leaves men unable to father female children."

"Yes, that's our problem," Hawkwood agreed. "That's why we have to bring women from the past to our time, as brides. Our situation isn't without precedent, you know. There have been many previous cases of entire species dying out due to infertility, the dinosaurs being one of the most notable. Dinosaur eggs, while incubating, changed sex based on temperature. The impact of an asteroid during the dinosaur's reign on earth, and the subsequent lowering of global temperatures, skewed the dinosaur population toward males and led to their eventual extinction."

"And now humanity is facing the same future, unless we can cure this plague," Conlean added. "Maybe this is nature's way of cleaning house every couple of million years, but I, for one, would like to avoid it."

"Extinction," she breathed. If the two men were to be believed, she was standing with the human species during its last moments on earth. She'd always thought that humankind would end up killing itself off with nukes. But good old Mother Nature was evidently going to take them out, and possibly make room for a species that wasn't intent on destroying her.

Payback, she thought, *is a bitch.*

She glanced down at the paper again. "How does this relate to me?"

Both Conlean and Hawkwood appeared surprised by her statement. "Don't you recognize the book cover?" the older man asked.

She began to feel as if she was missing something big. "No, I don't. I didn't publish my research."

Conlean took the book cover from her virtually nerveless fingers and set it back on the side table. "You *did* write this book. Perhaps you just don't remember doing it."

"I would recall something as significant as a publication."

"Does the name Arnold Rinehart mean anything to you?"

A sudden chill made her shiver. *Rinehart.* The name, spoken by such strange men in such a strange place, almost had the effect of a curse uttered by a witch. "Dr. Rinehart? Of course. He and I worked on a fertility study together. We were using gene therapy to increase sperm motility. How would you know about him?"

"He's listed as your editor on the front page of the book."

"My editor? That's not true. We weren't working on any book together . . ." She trailed off, remembering the months of study data she'd collected, the journals she'd kept regarding the gene therapies, and even her recordings of her personal experiences with the team. If he'd wanted to produce such a book, he'd have had enough information to work with.

"Are you remembering the book now?" Hawkwood prodded.

She refocused on the older man. "Dr. Rinehart and I worked for many months—years, actually—on increasing fertility using various gene therapies. He mentioned that he was considering working for a government facility but said nothing about the studies he might be conducting there."

"So you're denying that you wrote this book?"

"I suppose he could have edited a book based on our shared experiences," she slowly admitted. "So, yes, you could attribute the work to me. But I don't see why he would bother. The results of our therapies were far less than what we'd hoped for. In fact, our last desperate attempt at therapy had been my idea, and it failed so spectacularly that it led to our sponsors shutting the project down."

"I would say," Hawkwood told her, "that your last attempt at gene therapy was indeed spectacular. From what we've learned, Dr. Rinehart took your research material and the idea that a virus would be a good way to deliver genetically altered 'supersperm' to an infertile male. Evidently, he and a secret team of government-sponsored scientists created a virus designed to make all males within fifty square miles infertile, and thus eventually eliminate an entire population within a few decades."

She stared at him. "He created a biological weapon from my research?"

"He and other scientists," Hawkwood confirmed. "We've read that he modeled the plague after some of the more powerful insecticides used during your time."

Insecticides.

Hawkwood's words had a ring of truth to them. A headache began to pound at her temples. Her stomach began to feel sick. Her research had been used to create a biological weapon. Her research might lead to the extinction of the human race.

Her research.

"No. Tell me it's not true." She pressed a hand against her forehead. Both men were staring at her.

"I'm so sorry, Jordan." Conlean paused, as though weighing his words, before continuing. "You have to understand that the people of Blackfell wouldn't look very kindly upon you if they knew you had helped create the plague. To make sure you're safe, we're keeping your true identity a secret while you're here in Blackfell. For all intents and purposes, you were a librarian in your former life."

"I appreciate your concern for my safety," she managed, "but you've got it all wrong. My theories led nowhere. We weren't successful in curing infertility. Dr. Rinehart would have had no use for my research."

"Your research had the opposite effect from what you intended," Conlean said softly.

"Exactly! It didn't cure infertility at all."

"And that's just what the government team wanted. Something that created rather than cured infertility."

She grew quiet. "And now you're hoping I can cure this plague and save the human race from extinction."

"We're not hoping, dear lady. We're *praying*."

Heat washed over her, warming her cheeks and bringing perspiration out on her brow. "And this is the laboratory you want me to use to find a cure?"

"We call it a studio. It's very similar to the one you'll be using, and it's the best that artistry has to offer."

She glanced around at the primitive earthenware jugs and furnace and blotted her brow with her sleeve. "I don't have the equipment I need. Where are all the technological advancements? This place looks like it's from the Dark Ages."

"There hasn't been much technological advancement since the release of the plague," Conlean said. "Through the millennia, we've relinquished our hold on science—as it produced only suffering—and turned to artistry."

"Artistry. You mentioned that before. You use artistry to create your time portals." She struggled to understand, but her head was pounding so hard, she could barely think. "I don't understand artistry, or how it manipulates time and space."

Hawkwood shrugged. "You're from a time when science ruled, so we don't expect you to understand our ways all at once. Suffice it to say that upon discovering Prima Materia, we stopped worrying about how things work and started worrying about how they look and feel."

She clutched her glass. About an inch of liquid remained in it. She didn't think an inch would be enough. She needed a quart. And if she couldn't find a quart, she'd take ice water in its place. Her cheeks felt hot. Feverish. The furnace was heating the studio up to sauna levels. She wondered why the two men showed no signs of roasting. "I feel sick."

"Jordan . . ." Conlean sounded wary. He stared meaningfully at Hawkwood. "It's begun."

Hawkwood rose and went to a collection of vials on a shelf.

"What's begun?" she asked, and dropped the glass she'd been holding from a hand that suddenly felt weak. The glass hit the stone floor with a crack and shattered.

Baudrons fled from her chair and ran behind the furnace.

Jordan stared down at the fragments. She was just like that glass—broken into a hundred fragments that could never be glued back together. "Why do I feel so sick?"

Hawkwood moved to her side with another glass in hand, this one filled with a light pink liquid. "It's the plague. You need to rest. Drink this, Jordan."

Conlean's arm slipped around her back. She sagged against him. Her muscles felt sore; her bones ached.

The older man lifted the drug to her lips and poured

it into her. She hadn't the strength to resist him. Almost immediately she began to feel sleepy. Then, for the second time that evening, she found herself in Conlean's arms. "Is it going to kill me?"

"You'll be ill for a while," Conlean murmured close to her ear. "But you'll survive."

She hadn't any breath left to tell him that as long as she survived, she'd be all right, because the plague couldn't take her fertility away from her. She was already infertile.

"Take her to her room," Hawkwood directed, and then she and Conlean were moving out of the studio and into a dark stone corridor.

The cat, she saw, was following them.

Chapter Seven

Conlean brought Jordan through the lower levels of the Gallery, to shield her from prying eyes. Baudrons tagged along, skulking from dark corner to dark corner, but he paid the cat little attention. He was focused on Jordan.

She was very supple, her body molding itself to his as though he had painted her custom-made to his own measurements. He recalled thinking of her as tough yet delicate when he'd painted her portrait, and in reality she possessed that same contrary mixture he'd imagined, her strength that of a sapling that bends in a harsh wind but never breaks. As they passed through a particularly dark section of the corridor, he leaned forward to catch her scent. It was spicy, mysterious; something he'd never smelled before.

He had to admit, he found her fascinating. The determination in her eyes as she'd tried to convince them to let her go, her strength of mind in spite of the fact that he'd brought her through *between time* to an unfamiliar world—that alone had inspired him with a hundred ideas for painting vivid, unpredictable women. She was quick, volatile, and fiery; yet she had a certain vulnerability about her, a sadness that seemed to run very deep. Bright red and deep blue, he thought. No pastels here.

His first impression of her? He liked her. A lot. He knew she belonged to another man—his father—and yet he found himself enjoying the feel of her in his arms. Even so, it was hard to hold her, and see the youth and beauty in her face, and to think of her as vulnerable, while at the same time knowing that the fate of Blackfell lay upon her slender shoulders. Would she assist them in curing the plague? Remembering her earlier demands to return home and her flat refusal to marry his father, he suspected he was going to need every inducement he could come up with to win her cooperation.

He reached the door to her room. A guard sitting outside the door stood promptly and opened it for him. Seconds later, a white streak emerged from the darkness in the corridor and ran into Jordan's room. Conlean followed the cat inside and took a moment to glance around the room to make certain everything had been prepared as he'd requested.

The team of apprentice artisans he'd assembled had done an admirable job of bringing warmth and charm to the cold stone walls by adding natural elements and textures. Folding screens made of paper and beautifully painted with scenery depicting a local hillside brightened the darkest corners of the room, and a six-inch strip of highly polished wood carved with leaves formed a border around the ceiling. Textured silk the color of azure blue draped the glazed windows and simple woven mats protected feet from the cold marble floor, while an arrangement of polished stones atop a chest served as a decorative touch. The paintings in the room, Conlean saw, were simple, strong, and graphic, with the initial brushstrokes also serving as the final result; he detected no evidence of overpainting or redoing.

Pleased, Conlean brought her limp form to her bed, a wooden platform that rose a scant six inches off the floor and was covered with a plush mattress.

A page, one who had been altered so he might serve women without desiring them, moved forward to help Conlean undress her.

"Will you require my assistance, Artisan?" the page asked.

"Not this time. My father would expect me to look after her personally." Conlean laid her on the mattress and arranged a few silk cushions under her head. A black lacquered chest for her clothes stood next to the bed, and a basin of water sat atop it. The lighting was dim; as he'd requested, candles rather than lanterns brought a soft glow to the polished surfaces and a stick of burning incense filled the air with a brisk fragrance. Conlean dipped a cloth into the basin of water and wrung it out. He gently laid it on her forehead to cool her.

Judging by his raised eyebrows, the page had clearly expected to remain in Jordan's room to care for her.

"I've brought more medicine to reduce her fever. Will you need anything else?"

"No," Conlean replied. "I'll ring for you if anything comes up."

The Gallery was buzzing with the knowledge that the Patriarch's new bride had been retrieved, and everyone wanted a look at her. The page was no less interested. And in truth, it was the youth's task to care for Jordan. Pages were the caretakers of all brides newly retrieved, and Conlean was overstepping his bounds by insisting on caring for her himself.

In this one instance, though, he'd had no choice but to disregard tradition. Jordan was the key to their entire plan. If she even hinted at her "kidnapping" during her feverish ramblings over the next several days to anyone but him, he and Hawkwood would be found out. And so, this time the gossipy page was out of luck. Conlean only wished he didn't feel so much enjoyment in her presence. Why couldn't she have been unattractive and boring?

"She'll be hungry when she awakens," the page warned him.

"Then I'll feed her. That'll be all."

Moving toward Baudrons and making circling motions with his arms, the page tried to chase the cat from the room.

"Don't bother Baudrons," Conlean directed. "I'll see to her."

Lingering for a few seconds more, the page glanced repeatedly at Jordan. Just when Conlean thought he might have to throw the youth out, he finally left.

They were finally alone.

Almost.

Swallowing against a sudden dryness in his throat, Conlean walked to the window and opened it wide enough for the cat to leave. "Baudrons, would you mind . . ."

An eddy of fresh air curled around the room. Baudrons ran across the room and jumped out of the window.

Conlean closed the window and walked back over to Jordan. He stared at her unconscious form for a moment, marshaling his courage, before he kneeled at her side and set about removing her clothes, so that she might be easier to care for during her illness. This again was something that pages normally did.

Her outfit was completely shapeless and without any real color, a far cry from what he was used to. She would, he thought, look even more attractive once she'd put on something more feminine. He grasped the bottom of her shirt, to draw it up over her head. It moved reluctantly, as though it didn't want to allow him the sight of her bare skin, but he quickly realized it was simply caught beneath her weight.

Letting out a deep breath, he slid his hand between her back and the mattress and lifted her, at the same time pulling the shirt upward. Inch by inch the soft contours of her belly and ribs were exposed. Her skin looked so smooth, so supple, so pale.

He quickly looked away and focused on the windows while willing his pulse to slow. He knew he shouldn't be looking at her this way, thinking of her like this. She would soon be his father's bride, for

God's sake. And yet, this sneaking pleasure continued to taunt him. He wished the task of caring for her had remained with the page.

He dragged another deep breath into his chest, then reached beneath her shirt, the heat of her body enveloping his hands as he drew her arms from their sleeves. The scent of her drifted across his face like a warm summer breeze. Clearly uncomfortable in the sleep that the fever-relieving potion had induced, she turned restlessly, making his job easier by forcing the cloth up. He averted his gaze as he pulled the shirt over her head and set it next to the bed.

A few moments passed. Still, he didn't look at her. Instead he reminded himself how helpless and ill she was, and how much she needed him to look after her and protect her. He'd brought her here, and that made him accountable for her well-being. Keeping his responsibilities firmly in mind, he turned back to her and allowed his gaze to drift downward.

One of those contraptions called bras, he discovered, was girding her breasts. He'd seen these devices before. It forced her breasts upward in a way that made him want to forget all his good intentions. A bit kinder to a woman than the corsets of a still earlier era, the bra looked uncomfortable. He debated whether or not he should remove it. Would she be more comfortable without it? And how would she feel when she realized he'd taken it off her?

Caught in indecision, he slipped a finger beneath one of the straps. It pressed his finger into her skin. She was very warm, very soft. He grew still. The whiskey he'd been drinking before had created a fire in his veins. The sensations he felt now from touching her made him feel the same way. Hot. Reckless.

What would a page have done in this situation? The youth would have taken the bra off her, of course. The device was tight and constricting. Why should he do any less?

He had to get the damned thing off her. But he had to do it *fast*.

Moving quickly now, he tried to recall how they were secured. He seemed to remember hooks and eyes, but where? He tested the straps near her shoulders and the edges of the device along her breasts. There were no fasteners, no breaks in the fabric. Stifling a groan, he ran his fingers along the strap that went around her back and discovered the little metal loops he'd been looking for.

He lifted her up with one arm and fiddled with the loops with his free hand. He could tell from touching them that the fasteners shouldn't be difficult to disengage; a child could probably do it. But he seemed to possess only thumbs today; he fumbled with them like an idiot and gained not an inch of ground. The heat from her body, which curled around him like the smoke from a smoldering fire, didn't help matters any.

Muttering an oath, Conlean jumped up and strode over to a black lacquered chest, where he found a small sewing knife. Jaw clenched, he brought it back to her bedside, hunkered down, and carefully sawed through the straps in two places before he removed the bra. Then he sat back on his heels and gazed at her body, revealed to him from the waist up and as perfect as he could imagine any woman's.

After a while, he felt stupid, sitting there staring at her. Did he plan on gaping at her all day while she grew hot with fever? What sort of caretaker was he? Determined to finish undressing her, he went to work on the ugly blue garment encasing her legs. The cloth proved surprisingly stiff and difficult to pull off. Still, he managed to draw it down to her ankles and over her feet, revealing slender hips and long legs. He tried not to dwell on how exquisite she was and eyed the scrap of fabric that covered the small, remaining triangle of her flesh.

A wise man, he thought, would leave that scrap alone. But his hand seemed to have its own opinion and moved to touch her hip, where the fabric crossed. Frowning, he shook his head and drew his hand away. Silently berating himself, he rose from her bedside and retrieved a lightweight blanket from the cupboard. He brought it back to her and tucked it around her nearly naked form. Only when she was covered from neck to ankles did he finally relax.

Conflicting emotions twisted through him as he drew the basin of water within reach and sponged her forehead with a washcloth. He had no doubt that the end he and Hawkwood sought—a cure to the plague—was the best long-term solution to Blackfell's problems. He wouldn't have agreed to help the Grand Artisan had he felt otherwise, and the knowledge that he was doing the right thing gave him some satisfaction. But he didn't know if he could justify, to himself or anyone else, the means they'd chosen to achieve that end, especially when the means included lies, disloyalty, kidnapping, and treason.

Over the next few days, as Jordan's fever worsened, his mood continued to hover somewhere between relief that he was finally doing something about the plague and queasiness over the idea of betraying his father. He found himself gazing at her, memorizing the lines of her face and thinking that this was the bride he'd retrieved for his father . . . a woman whose efforts would, with some luck, topple the established order in Blackfell. What would happen to the Patriarchy and his father if Jordan found a cure for the plague and women became readily available? The most powerful and wealthy men in Blackfell, those who controlled the supply of women, would have their feet kicked out from under them. And if the supporters of the Patriarchy fell, so would the Patriarch.

So would his *father*.

Had any other son deceived his own father more thoroughly? Conlean imagined the older man's graying face twisted with hurt, darkened with the knowledge of treachery, the brows drawn together under the weight of the humiliation of being destroyed by his own son. He had no doubt that all his father's emotions would eventually gel into pure, simple hatred. The thought left him feeling almost sick with guilt and regret, two sentiments that stayed with him until the third night, when Jordan's temperature finally went down.

He'd been worrying that she might be one of the rare women who died from the plague, but that night, for the first time since her arrival in Blackfell, she fell into a natural sleep. Relief filled him and, almost as exhausted as she, Conlean drifted off right where he was, sitting next to her with his back propped up against some cushions. He didn't wake until the following morning when the page, whom Conlean had all but barred from the room, entered with a breakfast tray.

"She's waking, Artisan," the page announced as he placed the tray on a table.

Conlean jumped at the sound of the youth's voice and dragged his feet off the cushion he'd rested them on. He felt stiff all over, sore. None of that mattered, however, when he looked at Jordan and saw her eyes, as clear and blue-green as a mountain pond. Immediately he dismissed the page, and waited until the younger man had left before placing his palm on her forehead. Much to his relief, she felt cool. She didn't flinch or pull away from his touch, which pleased him even more.

"How are you feeling?" he asked, dropping his hand to his side.

She swallowed a few times, as though trying to work out a knot in her throat. "My head's pounding. What was in that drink you gave me?"

"Medicine to help you through your infection. Do you know how long you've been sick?"

She glanced out the window. "I see the sun shining, so I guess I've slept through the night and into the next day."

"You've been ill for nearly four days."

"Four days?" Her eyes grew wide. "I have to go home. People will be looking for me, wondering where I am."

93

He bit back a reminder that she wouldn't be going home again. "You've been sick, Jordan. You won't be going anywhere until you get your strength back. How about trying to eat?"

"I suppose you're right." She narrowed her eyes, and he thought he was in for another confrontation. But then her eyes cleared and she looked at the covered platters on the breakfast tray. "What do you have for me?"

"Let's find out." Relieved, he slipped a cushion behind her to prop her up and placed the breakfast tray on her lap. Then he lifted the tops of the dishes the kitchen had prepared.

Fragrant steam filled the room. Toast, eggs, a bowl of porridge, and a glass of fresh-squeezed orange juice made his stomach grumble about not being fed lately.

She examined the contents of the tray. "I know all these foods. My mother used to cook me this sort of breakfast when I was little."

He nodded, hoping she found some comfort in familiarity. "If the food displeases you, I'll have the page bring you something else."

"No, no, it's fine." Looking down at the robe that had replaced the clothes from her time, she murmured, "What am I wearing? Pajamas?"

"It's a very loose robe called a pao, made for comfort and often worn during sleep. You'll find many more gowns in your wardrobe, most of them fitted and appropriate for day wear."

"Who took care of me while I was ill?"

He took a moment to assess the sudden color in her cheeks, and heard what she hadn't said as well as what she had. She wanted to know who had taken her old clothes off, sponged her down, and looked after her while she lay there helpless. He wished he could tell her that the page had performed that duty, to spare her further distress. But lying to her didn't sit easily with him, so he decided to tell her the truth—or at least an edited version of it. He wouldn't mention how much he'd enjoyed the task, despite his best intentions. "I was here with you the entire time."

"You looked after me?"

She sounded so appalled that he rushed on to say, rather stiffly, "I didn't do anything that anyone would consider improper."

"I doubt you know the difference between proper and improper," she accused, her cheeks growing redder. "You've brought me here against my will and don't seem to have any problem with your conscience."

He did see her point. How could she know for certain that he hadn't taken liberties with her? She didn't know him or what he was capable of. Remembering that he had to win her trust before he'd gain her cooperation, he spoke in his most earnest tone. "I'm not happy that you're here . . . I mean, I'm happy that you're here but not that you don't want to be here . . ." Suddenly stopping, aware that he sounded like a fool, he drew in a deep breath. "What I'm trying to say is that my conscience *is* bothering me. I don't like keeping you here against your will. Still, I don't have much of a choice.

"And as for taking advantage of you while you couldn't defend yourself, I would never do such a thing. Here on Blackfell, women aren't easy to come by. Because they're so rare, they're treated with nothing but respect. Mistreating a woman would stain a man's honor forever."

Eyebrow lifted, she tilted her head. "You mean we're like precious diamonds, to be mounted in a fancy setting and admired from afar?"

He shrugged. "I'm not sure I like the analogy, but in some ways, yes."

"What about you? Do you have your own woman?"

"No, I don't," he admitted, feeling a little uncomfortable. The discussion was getting very personal. "I haven't qualified for a wife yet. I need a certain amount of funds in my account before I can commission a portrait of my bride."

"Oh, I get it. Women go to the highest bidder."

"Only men who have demonstrated financial stability can commission a portrait," he corrected her. "It works to the bride's advantage, don't you think?"

"I suppose. So how much more money do you need before you can retrieve a bride?"

"I have several years of painting ahead of me," he admitted.

"Several years ahead of you before marriage," she murmured, "and no girlfriend. Doesn't sound like much fun. Does Hawkwood have a wife?"

"Hawkwood never commissioned a portrait. He's unmarried and devoted to his work."

"So you're both single men. Bachelors. And yet, oddly enough, I believe you when you say that you wouldn't take advantage of me. There's something truthful in your voice and your eyes." After a slight hesitation, she grasped his hand. "Thanks for taking care of me while I was sick."

He slipped his hand out from under hers, at the same time returning her smile, so she wouldn't think he was rebuffing her. The truth was, her hand felt warm, and that warmth had seeped beneath his skin and set his nerves afire. He felt like a starving man eyeing a gourmet meal, and he didn't want to awaken a longing that could never be satisfied. "You're welcome."

She folded her hands in her lap and looked at him calmly. "So what's next? Who's going to show me around?"

"I will. You're my responsibility, Jordan, until you—" He'd been planning to say, *until you marry my father*, but unwilling to spoil the growing rapport between them, he hesitated.

"Until I what? Find that cure you're looking for?" She picked up her fork and speared a piece of omelet. "I have a lot of questions for you, Artisan."

"I have a few for you, too."

She paused, her fork halfway to her mouth. "I thought you knew everything about me already."

"My details are sketchy." He tried to bring the conversation to a more personal level. "I was wondering, will anyone miss you from your time?"

She narrowed her eyes. "A lot of people will notice my disappearance," she informed him. "My landlord, the bill collectors, the unemployment agency . . . What do you care? They won't find me, and can't come after me."

"What about family?" he pressed, his thoughts running ahead to her upcoming marriage. If she'd had feelings for someone back in her own time, those feelings would make it much more difficult to convince her to marry his father.

She lifted an eyebrow. "My father is dead, and my sister and I lost touch. As I mentioned earlier when you barged into my apartment, I don't have a husband. I'm divorced, in fact."

"Divorced?" Although not unknown to him, the word was so infrequently used that Conlean had to think for a moment to remember what it meant. "You and your husband ended your marriage?"

"That's right."

He shook his head. Divorce was unheard of in Blackfell. "Why did you divorce?"

"For a lot of reasons. What business is it of yours?"

He eyed her closely. "No one divorces anymore; marriages are far too precious to disregard so easily. I was merely curious about an anachronistic practice."

"Just about everyone I knew who married eventually got divorced," she said, a little defensively. "I wasn't so unusual."

"According to the history books, the practice reached its highest peak during the early twenty-first century. I've always thought it must have been hard for the children, to see their parents part."

"We didn't have any children," she said, a look of pain crossing her face.

"I guessed as much. I'm sure I would have heard about it from you by now if you had. Why did you decide against it?"

"I couldn't," she blurted out. Instantly, a flush reddened her cheeks.

"You couldn't?" Confused, he stared at her. "What do you mean?"

"I didn't mean to say that," she hedged.

"But you did. And now, of course, I'm even more curious," he said lightly, his tone at odds with the shock spreading through him. *Was she infertile?*

"Well, I guess I might as well tell you that I've had a problem conceiving children. Sad, isn't it? I wasn't even exposed to this plague of yours. I managed to be infertile all on my own. That's why my ex, Dennis, divorced me. He wanted a family."

"I'm very sorry," he managed. *Infertile!* His father had requested a bride in order to sire a new heir to the Patriarchy, and here he had retrieved a woman who couldn't have a child! He struggled to hide his reaction.

"Don't be sorry for me. I've gotten over it."

He heard the pain in her voice, the loneliness that she couldn't quite hide. Anger at the man who had clearly broken her heart chased away some of his shock. "This Dennis must not have been much of a man, to divorce his bride so easily."

"I don't blame him." She paused, drew in a deep breath, and then continued, "He wanted children, and I couldn't give them to him. Why should he give up all his chances for happiness because of a youthful promise?"

"Here, marriage is sacred," he reiterated.

"You've obviously never been trapped in a bad one." She narrowed her eyes. "There isn't any greater leap of faith than marriage. You're betting your entire future on the hope that love can survive the test of frustrated expectations and change. Few couples succeed."

He swallowed. The conversation had taken a bad turn, especially in light of the fact that he was supposed to convince her to marry his father. Now that he knew she was infertile, he felt even worse about his deception. What would his father do when her infertility became obvious? At the very least, the Patriarch would requisition another bride, and Jordan would be cast aside. Then she would be *his* responsibility.

What would he do with her then? Marry her himself? Preposterous! "There are other advantages to marriage, such as companionship . . ."

"Marriage is for fools," she cut in. "It creates too many financial and social penalties. Any woman worth her salt should avoid it."

"But you agreed to marry once. You didn't always feel this way about the subject."

"That was because I believed in the power of love to eclipse any hardship life could deal out. I don't anymore." She stated the last part with such finality that deep foreboding filled him.

"Would you, ah, ever consider marrying again?"

A sudden smile lightened her features. "Are you proposing?"

"No, not me . . ." he hurried to say, then realized she was teasing him. "But perhaps someday, here on Blackfell, you might find marriage convenient—"

"Oh, that's right, I remember now. You and your older friend brought me here as a bride. You want me to marry someone. You're quite the matchmaker, aren't you? All this talk about husbands and marriage. Thinking about trying it out yourself?"

Her husky voice sounded soft to his ears. His gaze flicked to her full breasts before he even realized where he was looking. Quickly he glanced away and angrily berated himself for ogling his father's future wife. But then, a moment later, he found himself wondering what it would be like to take her to bed with him every night. God knew his bed was cold now. She would warm it up pretty damned quickly.

For a second time, he caught himself. What was wrong with him? How could he sit there and daydream about the woman who was destined to marry his father? Something about her was far too fascinating for comfort. "I have no intention of marrying just yet."

"I have no intention of marrying ever again," she told him, her tone saying she would brook no further argument. "For any reason. I don't care what kind of scheme you and your friend have cooked up."

He gazed at her, unable to reply. He hadn't expected her to be so obstinately opposed to the entire idea of marriage, let alone a marriage of convenience. He was going to have to show her why the marriage was necessary, and convince her to help them.

And yet, even as he thought of how he might build a case for the marriage, he realized how difficult his task would be. Did women respond to cold, hard facts and logic? Something told him he was going to have to do better than that. He had to show Blackfell in its best light and appeal to her heart as well as her mind. The problem was, he didn't know the first damned thing about women, courtship, or marriage.

Obviously he was going to have to learn fast. Very fast.

A visit to the Counselor was definitely in order.

Chapter Eight

"Why are you staring at me like that?" Jordan asked. When she'd told him she'd never marry, he'd seemed to take her statement like a blow to the stomach. And then, his gaze fixed on her, he'd fallen into thought.

He blinked once. "Am I staring at you?"

"You are. In fact, you look as though I've just jilted you at the altar."

He visibly struggled to modulate his expression.

"What's the problem?" she pressed.

"There's no problem."

She narrowed her eyes. He clearly had a problem. Was he still actually hoping that she would marry someone in Blackfell, as he'd suggested earlier? Or did he have a different kind of problem? She'd noticed the way his gaze had flicked across her breasts. Hadn't he'd seen enough of her while taking care of her?

The thought should have pissed her off. Instead, she found herself intrigued by the idea. He might have kidnapped her and hatched this crazy plan that he expected her to become a part of, but he also had a tousled-looking attractiveness. He was like velvet and steel—velvet in the way he handled her and steel in his determination to bend her to his will. Some feminine part of her wanted to see exactly how velvety he would become in his effort to make her behave.

It was a dangerous thought. Very dangerous.

"I have something for you," he announced, distracting her. His shoulders relaxing, he reached behind him and grasped a book, which he then deposited on the foot of her bed.

She glanced down at the book and saw the cover he'd shown her earlier. "Is this the book I supposedly authored?"

He nodded. "I thought you might like to read it."

"I definitely would." She picked it up, and some of the pages started to fall out. "Not in very good shape, is it?"

"You can't expect much more from a book that's several thousand years old," he reminded her. "Please be careful with it."

She shuffled the pages back toward the spine before they fell out completely. "I'll treat it like a baby," she promised, then grimaced at her poor choice of words. "In the meanwhile, can you tell me a little more about your portals and *between time?* I'm fascinated by the whole idea. Who would have thought we'd come up with a way to actually travel through time? Give me the details, Conlean."

He smiled a little. "You really want to know?"

She nodded enthusiastically. "How in God's name did we figure it out? And how long has this bride business been going on?"

"Okay. First, let me put this away." His smile broadening, he picked up the book, walked over to one of the many lacquered chests in her room, and locked it inside with a small key. "Do me a favor and keep the book locked up when you're not looking at it. We don't want anyone knowing that you were involved in creating the plague." He handed the key to her.

A tiny shudder went through her at the thought of someone in Blackfell finding out that her research had been used to nearly decimate civilization. They'd string her up in one hot minute. She took the key and slipped it into a pocket of her robe. "I will."

"Good." He took a seat next to her, leaned backward against the cushions, and made himself comfortable. "So, you want to know how we travel through time."

"Yes! Was there a new scientific discovery? Another whopper like Einstein's Theory of Relativity?"

"Something *was* discovered. Not a new scientific law, though. Instead, we stumbled across a substance called Prima Materia. When used in its purest form, Prima Materia turns an artisan's portrait into a portal to the woman herself."

"Prima Materia?" She furrowed her brow. "I don't think I've ever heard of it. It's not on the periodic table of elements, that's for sure."

"Prima Materia is the most basic element in existence. In fact, it's a building block for all other elements."

She tried to imagine the chemical structure for such a substance and failed. "Where did it come from?"

"It didn't *come* from anywhere. Prima Materia has always been present, like air or water. It's in everything. It even formed the basis of the universe before the start of the expansion. But it doesn't usually exist in its purest form. Rather, it assumes the form of elemental qualities imposed on it."

"What sort of elemental qualities?"

"Earth, air, fire, water. Humidity, sunlight. Ice. Sound. Colors also have certain effects on it."

"I don't understand."

Animation lightened his face. "When ice and pure winter sunlight are applied to Prima Materia in the right combination, it takes the form of silver."

"The color or the metal?"

"The metal," he clarified. "We create copper—another metal—by passing Prima Materia through fire and adding orange tincture. Rubies are made by mixing in red tincture and blood; opals by adding sand and an extended exposure to moonlight; gold by adding a complex list of items, summer sunlight being the most important."

"You turn ordinary ingredients into gold just by mixing them properly and adding a little sunshine?"

"It's not so simple. Essentially, though, yes. We do."

Completely awed by the whole idea, she managed a nod. Clearly this Prima Materia had caused the people of Blackfell to think in terms of color and light, rather than in weights and chemical structures. She found the whole concept fascinating. "So, you somehow got your hands on this stuff in its purest form?"

"We did."

"How?"

"Well, we found it. Though maybe I should say *unearthed* it. In an archaeological dig. Along with the journal of the man who had created it, and his advice on how to use it. His name was Nicholas Flamel, and his journal is now known as *The Fundamentals of the Grand Artisan*."

"Nicholas Flamel," she murmured, rolling the words around on her tongue. "His name sounds familiar. What century did he live in?"

"Long before your time. During the Dark Ages, in fact. He was both an alchemist and a painter." Conlean continued on with a description of how Flamel had gained fame in his own time by manufacturing Prima Materia and then turning it into gold for a select few. News of Flamel's achievements, he explained, had quickly gotten around, inciting the jealousy and greed of kings and mercenaries and forcing the man to go into hiding. Before he died, Flamel had apparently hidden his cache of Prima Materia along with his journal, which contained a recipe for the substance; desperate men far in advance of Jordan's era had unearthed it.

As Conlean was giving her this explanation, she sensed that additional information regarding this Flamel character lay just beyond her grasp, somewhere in the recesses of her memory. She couldn't seem to draw it out, though. It just kept teasing her.

Flamel. *Flamel.*

Her gaze touched on an arrangement of simple gray stones in a bowl. It wasn't the sort of decoration she would have used in her own apartment. Still, it had an attractiveness about it, a peaceful quality.

Stones!

"I know where I've heard of Nicholas Flamel," she breathed. "He was the one who, according to legend, created the Philosopher's Stone!"

He nodded. "The Philosopher's Stone is just another name for Prima Materia."

"And I always thought the story of the Philosopher's Stone was just a fairy tale. I'd love to see how Prima Materia is manufactured."

"So far, we haven't been successful in manufacturing it according to Flamel's recipe."

"Well, then, where do you get it from?"

"We're still using the cache of Prima Materia that Flamel buried along with his journal."

Her brow furrowed. "You must have a lot of it."

"We did at one time. It's running out, I'm afraid."

"And you can't produce any more?"

"We haven't managed it yet."

"Are you close, at least? What are you going to do if it runs out?" She imagined their whole mail-order bride business coming to a grinding halt. Without Prima Materia, they couldn't make their portals, and without portals to the past, how could they bring women to Blackfell?

"When it runs out, we're going to be in trouble unless we either cure the plague or manage to reproduce more Prima Materia from Nicholas Flamel's recipe."

Silence momentarily filled the room as she digested this piece of information and its implications: the eventual extinction of the human species. "How much of it is left, exactly?"

"We've used about half of Flamel's cache. We're also continually attempting to make more; in fact, there are entire laboratories devoted to the task. So far, though, we've had no luck. We're not even close."

"That is not good." She narrowed her eyes as a sudden thought struck her. "Why don't you go back to Flamel's time and bring either him, or more Prima Materia, to Blackfell?"

"We'd need a portrait of him in order to construct the portal to his time and location. So far, the Seekers haven't been able to find a portrait. The man went into hiding to protect himself and did a very good job of it. Anyway, Hawkwood and I both think that we'd be better off curing the plague, and ending the need for Prima Materia, than manufacturing more of the substance and perpetuating the use of it."

"I agree. Prima Materia is simply a Band-Aid on a more basic problem." She tilted her head, interested by something he'd said. "Who—or what— are 'Seekers'?"

He paused to readjust a pillow behind him before continuing. "Seekers are men who go through a portal into the past and remain there. They are agents who find women willing to become brides in Blackfell. If a Seeker locates a woman who wishes to become a bride, he puts the would-be bride's picture and biography in a specialized vault. The picture and biography are used by artisans to create a portal."

"What sort of women have you brought here in the past?"

"We've rescued aristocrats from the French Revolution, retrieved women from the hinterlands of Siberia, taken prisoners from concentration camps, whisked away marriageable daughters threatened by the Aazimbi Uprising—"

"The Aazimbi Uprising?"

"Just after your time," he informed her. "All of our brides are from pre-plague eras, naturally."

"And you orient your time travel according to the woman's likeness on paper." She shook her head, fascinated by the substance he called Prima Materia. "What does Prima Materia look like? And what else can it do?"

"Prima Materia is devoid of all color and appears black to the eye. That's because it absorbs light. As far as its other properties go, we haven't really tested it beyond its ability to create portals. We need the portals to survive and only have a limited supply of Prima Materia, so it isn't used for anything else."

"What form does it take? Is it a liquid?"

"It's solid, like clay, unless it's raised to a certain temperature, at which point it becomes a liquid. If heated enough, it eventually evaporates."

She tapped her chin in a thoughtful manner. "A solid. Devoid of color. And capable of changing its basic structure depending on what other elements it comes into contact with. Interesting. It almost sounds alive. But how does it manipulate time? There must be some sort of mathematical expression involved."

"There may be. If so, I'm not aware of it. Although we've experienced Prima Materia's strange properties, including its ability to bend time and space, we haven't tried to assign numbers to them. We're artisans, not scientists. We don't need numbers and formulas."

She frowned. There had to be a way to quantify Prima Materia's effects.

A lopsided smile curved his lips. "I can see you're not satisfied with my explanation. Is it simply that you don't understand? Perhaps your science wasn't as advanced as our artistry."

She nodded slowly, her gaze touching on the simple, clean lines of the room's furnishings and the arrangement of stones on one of the bureaus. The selection of colors, materials, shapes, and lines combined to create a feeling of unequalled tranquility. She'd experienced nothing like it in the past. Clearly these people's understanding of artistry went far beyond anything dreamed of in her time. But could it completely replace science?

For the moment, she decided to give him the benefit of the doubt. The nuances and possibilities of artistry were clearly beyond her. "Your world appears several hundreds of years behind mine technologically. Maybe, though, things are just . . . different. This artistry is a whole new way of thinking. I'm going to need time to adjust to it. And I'd really like to examine some Prima Materia."

"Hawkwood and I would like you to have a chance to study it, combine it with other materials, whatever you'd like. But you're going to have to study it secretly."

"What?" Her eyebrows crept upward. She hadn't expected this. "Why?"

"Women have one purpose on Blackfell: to have children. That's why they're brought from the past.

They don't go into studios and experiment with Prima Materia."

"Are you saying that in Blackfell women are baby machines and nothing more?"

"The term 'baby machines' seems a little harsh, but essentially, that's what they agree to do when they come here. It's necessary for our survival. And it's in their contract."

"I remember someone mentioning that every bride signs a contract," she said. "Sort of like a prenuptial agreement."

"Contracts are standard with every retrieval."

"Where's my contract?"

He shifted uncomfortably against the cushions. "We have a false contract in your name, with details invented to protect your identity."

"I assume this false contract says that I'm going to marry some man and make him lots of children. Did you even forge my signature on it?"

He shrugged. "Yes."

Disgusted with his deviousness, she shook her head. "You'd better give me the details of this false identity you've constructed for me so I can answer questions without getting us both into trouble."

"Good idea."

For the next several minutes, Conlean described her former life in Philadelphia, as a librarian working in the Free Library; the fact that she'd been an only child; and other details that seemed to paint her life as a very lonely one, indeed. She repeated the history when he'd finished, and after satisfying him that she could successfully answer at least cursory questions, she broached a topic that she'd been wondering about while he talked about her fake life.

"You keep telling me that you want me to marry. Who, exactly, am I supposed to be marrying? Do you have a groom picked out?"

"The Patriarch of Blackfell," he said flatly.

"Who the heck is that?"

"He's the ruler of Blackfell . . , similar to a king or emperor."

She stared at him. "You've recruited me to become Queen of Blackfell? You're crazier than I thought. In any case, it isn't happening, so stop trying to make it happen."

"Your marriage must happen, Jordan. You will become Matriarch."

She sighed deeply. "All of this cloak-and-dagger stuff is making things a lot harder for everyone. I know you're worried that people will react badly if they find out that my research was used to create the plague, but surely they'll get over it after realizing that I might be able to cure the problem. Maybe we should just give folks the benefit of the doubt and be truthful? After the furor dies down, I'll surely be given everything I need to do some research."

"What you say makes sense, but you're missing one point. Not everyone feels that a cure is needed. In fact, I'd say that more than a few people would resort to murder to prevent that cure from being found."

"Murder? Are you kidding? They didn't murder Louis Pasteur. Why would anyone want to take me out?"

"Many rich and influential patrons rely on the benefits they receive from our bride retrieval system." He sat forward, his expression betraying tension. "Artisans and the Gallery exist solely to support the service. Studios of alchemists work around the clock to find ways to manufacture more Prima Materia. The Patriarchy of Blackfell stays in power mostly because it controls the supply of Prima Materia. In short, every aspect of our society is tied to bringing brides from the past to the present. If we cure the plague and women can be born naturally into Blackfell, all of these organizations will no longer be needed. We're talking revolution, Jordan."

"Sounds like the oil cartels that existed in my time," she remarked. "We knew that the fossil fuel supplies would eventually dry up, but very little was done to prevent it. The most powerful and wealthiest men had invested heavily in the oil fields and would have lost their shirts had the world found an alternative source of energy. Now women are the commodity rather than oil."

"I guess human nature never really changes," he murmured.

"No, it doesn't," she agreed. "You've got quite a setup here, with all these women serving as willing and happy handmaidens. It's a man's paradise."

A mild frown shaped his lips. "Not quite. Not everyone can afford a bride. There are a lot of men who would give just about anything to have a wife and family. Unfortunately only the most successful and favored men are rewarded with brides."

"Wow. I can't imagine living in a world where marriage itself is restricted . . . not that I believe in the institution, remember."

With a pained look on his face, he continued, "The men who don't have families have formed a grass roots party intent on making brides an entitlement rather than a reward. They call themselves the FFA Party, with FFA standing for Families For All. They've caused the Patriarchy a lot of trouble with their rabble-rousing and kidnappings."

Amusement made her smile. "Now I've heard it all: a socialist marriage party disrupting society in the tradition of Greenpeace. Still, if women are banned from laboratories, why did you bring me here? Even if I was to agree to stay—and I haven't yet agreed—clearly I'm not going to get access to the facilities I'll need in order to help you."

He opened his mouth to reply, closed it without uttering a syllable, and then looked at her fixedly for several seconds.

"What?" she asked. "What's the problem?" Sudden comprehension dawned, and she shook her head. "Oh, no. We're back to that marriage idea, aren't we? Somehow, it's tied in."

Visibly swallowing, he replied, "Your marriage to the Patriarch would provide you with the privileges you'll need. As Matriarch, you'll have permission to enter studios and libraries that the average woman wouldn't."

Frustration filled her. "Didn't we already discuss this? I said no way, not on your life—"

"Fine. We'll put it aside for now," he said, cutting in. "Your appetite is pretty good. I imagine you'll be up and about quickly. In a few days I'll give you a tour of the Gallery, and at dinner I'll introduce you to some of the other artisans. Eventually I'll have to present you to the General Assembly."

"Oh, great. You're going to present me to the General Asembly. Sounds like it's going to be a really fun time. Who's the General Assembly?"

"General Assembly is the name we use to describe all of the Artisans in the Gallery, brought together to vote and discuss Gallery business."

A sinking feeling gathered in her stomach. How the hell was she going to navigate through this presentation he'd planned for her without getting herself into a whole lot of trouble? Maybe she should just go to the presentation and announce that Conlean and Hawkwood had kidnapped her. Still, she'd also have to tell this general assembly *why* she'd been kidnapped and, according to Conlean, as soon as they found out about her expertise regarding the plague, they'd want her dead.

Playing along with Hawkwood and Conlean would be better for her health.

The only problem was, she didn't know the rules of the game, and more than a few pitfalls awaited her. "You mentioned I'll be meeting other artisans. What about the Seekers? Will you introduce me to them too?"

"All of our Seekers are in the past."

"Every single one of them?"

"The portals that we create only stay open for a short period of time, and only the person who created them can pass through. Seekers go through the portal and allow it to close behind them, trapping them in the past forever."

"But you brought me through the portal and I didn't create it. Couldn't you go into the past and carry a Seeker back through?"

"I suppose so. We haven't tried it. Seekers volunteer

for the job because they wish to be our agents in the past. It's understood that they are going to stay in the past. After rigorous training and a thorough study of the history of the time period they're going to, they create a portal to a woman and then travel back in time, melting into society and becoming our agents in procuring brides."

"So, what about me? When are you going to paint a portrait and bring me back home?"

"Although it is possible to bring an unskilled person from the past to the present, only an artisan—someone with artistic talent like me—can travel through the portal from the present to the past. The artisan's meditative skill allows him to select the right path the first time he travels, and prevents him from becoming lost in *between time*. On the way back, the path is already created, so there is no need for artistic talent."

Only an artisan can travel through the portal from present to past. His statement hit her like a revelation. Her eyes widened. She swallowed. "Does that mean I can't go home?"

He looked away. "Once we rescued the daughter of an aristocrat from the French Revolution. She decided she didn't like it here and wanted to go home. When we tried to bring her back through the portal, she became stuck in between time. The artisan escorting her couldn't bring her through. When he found her in between time and returned her to Blackfell, she had gone mad."

"Conlean." She said his name carefully. She felt as though her breath had gotten caught in her throat. "You're telling me that you brought me here against my

117

will, knowing full well you could never send me home. Is that true?"

He focused again on her fully, a world of sadness in his jade-green eyes. "Yes."

"Yes?" Her voice had risen a notch. A wave of disbelief and panic was building inside her. She glanced inanely at the tattoo on his cheek. Was it glowing brighter?

"Jordan, I wish there had been another way . . ."

I can never go home.

She blinked. His face seemed to be going out of focus.

"Jordan?" He sounded very far away.

"I'm trapped, aren't I?"

He shifted forward and placed his hand over hers. "Ah, God, Jordan, I'm so sorry. I seem to be saying that to you a lot lately, but every day I regret more and more what I've done to you. If there had been any other way, believe me, I would have taken it!"

His palm felt warm, preternaturally so. Or maybe her skin had become ice cold. "It's too late for sorry."

"I know. I know." He squeezed her hand. "I'm going to try to make it up to you, I promise. I want you to be the happiest woman in Blackfell. But first, the plague—"

"Yes, the plague," she muttered woodenly. "I have to cure the plague." Gently she withdrew her hand from his. "If you want to make me happy, Artisan Conlean, you'll leave my room now."

His eyes darkened. "Please, Jordan . . ."

Something very close to anguish squeezed her heart. "Go. Now."

He stood and walked toward the door. As he reached

for the doorknob, he glanced back at her. "You must stay in your room for the next few days. For your own safety. I have a few errands to run. Remember, no one knows who you really are outside of myself and Grand Artisan Hawkwood, and we'd like to give you some time to look over your research. When I return, I'll give you a tour of the Gallery."

Rather than reply, she looked away. After a moment, she marked his leaving by the sound of the door closing behind him.

Chapter Nine

Directly after his morning glass of mead, Conlean slipped on his coat, put on boots suitable for the mud that the springtime rains had brought, and made his way to see the Counselor. He walked down the road quickly, because the night before his sleep had been interrupted by visions of Jordan's face when she learned she could never return home. The whiteness around her lips, the shadowed anguish in her eyes . . . these things told him that his chances of getting her to cooperate were slim to none.

And so, he hurried through the sunshine to the Counselor's estate, with the idea that he had to start winning her over soon or the gulf between them would soon become too wide to cross. Apprehension filled him, effectively blinding him to the green sprouts of wheat that had begun to push up from the freshly tilled earth and the white buds that had replaced the snow covering the cherry trees just a few weeks earlier. The breeze was warm and sweet, and had the promise of summer in it; and the men who tilled the fields doffed their caps to him with a cheery wave as he passed, recognizing the roundels on his coat as those of an Artisan. But he kept his attention focused on the road ahead, and after an hour or so he came to a gate that led to a house of great size and elegance, one with a tiled roof that seemed to reach toward the heavens. Just at this point, the road changed from mud to cobblestones and, beyond a small rise, Conlean could see the outskirts of the city of Blackfell, whose homes were a patchwork quilt of roof styles: thatch for the poorest residents, tile for the wealthiest, and everyone else somewhere in between.

Very few men had enjoyed the privilege of consulting with the Counselor, a relationship expert who helped brides and grooms find love in their new marriages. Conlean supposed he ought to be grateful he'd avoided the man so far. He knew from talking to the men he'd procured brides for that the Counselor—otherwise known as Doc Juan—charged a very hefty fee for his assistance, almost as much as the cost of the brides themselves.

Still, most men swore the price was worth it, because once a groom married, he couldn't end the union without a great deal of pain. The bride's contract forbade disunion unless the circumstances between the two parties were grievous indeed, and the bride agreed to be put up for auction. This wasn't in the groom's best interest, because all monies gained from the auction automatically went to the bride, often leaving the groom flat broke, with nothing to show for his trouble.

Conlean turned off the road. He opened the gate

himself, as there were no servants about, and walked up the path to Doc Juan's manor house. Now that he stood on the Counselor's doorstep, he felt hope flare anew inside him. Schooling his face into a pleasant expression, he tapped on the door and soon stood face-to-face with an austere-looking man in livery.

"Hello, Dorset," Conlean greeted the servant, remembering his name from the recent discussion he'd held with Hawkwood on the Counselor. "I'm here to see the Counselor."

The man inclined his head in acknowledgment, and then raised his eyebrow in a significant manner.

Conlean knew immediately what the servant wanted. Doc Juan was a businessman, first and foremost. He untied the pouch full of gold coins from his belt and handed it over.

Dorset hefted the pouch once or twice to test its weight before untying the strings that held it closed and peering inside. After a moment, he smiled and nodded again. "This way, Artisan Conlean."

The man motioned him inside. Conlean paused in the entry hall and glanced around, noting the Counselor's subtle display of wealth. Fine artwork decorated the walls, and the sliding panels that divided up the space beyond the hall were made of paper-thin yet opaque cloisonné. Gold accents brought warmth to benches and tables made of rich, dark wood; and a collection of copper kettles sat on a shelf near a window that formed a tasteful frame for the picture-perfect garden outside.

Reassured by the Counselor's obvious success, Conlean decided that if anyone could figure out how to convince Jordan to do what he and Hawkwood wished her to do, Doc Juan could. He'd seen the man perform miracles for couples who'd clearly felt nothing but indifference toward each other, and Conlean had an idea that they were going to need no less than a miracle, at this point, to get Jordan to cooperate.

The servant led Conlean through a maze of rooms, bringing him ever deeper into the house until suddenly they came to a spacious chamber overlooking the same garden he'd seen from the entry hall. Three of its four walls had been pushed to the side, giving the illusion that the chamber and the garden were united in a single composition of geometry and nature. Against the one remaining wall sat a couch of immense proportions, its back and seat covered with silk cushions and embroidered throws.

Doc Juan reclined on the couch, his gaze fixed absently on the garden.

Dorset cleared his throat. "Excuse me, sir, but the Artisan from the Gallery is here to see you."

The Counselor swiveled to focus on Dorset first, and then Conlean. "Ah, good, you've finally arrived." He stood and held out a hand for Conlean to shake.

Grasping the Counselor's hand firmly, Conlean exchanged greetings before sitting down on a chair Dorset had discreetly brought into the chamber. As Doc Juan returned to the couch, Conlean took a moment to study him.

He looked a little older than Conlean had expected. He must be in his mid-sixties, judging by the gray streaks in his hair and the wrinkles around his eyes and mouth. He'd adorned himself in a court robe made of blue-black silk and sporting richly embroidered dragon designs. His wide-legged trousers matched the robe and black leather boots encased his feet. To Conlean's surprise, though, he'd eschewed the cotton waistcoat usually worn beneath the robe in favor of nothing at all. As a result, his thick pelt of grayish-black chest hair was visible near the top of his robe. Gold necklaces and a muscular build only served to emphasize his virility.

"Thank you for seeing me, Counselor," Conlean said, fighting the urge to flex his biceps.

Doc Juan made an expansive gesture with his hand. A sweet-smelling scent wafted from him. "You bring brides to Blackfell, Artisan Conlean. Without you I wouldn't have anyone to counsel. I'd have no job, no estate, and no beautiful woman at my side, ready to bear my children."

Conlean asked after the other man's health and his new wife, and responded to the same sort of pleasantries before he glanced out at the garden. "Do you spend a lot of time gardening?"

"I do, Artisan. It eases the soul."

"This is a moonlight garden, no?" he asked, noting that many of its plants had white blossoms that opened and gave off scent only in the evening.

"It's very special," the other man said agreeably. "Many of my flowers are subtropical. They don't much like the cold weather, so in the winter I have to install a plastic cover over the garden and heat it with specially built furnaces."

"Sounds like a lot of trouble."

"Not at all. In any event, the garden is worth the

trouble. It's a whole different world at night, full of un-expected things. Besides, I make soap from some of my flowers. The night jasmine smells the best." He shifted his position on the couch and sat up straighter. "So, I understand there have been some unusual events at the Gallery."

Conlean regarded him quizzically. Hawkwood had set up this meeting with the Counselor, and he didn't know how much the older man had explained to him. "What do you mean?"

"Oh, come now, Artisan, we both know what I'm talking about. You've retrieved the Patriarch's new bride, yet allowed no one to see her. And there's talk that she's very different . . . a scholarly type, in fact. I don't believe the Patriarch would have agreed to a con-tract with that sort of woman."

"She was a librarian in her time," Conlean said, re-ferring to the false past he and Hawkwood had con-structed to protect Jordan. "She knows a lot about books and has a passing knowledge of many subjects."

"Ah, but why not allow anyone to see her?"

"She is to be my father's bride. I feel a certain re-sponsibility for her safety."

"She isn't safe within the Gallery's walls?"

"The FFA has many resources, and even the walls have ears. I wouldn't want her to become the victim of a plot to cause trouble for the Patriarchy," Conlean murmured, thinking she was exactly that—the victim of a plot, spawned by himself and Hawkwood, to top-ple the Patriarchy.

"So, when will we finally get to see his bride?"

"I'll be introducing her slowly over the next few

weeks, to give her time to become accustomed to Blackfell." He raised an eyebrow. "Have I satisfied your curiosity, Counselor?"

"Not in the slightest." The older man smiled easily. "Still, I suppose we should get down to the business at hand."

Conlean relaxed in his chair. "Grand Artisan Hawkwood and I would appreciate your advice on how to make the Patriarch's new bride more comfortable. Neither of us knows all that much about women, as we are not married—"

"Oh, I think the Grand Artisan knows quite a lot about women," Doc Juan interjected. "But he isn't an expert like me."

Surprised that the Counselor would make such a statement, Conlean nevertheless let it go. Now was not the time for a debate. "That's why we need your help. She is to be the Matriarch. We want her to be completely happy. To do that, we need to understand what women want."

Doc Juan nodded. "Let me think." He steepled his fingers and stared at their tips for several moments before refocusing his attention on Conlean. "You want to know what women want. Well, it's a knotty problem that can only be solved by understanding a woman's emotional needs. What do you *think* they want?"

Shrugging, Conlean took a stab at it. "A man who can provide well for his wife and children?"

"Ah, the typical answer. Unfortunately, too many men come in here thinking that women want good providers, with boundless respect for their brides. I tell them not to be suckers, but they ignore me and then expect me to put out the fires when they get burned." Doc Juan's voice was smooth and persuasive. Gently he stroked the gold chains around his neck.

Conlean remained silent. He could see that he was about to get an education.

"Did you ever ask," Doc Juan continued, "one of the brides you retrieved what she wanted in a groom?" At Conlean's demur, he answered, "They'll talk and talk about the qualities they want, like honesty and sensitivity, a sense of humor. But if you watch them closely, you'll see them fluttering their lashes at the men they judge as louts. Cads. Jerks. These are the men they chase."

Surprised at this reasoning, Conlean urged him on with an affirmative shake of his head.

"My esteemed father," Doc Juan said, his fingers going from a steeple to a prayerlike clasp, "once said that there are two kinds of men: those who chase women and those who are chased by women. Your groom wants to be the second kind, Artisan."

"The groom should act like a lout." Conlean wanted to make sure he had it right.

Doc Juan nodded sagely. "That's right."

"Why do women prefer louts?"

Doc Juan pounded his fist lightly against the back of the couch, startling Conlean. "I've discovered that there's no point in asking them why. They're unable to tell you what masculine traits they respond to on the most primal level. Quite frankly, they don't know what they want. They don't know what they *need*. My understanding of women comes from years of careful observation."

127

"Well, why do you believe louts have such appeal?"

"I can best explain it by comparing the lout to the sensitive groom. The sensitive groom puts his bride's needs above all others. He's incapable of saying no to her and tries to please her even when it leads to his own misery. In short, he's the perfect mate and, as we all know, perfection eventually becomes boring." The older man's voice dropped to a hushed whisper. "Women need something to work for, but the sensitive groom does all the work. After a while, the sensitive groom is rejected by his bride, who's grown indifferent to him."

"What do you mean, women need something to work for?" Conlean frowned. He needed practical advice, not a philosophy lesson.

"Well, that's the difference between the lout and the sensitive groom," Doc Juan told him, his tone implying that he had a dunce on his hands. "If the sensitive groom does all of the work, the lout does very little. He makes the woman do the work. A woman might tell her friends that the lout is self-interested and egotistical, but she can't stay away from him because on a deeper level she sees him as a strong, dominant male who knows what he wants and can't be stepped on. He presents her with a *challenge.*"

"I don't get it."

"If a man remains a challenge, then the woman can never know for sure if she's landed her prey. Challenge keeps her coming back for more. It makes her laugh, it makes her cry. She yearns for the man she isn't sure she can have."

"This doesn't sound much like a recipe for success,"

Conlean murmured, thinking of the ancient texts on courtly love he'd once paged through, in a moment of idleness and curiosity. The men described in those books spent most of their time chasing after women.

"Believe me, it works," the older man insisted forcefully. "I haven't become the Counselor for no reason. Women like emotions, and louts give them lots of emotions . . . a regular storm of them. For example, a lout is often unavailable to a woman, forcing her to wonder if she's lost her man, and women crave what they can't have all the more. Have you ever noticed this?"

Conlean hesitated, suddenly finding a thread of understanding. "In fact, I have."

The Counselor gave an approving nod. "Louts are mysterious, too, and women love to pry information out of them. Why is this good? Because when a woman doesn't know much about a man, she spends a lot of time thinking about him, and wondering. He's always on her mind."

"True . . . I mean, I see that the groom has to be mostly unavailable to her and not give her much information," Conlean recapped. "I'm assuming she'll finally come to love him?"

"Don't assume anything with women —unless it's an unusual position. If you remember anything I've told you, remember this: A woman only wants what she can't have, so a man must retain a certain aura of unavailability . . . though it must be done subtly."

"I've never thought of women in this way," Conlean admitted. Doc Juan's approach had a strange sort of logic to it. "Still, I'd like to go back to what a woman wants. I understand that on an emotional level she needs a challenge. What about on a practical level? How do we make our future Matriarch happy? Should we give her gifts and fine apartments? Satisfy her every whim? Shower her with compliments?"

"No, no, and no! Those tactics work for a short time at best. Only a gold digger would be satisfied with endless gifts, and compliments eventually become wearisome to all women but those with low self-esteem. The only women I know who need their every whim satisfied enjoy dominating their grooms, and this isn't behavior you want to encourage. Instead, what you need to do is show her a whopping good time."

"Really?" Conlean smiled in spite of himself.

"Yes! Make sure she has fun all the time. Don't let her get bored, and keep her on her toes. But don't bend over backward for her, either. Give her a challenge, make her do the work. And if all else fails, come to see me again, and I have a small pill that she can take every morning, to even her out."

"I don't think I want to rely on pills—"

"Sometimes nothing else works," the Counselor cut in. He looked at Conlean with narrowed eyes. "How long until she meets the Patriarch?"

"A few weeks, maybe less."

"A few weeks is a long time for a woman to go without the attentions of a man. Here's another piece of advice, then: I know she isn't marrying you, but it wouldn't hurt if you played the courtier in her presence, in order to keep her interested and motivated until she is married."

"Played the courtier?" Conlean swallowed against a suddenly dry throat.

"Have you ever read accounts of courtly love in the ancient books we've recovered?" A reverent look transforming his features, Doc Juan closed his eyes. "Courtiers love their sovereigns, not with their bodies but with their minds, and not in a sensual way but in an honest and godly way. Their love is ruled by reason rather than appetite."

"Yes, I've read them," Conlean admitted sheepishly.

Doc Juan's eyes snapped open. He began to stroke his gold chains again. "So, flatter her, and demonstrate interest in her, but make certain she understands that you would never presume to act upon that interest "

"I'll see what I can do."

The older man shook his head in evident dissatisfaction. "You don't sound very sure of yourself." Abruptly, he slapped his knee in an authoritative manner. "If you'd like, I'll write up some notes for you that you can refer to for help. Consider it part of my fee."

"I'd appreciate it," Conlean admitted, relief in his voice. "How long will it take you to put them together?"

The older man smiled. "I could have it done in an hour or so. Would you mind waiting in the salon?"

"Not at all." Conlean stuck out his hand, which Doc Juan took in a firm clasp. "Thank you, Counselor."

They shook hands, and the older man's smile grew wider. "You're going to enjoy these next few weeks, Artisan. Just make sure you don't fall in love with her. Remember, she belongs to your father."

"I'm an artisan, not a lover," Conlean replied, forcing the words past a sudden knot in his throat as an image of Jordan formed in his mind.

* * *

Appalled, Jordan tossed the book onto her bed and stood abruptly. She'd been cooling her heels in her chamber for a couple of days now, recovering from her illness and regaining strength, and she'd occupied herself by studying the book Conlean had given her. Only a few hours into it, she'd confirmed that she was definitely looking at her own work. All of her notes, her research results, her journal entries . . . they'd been twisted into a narrative-style amalgam on male infertility. And yet, there were parts of it she hadn't authored, techniques she hadn't thought of. Clearly Dr. Rinehart had added his own ideas to hers and then most likely used the money he earned from the book to finance additional projects.

She glanced down at the bed and saw that the book had fallen open to the acknowledgments. That page, more than any other, galled her. Dr. Rinehart had made a big show of thanking her for her contributions, and then offered a quick biography that explained the motive for her single-minded effort to solve the problem of infertility: her own inability to have a child.

She picked up the book and threw it across the room. Why had Conlean acted so surprised when she'd admitted to him earlier that she was infertile? He must have already known, given that her most embarrassing and upsetting secret had been published by that old buddy of hers, Dr. Rinehart.

Feverish again, her agitation not caused by the plague this time but by the situation she was in, she walked over to the window. This prison they called her chambers felt stuffy. Hot. Uncomfortable. Grimacing, she opened the window and stared outside. Night had fallen some time before and darkness blanketed the fields and hills that rolled away from the Gallery, hiding the details of the landscape she now found herself in. A full moon hung near the horizon, however, its silvery glitter illuminating several smaller buildings whose windows glowed with light.

The outbuildings appeared to have been constructed in the style of a European castle, with stone walls, tiled roofs, narrow windows, and even a few squat turrets. From what she could see—and granted, she couldn't see much—they lacked even the slightest embellishment, suggesting that this wasn't the home of a nobleman intent on displaying his wealth, but rather an ancient fortress or monastery. Frowning, she turned and glanced around the room, noting that its furnishings and the clothes Conlean had found for her had a curiously Asian aspect to them: comfortable yet minimalist, and focused on nature. Maybe, she mused, the Gallery was an old Buddhist monastery where monks had once practiced meditation. After all, he *had* said that meditation was the key to creating a portal out of a portrait.

Putting things into neat categories had always helped her to tame her worry over this problem or that, and deliberately she continued to sort out everything within view: chairs, Shaker style; chests, black lacquer embellished with flowers, circa China in the 1950s; blue pajamas, a takeoff on the Japanese kimono; simple arrangement of stones suitable for meditation in the fashion of Tibetan monks, and a Korean gawain for hot beverages. Eventually, her heartbeat began to slow and she was able to think more clearly.

She didn't believe Conlean when he said that she could never go home. This was a premise that her mind simply refused to accept. He had no reason, in fact, to admit that a way to return did exist. By telling her that she had no choice but to stay in Blackfell, he circumvented all her pleas to return home and would gain her cooperation more quickly.

Even so, determination to return to her own era filled her like steel. She would get her hands on a sample of that Prima Materia and learn all she could about artistry. When the time was right, she would send herself back or, if necessary, recruit an Artisan to send her. And so, she had to start investigating the Gallery and establishing herself in Blackfell, in order to gain a few allies she could call upon in time of need.

Sighing, she moved away from the window and plopped down into one of the side chairs. Just having an objective made her feel a hell of a lot better. No longer would she be sitting around, looking at these four walls and wondering. Instead, she'd begin an exploration of the Gallery in the morning. Her mother had always told her she'd catch more flies with honey than with vinegar, so she'd put on her most charming face the next time she saw Conlean. Wouldn't he be surprised by the change in her attitude!

Her lips had curved into a slight smile. Conlean. His eyes had the clear green sparkle of a tide pool along a rocky coastline, and yet she sensed the deep currents beneath them . . . an underground river of emotion that he struggled to keep at bay. He seemed to genuinely regret the part he'd played in her troubles, but his worry for the people of Blackfell outweighed that regret, and she couldn't fault him for it. Not really. As much as she bitched and moaned, she understood why he'd done what he'd done, and a sneaking part of her admired him, for surely he'd sacrificed a lot to kidnap her from her time. Of course, she also couldn't ignore his dark good looks. Or his easy manner. Or the fact that he was a bachelor who didn't want to be a bachelor, judging by the gleam she caught in his eyes when he looked at her.

Restless at the thought of him, she glanced at the clock on a side table. It had a plastic housing and cartoonish moon face that reminded her of the *Honeymooners* TV series, and at the moment it was telling her that the hour had slipped past midnight. She stood up again and paced back to the window. This time the vista revealed nothing new. A cloud had drifted across the face of the moon, obscuring its light. She glanced back at her bed, knowing she should get some rest, but sleep was a thousand miles away. Her mind refused to stop thinking. What if she couldn't find a way home, what if she couldn't find any allies in Blackfell, what if, what if?

With nothing better to do, she walked around her room, running her fingers along the stone walls and stopping to examine the furniture she ran into. She paused at her wardrobe and threw its doors open, revealing several robes made of silk, satin, and velvet, all apparently close to her size. Shoes covered in fabric with little wooden heels hung in a neat row near the bottom of the wardrobe, and a few precious stones hung as pendants from silver chains. The part of her that she'd denied for so many years in favor of scientific pursuits wondered if they'd make her beautiful.

For whom?

That thought followed quickly on the tail of her wondering, and an image of Conlean's features formed in her mind, one she quickly banished.

She closed the wardrobe doors and wandered over to the door. She didn't really expect the doorknob to move, and when she grasped it, it stubbornly refused to turn. But then she noticed the key in the keyhole, and realized Conlean had locked the door on the inside, to keep people *out* rather than in. He wanted to protect her privacy, not imprison her.

She grasped the key with two fingers. Maybe now was a good time to begin her exploration of the Gallery. She couldn't sleep, and she didn't relish the idea of trying to calm her racing thoughts all night. And hiding out in her room wouldn't bring her any closer to an insight into Blackfell, its inhabitants, or Prima Materia, all of which she desperately needed to understand.

What if she ran into someone, though? What would she say?

She frowned. She just didn't have enough knowledge about her situation in Blackfell to say *anything* with confidence. Then again, what were the chances of her running into someone past midnight? She should be able to take a short stroll around the Gallery without engaging in conversation.

Particularly if she kept to the shadows.

Still, what if someone came to her room while she was gone?

She let go of the knob and hurried back to her bed, where she bunched up a few pillows beneath a blanket to look somewhat like a sleeping person. She didn't know if any older ruse existed, but despite its age and frequency of use, people still fell for it. The bunched-up pillows would pass a cursory inspection, at least for a short time.

That done, she walked back to the door and turned the key in the keyhole, unlocking it. Then she pulled the door open and stuck her head outside, with the idea of checking the hallway to see if anyone happened to be around. But instead of an empty corridor, she found herself staring at a bleary-eyed man sitting in a chair with a long, deadly-looking knife clipped to his belt. A pewter cup of dark red liquid—wine, perhaps?—sat near his feet.

A guard.

Oddly enough, she could smell a floral fragrance in the air, as though the guard had used women's perfume for aftershave.

He yawned and shook his head. "I'm sorry, miss. You're required to stay in your room until Artisan Conlean comes for you in the morning."

Frustration filled her. "I'd like to get something to eat," she invented, hoping that he hadn't seen the page take empty lunch and dinner trays from her room a few hours before. "I'm starving."

"The kitchen is closed. It's in a building outside of this one, anyway, and it's too dark to go wandering about the grounds. You'll have to wait until the morning."

"Fine." She closed the door on him, then leaned against it. Apparently Conlean *had* imprisoned her. Her mood plummeting, she slid down the door to the floor. How was she going to get through the night?

She sat there for a while and studied her room, looking for insights into Blackfell and its inhabitants. But after several minutes of scrutiny and categorization, nothing new came to her. Nothing, that was, except the sound of guttural rumbling from the other side of the door.

Careful not to make a sound, she stood and eased the door open. Just as she'd suspected, the guard had fallen asleep and sat there with his head resting against the wall and his mouth open, snoring. The pewter cup near his feet was empty and lay on its side. Keeping her attention on him, she slipped out through the door, shut it behind her, and tiptoed past him, again thinking that the perfume he wore was lovely. If she had to guess, she would have said he'd chosen jasmine.

The thought almost drew a laugh out of her. Somehow she managed to squash it and hurried down the corridor, her gaze now on the turn in the hallway that would hide her from his view completely.

Chapter Ten

Jordan realized almost immediately on her midnight foray through the Gallery that she should have brought a lamp with her. She couldn't see even one electric lamp, outlet, or switch; rather, paper lanterns cast uneven light into the corridor, creating shadows that danced as she passed by. Keeping as much to the shadows as possible, she passed a turn in the corridor and then paused to look around, so she would remember how to return to her room.

The corridor she was standing in had a white arched ceiling reminiscent of the kind one might see in a church. The paper lanterns hung from hooks in the ceiling, illuminating several doors, all painted black. A musty woven mat covered the floor, and muted conversation echoed from somewhere nearby.

If she had to guess, she'd say that these were the artisans' rooms.

Afraid that one of the artisans might enter the corridor at any moment, she hurried to the next bend in the corridor. Ahead, another long stretch of lanterns and doors led her to yet another turn. Starting down the third corridor, she began to think that the artisans' rooms were probably part of a dormitory, organized in a giant square around one central feature, like a staircase. One of the doors on the inside of the hallway, she reasoned, must lead to stairs rather than another room. She also assumed that if she kept going straight, she would eventually run into the door to her own room and the guard snoring at his post.

Since she didn't want to run into the guard again, sleeping or not, she started looking for a door that would open up to a staircase. All of the doors appeared exactly the same: painted wooden planks, with a worn black knob and keyhole. And yet, when she arrived at the corridor mid-point, she saw a door that was slightly different: It didn't have a keyhole.

A door to a staircase wouldn't have a keyhole, she thought.

This had to be the one.

She pressed her ear to the door and heard nothing, so she grasped the knob, her hand trembling. She eased the door open an inch and put her eye to the crack. A wide staircase, illuminated by the same lanterns that hung in the hallway, lay beyond.

The staircase led both upward and downward, its vertical sweep interrupted by landings on different floors of the Gallery. Far below, she heard several voices muttering and smelled incense . . . possibly artisans in their equivalent of a chapel? Pausing, she assessed the staircase and decided that if she moved fast on the steps, she could probably avoid detection by anyone who entered. But which way to go? Up or down?

Down. Conlean's laboratory had to be on the ground floor, or maybe in the basement. The furnace he used appeared too heavy to be sitting in a second-floor room somewhere. And she wanted nothing more than to explore his laboratory and get a look at Prima Materia.

She opened the door wider and slipped through. Keeping to the outer edge of the staircase, she counted the steps as she descended. By the twelfth step, she had reached the landing. Here, the voices had become very loud, and she could hear chairs creaking. Clearly the artisans kept very busy at night. She didn't dare exit the staircase.

She peered downward. The lanterns ended at this point, but the stairs continued to descend into darkness. The lack of light fixtures suggested that the artisans didn't often go past ground level, so there likely wasn't anything of interest at the bottom of the staircase. She didn't see much reason to explore further in that direction. Besides, she didn't like the look of that darkness. It appeared too murky, too opaque, as though it made a habit of swallowing up those who made the mistake of descending.

Suddenly, one floor up, she heard a door open and close, followed by two distinct sets of footsteps descending the staircase. Two men were talking in low voices. Pulling in a surprised breath, she hurried a few steps down, where she could hide in the darkness. When she looked back, she saw the bottom half of the men's robes come into view.

Feeling the bite of panic, she plunged further into

the shadows, reaching blindly for the wall to steady her. Then she stopped and said a silent prayer that the two Artisans would exit the staircase on the ground level rather than descend farther, into the darkened portion of the staircase where she now crouched.

Their voices grew loud enough for her to hear the conversation between them: the reasons why Artisan Conlean might be delaying the presentation of the Patriarch's future bride.

Her eyes narrowed. Conlean had mentioned this presentation business earlier, and had also mentioned that he wanted her to marry the ruler of Blackfell. Apparently everyone else also knew she was in town to marry this Patriarch fellow, and they were wondering why she hadn't happily announced her excitement over her coming marriage. She had a sense of time running out, of a noose tightening around her neck. How was she going to get out of marrying the Patriarch if she couldn't find a way to quickly return to her own time?

Growing irritation and a sense that she was trapped mixed with her panic, until her heart was beating in a hard and uncomfortable way. The two men were lingering on the landing above her, giving each other reasons why Conlean had kept her concealed so far: she was ugly; she was ditzy; her illness upon coming to Blackfell had lasted longer than usual; she had some sort of problem that would make her undesirable; and ten other unflattering reasons why Conlean would need to conceal her, if only to protect his reputation as Artisan extraordinaire, incapable of delivering anything but perfection. Disgusted with their gossip, she silently urged them to exit on the ground floor, so she wouldn't have to descend fully into the darkness.

Upstairs, another door opened and closed, and a new set of footsteps began to descend to the ground level. She heard the two who were talking on the landing greet the new one, and then all three began discussing her in terms any woman would consider unflattering. Then, after a minute or two, their voices dropped to a hush, as if their discussion had become highly secret and they suspected even the walls had ears.

The walls, in fact, did have ears.

She strained to hear what they were saying but could only distinguish the word *FFA*—an acronym for that Greenpeace-type organization, she recalled, the one that was promoting brides for all men. Losing interest in the conversation and feeling even more determined not to get caught, she assessed the darkness below her in the stairwell. It had begun to look inviting.

She crept down a few more stairs, counting them as she went and going deeper into the gloom. The artisans' voices became even more difficult to understand. Feeling her way along, she silently noted that the walls felt very dry, unlike the upper levels of the Gallery, and even a little warm. Remembering Conlean's furnace, she thought that maybe, just maybe, she was on the right track.

At the twelfth step, she reached the next landing and took a few tentative steps toward the area where she imagined the door might be. Sure enough, she found a doorknob after only a short inspection. Her luck ended there, though. The doorknob, she discovered, wouldn't turn.

Damn!

Silently she stood there, wondering what to do. Frustration made her take a few paces. Suddenly, the floor seemed to drop out from under her one foot, and she realized there was yet another staircase leading downward.

She hadn't yet reached the bottom.

The gloom became more complete as she descended. She barely avoided stumbling over the stairs, which unexpectedly changed heights on her a few times. She figured she must be entering one of the oldest sections of the Gallery. Pressing her palm against the wall to guide herself, she noticed that the stone had become very warm. Evidently the bowels of the Gallery shared a few rooms with Hell itself.

After several steps she reached another landing and another door, this one locked, too. A cautious investigation of the landing revealed that yet another staircase led downward. Confounded, she stared into the darkness below her and assessed the wisdom of continuing, her thoughts running a mile a minute.

How far down into the ground did this place go?

Frowning, she leaned one palm against the wall. It felt hot.

With a shrug that felt a little foolhardy to her, she decided that down she must go, if only to make sure that the stairs did, in fact, end, and the door on the bottom was locked like the rest.

Slowly, reluctantly, she walked down the stairs. The air around her seemed to cling to her skin. Beads of perspiration formed on her forehead. Had the heat caused the dryness in her throat, or had anxiety from the entire reckless experience done it? Probably a little bit of both, she mused, as she approached the spot where she thought the next landing must be. But unlike the previous sets of staircases, the steps didn't end after twelve. Thirteen, fourteen, fifteen . . . she kept moving downward until she reached the eighteenth step and another landing.

A nearly blind inspection of the area told her that she had, finally, reached the end of the staircase. She also found the edge of a door. She ran her fingers along the door jamb until she reached a waist-high spot and then moved left until she found the doorknob. She gripped it and, without much hope, rattled it to see if it was locked.

It turned easily, as if someone had just greased it.

Swallowing, she eased the door open.

Lanterns, much like the ones that hung in her hallway, but older-looking and blackened with soot, illuminated the corridor beyond. She slipped through the doorway and surveyed the lowest level of the Gallery.

The walls and floor were made of stone as they were upstairs. A light sheen of dust on the lanterns and large cobwebs along the wall suggested that not much foot traffic passed through here. She could see an open mahogany door ahead, looking thick enough to withstand a battering ram, and beyond that a passageway that widened into a larger space.

Alert for the sound of voices or footsteps, she passed the mahogany door and went into the wider hallway. At first, when she saw what appeared to be a series of stalls on both sides, she thought that horses or other stable animals were kept there. A closer inspection, however, revealed that iron bars intermingled with the wooden portions of each stall.

She hadn't stumbled upon a stable.

She must have entered a prison, complete with cells.

A flash of white inside one of the far cells caught her attention. She moved forward and squinted through the darkness, her attention settling on a small, sleek figure.

The cat, Baudrons.

Baudrons sauntered a little closer, until Jordan could see a hint of amber in its eyes. After a long look at Jordan, the cat started to walk away.

Jordan had the distinct impression that Baudrons wanted her to follow.

Grimacing, she peered into each cell to make sure it hadn't any occupants. Cobwebs wreathed most of them. Only two looked dust-free, as though they'd been recently used. Did the Gallery actually imprison criminals down here? What would an artisan have to do to merit a stay in one of these cells?

The prison had an air of menace about it, raising the hairs on the back of her neck. Realizing anew how dangerous her little tour could be if someone discovered her, she hurried through the prison after Baudrons, only to find that the cat had disappeared.

Thoroughly unnerved, she decided to try to find another way back to her room, one that would avoid the staircase, which apparently saw quite a lot of use even at this time of night. The heat grew as she left the prison area and continued down the main hallway. A few smaller corridors branched off to the left and right,

and she considered trying them out. Since she didn't
want to get lost in a warren of underground hallways,
though, she decided to see this corridor to the end and
then explore the others in a systematic way, at the same
time keeping watch for the white cat, who might decide
to return and lead her out of there.

After a short time, she reached a set of metal doors
that marked the end of the main corridor. The warmth
was emanating from behind these doors. Carefully she
pushed them open and eased her way inside, only to
face an immense boiler, an oil tank, and a series of copper pipes that led out of the room. She scanned the
room to make sure no one else was around, and then
walked inside. Remembering the baseboard heating in
her own home, she understood that this boiler, fired by
oil, must supply the artisans' dormitory with heat and
hot water. She circled around it, amazed by its size and
somewhat alarmed by the cranky hissing and clanging
noises it made.

Suddenly, she saw Baudrons again, outside in the
corridor. The cat had paused by the door, as if inviting
Jordan to follow her out. Jordan began walking in Baudron's direction when a male voice came out of
nowhere.

"Have you come for the warmth?"

At the sound of the scratchy old voice, she jumped.
Baudrons disappeared in a flash of white, and panic
seized Jordan in an iron grip. She swiveled around until she found the owner of the voice and then froze.

He had grizzled features, bulging eyes, and white
hair. His beard appeared ratty and unkempt. The artisan's robes hung limply over his gaunt frame. He nod-

ded toward the boiler, his expression sympathetic. "I come here for the warmth. The Gallery is such a cold place. I can never find a room where I'm comfortable. Besides, I don't like talking to fools, and down here I'm always alone."

She opened her mouth, then closed it again. The man looked half-crazed. Fear for her own well-being rose up in her. She glanced behind her, judging the distance to the door.

"No, don't leave," he pleaded, apparently unaware that he'd just contradicted his earlier comment about hanging out in the boiler room to avoid talking to fools. "You must be the new bride Artisan Conlean retrieved. Why don't you come into my studio and tell me why you're wandering around the Gallery in the middle of the night?"

Hesitating, she assessed him. He appeared slightly crazy, but not dangerous. And she didn't think she had much choice, anyway. She had to offer him a plausible excuse for her midnight jaunt . . . provided she could think of one.

"Where is your studio?" she managed.

"It's right here. Follow me." Smiling crookedly, he walked around the boiler to a wooden door on the opposite side of the room and disappeared inside.

She trailed after him and found herself in a long, narrow room that he'd furnished on one end with chairs and a cabinet and on the other with the same sort of painting and alchemistic equipment she'd seen in Conlean's laboratory. The old man stood near a bench, his gaze directed at a cluster of pots and alembics. Reassured that the door leading back to the boiler room re-

mained open behind her, she moved to his side but kept
a judicial five feet between them.

"So, you *are* the latest bride Conlean has retrieved,
are you not?" the old man asked.

She nodded her head affirmatively. "My name is Jordan. And you are . . . ?"

"Grand Artisan Tobias. A pleasure to meet you, Jordan."

After a slight hesitation, she shook the grimy hand
he thrust at her.

"Let me get you a glass of something warm." He
bustled toward a set of dirty mugs, hanging by their
handles from pegs on a shelf.

"No, that's all right, I'm fine," she interjected, eyeing
the spots on the mugs. They had a greenish cast, like
mold. "I had some water in my room not too long ago."

Appearing not to have heard her, he filled two mugs
with amber liquid poured from an equally grimy kettle.
"I put some tea on just a while ago. Here, try some. It'll
help you sleep. That *is* why you're up so late, walking
around, is it not?"

"Yes," she agreed, seizing upon the easy explanation. "I always have trouble sleeping in unfamiliar
places."

He thrust one of the mugs at her. "Well, how do you
like Blackfell?"

"I haven't seen much of it, so I haven't formed an
opinion yet." She took the mug and held it between her
hands, hoping it might warm them. They were ice cold.
"I've been recovering from the plague."

"All brides contract the plague when they come
here," he offered.

149

"So I've been told."

"Most are up and about more quickly than you, though. How long have you been in your room? Seven days?"

Feeling a little defensive, she shrugged. "I was only sick for four days."

"Then why haven't you been down to dinner yet?"

"Artisan Conlean suggested that I stay in my room."

"Oh. How unusual."

She shrugged. "Is it? I didn't mind." For the first time she really began to regret leaving her room without Conlean at her side. This old crazy was fishing for information and she didn't know what to say to him.

"Let's just say that in your case, he's not following the customary protocol for retrieved brides."

"What is the customary protocol?"

He squinted at her. "Don't you know? Hasn't anything been explained to you?"

"Not everything," she hedged.

"What a strange situation." A crafty look came into his eyes. "Would you like me to tell you more about Blackfell?"

"Yes, please." She tried not to sound too eager.

"I'd be happy to, but I do have one request. For every question of yours that I answer, you must answer one of mine."

She didn't reply immediately, aware of how dangerous his request could prove. If she gave too much away about herself, he might sense that she wasn't exactly a harmless librarian. And yet, if she refused to answer any questions at all, he would wonder what she was trying to hide.

"Well, Jordan?" he pressed, the craftiness in his eyes twisting his smile wider. "Do you want to play?"

"You make it sound like a game."

"It is."

She took a deep breath. *What the hell.* "Who goes first?"

"Why, you, of course."

"I can ask any question?"

"Any question at all. But understand that the deeper you dig, the deeper I'll dig."

"All right." She took several moments to think of something innocuous before asking, "How long has Blackfell been a province?"

He looked disappointed. "Oh, come now, surely you're more adventurous than that."

"That's my question."

"Well, then, the answer is, about two hundred years."

Equally disappointed in his reply, she abruptly realized that very precise questions would yield little information. She had to be more vague, and give him more freedom in the formulating of his answers.

She *was* playing a game, one that required strategy.

"So, Jordan, how old are *you?*" he asked idly.

"I'm twenty-eight years old." Now it was her turn. "What is Blackfell's history?"

A slight smile twitched his lips. "An explorer discovered the ruins that would become Blackfell some three hundred years ago. I believe the ruins were known as the city of Kyoto in your time. Because of their location, near a bay deep enough to allow our largest ships passage, and the excellent condition of many of the buildings, the ruins quickly became settled. The family line of that original explorer has ruled Blackfell ever since."

She nodded. *Kyoto.* She was in Japan, of all places. "Your turn."

"What is *your* history?"

"I was an only child," she replied, repeating the story Conlean had constructed for her. "My parents were both scholars and brought me up to love the sciences. After graduating from high school, I went on to college to study, er, library science. I worked as a librarian in the city of Philadelphia, with a specialization in cataloguing."

"A librarian." He rubbed his chin. "One who works with books. Oddly enough, rumors have been floating around the Gallery about a book that has been recently unearthed, one with many scholarly secrets in it." His voice dropped to a whisper. "One story even suggested that the book contained steps to create a cure for the plague. Perhaps once you become comfortable in your new life, you'll use your skills as a librarian to locate this book for me. I want to read it."

Completely unsettled, she dragged in a deep breath. She knew very well what book he was talking about—the one she had apparently authored with Dr. Rinehart. How had he found out about it? Had he discovered her true identity? "I'd be happy to put my skills to use in whatever way I can," she offered in her most congenial tone.

Although his smile stayed in place, his eyes narrowed. "What's your next question?"

"Tell me about Artisan Conlean," she said, the

thought of him never very far from her mind. He seemed a safe enough topic. "What kind of family is he from, and did they approve of his decision to become an artisan?"

The old man gave a grunt of surprise. "Artisan Conlean has told you nothing about himself?"

"Not yet."

The other man's face twisted into a peculiar smile. "Artisan Conlean is also a member of the ruling house of Blackfell . . . the House of Arador."

Now it was her turn to gasp with surprise. "Do you mean to say he's, er, descended from royalty?"

"His father is the Patriarch of Blackfell."

She gaped at him. Conlean, son of the Patriarch? She couldn't believe it. "Wow. I didn't know."

"Conlean was the next in line to inherit the Patriarchy," Tobias continued, "but then the Gallery discovered his talent at artistry. By law, anyone displaying talent must enter the ranks of the Gallery, and so he went to study artistry full-time. From what I understand, the Patriarch resented his loss of an heir, but Conlean rejoiced in the fact that he would be able to indulge his love of portraiture rather than spend his time administering to Blackfell."

"I see." Abruptly Conlean seemed taller, harsher, more enigmatic to her. And as she'd always possessed a logical mind, she also connected the dots and realized that if she married this Patriarch, she would also become Conlean's mother-in-law. What a kicker!

"So, Jordan, tell me about your life in your own time," Tobias said, interrupting her thoughts. "Your contract, and your own description of your past, is very thin on details. Tell me more about your family. Were you married?"

"I was married, but it didn't work out. We've since divorced."

"How long were you married?"

"Oh, about five years."

"Any children?"

An unexpected spasm of regret clutched at her. "No."

Sympathy softened his features. "Why did you divorce?"

He asked the question with such a tone of kindness that she almost confessed her problems to him. And yet, she detected a strange cunning behind the sympathy in his eyes. At the last second, she blurted, "Isn't it my turn to ask a question?"

The sympathy disappeared instantly from his face, replaced by lowered brows that clearly indicated his frustration with her. "Go ahead."

"Earlier you mentioned that in my case, Conlean isn't following the customary protocol for newly retrieved brides. What is the customary protocol?"

"Usually, once a bride is retrieved to Blackfell, her contract is immediately presented to the General Assembly for review and the date for her presentation is set. So far, we've only received an overview of your contract and have no date for your presentation. You're a bit of a mystery, Jordan," Tobias prodded.

She couldn't quite look him in the eye.

He tilted his head and examined her closely. "The handling of your prenuptial ceremonies is even more peculiar considering to whom you are betrothed. In fact, the reason why Artisan Conlean has refused you a page and left on an errand when he should be preparing you for presentation is confusing to all of us."

He paused, perhaps to give her time to defend herself. But when she said nothing, he added, "I confess that your reason for sneaking around the Gallery at night also perplexes me."

"What is your question, Grand Artisan?" she asked, unable to think of a single thing to say that might distract him. Involuntarily she glanced at the door.

"I have two questions, and they are very simple. Do you want to marry the Patriarch? Do you want to rule Blackfell? As the future Matriarch of Blackfell, we would all expect that you'd be embracing the people you are soon to rule; and yet, your own lack of knowledge or enthusiasm regarding the Patriarch and your upcoming marriage would suggest you don't want to marry at all, or rule Blackfell as Matriarch."

His gaze caught hers and held it. She fancied that his rheumy old eyes held both knowledge and suspicion. No wonder everyone was talking about her. She was going to be some sort of queen, and Conlean was hiding her in the closet.

"Of course I want to marry the Patriarch," she finally replied, silently cursing the gnarled old artisan for forcing her to commit to the marriage out loud. "What woman wouldn't be honored by such a proposal?"

"Were you brought here against your will, without even knowing you would be expected to marry? Is that why Conlean has been hiding you?"

Her heart began to pound. This guy really had her number! "I don't know what you're talking about."

155

"Usually the women we bring here are in desperate circumstances in their own times. That's often why they agree to come to Blackfell. And yet you described your life in your own time as very comfortable. Why were you brought here, Jordan? You can confide in me. I'll help you."

Jordan frowned. The crocodile look in his eyes suggested she wouldn't much appreciate his kind of help.

A sudden blast of heat from the boiler room interrupted them both. She swiveled around to stare at the door. A hooded black figure stood within the door frame. He walked into the room and stopped near a lantern. Dirt coated the hem and wrinkles marred the fabric of his cloak. He looked as if he'd been traveling.

Abruptly he threw back his hood. Intense jade-green eyes stared first at her, and then at Grand Artisan Tobias.

Conlean had returned.

Chapter Eleven

"Conlean! You're back." Jordan let out a gusty sigh. He had never looked as good to her as he did right now. She didn't even care that he returned her greeting with tight-lipped silence.

"Grand Artisan Tobias," Conlean said, ignoring her. He drew the cloak from his shoulders and hung it over one arm. Beneath he wore a nondescript tunic and narrow trousers that looked equally travel-worn. "I see you've been keeping Jordan entertained."

The older man frowned at Conlean. "She's very intriguing. I have to confess I'm piqued with you for keeping her to yourself for so long." With a sly glance at her, he added, "And, of course, from her intended husband."

"Jordan will meet with the General Assembly when she's ready," Conlean replied evenly.

Focused on Conlean, Jordan attempted a smile. "The next time I'm looking for entertainment, I'll wait for you. The Gallery is a maze of passages, and I wouldn't want to get lost again."

After a brief hesitation, Conlean grasped her hand. His skin was warm, yet slightly roughened. His touch conveyed strength. "I'll take you around myself tomorrow."

Grand Artisan Tobias darted a look at their hands. A smirk replaced his frown. "Will you be introducing her to the Patriarch tomorrow, Artisan?"

Conlean moved his hand to her arm, which he clasped lightly. "She'll be presented soon. When she's ready." With a nod at the older man, he gently urged her toward the door. "It's late. I should escort you back to your room."

"Keep us informed as to the date," the Grand Artisan demanded as they reached the door. "We're all very much anticipating it."

Conlean steered her from Tobias's studio. "You'll know as soon as it's decided."

Then they were out of the boiler room and into the hallway, where the stones smelled musty and shadows leapt as they passed each lantern lighting the way.

Conlean's clasp on her arm tightened considerably. "What did you think you were doing? Are you crazy? You'd have to be, to leave your room on your own like that."

She shrugged out of his grasp. "I've been stuck in my room for days. What did you expect me to do, twiddle my thumbs forever? Where have you been?"

"I've been busy. I told you I'd be back. I thought you understood how dangerous it was for you to leave your room."

"I understand very little. I'd like to know more, but you won't tell me. So I went to learn about the Gallery for myself."

"Clearly you see what a mistake *that* was."

In a moment they were climbing a staircase somewhat smaller than the one she'd descended, presumably en route to her room.

"How did you know I was in Grand Artisan Tobias's studio?" she asked, hurrying to keep up with him. "I have to admit I felt glad to see you when you came in."

"I'll bet you were. We'll talk about this when we get back to your room."

A comment about his patronizing attitude hovered on her lips, but she managed to keep quiet as they emerged in the artisans' dormitory and walked quickly to the guard posted by her door. The pewter cup he'd been drinking from still lay on its side by his feet.

Conlean nudged the guard in the shin with a wellworn boot. "Wake up, Murray. There's someone here you should see."

The guard opened bloodshot eyes and tried to focus on Conlean. After a moment he managed the task and jumped to attention. Just as quickly, his focus twitched over to her and he sucked in a breath.

"That's right, Murray," Conlean told him in dulcet tones. "You fell asleep and didn't notice your charge taking herself out for a walk."

He blinked, dismay entering his gaze. "My apologies, Artisan Conlean. I don't know what came over me. I was feeling fine, fully awake, and then . . . I just went out like a candle being snuffed."

"Maybe if you did less carousing during your off-hours, you'd be able to stay awake on the job. A replacement for you should be arriving momentarily. When he does, report to your superior at once."

"Yes, sir." The guard turned to face the hallway, his demeanor fierce, his back ramrod straight.

Jordan listened to their exchange with only half her attention. She was mulling over the idea that Conlean had royal blood in him, and had been forced to give up his future as Patriarch of Blackfell to become an artisan. This would have been a bitter pill for most men to swallow, but Conlean apparently hadn't fought his fate. He'd given up power and money to embrace the life of a simple man. His actions spoke of a deep love of artistry.

Still, he'd put it all in jeopardy—his relationship with his father, his future as an Artisan—by plotting with Hawkwood against the Gallery and the Patriarchy itself. He'd risked everything because he thought he could help the people of Blackfell, and his willingness to sacrifice spoke of a man with a strong ethical code. He was the kind of person she could trust, at least a little.

The insight surprised her, and also eased her mind. Relaxing a little, she followed him into her room. "What's going to happen to the guard?" she asked, noting that the strange perfume she'd smelled when she'd left her room still lingered, despite the fact that her window remained open.

He steered her to a chair and sat her down. "He'll probably have to clean the barns for a day or so."

"It's hard to take him seriously when he wears such feminine perfume."

Conlean appeared confused. "Who, the guard?"

"Don't you smell it?"

"I can't smell anything outside the stench of my own fear."

She started to rise from her chair. "Conlean, I'm so sorry. I didn't think . . ."

He pointed to the chair. "Sit, Jordan. We need to talk, and *I* can't think when you're walking around."

Sighing, she sat back down. "I *am* sorry. It's just that I've been sitting around for days, worrying about curing this plague and wondering if you've got the right equipment. Finally I couldn't take it any more and had to go have a look around."

He shook his head. "If you had said one wrong word, you could have put our entire plan in jeopardy, not to mention all of us in prison."

"I didn't say anything wrong, though."

"Hawkwood was crazy to suggest this plan of his would actually work." He pivoted away from her suddenly. She could hear him cursing beneath his breath.

Frowning, she stood up and followed him. "Why did you leave me alone for so long?"

"I went to see the Counselor," he growled, upon turning to face her again.

"Who's the Counselor?"

"He helps men and women understand each other. I went to see him because I needed to know what women want."

"That is the strangest damned excuse I've ever heard," she muttered.

"Never mind about the Counselor. What about you?" He chose a chair that faced her and dragged it so close to hers that their knees nearly touched when he sat down. "I need a step-by-step description of what you did when you left your room."

She glanced down at the position they'd fallen into. Although they weren't touching, he'd wedged his knees between hers. She felt dangerously intimate with him. But she didn't move. She wasn't going to even hint at how much he affected her. "I opened my door and the guard told me to go back into my room. So I came back and stayed here for a while. Later, I tried again and saw that the guard was snoring, so I went past him and walked around the hallways until I found a central staircase. What is this building I'm in, by the way. A dormitory?"

"This is the living area for the master artisans. Did anyone see you walking around?"

"Not then."

He sighed. "What happened next?"

"Well, I stepped onto the central staircase. I heard a lot of chanting and mumbling as I was going down, and I paused on the landing where the lanterns stopped."

"That would be the ground level. We call it the reredorter. It's a common area with groups of tables and chairs arranged to promote conversation. Artisans often go there to meditate or discuss ideas for new projects. Did you leave the staircase at that point?"

"No. I heard too many voices and I didn't want to be seen."

"And then?"

"I heard a door above me open and close. Two men came down the staircase. I hurried down a few more steps into the gloom, so they couldn't see me. The men paused near the door of the common area and started talking."

"What were they talking about?"

She allowed a beat of silence to pass before she replied. "They were talking about my marriage to the Patriarch."

He recoiled briefly, and then leaned forward until his face was a mere few feet from hers. "What did they say?" he asked, his tone urgent.

"They were wondering why you hadn't yet set a date for my presentation to the General Assembly. Your handling of my 'case' is apparently very irregular. And the reasons they came up with weren't very complimentary. They were assuming I was unacceptable in some way. Ugly, too studious, too much mouth . . ."

A little smile briefly twitched his lips before disappearing. "You're none of those things."

"Gee, thanks." She shot an annoyed look at him before continuing. "I didn't realize how much I would be in the public eye. Now that I'm finally getting the picture, I'm also getting chills. In my day, anyone who wanted to occupy an important position in the government had his or her entire life outed for the world to examine and laugh over. Every damned thing they did, from smoking pot in the restroom to the hooker they screwed during a bachelor party, became common knowledge. Do you really think my pathetic little librarian story will stand up to a second look? We're all going to end up in prison."

"Don't worry about your cover story being shown as false," he assured her. "In my time, a person's privacy is respected. Once we get you past the presentation, we'll be in the clear."

"What do you mean, 'get past the presentation'? I'm not going to be presented. Why? Because I'm not going to marry the Patriarch."

He put a hand on her arm, presumably to comfort her. She didn't feel very comforted, though. Wedding bells were ringing in her head, and they were giving her a headache.

"Maybe, with time, you'll change your mind," he said.

"I don't know that I have a choice. You've trapped me, Conlean. And you're damned eager to give me away!" A little ache formed somewhere near her heart. "By the way, you forgot to tell me that the Patriarch is your father. And I, if I married him, would be your mother-in-law. I don't want to be your mother-in-law, Conlean."

"I'll be honored to have you in my family," he said, after a brief hesitation.

She closed her eyes and fought for calm. Suddenly she felt like discarded trash. But what had she expected him to say? That he wouldn't give her up to his father, that he wanted her for himself?

Yes. That's exactly what she'd been hoping for.

Because at some point during the last several days she'd realized that she wouldn't mind Conlean's arms around her in the slightest. In fact, she'd welcome the chance to get naked with him, because he was one handsome piece of ass and seemed to care about her, at least a little. How long had it been since she'd had a man's arms around her? Too long.

She swallowed, then faced him squarely. "Oh, so you're looking forward to giving me away to your father?"

"No, I'm not," he said abruptly. "You're young, vibrant, beautiful. Smart. You need someone who can love you the way you need to be loved. And my father can't do that."

"Then why are you insisting I marry him?" she asked, her insides clenching.

"Because I don't have a choice, damn it!" He gripped her shoulders again and drew her close. She looked deep into his eyes, saw the pain he tried so hard to hide. "I don't want to give you up. But I have to. Your destiny lies with my father, not with me."

Her insides trembled at the passion he'd revealed. There seemed to be something between them, some connection that had only just budded. She wondered what that bud might become if given a chance to bloom. "I don't believe in destiny, Conlean, and I won't marry your father. I can't bring myself to do it."

"Then it's my job to change your mind," he told her, his voice low and tired-sounding. He released her shoulders and turned away.

She couldn't imagine a worse hell than having Conlean —the man she wanted- —spend all his time trying to convince her to bed down with his father. Her stomach roiled at the mere thought. "I know you said that I have to marry him in order to have access to the best studios and libraries, but you're royalty too. Don't you have access to these places? Why can't I marry you instead?"

He spun around, his expression shocked. "You would marry me?"

"Yes, I would," she said firmly.

"For God's sake, why? I stole you from your own time, brought you to a place you can never leave, and then asked you to marry against your will, all in an attempt to cure a plague."

"You know what, Conlean? You're a bastard for bringing me here, but I trust you. I don't know why, but I trust you. And I like you. That's as solid a basis for marriage as any I've ever heard."

A brief smile lit his face, and at the sight of it, her hopes soared. Just as quickly, though, he shook his head and began to pace. "We can't marry. Artisans aren't allowed to marry women whom they themselves paint and retrieve as brides. It's considered a conflict of interest."

"What would happen if you married me anyway?"

"I'd be thrown out of the Gallery and forbidden to ever practice artistry again. The fact that I'd be stealing my father's bride makes matters even worse. I'd probably be imprisoned for a long time."

She swallowed, all the hope leaking out of her. "Sounds like the kind of punishment horse thieves received in the Old West."

"It wouldn't be pretty." Frowning, he paced a few steps and then stopped. "There isn't a way around it. You have to marry him."

"Has there ever been a situation in the past when a bride has come to Blackfell and then decided she didn't want to marry the man who commissioned her retrieval?"

He nodded slowly. "I can think of a few instances,

but each time the couple has visited the Counselor until they became reconciled to each other."

Brow furrowed, she walked over to her bed and plopped onto the mattress. "You mentioned the Counselor once before. Sounds like marriage counseling from my time. Has the Counselor ever failed to convince a couple to marry?"

"Once, this happened," he admitted as he sat down next to her. "It caused one hell of a furor. Eventually the bride's contract went up for auction, and she married the highest bidder."

"Did the bidding go very high?" she asked, another plan forming in her mind.

"It went through the roof." He stared at her, his eyes widening. "Are you suggesting that you break your contract with my father and put yourself up for auction?"

"Why not?"

"Why not? Because you'd be selling yourself to the highest bidder. You'd have no control over who would win. You could end up married to the ugliest, meanest man in Blackfell, and there's more than a few of those."

"Wouldn't you bid for me?" she asked in a small voice.

"If I bid for you and won you, then I'd be thrown out of the Gallery, as I mentioned before. Our marriage would be a conflict of interest. In any case, I wouldn't have enough money to win you. There are many rich men in Blackfell who would jump at the chance to claim you as a bride."

"Damn. This is such a mess."

"It's not a mess. All you have to do is agree to marry my father." He looked away.

"How long do I have to decide?"

"A few weeks at most. I can't delay setting a date for your presentation to the General Assembly much longer."

"I still say it's a mess."

"I'm sorry." His voice became husky. "I hope to change your mind, as much as it may kill me. Before your presentation, I want you to know more about my world. I want you to see why it's worth marrying my father to save it. We also have to tour the Gallery, visit the city—"

"You're going to show me all these things?"

"I will."

"Good." Deliberately she moved closer to him, until their thighs nearly touched. She wanted to tempt him. She wanted to make it hard for him to give her up. She wanted him to fight for her, because she was starting to believe that unless she managed to win him over, she would end up married to his father, the Patriarch. "Tell me more about Blackfell."

He looked at the tiny space separating them, then back at her. A questioning look filled his eyes. "Jordan . . ."

She placed her hand gently on his arm. "Conlean, please don't push me away. You've put me in a terrible position with no way out, and now I need some of your strength, otherwise I don't know how I'm going to face another day."

His questioning look melted away. He put his arm around her. "I'm here for you, Jordan."

Her heart beating harder, she allowed her head to rest on his shoulder. He felt so warm, so strong.

Determined knocking on the door echoed through the room.

"Who is it?" Conlean released her and stood to face the door, his gaze distracted.

"Jerrod, Artisan," a youthful voice answered. "You're wanted in Hawkwood's apartment immediately."

"Thank you, Jerrod. Tell him I'll be there in a moment." He turned back to Jordan and placed his hands on her shoulders. "I have to go. As soon as I finish with Hawkwood, I'll come back. I need to know what you and Tobias talked about."

"I said very little to Tobias——"

"I still want to hear," he insisted. "I'll be back as soon as I can."

Shivering, her hand at her throat, she watched him go, and got up to turn the key in the lock as soon as the door closed behind him. Then she plopped back onto the bed, her thoughts on her upcoming marriage. She'd always said that she wouldn't marry a man she didn't love. And yet, here she was, contemplating a marriage to a man who would only marry her if she seduced him into giving up everything meaningful in his life. What a joke, that the scientist who once had her nose buried in her work now had to work at being a seductress equal to Helen of Troy.

Still, some part of her wondered what it would be like to have a traditional life, the kind her mother had told her that she ought to strive for, with a husband she loved and children to raise. She imagined what it would be like to wake up next to Conlean in the morning, to make love to him, to eat breakfast with him, and then spend the day chasing around after the kids like her other married acquaintances. A few years ago that kind of life hadn't appealed to her at all, but now she had to admit that the idea of permanently hooking up with Conlean intrigued her. Warmth, purpose, love . . . those things had been missing from her life for so long. She was ready for a change, and Conlean was just the man to help her.

Clearly, this seductress business was going to be enjoyable.

Chapter Twelve

Conlean hastened to Hawkwood's apartment, thinking the older man's summons a propitious one. They had to figure out what to do, considering the fact that Jordan had refused to marry the Patriarch and would likely continue to do so. The worst aspect of the whole situation was that some rebellious part of him cheered at her refusal to marry his father, and rubbed greedy hands together at the thought of spending extended amounts of time in her company.

Rounding the corner in the hallway, he recalled the urgency in the page's voice, and wondered if the Grand Artisan had even more bad news to share. He stopped before Hawkwood's door and knocked. Immediately the older man's muffled voice told him to enter. Gripping the doorknob and wishing he knew exactly what lay in store for him, he pulled the door open and stepped inside.

"Hello, Conlean. We've been waiting for you."

Hawkwood, his gaunt face giving nothing away, nodded toward another man sitting in the corner. "His Excellency, the Patriarch of Blackfell."

"Father." Conlean hid his surprise at seeing his father in the Gallery. As he inclined his head, he wondered what disaster had brought the Patriarch here. His father never visited the Gallery. The place gave him claustrophobia. "You're well, I hope?"

The Patriarch barely acknowledged Conlean's greeting. "No, Artisan, I'm not *well*. I'm *impatient*. Impatient to see my new bride. When will you finally allow me to meet her?"

Conlean darted a glance at Hawkwood, whose gaze revealed nothing. Taking a deep breath, he sat down. He couldn't tell his father the truth: that Jordan hadn't come here of her own free will and had flatly refused to marry the Patriarch. Instead, he took a few seconds to formulate a reasonable excuse.

"Make yourself comfortable, by all means," his father said with a glare when the silence apparently became too much for him. "We have all the time in the world, don't we, Artisan?"

"I realize how important your time is, Father." He glanced at the Patriarch, who'd chosen a gray robe today, embroidered with silver thread. The color choice made the older man's features look even more sallow than usual and darkened the circles beneath his eyes. He seemed thinner and more tired than ever before, his inner strength depleted.

The Patriarch waved his hands in an impatient movement. "You're damned right, son, and I'm tired of waiting."

"I also know how eager you are to meet Jordan," Conlean said, the words sticking a little in his throat. Every time he thought about marrying his father to Jordan, he wanted to choke. "She's taken longer than usual to recover from her illness, though, and I haven't had a chance to introduce her to Blackfell or prepare her for her presentation yet."

"To hell with her presentation. I want her presented to me. Now. Bring her here," the Patriarch demanded.

"She's still weak—"

"Then carry her in here." The Patriarch began to pace around the room, his attention unfocused. "I don't know why you artisans think you can live by your own rules. I'm the Patriarch of Blackfell. You're here to scrve me." He paused and fixed Hawkwood with a gimlet stare. "You retrieved my bride and now I want to see her."

Hawkwood stood and raised his arms, his palms facing outward. "Yes, of course we serve you. We do so with great pleasure. Without you, the Gallery would be nothing." He allowed his arms to drop to his sides. "But we also want to ensure your happiness. Your first impression of your new bride should be a good one, because it'll remain in your mind forever. Until we've given her at least some polish, I'd like to delay a meeting between you two for a little longer."

The Patriarch's gaze softened. He appeared to consider Hawkwood's argument.

"She also wants to look her best for you," Conlean added, sensing victory was at hand. "She's yet to visit the dressmaker, and hasn't learned the rules of etiquette necessary for her public appearances. We don't want to embarrass her by forcing her to stumble through a presentation before she's ready."

The Patriarch stroked his chin. "I can see your point." His voice dropped an octave and the stare he suddenly fixed on Conlean was full of need. "I've heard some talk that doesn't sit well with me."

Hawkwood stiffened almost imperceptibly.

Conlean didn't have as much practice as the Grand Artisan at subtlety. He couldn't prevent a flinch. "What kind of talk?"

"I've heard that my new bride is . . . unsightly."

"Unsightly?" Conlean thought of Jordan's ocean blue eyes and wavy brown hair that always managed to look tousled, as if she'd just enjoyed a romp in bed, and almost laughed aloud. "She's a very attractive woman."

His father tilted his head and regarded him more closely. "You say that with a lot of enthusiasm. She's charmed you, eh?"

"She's charmed everyone," Hawkwood cut in. At the same time he gave Conlean a look through narrowed eyes.

Conlean cleared his throat. "She'll be a great asset to you, Father."

The Patriarch didn't appear convinced. Still, his interest in his bride evidently managed to overcome his misgivings, for he dove back into the topic with some trepidation, but mostly enthusiasm. "So, she's not an ugly old matron?"

"No, no, no." Hawkwood shook his head to emphasize the point further. "She's young, fresh, attractive . . . all that a man could want."

"I've also heard that she's scholarly."

A smile that wasn't a smile stretched Hawkwood's lips. "Who's been spreading such nonsense around? She hasn't even met anyone yet."

The Patriarch hesitated before replying. "Well, there is that matter of her being a librarian with an interest in the sciences. In fact, she supposedly has some knowledge of the ancient science of biology. I understand the plague was discovered through the use of biology."

"She does have an interest in the sciences, but her knowledge lies in categorizing scientific books rather than in the sciences themselves. I don't think she could tell the difference between an alembic and a drinking glass," Conlean asserted, thinking this his biggest lie yet. Surreptitiously he wiped the sweat from his brow.

"So she won't be mixing up substances or trying to create another damned plague?" This the Patriarch directed at Hawkwood.

"Of course not!" Hawkwood managed to appear offended.

"And she'll be warmhearted toward me? At my age, I need affection."

Conlean swallowed. "She loves you already."

His father sat down heavily. "I have to admit, I feel much better now about my new bride."

"I'm surprised you've been listening to gossip," Conlean murmured.

"I know." The Patriarch took a moment to rub his brow. "You may be an artisan, Conlean, but you're also my son. My own blood. I trust you implicitly. I should have realized you'd retrieve a woman who will serve my best interests."

Conlean didn't know if he should cringe with guilt

or sigh with relief. But then his father muttered that one more thing about his bride bothered him, and Conlean stiffened.

Here it comes, he thought.

"What's bothering you, your Excellency?" Hawkwood asked, his tone one of utter calm.

"I have heard something terrible, though I can scarce believe it."

"What have you heard?"

The Patriarch leaned toward Conlean and Hawkwood. "I've been told that she may be *infertile.*"

Hawkwood's left eye twitched. "Infertile?" He glanced at Conlean. "Do you know anything of this, Artisan Conlean?"

Conlean grew very still. How had that information leaked out? As far as he knew, Jordan had told only him. "The seeker would have researched her ability to have children before he offered Jordan a contract," he reminded his father, after he'd recovered enough to sound normal. Just barely normal. "Only women who can be ninety percent guaranteed fertile are offered contracts. I think we are safe on this point."

"You're certain of this, son?" his father asked, a peculiar vulnerability softening his voice.

Conlean couldn't quite meet his father's gaze. "As certain as I can be. The seekers haven't failed us before."

"Good." The Patriarch slapped his legs with both hands, in the manner of a man who had just satisfactorily completed a nasty piece of business. "In that case, I'll trust your judgment and wait until my new bride is ready for presentation. When might that be?"

"Give us another few weeks," Hawkwood adjured.

"A few weeks at most, gentlemen." He stood, displaying some of the vigor that Conlean had thought he'd lost.

"A few weeks," Hawkwood assured him.

Conlean bowed, and Hawkwood followed suit. On that note, the Patriarch left Hawkwood's apartment.

As soon as the door had shut behind him, Conlean sank into a chair. He wondered if things could possibly get any worse.

His attitude quiet and thoughtful, Hawkwood wandered over to the window. "Your father is becoming impatient. And he's listening to rumors intended to discredit Jordan. I don't know who is spreading these rumors, but clearly someone is very unhappy at the idea of the Patriarch marrying Jordan. We have enemies, Artisan, and we're going to have to move quickly or we may have a problem."

Conlean rubbed his eyes and then focused on the older man. "We have so many problems, I've lost count. Brace yourself for a shock, Grand Artisan. Jordan *is* infertile."

Hawkwood nodded. "I know."

"What?" Conlean sat forward in his chair. "How did you know?"

"One of the pages in her book states that her own inability to have children motivated her to study infertility."

"And you didn't see fit to tell me this?"

"There wasn't any need for you to know. It won't affect her ability to study the plague."

"Right." Conlean slumped backward. He was filled with roiling emotions: regret, guilt, need for Jordan, a sick feeling at the thought of her marrying his father. "What else haven't you told me?"

"If there is something you don't know, it's for your own protection," Hawkwood said.

"Forget about protecting me. Just tell me everything, okay?"

Hawkwood lifted an eyebrow. "What I find interesting is the fact that your father questioned Jordan's ability to have children. I'd thought that only the people directly involved with Jordan or her book, including you, me, and your mother, knew about her infertility. Someone has been spying on us. God only knows what else has been uncovered."

"There is something *you* should know," Conlean said. "Tonight Jordan went on a little tour of the Gallery without me. She met up with Tobias. I still don't know the details of their talk, but Jordan claims to have said nothing incriminating."

A grim look entered Hawkwood's eyes. "Find out exactly what was said."

"I will."

"We're running out of time, Artisan Conlean. Has Jordan agreed to marry the Patriarch yet?"

"No. She's still refusing."

"Do you think you'll be able to convince her to marry him within the next week or so?"

"It's doubtful."

The older man muttered an oath. "I thought the Counselor was supposed to help with all this."

"The Counselor can't work miracles, and neither can I. At least not in a matter of days. She simply refuses to marry."

"Why?"

"Her previous marriage went wrong and she ended the union. Now she says she'll marry only for love. Obviously she doesn't love my father."

"Did you and the Counselor come up with a plan to bring her around?"

"He's given me some ideas, but I can't know for sure if they'll work." Conlean hesitated before adding, "Jordan did suggest, in so many words, that while she had no intention of marrying my father, she *would* consider marrying me, so she isn't entirely opposed to the idea of marriage. The situation isn't hopeless."

Hawkwood looked thunderstruck. "Marry you? Does she love you, then?"

"Of course she doesn't love me."

"But you just said that she'd only marry for love."

"That's what she said . . ." Confused, Conlean trailed off. Why had she suggested that she'd marry him but not his father? Could she have developed feelings for him? No, it wasn't possible.

Was it?

He shook his head, not liking how good he felt at the thought of Jordan wanting to marry him. "I told her that marriage to me wasn't an option. She asked what would happen if she broke her marriage contract, and I said she'd have to put herself up for auction to the highest bidder."

"That must have convinced her to marry the Patriarch," Hawkwood said. "No woman wants to go up for auction."

"She didn't seem too concerned by the idea of an auction, and hasn't changed her mind about the marriage."

Hawkwood shook his head slowly and then looked more closely at Conlean. "How do you feel about Jordan's proposal, Artisan?"

"I'm flattered, but I'm also committed to our cause. I know that she has to marry my father."

"And you know that if you married her, your right to study artistry would be revoked," Hawkwood reminded him in severe tones. "Still, in general, how do you feel about her?"

"I like her," Conlean admitted after a short pause. "A lot."

"Maybe you like her too much." Hawkwood began stroking his beard. "She's obviously enamored of you. We have to be careful, Artisan."

"This is a difficult situation. I'm doing my best."

"I can't ask for anything more. Just keep working on her. We need to get her married to your father as quickly as possible, before any more damaging rumors surface about her. In the meanwhile, I'll try to discover who's working against us, and how much they know."

Conlean stood. "She's going to need additional protection. Another guard posted at her door wouldn't hurt. I'll also find out what she and Tobias discussed."

"Just be careful," Hawkwood insisted. "I'm more worried about her forming an attachment to you than anyone trying to do her harm. She must be convinced to marry your father."

Conlean nodded. "I'll do my best."

Inside, though, he wondered if his best would be good enough.

Or if he even wanted it to be good enough.

* * *

Jordan was up to her neck in bedcovers and in the middle of a dream when a soft knock sounded against the door. She struggled up through sleep and, after a brief moment of disorientation—she had just been walking down the street with Conlean, who had on a twenty-first-century business suit—she wrapped a blanket around herself and staggered toward the door. She opened the door amid a volley of more soft knocks and found herself staring straight into Conlean's tense gaze.

"You were sleeping," he said, the tone of his voice making the statement sound like an apology.

She eyed the clock in a pointed way. "Uh, yeah, I was sleeping. It's after midnight."

"Can I come in? It's very important."

"Come on." She padded back to her bed. Conlean followed and paused by the edge of the bed to look down at her.

"Sit, Artisan. You look uncomfortable, standing there like that. No one should be standing at this hour."

Sighing, Conlean sat next to her. "I'm sorry I woke you, Jordan."

She snuggled the covers around her body and yawned. "That's okay. I'm used to artisans barging into my room. So, what's up?"

Conlean looked at her, his expression bemused. "You look nice."

"It's the middle of the night and I'm in my pajamas. I don't know if I believe you."

"Your face is pink and your hair looks soft. You're very beautiful, you know."

She smiled, heat curling through her. "Thanks. At least you didn't tell me I have bed head." Silently she wished he would lie down next to her and contribute to the warmth that was building beneath the covers. Still, she knew he wouldn't. Though his body might urge him to do so, in his mind, she was still his father's bride.

The trick now was to convince him that she wasn't going to marry anyone other than him. If she had to marry in this crazy world—and it was beginning to look as if marriage was definitely on the agenda—than she would marry Conlean. She knew him, trusted him, and felt a spark in his presence, one she hadn't felt with a man in a very long time. He remained her best, and likely her only, prospect for happiness.

"Conlean, I'm cold and I'm tired," she said softly. "I'll bet you are too. Now, I don't usually make this kind of offer, but because I like you, I'm going to suggest you lie down here next to me and let us both get some sleep. Can't the compliments wait until the morning?"

A sudden spark in his eyes made him appear fiercer, more masculine. "Your offer is very generous. I don't think it would be a good idea, though."

She feigned a yawn. "Come on, lie down. Whatever brought you here can't be that important. Besides, I need some help warming up this bed."

A slight flush invaded his cheeks. "It *is* important. I came to see what you and Tobias talked about."

"In the middle of the night?" She sighed. "If you agree to lie down with me for a little while and let me get some sleep, I promise I'll tell you every detail of the conversation between Tobias and myself. On the other hand, if you insist on questioning me now, I can't guarantee that I'll remember everything Tobias said."

Smiling, he shook his head. "You're one hell of a bargainer. I should take you to the market in Blackfell. You'd have the place bought out for a song."

Her heart beat a little harder. "So, do we have a deal?"

"How about I lie down next to you, so we're both 'comfortable,' and then you tell me what Grand Artisan Tobias and you talked about?"

"You're a pretty good bargainer yourself," she admitted. "All right, why not." She stretched, noting with satisfaction the way his gaze followed her movements. *Why not, indeed?*

His gaze never leaving her face, he stretched out and rested his head on the pillow next to her. A pleasant male scent drifted over her. Excitement quickened her breathing. His body was so close to hers, she could practically feel the heat coming off his skin.

Throwing caution to the winds, she moved closer until the sides of their bodies touched. Jade green eyes stared deeply into hers. She thought she saw a question in his gaze. She swallowed. "So, you want to know what Tobias had to say."

"Please." He picked up a stray lock of her hair and teased it between his fingers.

"Well, we played this game—"

Conlean's hand stilled for a moment, her hair caught between his fingers. "He's known for his games."

"It was a question-and-answer game."

He started to play with her hair again. "What kinds of questions did he ask?"

Tracy Fobes

His hands, she thought, looked like surgeon's, the fingers both sensitive and knowledgeable. She wanted them on other parts of her body. "He asked about my past. I managed not to tell him anything outside of the librarian story we'd discussed earlier."

"Good." He allowed her hair to fall back to the pillow. "What else did he say?"

"As I mentioned, he explained the customary treatment of newly retrieved brides to me, and how I've been treated differently. He acted as though he found the whole situation very suspicious."

"You *have* been treated differently from other brides," Conlean admitted. With a restless motion he picked up her hand and held it in his much warmer one, then began to trace her palm with those long fingers. "But then again, you're not the run-of-the-mill bride, either. You're going to be the Matriarch of Blackfell. Of course you're being treated differently."

Her palm tingled. "I'm not going to be Matriarch, Conlean."

He leaned close to her ear. "Please think about it some more," he whispered, tickling her.

She sucked in a breath and fought the urge to grab his face and pull it over to hers for a long and delicious kiss. "You're very persuasive."

Smiling, he moved away a little. His fingers traced little circles on the back of her hand. "Did he say anything else?"

"Nothing worth reporting." He was driving her crazy, touching her hand like that. She felt as if he was trying to seduce her. Hell, maybe he was. Maybe he figured that seduction was the only way to get her to

184

cooperate. If so, then they were both thinking along the same lines. And one good turn, she told herself, deserved another.

She smiled softly and pushed her fingers through his hair, scraping them along his scalp. "Your hair's all mussed. It looks funny. But cute." Gently she smoothed it back in place, running her fingertips along the edge of his ear as she did so. "There. All better."

"You, too." He released her hand and smoothed her hair back from her brow. "Yours doesn't look like it wants to stay put, though."

"It never does. It's always a mess." A swell of longing made her breath catch in her throat. He was definitely winning this little game of seduction. "I was wondering, why does Grand Artisan Tobias hide out in the Gallery's dungeons? He seems to be living in the boiler room."

"His studio is in the boiler room, but he has an apartment on the third floor. It's very luxurious."

She turned on her side, so she could look directly into his eyes, and moved closer to him, until their breath mingled. "Is Tobias friend or foe?"

"He can't be trusted." Conlean stared at her with a heavy-lidded gaze. "He and Hawkwood are at odds with each other."

"Why?"

"Tobias and Hawkwood are the only two Grand Artisans in the Gallery. They're vying for control of the Gallery, and they both have opposite ideals. Tobias believes a bride should be earned, while Hawkwood believes that all men are entitled to have a bride."

Unable to help herself any longer, she touched his

lower lip with the tip of her finger, then ran it to the corner of his mouth. "Whose side do you fall on?"

"Hawkwood's," he said, his voice husky.

She shivered at the promise in his eyes. It was becoming very difficult to keep her mind on the conversation. "How did you know I was in Tobias's studio?"

"The three Artisans you heard talking in the staircase saw you."

"They saw me?" She lifted her hand to touch his lips again, but he grasped her hand and brought it to his mouth. His gaze never leaving her face, he pressed firm lips against her palm.

"You'd make a terrible spy," he told her.

"I'll remember to stay out of the spook business," she murmured. "They told you where I was?"

"A healthy instinct told me where you were." He released her hand, only to pull her so close that their noses were practically touching.

She breathed him in. He smelled so good. "I have a healthy instinct too."

"What's your instinct telling you?"

"It's telling me to kiss you." Keeping her gaze locked with his, she wound her arms around his neck, pressed her body against him, and kissed him gently on the mouth. Then she leaned back and gazed at him.

At first, a look of surprise filled his eyes, as if this game between them had gone farther than he'd intended. Within moments, though, he wrapped his strong arms around her and held her close.

"I'm sorry I had to leave you, Jordan," he murmured. "I thought about you the entire time I was gone. I couldn't get you out of my mind. And I worried. I promise you, I won't leave you again. And I won't let anyone harm you."

Oddly enough, she believed him. Despite every crazy, dangerous aspect of this situation he and Hawkwood had placed her in, she knew that somehow, Conlean wouldn't let anyone harm her. Her heart hammering in her chest, she lifted her head until her lips were mere inches from his, and then kissed him again, softly, slowly, her touch a question he answered with lips that were gentle at first. But when she urged his mouth open with her own, a swift hunger darkened his gaze and he hardened the kiss between them, taking over, his tongue sliding around hers and making her light-headed. Everything about him pleased her—the way he smelled, the way he held her, the firm pressure of his lips, the bold exploration of his tongue—and she wanted more. Much more.

The place between her thighs grew warm and achy. She kissed him back, hard, feverishly pressing her lips against his, then dragging them away to plant rushed little kisses around his mouth and chin. He threw his head back and let her worship him for a moment, the muscles in his neck standing out, before dropping kisses on her hair, her ears, and her neck with the same kind of intensity.

She wanted him too much to speak; couldn't even think of any words. Moaning softly, she shoved her trembling hands beneath the edges of his shirt and pushed it off his shoulders, until the buttons were strained and ready to pop off. Her throat tight at the thought of seeing his naked chest, she released the buttons with fingers that didn't quite work right and then dragged his shirt back, so she could bury her fingers in the light covering of black hair. Impulsively she leaned down and kissed both of his nipples before rubbing her nose against him, drinking in his clean male scent.

"Ah, Jordan, we shouldn't," he murmured, his lips dipping to the hollow of her neck, his hands finding her breasts and cupping them briefly before slipping beneath her shirt to touch her bare skin. She jumped a little at the feel of his work-roughened hands against the sides of her breasts, but when his finger flicked her nipple, she grabbed his face and kissed him hard, the sensations going through her like nothing she'd ever felt before.

He explored her mouth slowly with his lips, while his hands began rubbing her nipples. She arched against him, wanting his hands between her legs, wanting to rip his pants off so she could taste him and drive him crazy with need, wanting him so badly that she threw all her inhibitions out the window. She would open to him fully, satisfy any of his fantasies, if only he would lay her down against the mattress and fill the aching void between her legs as deeply as he could.

"Please, Conlean," she whispered against his mouth.

He stopped rubbing her nipples and moved his hand downward, dragging his fingers across her skin to her waistband. At the same time, she eagerly grasped the top of his pants and fumbled with the buttons holding them closed. Soon, she had his pants loosened and slipped her hand inside. Not even hesitating slightly, she found his erection and grasped it in her palm, holding him with just enough pressure to draw a groan from him.

He broke their kiss and looked at her, his fingers finding their way beneath her waistband to the softness between her thighs. As he gently caressed her and found the center of her pleasure, she stroked his erection and felt him harden even more.

"You're so warm, so soft," he said quietly. "So wet. I want you, Jordan. More than I've ever wanted anyone or anything before. But this can't go any farther."

"Conlean. Please." She thrust her hips upward, and his finger slipped inside her. Intense pleasure washed over her. She groaned, long and deep, her touch on his erection becoming more insistent. "Take your pants off," she demanded, her voice breathy.

He hesitated. "You're my father's bride."

She sensed that guilt was dampening his passion. "No, I'm not." She kissed his neck. "Don't stop. Don't leave me like this."

He pulled his hand from between her legs, leaving her aching and desperate. "We can't, Jordan," he said, his voice husky.

"Please . . ."

"No." He kissed her swiftly on the lips, then released her entirely.

To her, it felt as if he was closing a book. Realizing that the battle was lost, she somehow managed a graceful retreat. "I understand. You're not ready." Gently she let go of his erection, which was still pulsing against her palm, and took some satisfaction in the knowledge that he was hurting just as much as she. Then she kissed him one last time, her tongue traveling across his lips before she sat back and found the strength to smile at him . . . in what she hoped was a seductive manner. "I want you, Conlean. All of you. And I'm willing to wait."

His face flushed, he pushed up from the mattress. "You need to get some sleep."

"Do you provide a tuck-in service?"

He stood and then stared down at her. "If I tuck you in, I won't be leaving."

She patted the mattress next to her. "I don't mind if you stay."

"My father wouldn't much appreciate my staying."

Frowning, she sat up. "I'll see you in the morning, then?"

"Bright and early." He glanced around her room. "You have your book locked up, right?"

"I locked it up earlier. I spent the last few days reading it, and I have to admit, a large portion of it *is* my research." She cast about in her mind for some kind of conversational gambit that would keep him from leaving, and abruptly recalled the other part of her conversation with Tobias. "You know, there's something I forgot to mention about my conversation with the Grand Artisan. We talked about the plague."

Conlean looked at her sharply. "About the plague? What did he say?"

"Only that he'd heard rumors about a recently discovered book that contains secrets about the plague. He mentioned my past as a librarian and suggested that I might be able to help him find this book, if it existed."

"Hawkwood and I have been hearing rumors about you that are far too close to the truth. I suspect that Tobias is behind at least some of them. We're all going to have to be very careful from now on. In fact, I'll take your book with me so I can store it in a safer place. Where is it? In the chest?"

She got up and went over to her wardrobe, mourning the loss of the closeness that had been between them minutes ago. "The key's in here." She retrieved it from a coat pocket and handed it to him.

He crossed the room and slipped the key into the chest's large brass lock. In a second he had the chest open and was gazing inside. "There's nothing in here. Are you sure you locked the book up?"

Her self-assurance faltered. She had locked the book up before leaving to explore the Gallery, hadn't she? She hurried over to the chest, oblivious of the fact that the room had gotten cold and she wore only a thin nightgown. It lay empty. "I know I put it in there . . ."

"I hope you misplaced it."

Together they began to search the room. It took her only a few seconds to discover the book beneath her bed, some of its pages fanned out across the floor. "Here it is," she called out, and began to put the pages that had fallen out back into their proper places.

Conlean rushed to her side. "You found it. Thank God. But how did it get beneath your bed?"

"I must have laid it close to the edge of the mattress." Frowning, she trailed off. The truth was, she couldn't recall what she'd done with it. She'd been too angry, too bored, and too interested in sneaking out of her room to notice.

"How did it fall?" he murmured.

She shook her head slowly. "I don't know."

Conlean ran a hand through his hair. "You can't remember?"

"No. Damn! I'm sorry, Conlean."

"Either you misplaced it or someone broke into your room and examined it. I hope you misplaced it, but I can't rule out the second option. You weren't here, and the guard wouldn't have stopped anyone from breaking into your room. He was too busy sleeping. Did you see anyone suspicious today? Hear anything? Notice anything different in your room?"

"No, nothing." She paused, remembering the perfume the guard had worn. "I did notice one strange thing."

"What?"

"Do you recall my mentioning the guard's feminine perfume?"

"Yes. I didn't know what you were talking about."

"When I left my room and passed the guard, I smelled a floral fragrance, like a woman's perfume. It was gone by the time we came back."

Conlean rubbed his chin. "That *is* odd. Murray is one of the more rough-and-tumble guards. The only thing I've ever smelled on him is sweat."

"How many times has he fallen asleep at his post?" she asked, remembering the pewter cup that lay askew at his feet . . . as if he'd fallen into a sudden stupor and dropped it.

"This is the first time."

"I suggest you check that pewter cup out there by his chair for a sedative."

He lifted an eyebrow. "He could have been drugged."

"Exactly." Shivering, she picked up the book and

gave it to him. "I'm sorry. I shouldn't have left my room."

He took it from her, at the same time enfolding her in an embrace. "It's okay. I don't blame you for wanting to get out of here. I don't like being cooped up in a room any more than you do."

She allowed her head to drop against his shoulder. To her surprise, she discovered she had tears in her eyes. "I might have put us all in jeopardy."

"We'll be all right," he murmured, his breath warm against her ear.

She trembled.

"You're cold," he said, his hands lingering on her shoulders and waist as he turned and moved her toward the bed.

"So you do have a tuck-in service," she said, trying for a smile but ending up wanting to cry instead.

"I guess I do." He bent down to pull the covers up over her. Then he pressed a soft kiss against her lips.

Closing her eyes, she opened her lips beneath his, trying to make more of what he'd no doubt intended as a platonic peck. She suspected that he'd end it quickly, but instead his mouth pressed against hers, in a slow and lazy way, like a hot summer day. Heat gathered inside her and a rush of heaviness flooded her thighs, in another good old-fashioned attack of lust. Maybe he would stay . . .

Without warning, he stood up, breaking their kiss.

She opened her eyes and saw him standing above her, looking at her with a troubled gaze.

He arranged the covers around her chin. "Get some

sleep. Tomorrow I'll be here first thing in the morning to take you outside."

"I'll be counting on you," she told him.

"Sleep well." With an abrupt nod, he turned and walked to the door.

Feeling lonely, she watched his tall form disappear through the door, leaving her by herself in the darkness.

Chapter Thirteen

Jordan woke the following morning feeling groggy and unsettled by dreams of people she didn't know chasing her. She hadn't had enough sleep, which meant that she would be in a bad mood all day, because she was the type of person who needed at least eight hours each night. True to form, when she dragged herself out of bed, she looked around with a frown and decided that her room was ugly, she was ugly, the day was ugly, and she was never going to get home.

Grouchily she picked through her breakfast, spearing her eggs with her fork and wondering how long Conlean planned to leave her locked up in her room this time. Even the kiss they'd shared didn't seem as magical as it had when she'd experienced it. All she could think of was how it had ended far too soon.

After breakfast she splashed cold water on her face and spent some time cursing Dr. Rinehart for appropriating her research without her permission. She couldn't

Tracy Fobes

believe he'd had the nerve to mention her infertility on the acknowledgments page. She hoped no one other than herself, Conlean, and Hawkwood had seen the book. They all had a vested interest in keeping her inability to have children secret. What would the Patriarch say if he found out he was marrying a barren bride?

Disgusted, she walked over to another tray with a teapot and made herself a cup of tea. She would have preferred coffee, but at least she was drinking something she recognized. Good old tea. Even after ten thousand years, people were still drinking it. Wondering if they still called the stuff in her cup *orange pekoe*, she glanced out the open window. The morning fog had burned off, leaving the sky a brilliant blue.

On the grounds surrounding the Gallery, sheep bleated, hammers struck metal, and voices ebbed and flowed in conversation. She walked over to the window and peered outside. Cobblestone paths connected the largest outbuildings and barns, suggesting that these places formed the backbone of the Gallery. Dirt paths veered off from the cobblestones, leading to smaller barns, pastures, and even an orchard. Wells for water dotted the grounds and flowers grew in well-tended beds around every corner, providing splashes of beauty, form, and color.

The Artisans obviously took very good care of their home.

Sighing, she turned away from the window and wandered over to her door. She felt cooped up. Stale. To amuse herself, she thought of some questions she could ask Conlean about Blackfell, but that quickly grew overwhelming, so she turned her thoughts to seducing him. Last night's kiss was an excellent start. Next, she had to encourage him to hit a home run. But how did women go about enticing men into their beds? She'd never wanted a man enough before to go through that kind of trouble. Even she and Dennis, her ex, had just sort of come together, first as colleagues at work and then as partners. There had been no chasing, no flattery, and nothing like the passion she'd experienced with Conlean.

Their arrangement had been serviceable.

At the time, serviceable had been okay with her.

Now, she couldn't imagine anything worse than a serviceable marriage.

She wandered over to her wardrobe to examine its contents. Maybe she could tempt him with some sort of slinky dress. Unfortunately, there wasn't much in her wardrobe . . . just enough to get by, she supposed. And the outfits she saw looked as if they had more in common with burlap bags than slinky dresses. With the exception of an emerald dress, they looked like tunics with matching loose pants. Talk about making a woman look unattractive! Then again, she supposed that a woman would have to be dumb to wear something tight-fitting in a world where most men didn't get laid, ever.

Smiling a little, she grabbed a navy blue tunic, matching pants, and a pair of leather-soled slippers. While she was dressing, a knock sounded at the door, and she heard a muffled "Good morning" from Conlean. Her heart beating faster, she yelled that she'd be there in a second, and once she'd finished dragging on the shapeless clothes, she ran to let him in.

He slipped into her room with a smile, his dark hair brushed back from his forehead in glossy waves and curling down past his chin. The dark circles she'd seen beneath his eyes the first few days had disappeared and a ruddy glow stained his features, giving him an aura of health. The best thing about him was his gaze, though. Happiness lit his eyes the moment he looked at her.

"Good morning," she said a little breathlessly. "I was hoping you would come soon."

His expression serious, he walked toward her, leaving a trace of his scent in the air. It was something simple, like soap, rather than cologne. She felt a new wave of lust fire up inside her.

But it wasn't just the physical with him, she silently admitted. She was honest-to-God glad to see his smiling face. She wanted to spend the day at his side. And she couldn't wait to see what sort of intrigue this renegade, in his mild-mannered artisan disguise, hatched today.

In other words, she had gotten herself in deep. Maybe too deep.

"I went over to see Grand Artisan Hawkwood this morning," he told her. "I wanted to know what he thought of the way Tobias had questioned you about your book, and the possibility that someone had broken into your room in an attempt to steal it."

"What did he say?"

"He said that we need to be careful. Very careful. But he didn't think someone broke into your room in order to steal the book. If someone wanted to steal it, why did he leave it lying on the floor by your bed?"

"Maybe we interrupted him in mid-steal. If we had

walked in a moment earlier, we might have discovered someone dressed all in black, hunched over my bed with their hot little hands on my book."

Conlean nodded. "That's possible. Still, it's not very likely. We would have found at least a few signs of forced entry and the subsequent search for the book."

"Like a jimmied lock and clothes tossed around the room?"

"Exactly."

"What about Tobias? Is Hawkwood worried that Tobias appears to know something about the book?"

"We aren't sure exactly what Tobias knows. He's probably only hearing bits and pieces about you through his network of informants, and a lot of those bits and pieces are speculation. Still, even if he manages to learn everything about you, I don't think he'll be our downfall. Tobias has a vested interest in the Gallery, and he wouldn't want to risk people knowing that a cure to the plague could be found. He wants to keep the Gallery intact, so he can keep collecting revenue from the painting of brides."

Jordan nodded uneasily. "I'll try not to worry about him."

"I will say that the faster we move, the better our hope of succeeding," Conlean offered. "Let's not dwell on it, though. I want you to enjoy yourself. Would you like to go for a walk?"

"I'd love to."

"Then let's go." He held out a hand for her to grasp.

She cast a worried glance down at her blue tunic, the scalloped embroidery across the front reminding her of lederhosen. "Am I dressed appropriately?"

"You look beautiful," he said enthusiastically. Then he coughed a little, as if to hide embarrassment.

She slipped her hand into his. "Thanks."

At the touch of her palm against his, his jaw tensed, then smoothed out just as quickly. He tightened his grip on her palm, not uncomfortably but firmly, so she couldn't let go. He had her trapped. With a little luck, she thought, the trap would close until their bodies were pressed together and he was kissing her hard enough to make her knees buckle.

Unfortunately, he seemed determined to keep at a distance appropriate for a mother-in-law and her new son. Thinking seduction, she closed the distance between them and tried to act as though there was nothing out of the ordinary in two people walking as though they were joined at the hip.

"Are you cold?" he asked, a look of concern on his face.

"No, I'm okay."

Slanting a curious look her way, he released her to open the door and say a few words to the man posted outside, then brought her into the hallway. The lanterns that had flickered on the wall last night stood extinguished, their glow replaced by sunlight, which filtered through a window down at the end of the hall. Again, the simplicity of the décor struck her. Where she expected to see old suits of armor and poleaxes, she instead found potted palms; woven mats replaced tapestries and rugs. She had to admit the hallway felt more open and airy than she ever could have imagined.

He led her down the corridor and around two corners before reaching the staircase.

They descended to the ground floor and emerged in a center hallway that evidently functioned as a gathering place. Chairs lay scattered about, some of them occupied by Artisans, and a fountain gurgled in the corner, the glasses stacked around it suggesting it provided drinking water. A magnificent stained-glass skylight reigned over the entire hallway, lighting the walls with rainbow shades that mingled with the pure sunlight drifting in from side windows.

She and Conlean paused on entering, and the muted conversation in the room stopped as every gaze turned toward them. Self-consciously she hung back. Conlean smiled and nodded his head at several of the Artisans before leading her through the hallway. She saw Tobias seated near a massive hearth. He winked at her as she passed, his gaze avid. She looked in his direction and gave him a nod.

"Aren't you going to introduce me to anyone?" she murmured.

"If we stop, we'll be stuck for a while, fending off questions instead of eating lunch and exploring the Gallery. Which would you prefer?"

"To look around."

He smiled. "I thought so."

She followed him into the entry vestibule. A youth stationed at the doorway opened one of the two wooden doors leading outside. Beyond, the cobblestone path wound through lawns and flowerbeds.

They stepped into the yard.

Jordan took a deep breath of fresh air. The sun shone directly overhead, its warmth a welcome change from the cold drafts inside the Gallery. A breeze laden with the scent of flowers brushed past her and, abruptly, a feeling of well-being surprised her with its intensity. Conlean, his features smooth and tanned beneath the noonday sun, smiled at her, and she briefly wondered what had improved her mood: the sublime weather or the man next to her?

"The dining room is this way," he murmured, his voice low, as though he too felt the dreamy pull of the day.

Together they walked along the cobblestones, pausing long enough to say hello to Jerrod, the young Artisan who apprenticed under Conlean. The youth smiled foolishly at her before stumbling away, and Conlean shook his head. "I think you have another admirer."

A smile curved her lips. "Another?"

His face reddening, he didn't reply.

She didn't have the courage to press him further.

After a few minutes, they turned up a walkway that led to a large stone building. Black smoke billowed from a chimney on one side of it.

"The kitchen and dining room," he informed her.

The scent of baking apples teased her nose. "Why is it so far away from the Artisans' living area?"

"I suppose the builders originally kept it separate from the dormitory in order to reduce the risk of setting everything on fire."

"You're never considered moving it closer?"

"We didn't see a need. Most artisans are more interested in craftsmanship than the menu."

Without thinking about it, she looked his muscled bod up and down and decided that more men should

NAME: _____

ADDRESS: _____

_____

_____

TELEPHONE: _____

E-MAIL: _____

_____ I want to pay by credit card.

__ Visa   __ MasterCard   __ Discover

Account Number: _____

Expiration date: _____

SIGNATURE: _____

*Send this form, along with $2.00 shipping
and handling for your FREE books, to:*

Love Spell Romance Book Club
20 Academy Street
Norwalk, CT 06850-4032

*Or fax (must include credit card
information!) to:* 610.995.9274.
*You can also sign up on the Web
at* www.dorchesterpub.com.

Offer open to residents of the U.S. and
Canada only. Canadian residents, please
call 1.800.481.9191 for pricing information.

If under 18, a parent or guardian must sign. Terms, prices and conditions
subject to change. Subscription subject to acceptance. Dorchester
Publishing reserves the right to reject any order or cancel any subscription.

take up craftsmanship. But then, when her gaze met his and she saw his interested expression, she suddenly realized how blatantly she'd checked him out. Her cheeks grew warm. "Craftsmanship is important," she agreed, sounding just like the tongue-tied idiot she was.

Again, he had no reply. Instead, he held out an arm in an old-fashioned gesture and guided her to the front door. She smiled at him as they sailed into the dining room with all the aplomb of Donald Trump and his latest wife.

As in the artisans' living area, a skylight made of stained glass topped the dining room and colored the space with diffused hues. Tables large enough to seat groups of four to six lay scattered about the wooden floor, and a highly polished buffet table of mahogany sat at one end. Earthenware bowls and pewter trays on top of the buffet contained various offerings—salads, pastas, and vegetable dishes, judging by the aromas that wafted across the room.

Artisans of every age lounged around the tables, some eating and some talking. A few spirited arguments punctuated the conversation that filled the room like a buzz. Conlean, an easy smile on his face, guided her toward an unoccupied table. Several of the discussions, she noticed, ceased as they passed. Feeling like a fly under a glass, she approached the table and tried not to return the stares directed her way. Suddenly she felt overwhelmed. She didn't want to talk to all these strange men whose experience of the past and hopes for the future were so alien to her. They had nothing in common, no basis for conversation.

"Easy, Jordan," Conlean said as he pulled out a chair for her. "Everything will be fine. Sit down and I'll bring you something to eat."

Gratefully she sank into her chair. "Am I that obviously nervous?"

"You're a shade paler than you were a little while ago." He brushed his hand across her arm. "Relax. I'll be right back."

She dropped her gaze, trying to hide her enjoyment of that little gesture and the brief closeness of his skin on hers. "Don't worry about me."

He walked away, and once he'd reached a safe distance she looked up and glanced around the room. She had the satisfaction of seeing several of the artisans divert their attention from her as she focused on them. Apparently they had the decency not to stare outright.

She studied the simple, clean lines of the hearth and the pot of water hanging from an iron hook above it. Steam that smelled like cinnamon and cardamom billowed from the pot, suggesting that the artisans were cooking up their version of chai tea. When Conlean went over to the pot and ladled some of it into a cup, she found herself relaxing more. At least she knew what she'd be drinking.

"Hello, milady," a deep masculine voice said.

Startled, she jerked her head up and stared into rich brown eyes. A tall, well-built man was standing over her, a solemn expression on his face. She gave him an automatic smile and silently wished him away. How was she supposed to negotiate a conversation without Conlean at her side, steering her away from the pitfalls that awaited her?

"I'm Adviser Erickson. A pleasure to meet you." He gave her a courtly little bow with such flair and grace that she knew he must have practiced long and hard to perfect it. A sweet scent wafted from him, reminding her of something, but she couldn't quite remember *what.*

"I'm Jordan Connor," she replied cautiously. The man had a smooth quality that suggested he usually got what he wanted. "Nice to meet you too."

He grasped the back of an empty chair at her table. "May I join you and Artisan Conlean for lunch?"

She glanced toward the buffet table and saw Conlean filling two plates with food. He appeared unaware of her predicament. "Well, I don't know . . ."

A smile made his features even more handsome. "I know Artisan Conlean would prefer to keep you to himself, but what about you? You don't look like the kind of woman who would enjoy being a princess in an ivory tower."

"Of course not," she replied instantly, and then silently berated herself for allowing him to manipulate her so easily.

Without further discussion he pulled out a chair and slid into it. "So, what do you think of our fair city?"

She swallowed. "I've seen very little of it so far. I've been staying at the Gallery these past two weeks."

"Ah, you *have* been the princess in the ivory tower." Another smile curved his lips and took some of the sting out of his observation. "Tell me what you think of the Gallery, then."

"It's very formal," she began slowly, thinking that he ought to have a suit of armor to go along with his flowery speech. "In fact, it reminded me of an old, drafty castle at first. For a while I kept looking for axes and lances in the hallways and wrought-iron chandeliers hanging from the ceilings. But the furnishings are softer, and very comfortable."

He nodded. "A lot of thought goes into every building we construct. It's our way."

"I've gotten that impression," she confirmed. "You're not an artisan, are you?"

"No, I'm an adviser. To the Patriarch," he clarified.

"And what does an adviser to the Patriarch do?"

"We help him make decisions. Each adviser has specialized knowledge of a different aspect of Blackfell, and when an issue regarding an adviser's specialization comes up, the adviser briefs the Patriarch with the information he needs."

"And what is your specialization?"

"I know about our roads and shipping lanes. I travel them frequently, and I make recommendations for new roads to be built, old roads to be fixed, and shipping lanes that need dredging. It isn't the most exciting specialization, but as the Adviser of Journeys, I receive income from a large estate that produces a considerable yearly sum. I live quite well."

Department of Transportation, she thought.

"Actually, I've just brought on two apprentices who are going to help me with inspections," he continued. "That'll free up my time and allow me to spend more of my days at Duncraven, my estate. Now I just need a wife."

She nodded slowly. "A wife. I see."

"It's time for me to start a family." His eyelids slid a little bit lower, masking the expression in his brown eyes. "I'm sorry you're already taken, Jordan. I think you'll make an excellent wife."

Warmth rose in her cheeks. Adviser Erickson had a way with the ladies, no doubt about it. He was handsome, charming, smooth, cultured, tall and well-built . . . he possessed every trait a woman could want. And yet, she had to admit, something about him just didn't appeal to her. She couldn't quite put her finger on it. Maybe it was his pencil-thin mustache, or maybe the smoothness that seemed more slick than silky had turned her off, but she kept thinking *snake oil salesman* when she looked at him. "Oh? How do you know?"

"It's in your eyes, and the way you move your body."

"Pardon me?"

"I can see the conflict within your eyes, the way you want to please but are afraid to do so. And your body . . . it moves toward me even as your mind insists you pull away."

She hid a grimace of revulsion. What a conceited ass! "You have a great imagination."

"Adviser Erickson." Conlean appeared near her elbow, two plates balanced in his hands. A small muscle in his jaw was flexing. He didn't look happy.

She stood. "Here, let me help you with that." She took the plate and set it down before her.

Erickson smiled, but his eyes had lost their warmth. "Artisan Conlean. Good to see you again. I was just talking with your latest bride."

"How are you, Erickson?" Conlean put his plate between her and the adviser. "Still mending roads?"

"Actually, I'm leaving the roads to my apprentices and settling down at Duncraven. I'll need a bride very soon." The adviser's eyes narrowed slightly. He moved away from her slightly to accommodate Conlean.

Conlean sat down in front of his plate, his body forming a wall that separated her from Erickson. His face showed no emotion. "Best wishes on your impending marriage, then."

Her attention glued to the men, she sat down.

Erickson glanced at her. "I'd like to find a bride like Jordan."

Conlean shook his head. "She already has a contract."

"As I well know." Erickson gave Jordan a crooked smile. "She wouldn't be here if she didn't. Perhaps if your circumstances change, Jordan, you'll consider me."

She managed a polite smile in return, though silently she wondered why he thought her circumstances might change. "You'll be the first on my list."

Erickson reached across the table, right past Conlean, to grasp her hand with his. He squeezed her palm, his gesture courtly yet somehow intimate. "Ah, charm as well as beauty. What a wonderful find you are."

Fighting off the urge to make a gagging sound, she picked up her fork and pushed some food around on her plate.

"Do you know those men?" Conlean abruptly asked Erickson, a frown hardening his features. He nodded his head toward a distant table. The men sitting at the table were motioning for Erickson to join them.

"They're friends of mine," Erickson admitted.

Conlean picked up his own fork and speared a piece of meat. "They're signaling to you. Maybe you should go over there."

"They want to know what I think of our lovely Jordan," Erickson said. "Naturally I'll put in a good word for her."

"Would you do that for me?" Jordan smiled sweetly and hoped he was too stupid to recognize the thick layer of sarcasm in her voice. She didn't care what he said to his friends; she just wished he would disappear.

Erickson gave her an oily smile. "Of course. I'd be happy to."

"Thank you so much," she said as he rose from his chair.

"Very nice to meet you, Jordan. Will I see you tonight, at dinner?" Erickson asked as he pushed the chair in.

"Jordan's taking her meals in her room until her presentation—" Conlean started to reply, but Erickson cut in.

"Why is she eating here in the dining room, then?"

"I'm making an exception this morning, so I can show her around the Gallery. Otherwise, I'll be keeping her safe within her room."

"So we won't be seeing Jordan at the festival next week?"

"Not likely." Conlean directed a frown toward the other man.

Erickson responded with a crooked smile. "I'll see you at your presentation, then."

"I'm looking forward to it," she managed.

With one last look in her direction, Erickson turned and picked his way toward the distant table. Once he'd passed beyond hearing range, she shook her head. "Is that what all the men in Blackfell are like? If so, I can't believe any marriage in Blackfell lasts. I don't think I've ever met a more ridiculous example of manhood."

Conlean nodded. "In Erickson's case, you're right. His marriages don't last. He commissioned a portrait right after he became the Adviser of Journeys, but his bride disappeared a few years after their wedding."

"Disappeared?" She studied him for a moment, then asked, "Do you think he had something to do with it?"

"There isn't any evidence to suggest that Erickson is responsible for his bride's disappearance."

"Still, you're suspicious."

"I don't like him. Maybe that's coloring my judgment."

"He struck me as a phony. He was saying all of those complimentary things to me, and he acted as though he liked me, but underneath it all I had the feeling that he didn't like me at all."

He nodded. "You're right. Phony is the word for him. I've never sensed any genuine emotion in him, even when his wife disappeared. I was far more concerned about her than he."

"Did you know his wife?"

"I painted her portrait." He paused, a shadow falling over his gaze. "I brought her here to Blackfell. The fact that she's missing has given me plenty of sleepless nights."

Silence settled between them as Jordan digested this piece of news. Clearly he felt responsible for whatever had befallen Erickson's first bride. Did he feel that kind of responsibility for all the women he painted? She wondered if he simply felt a sense of duty towards her; and if she'd mistaken his reaction to her as something more personal and deeper. With a start, she realized that tight feeling in her chest was jealousy over the other brides he'd brought to Blackfell.

After a time, she ventured, "Do you think Erickson is a threat?"

He frowned. "He can't feel empathy for others, and that makes him a threat."

"But not a threat in the same sense as Grand Artisan Tobias."

"I don't think he knows anything about our plan, but I do believe the man is smart and capable of anything."

"Lucky for me that I caught his eye."

"I'll keep him away from you."

Now it was her turn to frown. "I had nightmares all last night. I kept dreaming that someone was chasing me. I can't wait to find out what I'm going to dream about tonight, after this meeting with Erickson."

He groaned. "I'm supposed to be showing you a good time, according to the Counselor, and here you are, having nightmares and fending off compliments from a sociopath. I think we need to play a little. What did you enjoy doing back in your own time?"

"To be honest with you, I didn't do much for enjoyment. Most of my adult life I've either pursued good grades, a challenging position in biotechnology, or a cure for male infertility. I was a real workaholic."

"You were married once, weren't you? Didn't your ex-husband do things to make you happy?"

"No. That's why he's my ex-husband."

"Weren't there any good times in the marriage?"

She shifted uncomfortably on her seat. "I suppose that depends on what you consider a 'good time.' Dennis was just as driven as I. We were both scientists. We ate, slept, and lived biotechnology. We enjoyed research but didn't spend much time working on our marriage."

Conlean slowly shook his head. "I'm surprised your husband wanted children, since he evidently had little time for them."

"Dennis was an only child," she said. "He'd always said he wanted to have a big family because his own childhood had been so lonely. I imagine he would have found the time for them if I'd managed to become pregnant. *I* certainly would have found time for them. I wanted a big family too."

"That must have been very difficult for you."

Her eyes grew moist. "Difficult? That's an understatement."

He said nothing in reply. He didn't have to. His concern for her was written all over his face.

She drew in a deep breath and fought to banish the sudden rush of tears that threatened. "But my father and I did a few fun things."

"Oh? What kind of things?" He slid his arm around the back of her chair.

"When I turned twelve, he took me to an amusement park. I went on roller coasters, ate cotton candy, rode the merry-go-round, and in general made myself sick."

A perplexed look came into his eyes. "That was fun?"

"I loved it." She smiled. "It's hard to explain why. I suppose I enjoyed the thrill of danger, especially when I knew that I couldn't really get hurt."

"The thrill of danger, hmm?" A teasing smile turned

his mouth upward. "I guess I'll have to be careful around you."

"Don't worry, I won't get us into trouble." She glanced upward at the chandelier hanging from the ceiling. Small flames, rather than electric light bulbs, danced atop each branch. "Somehow, I don't think you'll be able to take me to an amusement park anyway."

He looked up too. "What do you mean?"

"This place is so backward," she explained. "In some ways, I feel as though I've stepped back into the nineteenth century instead of the future. There's no electricity, no gas-powered vehicles, no television, movies, cell phones, ATM machines, computers, or any sign of advanced technology at all. I haven't seen anything so far that I could classify as futuristic. So you'll hardly be able to bring me to an amusement park."

"Maybe we could find something close to an amusement park."

She shook her head. "It's not going to happen. How did the world get like this, anyway? Didn't anyone attempt to bring back some of the old technologies?"

"If you had stayed in your time, you would have soon been dealing with the effects of the plague," he murmured. "We believe it struck early in the twenty-first century. From what we understand, all of the brightest scientific minds from then on focused on curing it rather than inventing new machines. Government coffers were emptied on research to understand it. People simply didn't have the time or money to work on anything new. I don't think there was any technological advancement after your time.

"As far as electricity goes, as the population dwindled and the demand for it lessened, the government began shutting down generator stations. The nuclear power plants went first and then the coal plants, followed by hydroelectric power plants. Right now, all of our electricity is generated through wind power. We use it sparingly, in high-priority places like hospitals and enforcement stations."

"What about cars? Television? Phones? Email? How do you live without them?"

"You have to remember that our population dwindled to nearly nothing. In order to survive, we had to adopt new values that promoted community and family solidarity. Cars encourage families to spread apart. With a horse and wagon, though, you can only go so far. Families and communities end up staying together.

"As far as the other things go, artificial light can change the hue of paint and encourages garish or inaccurate portraiture, so we rely on gaslight, candlelight, or sunlight. Electronic methods of communication are impersonal and break down the closeness between people. Face-to-face communication is preferred because it keeps people together." He pushed back from the table and pointed to a small outbuilding in the yard beyond the dining room. "We do have terminals, though. They're very similar to the phones you're used to. We use them for emergencies only. Do you see that building over there? You can call the hospital, fire house, or law enforcement from the terminal inside."

"But what about the basics, like traffic lights?"

"Who need traffic lights? We've no cars, and not enough people on the roads to require them."

"You're really missing something without television and movies, though."

He raised an eyebrow. "Let a month go by and then tell me if you still miss them."

An assurance that she would, indeed, miss them even after six months hovered on the tip of her tongue. But then she remembered those last few episodes of *Friends* she'd watched, and how terrible they'd made her feel because she hadn't a single friend, while that group of buff, attractive twenty- and thirty-somethings never felt the slightest twinge of loneliness. Yes, the show had reminded her of all her shortcomings, of her dissatisfaction with her appearance, and the fact that she hadn't had a man in her bed for years. It had left her feeling like a damned freak. Now she knew a sneaking satisfaction that *Friends* was long dead and forgotten.

"You could be right about that," she admitted brightly. "So, what are we going to do this week in order to get me ready for this presentation everyone keeps talking about? What happens at the presentation, anyway?"

Conlean pushed his chair back, stood, and held out his hand to her. "I'll tell you on the way back to your room."

She too pushed away from her empty plate and stood. Hesitating only slightly, she slipped her hand into his. "I don't want to go back to my room. I've seen far too much of it already. Can't we do something else?" She dropped her voice to a whisper. "Maybe I ought to take a look at one of your studios, so I can see what I'll have to work with while I'm trying to get rid of the plague."

He narrowed his eyes. "Hawkwood and I have been mulling over the best time for you to begin your real work. At least until you're married, you're going to be under a magnifying glass and anything you do will be noticed. Still, a festival is planned for the City of Blackfell next week—"

"Is that the same festival Adviser Erickson was talking about?" she cut in.

"It's called Ostara," Conlean confirmed. "The celebration could provide us with just the distraction we need in order to get you inside the Imperial Studio, for a minute or two at least."

"What does Ostara mean?"

"Ostara is the goddess of spring and fertility, and the celebration coincides with the Spring Equinox. You called it Easter in your time, I think."

"Easter!" Everything seemed different, she mused . . . and yet everything was the same.

"On the Spring Equinox, day and night are the same length of time. After Ostara, the hours of light become longer than the hours of darkness. All beings awaken from winter and, well . . . begin to wonder about each other. Essentially it's a celebration of renewed life and fertility."

Excitement flared inside her. "And during the celebration, you're going to sneak me into a studio?"

Conlean nodded. "The Imperial Studio is the best-equipped in Blackfell. I'd like you to take a look around it, and tell me what sort of equipment and supplies you'll need for your own research. Hawkwood and I will try to acquire them for you."

"I'd like to know what I'm up against. We have to try."

They began walking toward the door. A few low voices became hushed as she passed. She suspected that more than a few were talking about her. "Sometimes, Conlean, I feel like I'm the last woman on earth," she muttered.

"You're living in a time where women *are* at a premium," he reminded her. Nevertheless, he shifted his body slightly so that he shielded her from the worst of the stares, and when they finally made it outside, he selected a path that appeared deserted, rather than the main thoroughfare.

"You said you didn't want to go back to your room. If you dislike it, please tell me. I'll have you moved to a new room," he said as they walked. "I want you to be happy, Jordan."

"You want me to be happy?" she asked softly as she crunched down the gravel path. Sunshine warmed her face and the scent of wet earth and growing things hung in the air, reminding her that she'd come to Blackfell in the springtime, when the cold barrenness of winter gives way to the birth of new things. "You'll do anything to ensure my happiness?"

A gleam entered his eyes. "Within reason, of course."

She took a deep breath and threw caution to the winds. "Is another kiss within reason?"

Without warning, he stepped off the path and pulled her with him. "You know I can't," he murmured, his gaze meeting hers.

She felt the heat of him, the pull of his body so close to her. Only a few inches more and they'd be touching. For a second she considered standing on her tiptoes and making the first move, but then decided to wait, to give him a chance to set the pace. Her heart pounding in her chest and her lips aching for his touch, she returned his gaze and silently urged him to give her the kiss she wanted so badly.

Chapter Fourteen

Though he tried very hard not to, Conlean couldn't stop his gaze from drifting downward to Jordan's lips. They looked moist and soft; their slight parting a deliberate invitation that excited him. He could see how much she wanted his kiss, and with something close to dismay, he realized that he didn't know if he could keep himself from kissing her.

Somehow he forced himself to look lower—anywhere but at her lips. His attention settled on her chin, which had just enough of a saucy thrust to predict that she was beyond prediction, and then slipped to her throat, which looked very slender compared to the thick-necked artisans with whom he spent his days. He could see her pulse pounding, another sign that she was just as affected as he.

Groaning silently—every place he looked seemed dangerous—he tore his gaze away and focused on her eyes. Their soft, dreamy quality did nothing to cool the fire in his veins. But why was there such a fire? He'd been around women for most of his adult life, painting them, bringing them to Blackfell, seeing them settled in their new lives. While some of them had hinted that they might be more than a little interested in his attention, he'd never been tempted before to risk the consequences of a stolen kiss.

And yet, with Jordan everything felt different. All bets were off. There was something about her that he just couldn't get enough of. Without quite knowing how it had happened, he discovered he was leaning a little closer to her, his mouth hovering a dangerous distance above hers. The fact that she would soon wed his father grew increasingly less important as other needs took over. Last night, he'd had a taste of her, and it hadn't been enough. Not nearly enough . . .

"Jordan," he whispered, his voice huskier than he'd intended.

Something flared in her eyes. Her only reply was to place her hands on his shoulders, the heat of her palms searing him through his tunic. Those fine-boned hands, softer than any he'd ever felt before, suddenly seemed to pull him down, as if they weighed far more than they should, and soon his lips were hovering a mere inch above hers. Her breath, warm and soft, brushed across his mouth.

God help him, he was going to kiss her, in public view. And risk everything . . . his relationship with his father, his future as an Artisan, his and Hawkwood's plan . . . everything.

The thought sliced through him like a sword, mixing

with his illicit desire until the guilt was too much to bear. With a muttered curse, he shrugged off her hands and looked away from the heat in her eyes. His groin felt like a hard, tight knot. Unappeased hunger flared inside him like anger. He swallowed and breathed deeply, striving for calm.

A surprised look tightened her features, and then melted away as color flamed in her cheeks. She cleared her throat. "I think I've made you uncomfortable," she murmured. "I'm sorry."

Desire still raged in him, but now he felt guilty too, over the distress he'd caused her. He debated trying to explain himself and decided against it. He wasn't going to be able to explain anything with his blood pounding like this. Rather, they needed a distraction. He wracked his mind for something to say that might deflect her attention, but his brain wasn't working very well.

"Would you like to have dinner in the Gallery this evening?" he finally blurted, stumbling over the words like a first-class idiot.

She looked at him with uncertainty, the color deepening in her cheeks, but gave no reply. Then she looked away. When he realized that she wasn't going to follow his lead and engage in a safe conversation, he became even tenser inside.

"Conlean, I'm confused," she said a moment later, confirming his fears that their discussion on this topic hadn't finished. "I thought you liked kissing me last night. And even though you told me that you weren't ready, I thought you wanted to kiss me just now. Did I make a mistake? If so, I apologize."

His gut twisted at her apology. She just didn't seem to understand that he couldn't be intimate with her because he intended to see her married to his father. And he didn't know how to make her understand. "Don't apologize. You haven't done anything wrong."

"Then why are you acting so strangely?"

"Because I can't kiss my father's future wife."

"I've already told you, I won't marry your father. I'm not his future wife."

He gazed at her, wondering what he could say to make her realize that she *had* to marry his father. In truth, he didn't think he'd be able to say the necessary words even if he knew them, and the reason for his reluctance gave him a stab of fear.

The reason, in fact, was simple. He couldn't say the right words because he'd fallen for his father's future bride, and the thought of becoming her son-in-law was as appealing to him as having a leg sawn off. Still, they all had very little choice in the matter. She *would* marry his father. And he wanted to treat her honorably in the short time they had left together, rather than steal kisses that could lead nowhere.

She was looking at him anxiously.

"Jordan," he muttered, "I brought you here. Your well-being is my responsibility, and kissing you again is out of the question."

"Is that all I am to you? A responsibility?" she asked in a quiet voice. "Do you force yourself to spend time with me out of a sense of duty?"

"Of course not," he replied quickly. "I enjoy being with you."

"Do you like me, then?"

"Of course I like you."

"I mean, do you *really* like me?"

"Yes, I really like you." When he saw that she would need more than a simple affirmation, he added, "You're different from any woman I've ever met. And you're very unpredictable. I never know what you're going to do next."

She was still looking at him with those vulnerable eyes and a mouth that demanded he kiss it. Swallowing, he grabbed her hand and started leading her down the path, back toward the dormitory. They needed movement . . . a change of scenery . . . and other people around them to stifle the intimacy growing between them.

Lagging a little, she sighed. He heard her frustration in it. "I know I'm not as pretty as the other women around here, but at least I have a quirky personality to make up for it."

He couldn't stop a smile from forming on his lips. How could she think she wasn't attractive? "You're very attractive."

"So are you. Too bad we're letting the rules stand between us."

"Rules are necessary. Without them, life would be chaos."

"I think you worry too much about rules. Rules aren't always right or proper. Sometimes they need to be broken. Would you kiss me now if I were *your* bride, and you hadn't painted and retrieved me?"

"I would wait until our wedding day," he insisted. "A bride is like an apple. If someone takes a bite out of an apple before it's sold, then no one wants it."

She stopped in her tracks. "Are you kidding? That sort of attitude went out of fashion back in the Stone Age, along with knights in armor and jousting."

He shrugged and gently urged her along again. "It's the best way for a groom to make sure that any children born soon after the marriage are his."

Eyebrows arched thoughtfully, she fell into step with him. "What if the groom gets a sour, worm-infested apple? Maybe a taste-test before marriage is the best option for everyone."

He managed a laugh. "Maybe it is. Still, couples in Blackfell take their chances. That's why we have the Counselor."

"Who's the Counselor? That marriage guy you were talking about?"

"Yes. He's the Adviser of Marriages. He has a reputation for helping husbands and wives fall in love."

"I think *we* need the Counselor's help," she muttered.

He didn't answer, but silently he vowed that if he were lucky enough to have Jordan as a bride, the Counselor's doorstep was the last place anyone would find him.

Rather than pursue the subject further, she gave his hand a squeeze. They walked onto a cobblestone path, Conlean wondering with a bit of embarrassment if she'd noticed how sweaty his palm had become. Ahead, the dormitory's gray stone sparkled in the sunlight, as though it had been dusted with crushed quartz. Trees and bushes surrounded its foundation and created inviting patches of shade.

"What are we going to do for the rest of the week?" she asked as they approached the front door.

"We'll tour the dormitory some more, and I'll show you inside the other buildings," he promised. "We have a couple of fairly interesting gardens I'd like to take you through too. Maybe we'll even have time to visit some of the families who live on the Gallery grounds, and help with the fieldwork."

"I'd like that." She gave him a smile full of happiness, one that rocked him to the core. "I want to get to know your world better, Conlean."

"And then, at the beginning of next week, I'll take you into the city to see the festival."

"That sounds good."

He escorted her through the center hall, past the other Artisans, who were inevitably having their arguments and discussions, and up the stairs to her room, where he deposited her outside of her door.

"Do you want to come in for a while?" she asked, another kind of invitation in her eyes.

He sighed. "I don't think that's a good idea."

"When will I see you again?"

"Tomorrow morning, at the same time."

"Tomorrow seems so far away."

He wanted to agree wholeheartedly. Instead, he simply gave her a short bow and left for his studio, where he could try to lose himself in his artistry.

The following morning, Conlean showed up exactly when he'd promised. She'd barely finished her breakfast and gotten dressed before he presented himself in her room, looking darkly handsome and very masculine despite the basket he gripped with one hand.

He greeted her warmly. Remembering how he'd rejected her the previous day, she couldn't find anything other than a meek good morning to say in return. Still, after he chatted with her a bit she could see that he wasn't acting any differently toward her and she finally relaxed.

"So, what are we doing today?" she asked.

"We're going to the gardens."

She glanced out the window. Sunlight brightened the lawns and trees, and the sky was a light azure blue. "It's a beautiful day. I can't wait to see them."

He sheepishly indicated the basket he was gripping with one hand. A flowered cloth covered the top, hiding whatever the basket contained. "The cook gave this to me to take with us. In case we get hungry."

"So we're having a picnic too. Sounds heavenly."

He held out one arm. "Ready?"

Smiling, she hooked her arm around his, and together they made their way into the warm spring sunshine. For the rest of the day, they spent their time exploring the various gardens around the Gallery, including one that contained her favorite herbs—lavender and basil—and another that overflowed with flowers that looked remarkably like the peonies that used to grow in her mother's garden. They stopped for lunch, and Conlean reminisced about his childhood spent at the Imperial Palace.

At first, he spoke in positive terms about his father. Still, she could see how much the Patriarch's duties had kept him away from his son, and could only imagine how lonely Conlean had been. Part of the Gallery's attraction for Conlean, she guessed, had been the idea of having a family for the first time in his life. Her opinion of the Patriarch was not improved.

They finished lunch and their tours, and Conlean delivered her to her room when the sun began to set. The next morning he again appeared at her door just moments after she finished eating breakfast and getting dressed. As he escorted her through the Gallery with basket in hand, he told her they were going to visit an old tunnel near the back of the property. Baffled by the idea, she asked him why he thought she'd want to see a tunnel, but he refused to answer, a curious smile on his lips. A half hour later, though, when they approached the site and she discovered an old railroad cart sitting on tracks, with a couple of mules hooked up to it like reindeer to Santa's sleigh, she began to see the light.

An elderly man in a rough tunic and pants stood near the mules, feeding them handfuls of hay. He saw them coming and doffed his wide-brimmed hat.

"Good morning, Artisan. I've gotten everything ready, just as you asked."

Conlean reddened slightly. "Thanks for helping me, Joe."

Joe smiled, displaying white teeth so perfect they had to be dentures.

Conlean turned his attention to her. "There aren't any lift hills or steep drops, but it's a pleasant ride through the countryside, and I thought you'd enjoy it."

Lift hills? Steep drops? She looked at him open-mouthed, then focused on the little platform before her, which looked like a primitive train station.

227

"I read some books on roller coasters," he admitted.

Roller coasters? Abruptly she remembered talking to him about roller coasters a few days earlier, and mentioning how much she'd enjoyed them. Clearly he'd taken her discussion to heart and had set out to recreate the experience for her. Impulsively she grasped his hand and pressed a quick kiss on his cheek. "Thank you."

The elderly man turned away.

Conlean cleared his throat, his face reddening. "Let me help you climb in."

Conlean held her arm as she hopped into the little car and then joined her. Joe perched before them and urged the mules into a walk. Slowly, the car began to move, and then picked up speed as the mules found a comfortable pace. For the next few hours, they toured the countryside on railroad tracks, and they even went through a tunnel that looked as though debris had recently been cleared from it. When she mentioned this to Conlean, Joe admitted from his spot in front of them that he'd cleared the tunnel just the previous day so they could pass through without incident.

As the journey continued, she felt more and more impressed by the effort the two men had put forth just to see that she enjoyed herself. "Thank you, both of you, for giving me my best day in Blackfell yet," she told them as they pulled back into the "station," their ride finished.

Joe doffed his cap again, and Conlean gave her a wide grin. "It was our pleasure."

The elderly man looked as though he wanted to say something, but he leaned in toward Conlean and spoke in a lowered voice. Conlean nodded in agreement with whatever Joe had said, and then Joe was facing her with a serious, yet hopeful, expression. "It's my wish that you'll join me and my family tomorrow night for dinner."

She glanced at Conlean, who nodded almost imperceptibly, telling her that he was okay with the idea. "Thanks, Joe. That sounds nice. Does the invitation include Artisan Conlean?"

Joe nodded. "Yes, it does."

"In that case, we both accept," she said.

Conlean was smiling. "Is seven o'clock all right?"

Joe nodded. "My wife and I will see you then."

With a few final thanks, she and Conlean left Joe with his mules and began to walk across the Gallery grounds toward the dormitory. Impulsively she grasped his hand. "Conlean, I can't thank you enough for going to such trouble to make me feel comfortable. I don't feel as though I deserve it," she admitted.

Conlean slanted her a look that she couldn't quite decipher. "This is the kind of treatment you'd receive every day as Matriarch. You'd be the most important woman in all of Blackfell. The life you'll have if you marry my father will be enjoyable, to say the least."

Some of her joy faded. "Is that why you planned today's outing? You wanted to show me the benefits of being Matriarch?"

"No," he replied slowly. "I wanted you to be happy."

"I don't want people doing nice things for me because they're impressed with my title. I want people to do nice things for me because they love me and care for me."

He had no reply for her. Silently, they returned to the

229

Gallery, and Conlean paused at the front entrance. "I'm going to leave you here, to make your way to your room alone. I have a couple of things to get done. Do you mind?"

"No, that's fine," she said, slightly miffed with him. "Will we be doing something tomorrow during the day?"

"Not during the day. Several dressmakers will be here to fit you for the proper clothes. I won't be around to collect you until about six o'clock, so we can go eat at Joe's."

"I don't want any more clothes," she said, thinking of the ugly pants and tunics in her wardrobe.

"Maybe you'll change your mind about being Matriarch," he insisted with a grimace, as if the admission pained him. "If so, you'll need to look the part. Besides, your presentation is just a week away, and the dressmaker will need time to complete your presentation gown."

"So you're still hoping I'll change my mind and marry your father?"

"Is there reason to hope?" he asked carefully, his face tight.

"No," she answered flatly.

The tension left him, making him appear younger. "You *are* stubborn."

"Yes, I am. Why do I have to go through this presentation ritual?"

"Because we don't have an acceptable alternative. At least not yet."

Acceptable alternative? She liked the sound of *that.* "I'll see you tomorrow night, then?"

"Tomorrow night." He grabbed her hand and kissed it. His lips felt very warm and insistent against her flesh, and when he dropped her hand, he looked at her with barely concealed passion. She watched him go, and as soon as he disappeared from sight, she calculated how many hours would have to tick by until she saw him the next evening.

"Excuse me," interjected a footman she hadn't noticed. "I'm to see you to your room."

She accepted his assistance and, a short while later, found herself in her room, in bed, buried in bedcovers and with one silent admission in her head: Though she'd been kidnapped and brought into a wacky situation beyond her wildest dreams, she'd never had a better time in all her life.

Chapter Fifteen

The next morning began as all the others, with her in bed, breakfast tray over her legs and a steaming bowl of porridge sending its fragrance into the air. She was looking at the tray and thinking that she could get used to someone serving her in bed each morning, when suddenly the door burst open and a small man dressed in a garish tunic entered the room and looked around like Napoleon surveying conquered territory. His gaze zeroed in on her and he strode toward her, his attention slipping toward her breakfast tray.

"Are you done?" he asked in a peremptory tone.

The suddenness of his entrance had made her heart jump. Somewhat irritated, she shook her head.

"Then you must finish at once. We've work to do."

She lifted an eyebrow. "And who the hell are you?"

He too lifted an eyebrow. "I don't think I'm in Hell, my dear lady, and I'm hoping this day doesn't end up making me feel like I'm in Hell. Are you going to be one of the fussy ones?"

"Fussy?" Despite his arrogant attitude, she started to smile. His words were annoying, but his delivery of them made her want to laugh. "I'm very fussy, and a real bitch when I want to be."

"Then we'll get along perfectly," he declared, clapping his hands twice, like an old dame giving a summons. "I can't stand brides who don't care about their appearance. Their grooms care, believe me."

Two more men—youths, in fact—entered the room on cue, their arms laden with bolts of material and all sorts of trimmings.

All of a sudden she understood who the Napoleon wannabe was. "Oh, you're the dressmaker."

"Yes, I'm the dressmaker. Mr. Vogler." He strode over to her bed and removed her tray. "You can eat that later. Right now I must have measurements."

Eyes wide, she assessed him. "You're going to measure me?" Then she glanced at the open door.

He followed her gaze and clapped his hands again. "Claus, you idiot, close the door. Do you want everyone to see our dear lady being measured for her presentation gown?"

Red-faced, one of the youths hustled over to the door, shut it, and locked it.

Vogler stared at her impatiently. "Well, come out of that bed and let me see you."

"I'm wearing only a nightgown," she told him indignantly. "And I'm not in the habit of allowing strange men to see me dressed this way."

"But I'm the *dressmaker,* dear lady. I see women in all states of undress. I even see them naked."

"Aren't there any women dressmakers?"

He threw his hands upward. "Women, dressmakers? They don't make dresses. They make fine, strapping sons."

"Where are all the women, anyway? I've seen nothing but men since I got here."

"You're in the Gallery. There are no women in the Gallery, only brides who have yet to be presented."

"So I'm stuck with you."

"Didn't Artisan Conlean tell you I'd be coming? Why all this commotion? I'm the finest dressmaker in all of Blackfell. I'm starting to feel insulted."

"I'm so sorry, Mr. Vogler. I didn't fully understand what the Artisan meant when he said that I'd be seeing the dressmaker," she murmured. "He just muttered a lot of things about my becoming Matriarch and needing to look the part."

"Ah." Vogler nodded in comprehension. "You're a little shy, I see. Perhaps you haven't fully woken up yet." He gave his other assistant a conspiratorial look. "Jude, go to the kitchen and bring us back a pot of chocolate. Be sure to make it the way I usually do."

She lifted an eyebrow but didn't complain as the assistant scurried off to do his master's bidding. After the youth had closed the door behind him, Vogler returned to Jordan's side, pulled the covers up over her lap, and returned her tray to her bed. "You will need careful handling, I see," he muttered, and then added something under his breath that she couldn't hear but suspected was far from complimentary. "Finish your breakfast, and I'll tell you about myself while you do."

Cautiously she picked up her spoon, but when Vogler nodded approvingly she began to eat her porridge. He chatted while she ate, talking about his life in the poorer section of town, and his decision to become a dressmaker, one that had elevated his status in life and brought him many rewards.

She asked a few questions, just to be polite, and inquired as to whether or not he had a wife and family, at which point he pulled away and studied her closely. "I think you are missing something very important here, dear lady."

Her porridge finished, she picked up the tray and put it on the floor. "What am I missing?"

"Well, your questions about a wife and children suggest that you don't know I've been altered."

"Altered?" She had no idea what he was getting at.

"All of the men who attend to the brides in the Gallery are altered except the Artisans. We agree to the procedure, of course; it's a small price to pay when one considers the rewards that an altered assistant can reap in the service of women."

She tilted her head. Altered? She still didn't know what he meant. The term brought to mind visits to the veterinarian, where male cats and dogs were neutered to prevent more unwanted kittens and puppies from being born . . .

"Ohmigod," she breathed suddenly. "You mean you're . . . *altered*."

He appeared confused. "Didn't I say that?"

"You did." She shook her head, shocked that he would agree to such a thing. There was so much she didn't understand about this society! Clearly, she had nothing to worry about regarding Vogler. She could undress in front of him and swing naked around a pole and he wouldn't want to do anything about it. In an effort not to insult him, she hid her shock and nodded sagely. "I'm sorry, my brain simply isn't working yet. Too fuzzy from sleep, you know. Are your two assistants, uh, altered too?"

"Of course they are." He shook his head. "I'll have to speak to Artisan Conlean. He hasn't done a very good job of introducing you to Blackfell. He should have allowed the page to do his job, rather than insisting on taking care of you himself. Well, I'll do what I can to correct the situation while we work today on getting you ready for your presentation."

"I'd like that," she admitted with a smile.

He smiled too. "Very good."

Just at that moment, a knock sounded at the door. Vogler's assistant was allowed into the room, and he placed the huge pot he was carrying on a side table. From a little basket hanging on his arm he produced four cups and soon had poured steaming chocolate from the pot into cups for all. His gaze averted, he offered a cup to Jordan first, and then passed one around to his boss and his co-worker.

Jordan took a sip. It was hot chocolate all right, with less sugar than she expected and a sharp undertone that suggested someone had spiked it. "Very good," she said, echoing Vogler's earlier statement.

He drank a sip and sighed. "Just what we needed, don't you think?"

"At this time of day? I'm not sure."

"Give it a try," he urged.

"Why not?" Laughing, she lifted the cup to her lips and drank again, the liquid pooling in her stomach like fire. Oh, yes, it was spiked.

"Now, will you stand up for me and let me measure you?"

"Since I'll have to do it sometime, I might as well do it now." She pushed the covers back and stood.

Vogler walked a tight circle around her. "You're very slender, and taller than most of the women I've fitted," he muttered in a businesslike way. "We'll need gowns with straight, classic lines that will emphasize your slenderness. No poofs and bangles for you. You don't need them."

Not sure if she'd been complimented, she lifted her arms as he directed. "I've been wearing tunics and pants since I got here, and I have to tell you, I think they're the ugliest clothes I've ever put on. Those gowns that you're making me—are they along the same lines as the clothes in my wardrobe?"

"Please," he chided her. "I wouldn't allow a married woman to dress in a way that her new husband would consider *ugly*. Unmarried women are a different story, though. They need to hide their curves with the tunics and pants you mentioned until their wedding day."

"That sounds positively chauvinistic," she remarked as she allowed him to run a tape measure over various parts of her body.

While he did this, his assistant kept his gaze averted and her cup of hot chocolate filled. After a while, she relaxed and discovered that she was enjoying all this fussing. She didn't even complain when he asked her to take off her nightgown and pull on some under-things that would leave most of her body bare. She only asked that the three men turn around while she changed; and though Vogler raised his gaze heaven-ward, he did as she requested. Soon she stood in front of him in a lacy camisole and panties, listening to their oohs and aahs and compliments regarding her beautiful body, none of which she believed. But she didn't ask them to stop, either.

Later, when they'd finished poking and prodding her with the measuring tape, she threw on a silk robe and sat down on the bed to go through fabrics. Every color and texture seemed to be represented and, with Vogler's help, she chose the fabrics that appealed to her most. Then they went through several sets of shoes, and underthings, and jewelry, and hats . . . until she was nearly exhausted from all of it and Vogler called for lunch.

"After lunch we'll have your hair styled and nails buffed, and then have you outfitted for your evening with the Artisan. He mentioned you would be visiting one of the Gallery's tenants for dinner." A disgusted look crossed Vogler's face. "We'll have to go very sim-ple this evening. More tunics and pants. I'm sorry, dear lady."

"I like simple, but not the simple that's in my wardrobe."

"Ah, but you must dress as befitting your status," he

Portrait of a Bride

warned, then broke off as his assistant returned with a tray filled to overflowing with food. The assistant placed the tray before her, and Vogler declared, "Eat, dear lady, and I'll tell you more about Blackfell."

While she munched on fruits and cheeses, Vogler talked nonstop about Blackfell: its recent history, political structure, and leading families; the basic rules of society, geography, and the other kingdoms he knew about besides Blackfell; and the duties she'd have as Matriarch of Blackfell. He finished as she selected one final piece of fruit and ate it, and she silently congratulated herself on refusing to marry the Patriarch, because anyone who married that man would have difficulty finding the time to sleep, let alone have one moment to herself.

Then Vogler's assistant Jude was washing her hair, and cutting it, and rubbing it dry with a towel before styling it with a curling iron and catching it behind her ears. Vogler's other assistant worked on her nails and skin, placing just the right amount of makeup on her face and the perfect touch of color on her nails to give her a polished yet natural look. When finally they'd completed their jobs to their own satisfaction and Vogler had dressed her in a tunic and pants made of a suedelike brown fabric with gold embroidery, Jordan felt as though she were in competition for Miss America's crown. She told them as much, but they just shushed her and dragged her in front of a full-length mirror.

"Look at yourself first, and then complain to us," Vogler demanded.

The tunic appeared closer-fitting than the others

239

she'd worn, revealing some of her curves, while its color brought out rich highlights in her brown hair. Her skin looked pale and dewy, with just a touch of roses in her cheeks, and her eyes sparkled with a zest for life that she'd never noticed in her reflection before. Amber-colored diamonds hung from antique settings around her neck and matching diamonds sparkled at her ears, giving her the appearance of someone born to luxury.

She smiled, transforming her likeness in the mirror. "You people are miracle workers. I can't believe how wonderful you've made me look."

"We just polished the jewel," Vogler declared in a soft voice. "Its beauty was always there."

"I'm no jewel—" she began, but then a deep male voice cut her off.

"Yes, it was," Conlean agreed.

She spun around to face him in the doorway.

"Artisan Conlean," Vogler murmured in reverent tones. "Look at our future Matriarch. Isn't she beautiful?"

"Very." Conlean walked into the room, his gaze never leaving her. He'd exchanged his casual shirt and pants for a formal-looking black jacket and creased trousers. He looked very polished, his phosphorescent tattoo giving him an exotic, even slightly dangerous aspect. "I see you've had a productive day."

She smiled at Vogler. "Mr. Vogler has been wonderful."

Vogler, for his part, had his attention fixed on the Artisan.

Conlean walked over to her, took her hand, and kissed her palm. "Are you ready to go to Mr. Wargate's?"

"I feel like I should be going to a museum opening or something. Aren't we dressed too fine for a simple dinner?"

"You will be the Matriarch," Vogler reminded her, a thoughtful look on his face as he dragged his attention from Conlean. "At the moment, you are dressed very simply for a bride in your position."

Reluctantly Conlean released her hand and turned to Vogler. "Does she have something she can wear in case it gets cold?"

"Of course, Artisan." He waved a hand at one of his assistants, who produced a brown velvet wrap and handed it to Conlean. "Your father will be very pleased with his new bride, no?"

A spasm of pain crossed Conlean's features. "He'll be very pleased."

"Ah." Vogler nodded knowingly. "You'll take good care of her until then."

"I'm taking her to dinner for now." Giving Vogler his thanks for a fine job, Conlean escorted Jordan toward the door. Just as they were leaving, she turned to give the dressmaker a wave of thanks.

Vogler was in the middle of winking at one of his assistants, and she didn't have to have any experience in lip reading to understand the one word he whispered.

Love.

Conlean wrapped his arm around hers, distracting her. "Did you enjoy your day with Vogler?"

"I didn't think I would at first, but eventually I got

into the spirit of it. Yes, I had fun. And I feel like a million bucks."

"You look very beautiful," he said in a low voice. "Joe and his family will be dazzled, just as I am."

"Not too dazzled, I hope."

He smiled and led her through the Gallery and out into the cool night breeze. A cart awaited them, and Conlean handed her in before seating himself next to her and directing the footman to take them to Mr. Wargate's house. The night sky sparkled with a spray of stars above them as they set off across the Gallery's grounds, the path taking them into a forest before they emerged on the road again, with fields on either side. A layer of mist hung close to the ground and gave the landscape a magical aspect. She wouldn't have been surprised to see some garden gnomes cavorting around in it.

Conlean talked of everyday Gallery matters as they drove along, and she managed to make him laugh once or twice with her descriptions of Mr. Vogler and the day they'd had together. In the few comfortable moments of silence that stretched out between them, she couldn't help wondering what Vogler had meant by mouthing the word *love*. That's all she needed—Vogler telling everyone she was in love with Conlean.

Was she, in fact, in love with Conlean? She didn't know. She'd never experienced love. She'd heard, though, that it wasn't a mild emotion. It hit right between the eyes. And so far, with Conlean, she'd walked around perpetually dazed, like a prize fighter. So maybe it *was* love.

She had to admit that she'd never before experienced

anything like the feelings she had for Conlean. She was up, she was down, she was laughing, she was crying, she was dreaming about getting down his pants . . . what a roller coaster of emotion! God knew she'd never felt this way about Dennis. In fact, she'd always believed him when he'd called her an ice maiden. He'd insisted that she was one of those women who didn't like sex, subverted all emotion and preferred work to romance. At the time, his assessment had seemed accurate. It'd become the truth after she'd discovered her own infertility and the fighting between them had begun. But the feelings running through her now—the longing for Conlean, the almost painful desire to have his arms around her and feel his mouth against hers—suggested that her flame for Dennis had burned low more because of their incompatibility rather than because of any flaw on her part.

A short while later, they pulled up outside a small house set only a few feet back from the road. Flagstones led up to the front door and lanterns stood near the road, lighting the way. As soon as they began to step down from the cart, Joe came out of the house and greeted them formally. His wife joined him moments later and, after brief introductions were made, the couple directed Jordan and Conlean into the house.

Inside, a fire was blazing in the hearth and the smell of roasted turkey filled the room. Three healthy boys were wrestling on the braided rug set in front of the fire, but Clara, their mother, quickly drew them to attention. When they saw Conlean and Jordan, their eyes widened. They bowed.

"I'm glad you both could come," Clara said. "I hope you like turkey."

Jordan hurried to make the woman feel more at ease. "It's kind of you to have us. And yes, turkey is one of my favorites."

Clara smiled, her thin face lighting up. Jordan judged her to be somewhere in her thirties, her hair betraying signs of gray but her skin still smooth and supple-looking. "Sit down, then, and I'll pour you a glass of amber. Joe, will you please take the turkey out of the oven?"

Joe nodded and grabbed a pair of mitts from the countertop.

Since the kitchen and living room formed one big room, Joe remained within earshot as they sat down and made themselves comfortable by the fire. After taking care of the turkey, he joined in the chitchat about the weather and the happenings at the Gallery as Clara served them glasses of amber. Shortly afterward, Clara and her husband began putting out dinner, rejecting Jordan's offer of help as they placed steaming dishes on the table.

The boys kept goggle-eyed stares on Jordan and Conlean the entire time.

Soon, dinner had been served and Jordan and Conlean joined the Wargate family at the table. Jordan recognized several of the dishes served as typical of a Thanksgiving dinner, right down to the homemade cranberry sauce that tasted better than anything she could remember. The knowledge that Clara had made a Thanksgiving dinner intrigued her. The woman must have come from the past as a bride, and Jordan wondered exactly what era she hailed from.

"Clara, I'm very curious," Jordan admitted between mouthfuls of chestnut stuffing. "I know you must have come here as a contracted bride, but I'm wondering what time period you used to live in."

Clara glanced at her husband and then back at Jordan. "I lived in the latter half of the eighteenth century, in what would later become the United States."

"Really! So you lived before the Revolutionary War."

The other woman nodded. "I came from a poor family in Boston."

"What brought you to Blackfell?" Jordan asked.

"We took part in what's now known as the Boston Tea Party," Clara revealed. "When the British discovered our involvement in the revolt, they came to put my family in jail and try us for treason. Just about that time, I met a woman who asked me if I'd like to come to another place, where I wouldn't be held liable for any of the crimes my family had committed. With my parents' permission, I came to Blackfell, and they received a dowry that helped them mollify the British. I guess you could say my coming to Blackfell saved us all."

"That's wonderful." Jordan glanced at Conlean, noticing his half-smile, before turning back to Clara. "And so you came to Blackfell and married Mr. Wargate."

Joe chose that moment to speak up. "I know what you're thinking. You're wondering how a poor man like myself could have afforded to have a bride painted, especially since my brothers have no families. Well, I just got lucky . . ." he trailed off, as if unsure how to continue.

"What Mr. Wargate—Joe—means is that he saved my father from drowning in the river that flows near the Imperial Palace, and he received a bride contract as a reward."

Joe nodded vigorously. "The day I saved your father, I was blessed a thousand times over. Not only did I save our Patriarch, but I won this beautiful, wonderful woman's hand as well." His gaze touched on his sons, and his voice swelled with pride. "We've had three sons, all healthy, and all determined to make their way in the world."

"Only their way is not so certain," Clara added, her voice bitter.

"What do you mean?" Jordan asked.

"We've not the resources to purchase bride contracts for our sons, so they'll never know the kind of joy Joe and I share," she said in low tones. "My youngest, Aaron, wants to be altered, so his way in the world will be assured. My older sons haven't made any decisions yet on what they wish to do, but both are determined to try to gain the Patriarch's favor so they might win brides."

"Oh." Jordan heard the pain in the woman's voice, and tried to imagine the kind of life her sons would have—a life striving for what should have rightfully been theirs, with little chance of actually succeeding. And the thought of the youngest son, whose red cheeks and rambunctious wrestling spoke of a spirited nature, willfully castrating himself so that he might have enough food to eat and a place to live, made her want to throw up that lovely Thanksgiving dinner. "What about your brothers, Joe? How are they doing?"

Joe looked down at his hands for a moment before returning his attention to her, his gaze raw. "I had three brothers. Only two survive. One has altered himself and works in the household of an Adviser to the Patriarch. The other has disappeared."

"I'm sorry," she blurted, unable to think of anything else to say.

"My oldest brother committed suicide some ten years ago," Joe added.

"Oh, dear." She turned to Conlean, hoping that he might give her some indication as to how to deal with the situation, but he only looked back at her, his gaze steady. At that moment she understood why he was willing to sacrifice everything in order to cure the plague. And she also understood why he'd brought her to this home: so she might understand how important her role in Blackfell was. These two people, Clara and Joe, had communicated Blackfell's need more eloquently than Conlean, Hawkwood, or anyone in the Gallery could have managed.

Maybe she *should* marry the Patriarch.

She glanced at Conlean again, and this time he looked away from her.

Impulsively she turned to Clara and grasped the woman's hand. "I'll do what I can to help you."

A ray of hope entered Clara's eyes. "I couldn't possibly ask you for anything—"

"I won't forget you and your sons, Clara," she said,

though she knew that a thousand Claras with a thousand sons needed the same kind of help.

Clara bowed her head. "Thank you. You are indeed a great lady."

"She is," Conlean echoed.

The rest of the meal passed in a more somber mood. Clara and Joe's boys, as soon as they finished dinner, disappeared outside to clean the horse barn, while Clara and Joe cleared the table and offered Jordan and Conlean a cup of tea.

Conlean politely declined, explaining that Jordan had a very full schedule awaiting her in the morning. Shortly afterward, heartfelt thanks and good-byes were exchanged, and Jordan and Conlean began the trip back to the Gallery.

About halfway home, Jordan sighed deeply and looked up at the stars, as if they might have some answer for her. "I know why you brought me to the Wargates. You wanted me to experience firsthand the suffering the people of Blackfell have to withstand because of the plague."

Conlean said nothing.

"I felt their suffering," she continued, "and now I understand why you're willing to sacrifice so much in order to cure the plague."

The Artisan remained silent.

She sucked in a deep breath. With the feeling that she was stepping over a precipice, she whispered, "I'm going to consider marrying your father. *Consider,* I said. I'll need to think about it some more, though, and I'd prefer to find another way."

Conlean grew very still, and then his shoulders slumped. "Thank you, Jordan," he said very softly.

She thought his voice had deepened. "That's what you want me to do, isn't it?"

"Yes."

"Then let's get on with this whole presentation business, so I can start to work on finding a cure for this damned plague," she announced angrily.

He didn't respond.

The rest of the trip home passed in silence.

The moon had nearly reached its peak when they pulled up in front of the Gallery and stepped down from the cart. Conlean, his expression grim in the pale moonlight, informed her that on the day of the festival of Ostara, he would take her into the city of Blackfell. Until then, however, she would be occupied with pages and servants who would prepare her for her presentation.

As he turned to go, she felt as if a great void had opened between them. Gone was the Conlean of the heated gaze, the one who smiled at her and complimented her and told her with his body, if not with his voice, how much he wanted to kiss her. An impassive servant stood in his place.

"Conlean," she said, "you do want me to marry your father, right?"

"You have to," he agreed, an edge to his voice, and turned to go.

"Can you come to see me tomorrow, so we can talk about it some more?"

"I don't think that's a good idea," he said softly in reply. "I don't want to distract you at this point. But I'll

249

see you at the end of the week. Remember what we have planned, and dress accordingly."

With that, the darkness swallowed him up, and she stood near the front door to the Gallery, all dressed up in her finery with no one but the footman for company.

Chapter Sixteen

Conlean stalked away from the Gallery. He should have been happy. Hadn't he accomplished his mission and finally convinced Jordan to cooperate with their plan? Hawkwood would be proud of him. And yet, now that Jordan's marriage to his father had become a reality, he felt as if someone had knocked the wind out of him. He couldn't imagine her in his father's arms, her beautiful smile wasted on a man who could only think of duty and routine. Still, what choice did either of them have? The plan was already set in motion, the proper papers drawn up.

He grimaced and walked into the woods. He knew of a cold stream that ran through the trees. Paying little attention to the ferns and twigs he was crushing underfoot, he hurried to the stream, stripped off his clothes, and dove into a section that had formed a pool. Ice-cold water drove all thought from his mind. He swam until he couldn't feel his legs anymore and then dragged himself on shore.

It took only a few minutes for the chill to recede, and images of Jordan to form in his mind. Images of her laughing, looking beautiful, looking vulnerable, needing him. He recalled how her eyes had flashed when he'd angered her, and how a little pout had formed on her lips when he'd refused to kiss her, even though she'd begged him . . .

Damn!

Cursing all the way, he returned to his studio in the Gallery and managed exactly zero sleep that night. The next day he had a meeting with Hawkwood, and he told the older man that Jordan was seriously thinking about marrying the Patriarch. Hawkwood's congratulations did little for him, however, and he left the older man as soon as possible so that he could spend some more time in his studio. He spent the next few days trying to come up with an acceptable alternative to Jordan marrying his father but failed utterly. His assistant Jerrod, clearly sensing his mood, had kept the stock of amber in the studio well-supplied, and Conlean basically drank himself into a stupor each day until the morning of the festival, when he was to see her again.

That morning, he woke up and took a bath, washing away the excesses of the last few days. He ate a hearty breakfast and took a long walk around the grounds, bringing a ruddy glow back into his face. He spent the rest of the day working on a portrait of Jordan, a study done in fiery oil colors that he thought best reflected her vibrant spirit. And when the time came to take her into the city, he dressed carefully in a tunic and pants that wouldn't attract attention but also made him look his best, and presented himself at her room a full five minutes early.

After her evening at the Wargates', Jordan had spent the next few days regretting her promise to consider marrying the Patriarch. Considering was damned close to agreeing, and anxiety filled her at the thought of living with a man she could never love, whose son invaded her every dream and made her ache with longing.

At some point during the stretch of days, while she'd been sitting there waiting for Conlean to come and tell her that her marriage to the Patriarch was off, that he loved her too much to give her up, a page arrived with a beautiful jeweled box. Inside the box, three gold rings sparkled like pure sunshine. She took out the rings, and the page told her that they were from the Patriarch, and that she was to wear them. Swallowing, she slipped them on her finger. They were a size too big.

As soon as the page left, she gave in to a few tears.

When the day of the festival arrived, she spent the morning resting and thinking that this would likely be the last time she spent alone with Conlean. All through breakfast, she mulled over the moments he'd stared at her with hot need, and how quickly her body had responded even to the thought of him. The sense that her one opportunity for happiness was slipping away from her grabbed hold of her and she began to wonder if just once, just this one night, she and Conlean might steal some happiness and make love, before she married a man she could never love and had, in fact, never even met.

Later in the day, she started looking through her wardrobe for something comfortable and understated to wear, clothes good for both physical activity and the modern equivalent of industrial espionage. She forced herself to stop obsessing about Conlean and began to feel some excitement about the idea of sneaking into a studio and finally getting a look at what sort of equipment they had. That was her real purpose here in Blackfell—to determine how the viral vectors and genetic alterations she'd researched had contributed to the plague.

A discreet knock sounded in the room. She walked toward the door, pausing long enough to confirm in a mirror that her cheeks were flushed and her eyes bright, as hope flared anew that Conlean had come to steal her away. Calling herself a fool, she quickly twisted the knob and pulled the door open.

Conlean's apprentice, rather than the man himself, stared at her.

She couldn't keep the disappointment off her face.

He coughed a little and averted his gaze, a paper sack held tightly in his hands. When he spoke, his voice trembled. "Artisan Conlean asked me to deliver this to you."

"Thank you, Jerrod," she said as gently as she could, aware that the guy thought he had made her unhappy somehow. "Did he have any message for me?"

Jerrod shifted from one foot to the other. "No, he didn't. Here's your package." He thrust the sack at her, tossed her a quick nod, and then forcibly shut the door between them.

She stared at the closed door. *Nerves,* she thought.

The guy's nerves were a wreck. Outside, she heard the guard mutter something that had a sarcastic edge to it. Clearly this was not Jerrod's day.

Shaking her head and thinking that it wasn't her day either, she opened the top of the sack. A dark brown tunic and matching pair of cotton pants lay folded inside, along with a pair of ankle-high boots and a slouchy hat that conjured up in her mind a few disco tunes from the seventies. Not quite as comfortable as old jeans and a sweatshirt, but they'd have to do. Quickly she shucked her silk tunic and slipped into the cotton farmer outfit and disco hat. Everything fit pretty well, even the boots, which reminded her of the kind Peter Pan supposedly wore. She took a minute to check herself out in the mirror and had to smile.

So much for provoking him into a kiss, or more!

The smile quickly faded from her lips as she sat down and began to read one of the books she'd requisitioned from the Gallery library. He finally came to her later in the day. His manner seemed subdued as he walked into her room, but she could see a spark of excitement in his eyes. She wondered how he could feel any kind of happiness, considering their circumstances. Was there something she didn't know?

"Are you ready?" he asked, his dark stare sliding up and down her form.

Her heart beat a little harder. "Ready for anything. Anything at all."

"Good." He studied her some more, his gaze anything but critical. "Let's go."

Feeling light-headed at the desire in his jade green eyes, she took his outstretched hand.

A short while later, they exited the building onto a cobblestone porch. Two large brown horses, tied to a post near the door, waited patiently nearby.

"Are we riding horseback?" she asked, suddenly appalled.

He nodded, then caught himself. "Why shouldn't we?"

"The last time I rode a horse, I got thrown and had the wind knocked out of me."

"Horseback riding is a necessary skill here." He lowered his voice. "We may need to make a quick escape at some point, and I can't guarantee that a cart will be at hand, or that we'll have time to hitch one up. So you have to ride."

"I'll take my chances with the cart," she told him, eyeing the horses up. They looked mild-mannered, but she knew they could turn into hoof-stomping, bucking demons with the slightest provocation.

"How far did that horse throw you? A couple of miles?"

"I can't do it," she announced, and started walking back inside.

He grabbed her arm before she'd gone more than a few feet and eyed her closely. "How can you be so eager to visit the Imperial Studio, which will be more than a little dangerous, and yet refuse to ride a horse?"

"At least tell me that horses have evolved to the point where they give you a comfortable ride."

"No such luck," he said. "Horses are pretty much the same as they've always been. In fact, they almost became extinct after the plague struck. People lost interest in them. Horses were a luxury, not a necessity, and instead humanity poured its money into crackpot cures for the plague."

"Cures? Like what?"

"Like bat dung and salt from the Dead Sea, both harvested on the night of a full moon and mixed into a fine powder." He smiled, giving her the idea that he was teasing her.

She played along. "I'm guessing that didn't work."

"It didn't taste very good, either." He walked over to one of the horses. "Come on. I'll help you up."

"No way."

"We'll take one horse, then. You'll ride with me."

At his offhand pronouncement, her body became several degrees warmer. "With you?" She couldn't keep her voice from rising an octave.

"Yes, with me." He shot her a sideways glance. "On the same horse. Is that all right?"

"Well, uh—" Images of her bouncing lightly against his tall, sturdy form filled her mind. She swallowed against a dry throat. Yes, she'd brave a hoof-stomping, bucking demon if it meant they would ride *together*.

"Would you prefer your own horse?"

"No, I'll ride with you." She moved a little closer to him, anticipation running riot through her body. She'd be close to him. She'd feel him pressed against her. The realization made her giddier than any bottle of champagne could have.

"You'll be fine. Don't worry." He smiled, warming her blood even more, and put his hands around her waist.

She certainly weighed more than a feather, but he tossed her up toward the saddle as if she didn't, and she landed on the hard leather with a thump. Trying to appear graceful, she attempted to pull her leg over the horse's back, but it wasn't the easiest thing she'd ever done. In fact, she suspected yoga practitioners might have had a hard time bending their legs the way she did as she struggled to get settled. After several embarrassing moments during which she knew she had his complete attention, she got her leg into proper position and offered him a brave smile even though she felt like a total klutz.

He watched her from beneath hooded lids. "Move back a little."

She complied, wondering if he could see the flush of embarrassment that was turning her cheeks lobster red. To her great surprise, he managed to mount the horse without crushing her, and also avoided banging his groin against the saddle horn. Actually, he landed so that his backside pressed ever so lightly against her spread thighs, and for this she gave him extra points.

Wow, was he smooth.

"Hang on," he told her as the horse danced nervously beneath them.

She didn't need a second reminder. Eagerly she grasped him around the waist, feeling the muscles in his back stiffen at her touch. Then he muttered something that the horse evidently understood, because they began to walk down a dirt path, away from the bustle at the center of the Gallery grounds. In just a few minutes they left the dirt path and entered the woods, their passage unobserved, as far as she could tell.

"I guess we're taking the less-traveled path," she said, leaning forward, her mouth near the back of his neck. He smelled great—like soap and leather. She only hoped he didn't realize what she was doing: breathing him in. Did sniffing someone without their permission constitute bad manners? She suspected so.

"We are. I don't want to be seen if I can avoid it," he confirmed, and then fell quiet.

For a while, she said nothing; their silence was companionable and she wanted to take a moment to look around herself. The woods had the same qualities of those she'd grown up with: shade that permitted an occasional ray of sunlight to shine through, crackly underbrush, vines wrapping around tree trunks, ferns, shy flowers, and in general a feeling of moistness and secrets. She did, however, notice very few signs of wildlife. The woods she'd explored as a child had been teeming with pesky deer, squirrels, mice—all sorts of creatures.

"These woods seem deserted," she remarked, the horse's slow, plodding pace forcing her to roll gently against his back.

"No one lives here," he replied, his hands steady on the reins.

"I mean, I don't see any sign of animals. In my time, I saw a lot more."

"What kinds of animals?"

"Deer, mice, and squirrels, I suppose. They didn't come right up to me and shake hands, but I always knew they were there."

"There aren't many wild animals around here anymore. They've been hunted nearly to extinction. That's what happened when there wasn't enough food to go around."

"Oh. That's terrible. What about animals like tigers? Or alligators?"

"Anything that ate dead human flesh contracted the plague," he revealed in a grim voice. "So there aren't any tigers, alligators, or any other carnivores around. What was the earth's population in your time? Six billion? Most of those six billion people died. Think about it, Jordan: all of those dead bodies. That's one helluva food source. The only problem was that the food was contaminated."

"Wow. I hadn't thought of it that way."

They both fell silent, Jordan both repelled and saddened at the idea of six billion dead bodies. At the same time, the wheels in her mind were turning. What kinds of viruses could infect animals through a food source?

"Tell me about your time," he said suddenly, breaking into her thoughts. "I want to know what it was like to live in the twenty-first century."

She realized then that she hadn't said much about her own life, and had only given him grim bits and pieces about her marriage with Dennis.

"Well," she began slowly, "life was very different then. We weren't worried about the survival of our species. There were too many of us. Instead, we worried about the woods and parks that were slowly being overrun by housing developments. We worried about the streets not being safe enough for kids to play in, and about people in foreign lands who were dying in droves of starvation. We were nervous about crazy terrorists and serial murderers and rapists who preyed upon small children . . ."

"Was there anything positive about living in the twenty-first century?" he asked, as they emerged from the woods and onto a road that led through a series of tilled fields, each one surrounded by a hedgerow.

She smiled. "Of course." Looking around with the setting sun in her eyes, she couldn't help thinking that the hedgerows acted as frames around rectangular wheat and hay canvases. The smell of freshly turned earth and growing things lay heavily in the air, and insects buzzed through the redolent currents as they went about their daily business. "In my time, people finally started to accept and value the differences between them. Ethnicity and the color of a person's skin meant less than his or her words and actions; and all living creatures, not just humankind, were for the most part treated with compassion and tolerance. There were also great technological advances. We came closer to understanding both the universe and the smallest particles in our bodies."

"Sounds like an exciting time."

"It was." Slightly homesick, she continued to describe her world to him, trying to paint a balanced picture. So caught up was she in the telling of the story that she had no idea how much time had passed when she realized that the traffic on the road had increased and the outline of a city lay far in the distance. A glance at the lowered sun on the horizon suggested that she'd been talking for an hour at least. Suddenly embarrassed, she squeezed his waist in a friendly way. "I must have been going on for a long time. Sorry to bend your ear like that. You haven't been able to get a word in edgewise."

"I love to hear you talk," he murmured, his voice husky. "Don't stop. Tell me about your family, and what you were like growing up."

A flood of warmth rushed through her at the sound of his voice, at the longing he conveyed with just a few words. She'd thought that he'd be more distant toward her, and perhaps less accommodating, now that he'd nearly gotten his way and gained her cooperation regarding marrying his father. But he seemed more attentive than ever. Apparently her surrender to the idea of marriage hadn't dampened the desire he felt for her, probably despite his best intentions.

Abruptly she realized how good it felt to be desired, and appreciated the influence she possessed simply by being a woman. The revelation was so primal, so powerful, and so very different from any she'd ever had before that she felt as though a whole new world had opened up to her.

Hoping to tease him, she snuggled a little closer until her breasts pressed into his back and her thighs rested against his. His slight shudder at her touch made her smile. "I hope we never reach the city."

"Why?"

"Because I'm so close to you now, I could taste your skin," she told him in a low voice. "I don't want this moment to end, ever."

He groaned. "Neither do I."

Her smile softening into a sigh, she rested her cheek against his broad back. "So, you want to know what I was like growing up?"

"Yes." His affirmation sounded shaky.

Pressing her breasts more firmly into his back, and

encouraged to continue the contact when he didn't stiffen or pull away, she began to tell him where her parents raised her, and what they were like, and how she'd managed to survive her teenage years. As she talked, she held him close; and when they left the fields behind for the outskirts of the city, she could feel the tension running through his entire body, and noticed the way he subconsciously leaned into her.

She felt good, so good, being with him like this. And she knew that he was enjoying her closeness, too. Maybe, she thought, just maybe, he would allow them a single night together, now that she'd all but agreed to marry his father. Because she'd finally come to realize that she *was* going to marry the Patriarch, if only to try to undo the damage done in her own time.

Before she married the Patriarch, she wanted one night of bliss with a man she was beginning to believe she loved. If she had to, she would demand that one night, so she'd have a memory she could hold close on all the barren nights to come. But she didn't think that a demand would be necessary.

Chapter Seventeen

Twilight had fallen by the time Jordan finished telling Conlean the story of her life. "At that point, when you came through the painting, I didn't know what I was going to do with my life," she recalled, her voice wistful. "All my experimentation and research appeared to have led nowhere. So you saved me, in a way, when you came for me." Telling him about her life had reminded her of the chances she'd had and ignored.

Conlean glanced back at her, his gaze dark with some unreadable emotion. "We both needed each other, I think."

"Yes, we did." She put her arms around his waist and laid her cheek against his back, his admission echoing the truth that hid in her own heart. As much as she'd initially resented being brought to Blackfell, at least now she had a job to do, an important one that could help make a real difference. And not many people back in her own time had really cared about her as Conlean did. She didn't feel so lonely anymore, and the future didn't seem so bleak.

"Jordan, there's something I should tell you," he said suddenly.

She sat up. She could tell by the intensity in his voice that he had something difficult to tell her, yet very important. "What is it?"

He hesitated, clearly considering his words.

Several nerve-wracking seconds passed.

"Conlean, what is it? What do you want to tell me?" she finally asked, sitting up straighter. Either he was going to tell her that he loved her or drop some bomb on her that was going to ruin her day.

A deep sigh dispelled the tension in his face. "We're moving into the Sonogawa River basin. This is where the city officially begins. Blackfell is oriented from south to north, with the southernmost part—the river basin—serving as both a harbor and an agricultural region."

"Never mind where we are. What were you going to tell me?"

He shifted slightly in the saddle. "The time isn't right. It's too soon. I should wait."

"Excuse me." She loosened her grip on him and moved back until their bodies were barely touching. "You can't leave me hanging like that. My imagination will come up with something much worse than whatever you'd planned to say, so you might as well just say it."

"It won't help either of us. It's selfish of me, in fact."

"Conlean, I insist you tell me. Now."

He sighed again, but this time it had an angry edge to

it. "I don't want you to marry my father. It's killing me to think of you with him."

"Why don't you want me to marry him?" she asked. "You know how important the marriage is to our plan."

He kicked the horse into a trot, forcing her to move closer again and hold on tightly. "Even though I painted your portrait and brought you to Blackfell as a bride, I've developed feelings for you, Jordan. Every artisan is warned about this moment, and told to guard himself against it, but in your case, I just couldn't stop myself from feeling the way I do. I don't want to give you up."

"Oh, Conlean." She pressed her cheek against his back. A warm feeling swelled inside her. She wondered if this was what love felt like. "I love being with you. I've never felt this way about anyone else, not even my ex. I think we were made for each other."

He groaned. "I know. I know."

"Are you sure I have to marry the Patriarch? There isn't another way?"

"I'm going to look for another way. I'm going to look hard."

She swallowed. There was at least one other way: She could marry *him*, not his father. But that would entail his sacrificing his artistry and possibly their plan to cure the plague. That was asking a lot of anyone. Was love worth such a sacrifice?

Relaxing against her, he slowed the horse back into a walk.

A few horseback riders, some carts, and even a bull had begun to compete for a space on the dirt road. She couldn't see much detail in the fading light, but judging by their clothes, she'd be willing to bet that all the riders and drivers were male. "Tell me about the city. Is there some sort of central marketplace? Where's the festival held?"

"There is a central marketplace, right on the dividing line between the north part of the city and the south," he said. "The southernmost part of the city has a harbor, so that's where you'll find the commercial district. We grow rice, wheat, and other crops on the outskirts of the city, and trade them for products from other provinces."

"How many other provinces are there?"

He shrugged. "I'm not certain. There are four provinces that are close enough to trade with us. Sometimes we hear stories about provinces farther away too."

"Has anyone gone exploring?" she asked, startled by the idea that the world was once again unmapped and in need of a new Christopher Columbus.

"We're too busy trying to survive," he told her, his tone dry.

She glanced at a terraced rice field on the left and at the many small tributaries that wound their ways on either side of the road. Birds flew among the reeds close to shore and a crowd of small fishing boats bobbed on the waves. A glow on the horizon caught her attention, and she realized that gas lamps lined the road ahead. "Everyone seems to be fishing."

"A school of perch or bluegill must have swum into the area," he suggested. "The road's pretty busy too, so keep your head down. I don't want to attract any undue attention."

She hunkered down in the saddle as he urged their horse into the left lane, the one next to the river basin. In a moment they had moved onto the lighted section of road. Faster horses and carts rushed by them on the right, their numbers increasing as they moved deeper into the city. Dust clouds rose from their wheels. Sneezing once or twice, she pulled her shirt up over her nose to block the dirt.

"The road becomes cobblestone just ahead," Conlean said.

"That's good news," she replied with another sneeze. A few gaily decorated carts that reminded her of gypsy wagons also shuddered past, the notes of high-spirited flutes lingering in their wake. "If the commercial district's in the south, what's up north?"

"The wealthier district. The Patriarch's Imperial Palace and Gardens are in the northernmost section of the city, with the mountains behind the palace acting as a natural defense. At the halfway mark between the north and south, we'll find the market, shrines, a few government buildings like the tax collector's office and the museum; and also the studio we're planning to visit: the Agricultural Biotechnological Research Studio."

With a bump, they left the dirt road behind for smoother pavement. She began to see evidence of the commercial district. Lights, large buildings that looked like the warehouses Conlean had mentioned, a maze of roads, and ships with tall masts filled her view. Some smaller buildings with even brighter lights appeared to be hangouts for the citizens of Blackfell, judging by the crowds lingering in front of them.

Keeping to the shadows and the outermost lane, they

walked through the city gates. Jordan took in as much as she dared. In her experience, nothing said *stranger* louder than wide eyes, a gaping mouth, and a habit of staring at skyscrapers, so she kept her gaze low and her mouth closed. Still, she couldn't quite harness her curiosity when they passed a two-story building where the lights were shaded red and the sound of clinking poured out of the window. "What's going on in there?" she murmured.

"It's a gambling hall."

"I thought you were going to tell me it was a brothel."

"We have no brothels in Blackfell."

"And no prostitution either, I'll bet."

"Diamonds were precious in your day, right? Did you use diamonds to pave cobblestone roads?"

"Not where I lived."

Rather than continue in this vein and betray her ignorance further, she remarked on the many flowers, trees, gazebos, statues, and other decorative items that seemed to flourish everywhere. "For a city, Blackfell is really very beautiful. I can see that someone put a lot of work into turning it into a work of art. The cities in my time were more functional than attractive."

"In your time, you relied on science. With Prima Materia, everything is accomplished through artistry."

Thus reminded, she said little else, preferring to gaze around rather than engage in conversation that was difficult to hear anyway, with all the city noises around them. After a while, the buildings became more solid and stately, and she guessed they had arrived near the center of the city, where the Imperial government had its offices. The Studio had to be near too, then. Confirming her suspicions, Conlean guided the horse toward a stable and stopped in front of a lounging youth.

"This should be a good place to stable the horse," Conlean remarked. He threw the reins to the youth, who now stood at their side. "Hold on, I'm going to dismount. Then I'll help you down."

Without further warning he dismounted in one graceful movement. He handed the youth a couple of coins retrieved from a pouch around his waist and then held his arms out to her. "Come on."

She looked down at him. "What am I supposed to do, fly out of the saddle? How do I get down?"

The youth snickered.

He raised an eyebrow, then cut a significant glance toward the boy. "I'd prefer not to make this moment a memorable one," he said, his voice lower than usual.

She understood by his tone that he didn't want the boy to be telling any stories about the dumb lady who dressed like a man and didn't know how to ride horseback in a world where everyone apparently rode horseback. "Oh, right. Sorry."

Even so, the trip down to the ground appeared awfully long.

Screwing up her courage, she mentally reviewed the motions he'd made to dismount and then attempted the same thing. As she was swinging one leg over the horse's back, she stood up in the other stirrup and tried to leap away from the horse. Unfortunately, she hadn't any fairy dust, and her Peter Pan act sent her flying down onto Conlean's unprepared body.

With a grunt that had a lot of wind behind it, he staggered backward beneath her weight, at the same time throwing his arms around her waist. "Damn!"

Her equilibrium completely lost, she clung to him, even though logic said that the best thing would have been for her to let go. They both seemed to dance a tango for one brief moment before she fell to the ground, her body cushioned by Conlean's.

This time she was the one who grunted. "Ow!"

His arms tightened around her. "Are you okay?"

She stopped thinking about the fall and started thinking about the fine masculine body beneath hers. "I'm really okay."

Her gaze joined with his, and again magic danced between them. The heat from his body rose up to envelope hers, and the whole world faded away as she stared into blue eyes darkened with desire, and thought about him kissing her, and how wonderful it would feel . . .

"You two need help?" the boy asked, amusement evident in his tone.

"No, we're fine," Conlean replied, after a moment's hesitation.

Seeing the desire in Conlean's eyes fade to a silent appeal, she reluctantly sat up on her elbows and then rolled off him, but not before she noticed a suspicious hardness pressing against her stomach. He sat up too, and then they both stood and dusted the grime off their clothes.

"I've never seen someone get off a horse like that," the stableboy remarked. "The lad needs some practice."

She raised an eyebrow, surprised that the stableboy

thought her male, considering the way she and Conlean had looked at each other just moments ago. Then again, in a world with few women, she supposed men frequently turned to other men for comfort and satisfaction.

"My little brother needs a lot of practice," Conlean muttered, with a secret wink in her direction. "How much is the stabling per hour?"

The stableboy answered with a figure that meant nothing to her and, after another exchange of money, took the horse off to his stall.

"We called structures like these parking lots in my time," she mentioned, seeing row upon row of horses stabled neatly within the wooden walls. "Only we parked cars, not horses."

"Come on, little brother." Conlean pulled her away from the stable. "Let's forget about the horse for a while and visit the market. It's a little too early yet to consider sneaking into the Imperial Studio."

"I'm really thirsty," she admitted.

"We'll drink from the fountain at the market." Grasping her hand tightly in his own, he led her down a couple of side streets before they emerged onto the main thoroughfare. Ahead, she could see that the road led to a cleared area where gardens, fountains, gaslights, and kiosks ruled. She and Conlean stuck to the shadows as they approached the market square, and then they paused in a darkened niche created by two buildings. He released her hand and she simply stared.

Beautiful, bejewled women in satin gowns caught her attention first. There weren't many of them, but they stood out like peacocks among a flock of crows, their gowns flashing in the lantern light, their laughter rich and delightful. Their companions' clothes, though clearly luxurious, had a drab appearance that made the women seem even more brilliant. They were the center of everyone's attention, in fact, and she couldn't help noticing that some of the poorer-dressed citizens of Blackfell fixed avaricious gazes on them.

Once she'd gotten her fill of looking at the women, she realized that the kiosks offered all sorts of interesting items for sale, everything from oranges to silks to wooden oars. Flowers and greenery danced from gardens around every corner and cleverly positioned bistro tables offered passersby the chance to sit down and enjoy some of the delicacies that filled the air with the smell of baked goods. The fountains, she saw, spewed silvery water, and suddenly she had to have a drink. She slipped her hand into Conlean's and tugged him in the direction of the nearest fountain.

"I need a drink. Can we go over there without attracting too much attention?"

"I think we can. Why don't we find a table while we're at it, and have something to eat?"

Her mouth began to water at the thought of sampling some of the lush fare she saw sitting on the countertops. "I'd love to."

Her hand once again enfolded tightly in his, they slipped in and out of the shadows until they reached a likely looking table, one that sat on a porch outside an establishment. "Stay here. I'll get some water and something to eat."

She nodded, and he slipped into the crowd. For a while she managed to follow his progress, but then he moved beyond her field of vision, and she contented herself with watching the antics of the people around her. This section of the market didn't seem to attract the peacocks with their crow attendants; rather, a rougher sort of crowd—all male—appeared to prefer this area. The establishment they were sitting near might have been the source of the attraction, because the men who entered were much more sober than those who exited. A few of the men who left even hailed her as a "wet-eared laddie" who ought to be home in bed rather than out drinking at such a late hour.

Favoring these obviously low-class louts with disgusted looks, she kept her attention focused on the kiosks closest to her and breathed a sigh of relief when she noticed Conlean approaching. Relief quickly became anticipation when she saw what he was balancing on a tray: a decanter, two crystal glasses, and a plate full of appetizers worthy of any high-society function.

She smiled at him as he sat down opposite her and lifted a crystal glass. "They serve food and drink in crystal here? That's outrageous! Why not paper cups and plates?"

His eyebrows lifted in an expression of curiosity. "Why not crystal?" He put a plate in front of her and lifted a few little pastries onto her plate with a spoon that looked like pure silver.

"Why not crystal?" She shook her head. "Crystal's expensive. It breaks. People steal it. Do you need any other reasons?"

He poured some amber liquid into one of the glasses and pushed it toward her. "Here in Blackfell, it's all about presentation. We like things to look good. No one would dream of serving food or drink in paper. I can think of no bigger insult."

"Wow. You people have really taken artistry to a new level."

"I don't think I would have liked living in your time, Jordan."

She briefly covered his hand with her own and fixed him with an earnest stare. "Trust me: you wouldn't have."

He smiled. "Let's enjoy the crystal, then."

She watched as he poured amber liquid into his own glass. "That's not water."

"It's amber. I thought you might enjoy it more. If you don't like it, I'll get you some water."

She took the glass he had poured for her and swirled its contents. "What's amber . . . an alcoholic drink?"

"It has a touch of alcohol in it," he confirmed. "Not enough to impair your judgment, though. Just enough to give it a taste."

"I can hold my drink. Stop worrying."

"Still, I'll get some water." He moved as if to rise, but she motioned him to stay seated.

"One glass won't kill me." She brought the glass to her lips and sipped It tasted like pure, honeyed warmth, just perfect. A sigh escaped her lips. "That's good."

He smiled. "There's no equal to a well-fermented barrel of amber."

She matched his smile with one of her own. The amber seemed to slip through her veins, making her warm all over. "So, what did you bring for us to eat?"

Silver fork in hand, he speared a small, croissantlike pastry and held it up to her lips. "Try it."

She parted her lips and, gently, he placed it on her tongue. She pulled it from the fork with her teeth and chewed slowly, savoring the flavor. Chicken. Berries. Honey. "It tastes wonderful." Selecting a fork, she speared another appetizer and held it up to his mouth, brushing it softly against his lips. "Your turn."

He allowed her to put it in his mouth. Chewing slowly, his gaze never leaving hers, he finished it and then offered her a smile with a touch of wickedness to it. "Mmm."

Seeing the advantage that their al fresco dinner gave her, and the possibilities that the amber brought into play, she put her fork down and refilled both their glasses. "You've quite an appetite. Would you like more?"

"Please." His eyes hooded, he handed her the fork, his fingers lingering against hers for longer than necessary.

Excitement and amber combined inside her, creating a heady sensation that she scarcely knew how to manage. Instinct demanded that she drag him off to a darkened corner, strip the clothes off him, and make love to him until they both collapsed from exhaustion. Another part of her insisted that she tease the hell out of him until he lost control and dragged her off to a corner himself, so that she wouldn't have to take responsibility for it. Neither option seemed to be stronger or have any advantage over the other.

Taking a deep breath, she took the fork and selected another appetizer. "Want to try this one?"

"That's my favorite."

Her smile a little shaky now, she lifted it to his lips,

but this time, he didn't gently accept it as he had before. Instead, with one quick motion he grabbed her hand to hold her steady, then pulled the appetizer off himself. He ate it slowly. Purposefully. "Very good."

She swallowed, the warmth inside her becoming all-out heat.

"Are you still hungry?" he asked softly.

"Unbelievably so."

"Which one would you like?" Even though he referred to the plate of appetizers, his attention never left her.

Her gaze fell to his lips.

"Well, Jordan? Which one?"

She moistened her own lips. "I want—"

A ruckus inside the establishment interrupted her. Four men who were stumbling all over each other and reeking of amber spilled out of the establishment. Slapping their comrades on the back and apparently full of bonhomie, they paused near the table she shared with Conlean. With a spurt of anxiety, she recognized one of them as the youth from the stable . . . the same one who had parked their horse.

"Well, look here," the stableboy said, his face sporting a grin. "It's the two *brothers* I helped out earlier."

Conlean just stared at him in reply.

"The *little* brother seemed mighty taken with his big brother when I saw them last," the stableboy announced in ringing tones. "Maybe the little brother is a little *sister*."

With owlish expressions, the other men grew quiet and examined her anew. "You know, you could be right

277

about that," one of them said. "He's awfully pretty. Look at those lips! He's a *she,* all right."

Jordan fought the urge to cover her mouth.

"I'd say the Artisan can't keep his hands in his pockets," another of the stableboy's companions slurred, his voice just as loud.

"But they're just sitting there, staring at each other," a third man observed belligerently. "Why are you staring at her, man? Go ahead and kiss her."

Conlean shrugged. "I don't make a habit of kissing my brother."

A round of raucous laughter erupted from the men. "Aw, come on, Artisan. We know she isn't your brother," a bearded man said.

Conlean dismissed the bearded man's accusation with a lift of his eyebrow. "You're wrong about that. Go home. You've had too much to drink."

"If you don't want her, we'll take her," the bearded man said. Without warning, he pulled the hat off her head.

Jordan felt her hair cascade down around her face. She looked guiltily at the bearded man.

A moment of silence descended over all, and then the drunken men accosted Conlean with a barrage of monetary offers for her.

His jaw tight, Conlean snatched her hat from the bearded man. "She's not available."

"Oh, she's yours, is she? Kiss her and prove it."

Despite her worry at the their aggressiveness, Jordan had to laugh softly. She couldn't believe she was sitting here being harassed into kissing Conlean by a bunch of drunks. She turned to Conlean and shrugged. "Why don't you just give me a quick kiss? That'll get rid of them."

A fierce look sharpened his features. Abruptly, he leaned forward and grasped her chin between two long fingers. His gaze captured hers. She stared back without flinching.

The men let out a volley of encouragement.

She parted her lips as he dipped his head in close. His mouth brushed against hers, as if he meant to give her a brotherly kiss and nothing more. And yet, she wanted more from him and didn't care that a few drunks were standing around watching. They wouldn't remember anything in the morning!

Caught up in the moment, she wound her fingers around his neck, and when he tried to pull back, she held him fast and deepened the kiss, pressing her lips against his. She saw the surprise in his eyes blossom into something hotter, more impatient, more demanding. He remained perfectly still for several seconds, allowing her to press harder against him, to suck his lips gently and lick them in the most sensual kiss she'd ever given in her entire life. And then he was taking over, the tip of his tongue running along her lips, then slipping inside to greet hers.

She clung to him, her heart pounding so hard in her chest, she felt giddy. When he lifted his mouth from hers a few seconds later and gazed at her, she could see the passion in his gaze, and the knowledge of how good, how right it felt between them.

"Now that was a kiss," the stableboy pronounced, his

tone hushed. His companions were staring at them with the kind of dreamy lust that a youth displays when he's studying his favorite pinup.

Conlean fixed them with an intense stare. "Go away."

Reluctantly, the drunks turned and shuffled away, muttering to themselves about the lack of women and how to get one . . . cheap.

Shaking his head, Conlean ran a hand through his hair. "Did you hear the way they were talking? The FFA will probably get a few new recruits this evening. That kiss may not have been such a good idea."

She grasped her hand and held it tight. "It was perfect."

He looked away. "I know."

A sigh slipped out of her. She held his hand up to her cheek and nuzzled it. "Oh, Conlean, why do we have to listen to the rules? Let's go somewhere. Alone. I want you to hold me. And I want to hold you. Just this once. Just for tonight. Tomorrow we'll worry about the plague."

He returned his attention to her. A shadow she couldn't decipher darkened his eyes. "Do you want to skip the Imperial Studio, then?"

The old Jordan would have said *no, this is our best chance to get some work done.* But the new Jordan couldn't have cared less about science or duty. "The Studio can wait."

Instead of replying, he grew still and made a quieting motion with his hand. She followed the direction of his gaze to see what had alarmed him, and noticed three men mingling with the crowd around the town square, their blue phosphorescent tattoos glowing in the darkness. Artisans, out to enjoy the festival, no doubt.

"We should go, before they recognize me and wonder who you are." He slid out of his chair and motioned her to follow him.

They left the market square and made their way onto a side street. Brownstones lined either side of the street, and gas lamps lit the sidewalk that passed through several plantings of bushes and trees, reminding her of the Rittenhouse Square neighborhood in Philadelphia where she'd rented an apartment.

"Where are we going?" she whispered, slipping her hand into his.

"To the Studio."

"But I thought we were going to go somewhere private—"

He squeezed her hand. "We'll find somewhere private near the Studio."

As he led her down more side streets, the residential buildings gave way to larger, sturdier structures that reached higher into the sky and had arched windows that made her think *cathedral*. She guessed that these were the government offices Conlean had spoken of, and that the city's midpoint lay somewhere ahead. Even the office buildings possessed the clean lines and expensive stonework of a museum or art gallery that might have existed in her time. Everything had a touch of beauty to it, and she liked that particular aspect of Blackfell. It made her feel good just to look around.

"The Studio is up ahead," Conlean told her after a

few more minutes of stealing down side streets. "Stay in the shadows."

"What's the plan? How are we going to get in?"

"Through a few passageways underground."

"Passageways?" She thought of the subways back home. "Is there any other way?"

"What's the problem with passageways?"

"I don't want to be brushing shoulders with cockroaches and rats."

"These are clean. You won't have to brush shoulders with anyone but me."

She shot him an appreciative look. "Who uses them?"

"No one."

"They're secret?"

"Yes. They were designed as an escape route for the Patriarch, just in case."

"How do you know about them?"

"I explored them when I was growing up."

She nodded, remembering their discussion about his past. Oddly enough, she rarely thought of him in this context. "Ah, the royal connection. You're the son of the Patriarch. You probably know all sorts of secrets."

A smile lit his face. "A few. I'm glad I know this one."

"Is there any chance we'll run into someone at the Studio?"

"I doubt it. It's late, and everyone should be at the festival."

"I always chose work over festivals," she said dubiously.

"We'll be all right. If I didn't think we had a ninety-nine percent chance of getting in and out undiscovered, I wouldn't have brought you here."

She shivered. "It's that one percent that I worry about."

Pausing before a stone wall carved with intricate designs, Conlean stuck his finger into a niche cleverly hidden in the center of a flower. When he pulled his finger out, a portion of the wall opened, revealing a black maw that led into even deeper darkness. "Trust me."

Chapter Eighteen

Conlean had explored the underground tunnel network beneath the city many times during his childhood. Of course, he'd always had some Imperial retainer following him around, ensuring that he didn't get lost or into trouble; still, he'd managed to scare himself by imagining he was on a secret mission he had to finish or die trying. The scenario had always come complete with the darkest, ugliest villain he could imagine, and this villain would inevitably be determined to stop him at all costs. Tonight, however, he found that he didn't need to make up any stories to scare himself. He already felt worried . . . and not over what lurked in the tunnel.

The strength of his feelings for Jordan were enough to keep him on edge. When did it happen? When did he stop thinking about his life as an Artisan and the fact that Jordan was destined to become Matriarch and start seriously considering a way to keep her from marrying his father? When had he decided that marrying her was worth sacrificing everything he held dear? When had he fallen in love with her?

From the moment they'd first met, he thought darkly.

Swallowing against a dry throat, he glanced at her as he led her into the tunnels and felt a hot glow in his gut, one that had become familiar to him. But it wasn't just desire. He wished only lust bound him to her. Unfortunately for him, so many different things about her attracted him that he felt her pull like a lodestone, even when he wasn't in her presence. And so, at some point during the last few agonizing days, he had decided that he wasn't going to allow her to marry his father.

He would marry her himself, regardless of the consequences.

If she agreed.

He pushed the lever to shut the tunnel door, and as it was shutting, he grabbed a lantern that the Imperial footmen kept near the opening. He lit it with matches he'd brought for this purpose and then he took her hand. "You're not frightened, I hope."

"I trust you, Conlean," she said, her voice soft.

Lifting the lantern high, he led her downward into the dry, dusty tunnels that criss-crossed beneath the streets. When the tunnel leveled out, it was very dark, with a closed-in feeling. Conlean glanced at her. "Still all right?"

"I'm fine. I can't believe you know your way through these tunnels. We've taken so many turns I'd be completely lost without you."

And I'd be completely lost without you, he thought. "We're almost there."

Mentally he reviewed the tunnels that led in the direction he needed to take her, and also noted the storage rooms along the way, the ones with the goods that the Patriarch kept hidden away in case their aboveground storehouses were ever plundered. He wanted to take her to these rooms filled with treasures just to see her amazement when she viewed them.

He wondered if her amazement would be any greater when he gave her his mother's ring and asked her to marry him.

Resolution filled him. He touched the ring he'd placed in his pocket earlier.

This was the choice he wanted to make, and he'd live with the consequences. When the General Assembly kicked him out of the Gallery, he'd collect his paintbrushes and go. If he had to resume his title as heir apparent to the Patriarchy, he'd put on the royal crown. If he had to go into hiding, he'd deal with it. He could deal with anything if Jordan stood by his side.

He stopped and turned to face her. "I'm taking you to the Studio, and then I have something else to show you. The Patriarch keeps several storage rooms underground, and a few have some artifacts in them. I think you'd enjoy getting a glimpse of some things from your own time."

"I'd love to see them." Enthusiastically she squeezed his hand. "Are we close to the Studio?"

"It's only a few minutes more." His body tight with anticipation over his upcoming proposal, he led her around two corners, down one very long passageway that forced them to hunch over when the ceiling dropped, and then through a tunnel that slanted upward, until they came to a stop at an iron door that didn't really look like a door, but rather an immoveable wall. He pressed an ear to the wall to make sure no one stood directly outside, but he didn't really expect to hear anyone as the door opened into a deserted section of the Studio's basement. Satisfied that they remained alone, he pushed the lever, and the wall swung open.

Beyond lay various tools and machines he didn't recognize and wouldn't know how to operate if his life depended on it. They were all from an era before the plague, antiques kept in the basement because someone thought they might have some curiosity value.

Jordan gave a little gasp of appreciation. "Wow."

"We're in the Studio," he said needlessly, and brought her into the basement. Clumsily he bumped into a machine near the door, earning a little gasp from her.

"That looks like a personal computer!"

"Looks like junk to me," he admitted.

Her gaze darted from one corner to the other. "Isn't that a cryostorage unit? And that, an electron microscope, though it's so rusty I doubt it works. And there . . ." She fixed her attention on a silver shelf that contained row after row of glass beakers. "They're all filled with liquid. They could be reagents or something. Who works here?"

His mouth lifted in a rueful smile. "No one. This is the basement, where they store junk."

"Junk! I can't wait to see the Studio with the cutting edge equipment."

"I don't think you'll be impressed with our Studios,"

he murmured, remembering her preference for science over artistry. "Not unless you enjoy working with paint and Prima Materia."

"I did forget. You're all *artisans,* not scientists." She glanced around the basement. "There's a lot of dust. I guess no one comes down here much."

"Not very often. We'll stick to the shadows, though . . . just in case." Her hand still held in his, he lifted the lantern and threaded his way past the out-dated equipment, stopping long enough for Jordan to examine a piece of machinery when she whispered her interest. The lantern offered just enough light to get them through the basement without bumping into any-thing, and when they reached the corridor, it revealed another iron door ahead. "Here are the stairs."

He handed Jordan the lantern and turned the door-knob. The door needed a firm yank before it would open and it did so reluctantly, with a low screeching noise. He froze, glancing at Jordan, his ears attuned to any noise upstairs suggesting that someone had heard them and was coming to investigate.

Holding his gaze, she returned the lantern to him. "I think we're safe," she whispered.

Nodding, he recaptured her hand and they crept up the stairs, twisting the doorknob at the top with great care. This door didn't want to let them in either, but he pushed firmly and finally it surrendered with a high-pitched whine.

Her eyes were very wide. "Someone should oil the doors around here."

"I'll suggest it at the next General Assembly meet-ing." He edged into the hallway and glanced both ways.

Gaslights stationed evenly apart on the walls were turned to their lowest level, as they were left during the nighttime, when the Studio was deserted. The glass doors along the corridor were shut. As before, he heard not a single noise.

"Are there any security guards?" she whispered.

"One, from what I remember. He makes his rounds once an hour. But the security company isn't very thorough. I snuck past the guard many times as a boy."

"Where does the guard sit when he isn't touring the Studios?"

"In the reception area out front." He grabbed her hand and pulled her into the hallway behind him. "Try to walk as quietly as you can."

Jordan stepped even more softly than he did as they slipped down the corridor. "Each of the laboratories is working on a different problem," he whispered as they passed the closed doors. "Most of them are agriculture-related. One or two studios, though, are trying to develop more Prima Materia using the recipe left by Nicholas Flamel."

Her head tilted to one side. "What kinds of agricultural problems?"

"Micropropagation techniques, mostly. Some of the species of grains that were plentiful in your time are now on the edge of extinction. We're trying to bring them back."

"Really? Which species?"

"Wheat, for one," he said.

"You know, I didn't realize it before, but I haven't had a single piece of bread since I got here." She shook her head. "What happened?"

"A specific kind of blight is killing off the wheat stalks before they can mature."

"Hmm." She shook her head. "And what about the attempt to duplicate Flamel's recipe? Any success there?"

"Nothing yet."

"Jeez. Sounds like the laboratory I worked in." She offered him a smile. "We'll have better luck, though. With my knowledge of the past, and your experience in artistry, I think we'll be able to pull something together that will really help."

At the confidence and enthusiasm in her voice, excitement stirred in him. "I *know* we can."

A moment later they reached the Studio. After ensuring that it was empty, he ushered her inside and shut the door behind them. Then he turned up the wick on the lantern to allow light into the room.

She made a little noise somewhere between a gasp and a sigh. "So this is what a laboratory of the future looks like."

"The Imperial Studios have the greatest selection and variance in hues of paint, materials for canvas, and collection of substances, in order to produce the most diverse reactions of Prima Materia. This is where we do our most intensive research." He edged closer to her, until he stood almost directly behind her. "Do you think a studio like this will be adequate?"

She took a few more steps into the room. "I don't know. This is very different from what I'd been expecting."

Standing back, he examined the room with a critical

eye. The windows along the far wall were very narrow, and even in daylight they didn't admit much light. Now they looked like black slashes across a somber stone wall, their darkness relieved only a little by the feeble lantern light. Above, the alchemical lantern—a star with a flame above each of its seven points— swung slightly in a draft, contributing a rhythmic squeak to the room.

On shelves, an assortment of compasses, alembics, canvases, bottles, paints, cachepots, skeletons of animals, leather-bound books, brushes, cauldrons, and everything else needed for the practice of artistry stood arranged in groups. Behind the shelves, paintings covered the walls—sketches of the constellations, geometric figures, portraits of women, and a rainbow of colors. Nothing here had the look or feel of a twenty-first-century laboratory, he mused.

She wandered over to the table that held the scales and a few musical instruments. "Is this where the musicians practice too?"

"Sacred music disperses artistic melancholia. Sometimes we ask an apprentice to play the instruments for that purpose."

Nodding, she ran her fingers over three plaques mounted on a nearby wall. "This looks like Latin. What do they say?"

He watched the way her fingers trailed across the plaque and took a deep breath. "The first one, *homo homini monstrum,* translates to *man is a monster unto men.* The second one means *dare to be wise,* and the last one says *neither rashly nor timidly.*"

291

Head tilted, she moved to a shelf that contained row upon row of bottles. "What do all these bottles contain?"

"Paints and tinctures, mostly. Some of them contain more exotic ingredients."

"Like what?"

"Well, *hyle* is primordial matter, or Prima Materia. *Ros celi* is dew of the sky and *azoth* is sophic mercury."

"What are 'dew of the sky' and 'sophic mercury' used for?"

"We mix them with the paints to produce different effects."

"What kind of effects? Do they accelerate isomerization or bind proteins?" A hint of frustration had crept into her voice.

He grimaced. "I don't know what you mean by isomerization. Maybe some of our tinctures will perform the way you need them to, if we can just figure out what you're trying to do."

"Right now I'd give a lot for a kit containing all of the reagents needed for a first-strand DNA synthesis reaction."

"I don't think I can supply you with that. I'm sure we have the equivalent, though, in artistry."

She raised her eyebrows at him. "We need to find some old-fashioned biotech tools or I'm not going to be able to help with the plague one iota."

"You'll have to describe the tools to me." He glanced at the clock, then returned his attention to her. Her cheeks looked pink and her eyes sparkled in a way that made him want to kiss her again. "Are you ready to go, or would you like to look around some more?"

"I think I'm done here. I'd like to see those treasures you mentioned earlier."

He nodded once. "Let's go, then. The guard should be making his rounds soon, so we have to be quiet."

On silent feet, he led her back to the door. His pulse began to pound at the thought of their trip back through the tunnels. He had some treasures to show her, and he planned to steal a few from her too.

He'd grasped the doorknob and had begun to turn it when suddenly the sound of two male voices drifted toward them. The voices were raised in an argument, and they seemed to be growing louder.

Both he and Jordan froze.

"Someone's coming," Jordan whispered. She moved in closer until she was brushing against him. "What do we do?"

He strained to listen to the men, trying to figure out who they were and where they might be going. The panic he'd detected in Jordan's voice reflected the feeling he had in his gut. He didn't really have a good explanation for his presence in the Studio, and though he might avoid being detained simply because he could call upon his relationship to the Patriarch, he had no explanation for Jordan's presence. Discovery at this point would be a complete disaster.

"Either you have to hide, and I have to talk my way out of here as the Patriarch's son, or we both try to escape without being seen," he whispered back. "Since I don't feel like leaving you stuck here in some hiding place, we'll try to escape."

The voices increased in volume. Conlean could tell

from their discussion that both artisans studied bioartistry. The studio he and Jordan were hiding in was a bioartistry Studio. He cursed softly but vehemently.

"What's wrong?" she asked, pushing even more closely against him.

He eased the door open and peered out. The light in the hallway was increasing in brightness. The two men, one of them with a lantern in hand, were on the verge of turning the corner and coming into full view of the bioartistry Studio. "They're coming here. To this Studio. We have to go. Now." He grasped her hand. "Don't turn toward them, don't say anything, just walk. And follow my lead."

Without waiting for her reply, he stepped boldly into the corridor, just as the artisans turned the corner. She followed him, but no sooner had she stepped out of the doorway than the heated discussion between the artisans stopped and they slowed their pace.

"Hello! Who's there?" one of the men called out.

Conlean said nothing. Instead, he grasped her firmly by the elbow and steered her quickly around. He began to walk away, Jordan matching his pace.

"Who's there?" the artisan called out again. "This area is restricted. Answer, please!"

Slipping his hand from her elbow to her palm, which he grasped with gentle pressure, he increased the pace to the point where they were moving fast but not fast enough to encourage the artisans to pursue. At least, that was what he hoped.

"You two—stop and identify yourselves!" the artisans called.

Conlean broke into a light run. Jordan kept up with him.

A moment later, the lights on the walls began to flicker wildly. Conlean heard footsteps behind them and knew that the artisans were following.

"Artisan Felder, call the guard," a male voice bellowed.

Aware that even more trouble would soon catch up with them, he raced around the corner with Jordan and ran full-out for the door leading to the basement. They reached it just as the other man turned the corner.

Conlean yanked the door open. He and Jordan rushed into the staircase. Darkness closed around them.

"Where's the lantern?" she hissed.

"In the Studio. Grab the railing!" He took a second to confirm that he couldn't lock the door behind them and then started down, one hand on the railing and the other gripping hers. They stumbled down stairs that seemed to have grown longer since they'd climbed them last, and even as they reached the bottom, the door at the top opened and light flooded the staircase.

"There they are!" a panting voice announced triumphantly. "In the basement. There's no other exit."

"Did you recognize them?" a new voice asked.

"No. One was taller than the other, I can say that much."

"The guard," Jordan choked out. "He's coming after us too."

"He must have been close by, on his rounds," he muttered as they stumbled past the artifacts piled high in the basement. "They don't know about the underground passageways."

"A security guard is going to know everything about a building."

Silently he admitted that she stood a good chance of being right about that. Jaw clenched, he maneuvered them to the general location of the passageway. He couldn't be exactly certain as to the location of the lever—the darkness in their corner of the basement was just too thick—so he began pushing stones with the hope that he'd find the right one before the guard found *them*.

She tugged on his sleeve. "Open the door, quick. They're coming!"

"I don't know where the lever is." He began pressing random stones as fast as he could, looking for the stone that would open the passageway. "I can't see anything. Help me out. Push the stones and see if one moves. And watch for temperature differences. The stones in front of the tunnel are colder than the others."

Drawing in a ragged breath, she began pressing the stones with her palms. Together, they groped along the wall like two blind people. At the same time, footsteps hammered down the stairs from the other corner of the basement, and the guard's and artisans' voices sounded urgent . . . as though they knew how close they were to catching Jordan and Conlean.

"These stones here feel cooler than the others," Jordan whispered.

He immediately abandoned the area he'd been searching and moved next to her. They both ran their fingers over the stones, their movements growing more urgent while the guard's lantern began to chase away the darkness. At the same time, Conlean glanced around, trying to gain his bearings, and saw the old computing machine he'd bumped into when they'd arrived.

"I think it's over here," he said, just as the guard and one of the two artisans came into view. Suddenly, he stumbled across a stone that stood out a little from the others.

"Damn!" Keeping his head low and hoping they couldn't identify them, he jammed his palm against the lever. With a nearly silent hiss, the door slowly swung open.

The guard and one artisan ran toward them. "Stop!"

He grabbed Jordan by the arm, dragged her into the tunnel, and pressed the lever before the door had finished opening. With a shudder, the door stopped suddenly and then began to reverse.

"They're going into a passageway." The guard raced across the room toward them, his lantern swinging wildly. Still, the door had already closed enough to block him from entering the tunnels.

Conlean took a second to grab the guard's lantern, and then slipped his hand into hers. "We have to hurry."

Together, they began to run, Conlean holding the lantern high so they could see where they were going. Behind him, the guard's and Artisans' shouts grew fainter as he and Jordan turned a corner and ran down a hallway with a ceiling so low they were forced to stoop. When they reached the end, they turned again, the smell of dust growing thicker as they moved into an area that even the Imperial servants who knew about the tunnels rarely visited.

"Are they going to follow us into the tunnels?" she asked between gasps for breath.

"I don't think so. If the guard knew about them, he'd already have the door open. Still, he might find the lever. We have to keep moving."

"For how long?"

"Until I feel we're safe." He scanned the corridor, trying to remember if he'd ever gone in this direction before. "I've been avoiding the main tunnels, just in case the guard was familiar with them."

"So you don't know where we are?" She sounded shaky. "I don't want to get lost."

"We won't. Stay close. I'll try to find a place where we can rest."

She sagged against him. "I need a rest."

He put an arm around her and hugged her close, then led her more slowly down the corridor. The ceiling grew lower, forcing them to walk hunched over for a while, and when it started leveling out, he saw that the stones in the walls fit together better and had a sheen to them. When wall-mounted lanterns started to appear every ten feet or so, he knew they had reached the tunnels closest to the Imperial Palace.

"We're near the storage rooms beneath the palace," he told her, his pace slowing. When they turned the corner, he surveyed the passageway ahead. "I've been here many times."

She sighed, the sound full of relief. "So, I might get to see the treasures you promised to show me?"

He gave her a smile in reply and continued down another few corridors, making turns as needed, until they arrived at a passageway lined with doors. Fishing the key he'd brought out of his pocket, he stopped in front of the first door and unlocked it. The door swung open and he stepped inside, the lantern held high.

"Some old paintings," he remarked.

She followed him in and suddenly stopped short. "These look like Rembrandts. Renoirs. Picassos."

"Yes, they are," he said with some pride.

She looked around with wide eyes. "Unbelieveable." Lips parted, she walked up to a picture of a woman with soft-looking eyes and whispered, "Mona Lisa."

"Most of the Old Masters are represented here," he said. "Every artisan is escorted down here when he graduates from his apprenticeship to view this ancient work. It's quite an honor."

"This is tremendous." She continued to move from painting to painting, and he stayed close by, lifting the lantern so she could better view each canvas. When she stopped to look at a scene of Aphrodite and Zeus locked in an embrace, he moved closer and studied her with as much interest as she studied the painting. She looked very pretty, with her cheeks faintly red and her eyes shining with excitement, and heat built in his loins.

Without really thinking about it, he leaned down and kissed the top of her head. He could smell her shampoo, smell her. Her hair felt so soft. He drew in a deep, ragged breath and told himself that he had to go slowly.

She grew very still, her gaze intensifying as it had when she'd first come into the room. But then a little smile began to play about her mouth, and she slanted an uncertain look at him before refocusing her attention on the painting and leaning ever so gently into him.

"This painting is kind of intriguing, don't you think?"

"Very," he agreed, his voice low. "Are you ready to move on?"

"There's more?"

"Much more," he promised with a smile.

She grasped his arm and pressed her side against his. "Lead on."

Swallowing, he drew her out of the room and locked the door behind them before taking her to another room two doors down. "Let's try this one."

Again, he unlocked the door and held the lantern high as they entered.

She gasped with delight.

Jewel-encrusted golden goblets, plates, pitchers, and bowls lay in artful disarray across a massive oak table. Silver urns, forks, knives, and spoons on a matching oak sideboard provided a sparkling counterpoint to the gold. Casks and bottles fought for space with baskets containing lace, silk, and other fine fabrics, while etched glassware competed with porcelain dishes for the prize of most delicate and graceful. In one corner, a basket woven with bits of straw and dried flowers overflowed with strands of pearls and jeweled baubles of every kind. Everything sparkled in the lantern's light, giving the room a magical feel.

"What's this, the room of dining treasures?" she asked with hushed reverence.

He laughed. "That's a good description of it. When I was a kid, I used to come here with a sandwich I'd filched from the kitchen and eat on one of these plates.

Later on, I discovered these jugs and started coming for a different reason."

Her brow wrinkled. "What's in the jugs?"

"Do you really want to know?"

"Of course."

"In that case, pick out two glasses," he directed.

A knowing look smoothed out the wrinkles on her brow. "Oh, I get it. This is where the Imperial stash of liquor is stored." She selected two jewel-encrusted goblets from the shelf and handed them to him. "Let's try not to break these. I don't think I can afford to pay for them."

"Neither can I," he said as he took the goblets and filled them with the sweet brew from a cask he'd chosen from the pile. "Try this."

"What is it?"

"The jug has a metal label that's rusted over, so I don't know exactly what it is. But it's good."

"Are you sure it won't make us sick?"

He shrugged. "Never made me sick."

"Well, here's to us, then." She lifted the goblet to her lips and sipped cautiously. After a moment, she nodded and took a bigger sip. "Hey, this is really good."

"I know. It isn't very strong, though." He too swallowed a mouthful, his mind swirling with fantasies. He was thinking of laying her down and staring at her, naked, while she offered her body to him, spreading her legs and lifting herself up so that she could kiss him easily. She looked so crisp, so clean, so innocent . . . and he wanted to replace her innocence with a look of knowledge when she discovered how it felt to have him inside her; and to be as exhausted and as satisfied as a cat with a belly full of cream.

For the next few minutes, they rehashed the evening and agreed they were very lucky to have escaped, while finishing off their drinks. Conlean felt himself relaxing and could see that she was too, judging by the way she stretched and then slouched against the wall. She was very sinuous, very slender.

"It's not too comfortable in here, is it?" he remarked, aroused by the sight of her and eager to see if she would accept his ring.

"Not at all," she agreed, her gaze alight with hope. "Is there a 'living room' of treasures too?"

"There's something similar," he offered.

"Let's go there, then. Can we bring the jug?"

"Of course." He handed her the lantern and picked up the jug.

"This evening is turning out to be really special, now that we've escaped the Studios. Do you think that's an omen, to stay away from work and devote ourselves to pleasure?"

"Could be." He studied her with a heavy-lidded gaze. "Let's give it a try and see what happens."

She drew in a quick breath, then nodded.

He led her into the passageway and closed the door behind them, only to open another a few feet away on the opposite side. A smile formed on his lips as he lifted the lantern and threw a soft glow on the contents of the room.

She squinted. "What are all those piles?"

"Go inside and have a look."

She glanced at him for reassurance. "Are they animals of some kind? They look like furs."

"That's right. They're furs."

"I didn't see any artisans wearing furs in the Gallery." She walked forward and rubbed her hand across one.

"We don't use fur for garments anymore. These are all very old."

"They're so soft." She buried her fingers in it.

"And warm too," he added. "Want to roll one out and see for yourself?"

She looked at him, a question in her eyes.

"It's all right, Jordan," he said softly. "We won't do anything you don't want to do."

A little smile began to tug at her lips. "Okay. Let's roll one out."

A hot wave of desire burned through him. He realized he was curling his fingers against his stomach. He wanted to be on top of her, pushing her naked body into the furs with his own, pleasuring her like that idiot ex-husband of hers never had. Managing a terse nod in her direction, he grabbed the softest, largest fur he could find and shook it out. Cedar shavings flew in all directions and filled the room with a clean fragrance. Dropping the fur for a moment, he found a few smaller furs and made a mattress of sorts, then spread the big one on top.

"That looks comfortable," she murmured.

Instead of answering, he spread his arms. Immediately she fell against him, sighing in contentment, and he enveloped her in a hug. "We've had a rough evening," he whispered against her hair.

She fixed him with her clear amber gaze. "So much has happened in a short time. A month ago I didn't even know you. Now I find I want to spend all my time with you. How can I feel this way?"

"It's strange, isn't it?" He pulled back so he could lock gazes with her. "I feel the same way . . . as if you and I were meant to be together."

She snuggled in closer and laid her head on his broad chest. "Since I've met you, Conlean, I feel better about myself. I mean, I used to think I had no purpose in life. But you gave me a purpose. And you reminded me how to laugh. Life seems worth living again."

He tightened his arms around her. "I didn't know you before you came to Blackfell, but you're a beautiful person, both inside and out. It hurts me to know that you thought, at one time, life wasn't worth living."

"Oh, Conlean," she breathed, her cheeks flushed pink. She melted against him. "I love being with you so much."

He slipped his hand into his pocket and curled his palm around the ring. "I have something I want to ask you."

"Hmm." She pressed her cheek against his chest.

"Would you really consider marrying me instead of my father?"

"Hmm."

"Jordan?"

She looked at him dreamily. "What did you say?"

"Would you consider marrying me instead of my father?"

"Would I consider . . ." She trailed off, her eyes

growing wide, and then she locked gazes with him. "Did you just ask me to marry you?"

He grinned. "I did."

"But how? Why?" Confusion marred her brow. "I don't understand."

"I want to marry you. I won't give you up to my father. Would you consider allowing me to purchase your bride contract?"

She pushed herself away from him. "Conlean . . . how can you purchase my contract? I thought you'd be kicked out of the Gallery and forced to give up artistry if you married one of your own brides."

"You're right, I will be. But I have no desire to be an Artisan if I can't have you by my side. I'd rather give it all up if it means I can marry you. You're that important to me."

She hugged him tightly. Tears slipped down her cheeks.

Trembling, he kissed the top of her head. "I love you, Jordan."

"Oh, Conlean, I love you too. I love everything about you. I just can't help it. You're so special to me."

"I am?" Happiness brought a smile to his lips.

"You are."

"But why? Why this change?" she asked, sniffling. With one hand she rubbed the tears from her cheeks. "And how can I possibly get out of marrying your father? What about finding a cure for the plague?"

With gentle fingers he traced the line of her jaw. *She loved him!* "We can figure everything out if you'll just tell me that you'll marry me. Will you?"

"Oh, yes, Conlean. Yes!" Without explanation, she pulled a stack of gold rings from her ring finger and allowed them to fall to the floor.

His hand steady, he withdrew his mother's ring from his pocket and slipped it onto the same finger on which she'd worn the gold rings. Then he cupped her face with his hands, pressed his lips against hers, and kissed her.

Chapter Nineteen

Groaning low in his throat, Conlcan broke their kiss long enough to sink to the furs, drawing Jordan with him. Their bodies were pressed so tightly together that even air couldn't fit between them. She tilted up her head and he kissed her again, more deeply this time. When her lips opened beneath his, he suddenly felt light-headed. But the dizziness only lasted a second before his body took over.

He ran his hands over her silky brown hair, down past her shoulders and hips, marveling all the while at her slim suppleness, at her delicate form. Her breasts, a temptation he'd struggled hard to ignore from the very moment he'd retrieved her, were crushed against him, and now he allowed himself the luxury of touching them, cupping them in his palms and rubbing her nipples until they hardened against his fingers. Satisfied with her little moan of pleasure, he moved his hands upward, gently cradling her cheeks as he slipped his tongue past her lips.

Boldly she touched his erection, as though claiming him for her own. When he made an encouraging sound and pushed against her hand, she rubbed him harder, creating friction and heat that socked him in the gut. He plundered her mouth with his tongue, feeling wet velvet and warmth; for several seconds he tasted her as her tongue teased and danced around his. When they drew apart, she began to lick his lips, his chin, and down to his neck with the same frenzy he was feeling.

He didn't know much about pleasing a woman. This was only the second time he'd actually had an opportunity to do so—and the first time had been with Jordan a few nights before. Tonight he wanted to make her scream with pleasure, to moan with satisfaction. He wanted her to think of nothing but him and the way his hands felt on her body. But how to accomplish it?

He didn't get much of a chance to think it over, though, because she was creating a trail of fire down his neck with her kisses and driving all coherent thought from his mind. Her lips stopped at the top of his tunic, and urgently she grasped the bottom of the garment and brought it upward. Clearly she meant to drag it over his head but couldn't.

Quickly he pulled off the shirt, exposing his skin to the cool air inside the room, and cupped her breasts again. The tunic she had on was made of silk and did little to hide their hard peaks. Abruptly he wanted to see all of her, at once. In one swift movement he grabbed the hem of her tunic and brought it over her shoulders. She shifted in order to make the task easier for him and tossed her hair as he threw the tunic onto the ground and drew off her trousers. Then he sat back to drink her in.

She was smiling, her lips red and soft, her eyes very dark and luminous. Her skin had a honeyed color to it, a healthy glow that made him think of mornings spent in the sunshine. His gaze dropped lower, and he saw that she was very slim and leggy, her curves under-stated. Her body didn't scream sex, but no man could look at her and think of anything but having those sin-uous legs wrapped around his own. Throat dry, he eyed the lacy pink top and underwear that hid the rest of her from his view, and then refocused on her face.

Her cheeks reddening, she grasped the ribbons that held her top closed and pulled on them. The lace fell open. Groaning, he took over the job, kissing her as he drew off her top. His erection rock-hard, he touched her nipples, and she immediately moaned into his mouth. Taking his cues from her, he moved his fingers over the soft curves of her breasts, eventually settling the motion over the hardened peaks, caressing them in small circles with his thumbs. Soon, her soft moans came faster against his lips.

His own excitement built at the effect he was having on her. He covered her breasts with his hands and squeezed a little, intrigued by the feel of her hardened nipples against his palms. Then he moved his hands lower and slipped his hand inside her lace underpants. As soon as he touched her, another groan escaped him as he felt how soft she was, how moist and warm. She arched into his fingers, at the same time running her hands up and down his back, then moved on to squeeze his buttocks, before going back up to his hair, which she pulled gently, sending chills down his spine.

"Take your pants off," she whispered against his mouth as his fingers slid over her, exploring, gently teasing and caressing, learning what she liked. "They're in the way."

Reluctantly he left her, pulling his hand away but stopping long enough to run his fingers across the tops of her thighs and admire their softness. Then, his attention remaining on her, he tore off his pants and lay down next to her so their naked bodies could touch from head to toe and everywhere in between. The sensation of her naked skin against him was as wonderful as it was indescribable. She felt soft and warm—like silk, only better, sexier, with a heated scent that stoked the hunger gnawing in his gut and made it impossible for him to lie still.

Acting on impulse, he lowered his head to her nipples and began to suck gently on one, drawing a gasp from her. As if in a fever, she ran her hands through his hair and across his upper back, her legs snaking around his waist to hold him tight. His erection pressing against her softness, he took her other nipple into his mouth and nibbled gently. He heard her sigh, and it was a sound of pure happiness.

"Jordan," he said against her skin. "Jordan, I love you."

"Touch me again, Conlean," she whispered urgently, wrapping her hand around his erection and squeezing gently.

A pulse of pleasure shot through him. He moaned.

Following her directions, he brought his hands down to the softness between her thighs and began to caress her.

"Right here," she said, directing his fingers to a small nub of flesh. When he touched it, she bit her lip and nodded. "Oh, God, yes."

His erection beginning to ache with need, he caressed her where she wanted, drawing little circles and then rubbing gently. She arched into him more violently, rhythmically, and suddenly he could take no more. He positioned himself over her and, looking deeply into her eyes, entered her with one smooth thrust. She cried out and clung to him, while he felt tremor after tremor rock his own body. Unable to stop himself, he started to thrust against her hips, and she rose to meet him each time, until suddenly she cried out his name and buried her face in his neck.

She held him tight and began to tremble against him, and the sensation of her moistness tightening over his erection was his undoing. A deep, almost painful pleasure welled up from inside and blasted through him, making him say her name over and over as he spent himself inside her. And when the last of the shuddering waves of pleasure left him, he held her tightly in his arms and asked himself how he had ever lived without her, without the joy she brought him.

Surrounded by furs and Conlean's strong arms, Jordan snuggled against his chest and wished the moment would never end. She felt so right, so complete, and so incredibly satisfied that she knew Conlean had always been her destiny; everything that had happened in her life had been leading her to this point, to him. Briefly she thought of Dennis, and recognized that she'd shared more intimacy with Conlean in one evening than she had during her entire marriage to her former husband.

Where once she wanted to return home, now she wouldn't leave Blackfell. The life Conlean had offered her was one of love and purpose. They would marry and work together on curing the plague. Once they'd found the cure, they could simply focus on loving each other, and exploring other possibilities that the combination of science and artistry presented.

He kissed her forehead and gathered her closer against him. She nuzzled his neck, then looked into his eyes, enjoying the clean smell of him and the tenderness that softened his face. "When did you fall in love with me?" she asked, a smile on her lips because she already knew the answer.

A long, shuddering sigh went through him, and he tightened his arms around her. "When I first saw your portrait."

Her smile widening, she knew she should press him for the details as to how they were going to solve all of the problems that still existed for them, but she didn't want to ruin their happiness, so she remained quiet. Conlean too said nothing. Instead, he loosened his hold on her and sat back far enough so he could trace her features with the tips of his fingers.

She looked at him with a lifted brow. "You were pretty good for a guy who'd never made love to a woman before," she teased.

His fingers wandered lower, down her neck and toward her breasts. "You made it easy for me. You told me what you like."

She grasped his hand and pressed it against her skin, over her heart. "I trust you, Conlean. With you, I'd do anything."

He put his arms around her again and held her close. "I only want to make you happy."

Warmth rushed through her at the sincerity in his voice. Sighing deeply, she snuggled against his naked body. "I wish I could just melt into you, so we'd never have to be apart. When do we have to go back?"

"I'm going to keep you here as long as I can," he murmured, arranging the fur around them. "I've been waiting for this moment for too damned long."

At the fervor in his voice, she pushed his hair back from his forehead, then dragged her fingers downward across his lips before settling them lightly against his chest. Although she didn't know exactly why, she felt the need to reassure him. "We'll have plenty more moments like this."

Rather than respond, he began to kiss her again; slow, deep kisses that stole her breath away. Soon their tongues were tangling together. Heat coiled deep inside her and she kissed him back, harder, her lips more demanding, until finally he broke away and ran his lips down her neck. Her breasts ached for his touch and her nipples hardened at the sensations she felt as he kissed them. When she wrapped her palm around his erection to caress him, he groaned low in his throat and buried himself deep inside her. Her body became a throbbing mass of need and she rose to meet every one of his thrusts until finally the ecstasy was upon her again and she collapsed against him with his name on her lips.

He reached his peak only seconds later, and the sensation of him pulsing inside her felt so good that waves of bliss washed through her and she shuddered. They were so perfect together; she thanked her lucky stars that she'd finally found someone she could trust and love without reservation. Exhausted, she snuggled next to him and drifted off to sleep, his male scent in her nostrils and the feel of his warm breath against her forehead.

"Jordan, wake up," Conlean said softly against her ear. "We have to go."

Jordan stirred in her sleep, her lips curved in a smile. Eyes still closed, she reached out and dug her fingers into his hair, sending chills down his spine. Conlean stared hungrily at her, trying to memorize every aspect of her face, because he knew he wouldn't see her again until after he'd made the proper arrangements and he claimed her at her presentation.

First he had to see Hawkwood, and explain what had happened between Jordan and himself. And then he would have to meet with his father. Guilt at the thought of having to tell the Patriarch that he'd fallen in love with the same woman the older man had planned to marry twisted inside him. And yet, there was no help for it. It had to be done. Afterward, he would have to publicly embarrass his father by insisting on an auction and buying his father's bride's contract, and for this he'd need Jordan's help.

Suddenly he realized her eyes were open. She was looking at him, a little furrow between her brows. "What's wrong, Conlean?"

He leaned down to kiss the furrow away. "It's getting late. We should head back. I wouldn't want anyone to know that you've been out all night."

"I don't give a damn if anyone knows."

"But I do." Slowly he pulled away from her and reached for his shirt, despite the quiet protest that his heart gave.

Grimacing, she shook her head. "Blackfell could give Victorian England a run for its money where society's rules are concerned."

"For both our sakes, we have to follow them. Once we're married, though, all rules are out the window." He handed her clothes to her.

Smiling, she pulled on her lacy underthings while he watched from beneath hooded lids. In his mind, he was planning out a sketch of this exact moment, a token of his love for her, one he'd keep private from the world. When she reached for her tunic and trousers, he shrugged on his own clothes, then stepped behind her to help her slip the tunic over her head. Together, they pulled on their shoes, and then her hand was in his and they were walking through the underground tunnels.

About a half hour later, they emerged into a city lit by pre-dawn light. Keeping to the shadows, he led Jordan back to the stable that held their horse. He collected the animal from a youth he didn't recognize and, after helping her mount, jumped into the saddle and began the trip back to the Gallery. While they traveled the more heavily used roads, Jordan kept herself at a discreet distance from him, but as soon as they moved onto the path that led through the fields and then to the woods outside of the Gallery, she nestled against him, the feel of her beautiful body driving everything but the thought of the pleasure they'd shared from his mind.

When at last they arrived at the Gallery and Conlean dismounted, he did so with an exquisite sense of both pain and relief: pain at the fact that he'd have to be parted from her, and relief that they would soon be married. Sticking to the least-traveled hallways, he escorted her to her rooms and steered her past the guard, who nodded at Conlean before averting his gaze.

She moved into her room and yawned. "Well, we had a close call in the basement, but in the end, I'd say the trip was successful, wouldn't you?"

He followed her in and shut the door behind him. "It was successful beyond belief."

"Come on over here and sit down with me," she invited, flopping onto the bed and patting the mattress next to her.

His smile became regretful. "I'd like to, but I have a lot of people to talk to, and things to set in motion, before I can claim you at your presentation. I also have one thing for you to do."

"What do you need? I'll do anything."

"At the presentation, your bridal contract will be read aloud. When my father is announced as your husband, you must make an objection to the union. You have to say that you'd like to have your contract auctioned. I'll take it from there."

"Object to the union, no problem. But what reason do I give for my objection?"

"Just say that you've become interested in another suitor and cannot marry my father in good conscience. That should be enough to force an auction."

"I'm a little frightened about this presentation," she admitted, her eyes wide. "Please make certain that you're the winner of the auction."

"Don't worry." He faced her resolutely, though inside, he did exactly what he'd told her not to do: worry. "I *will* win."

Chapter Twenty

After leaving Jordan in her room, Conlean went directly to Hawkwood's quarters and knocked urgently on the door. Almost a minute passed before it opened and Hawkwood, still in his sleeping robe, peered out at him.

"Artisan Conlean," he said gruffly, "I'm old and need my sleep. I hope you have a good reason for knocking on my door at daybreak."

"It's an emergency." Conlean pushed his way into the room and shut the door behind him.

His robe hanging loosely on his thin form, Hawkwood stared at Conlean. "What kind of emergency?"

"I've fallen in love with Jordan," Conlean said in a rush.

"Tell me something I don't know," Hawkwood invited in dry tones. "Only an idiot could fail to see that you've grown attached to her."

"I'm not *attached* to her. I *love* her."

The older man waved his hand in a dismissive gesture. "You'll get over it."

"And she loves me," Conlean added.

Hawkwood allowed his hand to drop. "This sounds a little more serious than I thought."

"We want to get married."

Hawkwood's gaze focused on him like a beam of light. "You're not serious, Artisan."

"I am."

"Do you realize the difficulties you will cause if you persist in this irrational, irresponsible behavior? If you steal your father's bride away from him, you'll insult him publicly. He could decide to ostracize you. You'll both be social outcasts. And you'll lose your ability to practice artistry if you marry a bride you painted and retrieved for someone else." Hawkwood paced away from Conlean and then back toward him. "Jordan was retrieved for your *father,* not *you.* For God's sake, tell me you're going to forget this attraction."

Conlean faced him squarely. "I'm not."

"You're not? Let me give you some reasons why you should!" Hawkwood began to jab at Conlean with his finger, trotting out several perfectly sound reasons why Conlean's love for Jordan, and her love for him, were going to cause no end of trouble for their scheme, for the Patriarch, and for the province of Blackfell itself. He went on for several minutes, and by the end of his tirade, he'd blamed Conlean for just about every evil that could befall mankind.

Conlean simply shrugged in reply. "Jordan and I are going to marry."

319

Abruptly Hawkwood's shoulders slumped. "I guess there's no talking either of you out of it."

"I'm afraid not," Conlean said, his voice firm.

"And you're willing to accept the fact that your father might send you into seclusion as punishment for stealing his bride? That you'll never again practice artistry at the Gallery?"

"I would rather be ostracized from society and never pick up a paintbrush again than have to give up Jordan. I've thought this thing through over and over again. My mind is made up."

"And Jordan—she accepts all this?"

"She does."

Hawkwood studied Conlean thoughtfully. They were both standing in the middle of his apartment, in a large room with a bed and a desk and little else. Hawkwood began pacing slowly around the bed, his forehead creased in thought for several moments until finally it smoothed. "If we can figure out a way to prevent his marriage to Jordan without turning it into a public insult, he might not ostracize you. In fact, he could very well reinstate you as heir apparent to the Patriarchy. There are many advantages to having you rule Blackfell as Patriarch."

"That has occurred to me," Conlean admitted. "I'm not very keen on taking on the responsibilities of the crown, but I'm willing to do it if I have Jordan at my side."

"Have you discussed with her what she must do?"

"She knows she has to reject my father as her groom and ask for an auction. Then all I have to do is purchase her contract."

"There will be other bidders at her auction," Hawkwood reminded him. "Men with more money than you. Women are too scarce to expect anything else."

Conlean's jaw tightened at the thought of Jordan being purchased by someone other than himself. "I have quite a bit of money saved. I hope it'll be enough."

"I have some money saved too, Artisan Conlean. I'd be willing to give it to you. You're a good cause." Hawkwood's half-smile slipped back into a frown. "But how do we accomplish your marriage to Jordan without insulting your father? What can we possibly say?"

"I'm not sure," Conlean said, feeling guilty as hell. "Maybe I should just be honest with him, tell him that Jordan and I have fallen in love."

Hawkwood eyed him doubtfully. "Love? Since when does love have anything to do with marriage? You need something more convincing than that."

"I'll try to come up with a good argument on my way to the Imperial Manor House," Conlean said. "I'm going to see him as soon as I leave here."

"What if he refuses to allow her to break her contract? She must have the bridegroom's agreement for a legal separation."

Conlean stared grimly at the Grand Artisan. "I hope I can convince him to let her go."

"See him at once, then," Hawkwood urged, "and return here afterward, so you can tell me how your meeting went."

Conlean nodded and was halfway out the door when he heard Hawkwood's murmured, "Congratulations, Artisan, on your impending marriage."

* * *

His interview with Hawkwood concluded, Conlean left the Gallery for the Patriarchal Manor House. Usually he walked, appreciating the five-mile trip through the woods and fields, but today, he'd taken one of the Gallery's fastest horses from the stable. His mission was too urgent for him to enjoy anything at all.

Throughout the trip, he thought of and then discarded many different ways to present his case to the Patriarch. He wished he could give some solid, logical reasons why he had to marry Jordan rather than his father, some political or business necessity that the Patriarch, with his logical mind, could accept without argument. And yet, the true reason why he wanted to marry Jordan seemed time-worn and, in fact, melodramatic:

There's no other woman in the world like her, Father. I fell in love with her. I couldn't help it. And she fell in love with me. Now I can't bear the thought of spending a single day without her. What did that poet once say? The heart wants what the heart wants?

It all came down to love, pure and simple.

Still, as he cantered down the road leading to the Manor House, his horse clattering across stones embedded in moss, he wondered if perhaps love *was* a good enough reason.

As a child, he'd experienced years of loneliness, and he'd been taught that although people lived together, everyone was basically alone. How could it be any other way? People were separated by the physical barriers of flesh and blood and ruled by a survival instinct that encouraged them to place themselves above everyone else.

In the end, he'd assumed he could only count on himself.

But now, he began to see that he might have been wrong about that. Yes, the physical barrier of flesh and blood did keep people separate from each other, but maybe love could bridge the gap.

Conlean turned the horse past the tall grass that the Imperial gardeners had woven together to form a hedge and approached the Manor House at a walk. Forehead creased in thought, he dismounted and handed the horse's reins to a youth who'd come out to greet him.

For too long the men of Blackfell had been marrying for every reason but love. Though they counted themselves lucky to have a wife and family, he suspected that those same men were missing out on the most basic, fulfilling, and precious of all human experiences: a deep, loving connection with a spouse that bridged the physical barriers of flesh and blood until the two became one.

This was the kind of connection he wanted to seek out with Jordan.

And with Jordan, he knew it was within his reach.

He knocked on the door.

Willmen, looking very regal in his high-pointed starched white shirt and navy pants, swung the door open a few moments later. "Artisan Conlean. Come in."

"Did you get my message that I'd be coming?" he asked as he followed Willmen in.

Willmen nodded. "We did. The Patriarch is most eager to meet with you. Indeed, he's sitting in the resolving pavilion, waiting for you."

"Good," he said, a tight feeling in his gut. A lot depended on the outcome of this meeting. "Take me to him."

Willmen directed Conlean toward the receiving pavilion with a gesture, and Conlean took the lead. Having grown up in the Manor House, he knew exactly where to go, and found his father reclining on a couch in the viewing room.

"Conlean, how good to see you," his father said as he walked into the room.

"Hello, Father." Conlean walked up to him and they clasped hands for a second or two before Conlean sat down and studied his father.

The older man appeared to lack the vigor he'd once displayed. His brown robe, edged with copper, brought out a yellow tinge in his skin, and his cheeks looked drawn. Suddenly Conlean hated himself for having to bring the clearly exhausted man down even more. Still, when he glanced at his mother's picture, which hung on the wall, and saw the gentleness and empathy in her eyes, he knew that she would want him to pursue exactly the course he'd planned out.

"You look tired," Conlean said. "Keeping late nights?"

"It's the damned FFA," his father groused. "They're always starting trouble and making demands. Now they want me to guarantee that at least one son from every family will have a wife. What will they want next?"

"No doubt, for every man to have a wife."

His father barked out a laugh. "No doubt about it! I've heard that they've the nerve to plan a meeting the same night as my bride's presentation, in an old warehouse on the docks. I'm going to make sure more than a few of my Imperial guards are there to attend."

"What will you do with them once you catch them?"

"Imprison them, of course. For treason. Anyone who plots against the Patriarchy will find himself in the bowels of the palace very quickly." His father rubbed his eyes. "This aggravation is going to kill me, and then Blackfell will be left without a Patriarch. Jordan had better give me a son quickly."

"Jordan is the reason I'm here."

"Oh. She's being presented soon, right?" His father shook his head. "You'd think I'd know when my own bride is being presented. I apologize, Conlean. I know you've been working hard to prepare her for me. I've been so busy, though. No time for anything."

"Yes, she is being presented. In two days." Conlean took a deep breath. "We need to talk about her."

His father frowned. "Talk about her? Why? I thought you said everything was going well."

"There's a problem."

"Problem? What kind of problem?"

"Well . . ." Conlean took another deep breath. "I've fallen in love with her."

"You've *what?*"

"I love her."

The Patriarch stood up from the couch. His face had gone gray. "Are you telling me that you've fallen in love with *my* bride?"

Conlean stiffened his spine. "I have."

"Good God." The older man turned away. "How could you do this to me? Me, your own father? Your own flesh and blood?"

"I'm sorry, Father," Conlean said, a cold, hard knot of misery in his gut. "I didn't want to fall in love with her. I couldn't help it. She's . . . wonderful. Beautiful."

"This is my fault," his father said in loud tones. "I should have married you off years ago. But the Gallery—they took my son from me. I couldn't have helped you, even if I'd wanted to. I can't purchase a bride for you. You have to purchase her yourself, with your own money. It's the rule. You understand that, don't you?"

"Of course I do."

"You mustn't have any more contact with *my* bride, of course," the Patriarch continued in a more conversational tone. "And once I'm married, you'll have to stay away from the Manor House and the Imperial Palace. If I need you, I'll come to the Gallery—"

"She loves me too," Conlean broke in, feeling sick over the pain he was inflicting on his father.

The Patriarch froze, his gaze riveted on Conlean.

"I'm so sorry," Conlean hurried to say. "I don't know how it happened."

"Are you telling me that you . . . and Jordan . . . are in love with each other?"

Conlean didn't answer. He couldn't. The lump in his throat wouldn't let him talk.

Shoulders slumping, the Patriarch returned to the couch and sat down heavily. "Have you slept with her?"

"Yes," he answered, his voice shaking despite his determination to remain firm.

"Ah, Conlean, you've betrayed me terribly," his father said in soft tones.

326

"I know." He looked down at the ground. "I'm sorry."

His father shrugged. "You can't see her again, of course. I'll have her brought to the Manor House immediately. She'll stay here and only return to the Gallery for her presentation. Later, you'll thank me for intervening and preventing you from throwing your life as an Artisan away."

Conlean stared at the older man. Shock filled him. "You still want to marry her? After all I've told you?"

"I'm an old man, Conlean. I need an heir right away. Yes, I'm still going to marry her. I have no choice."

"But you don't love her. I do. I want to marry her."

His father shook his head. His face, which had looked gray, began to take on a red tone. "You're an idiot, Conlean. Love means nothing in our world. We don't marry for love; we marry to have children. Why would you place value on something that doesn't last? Love is like fog: it rolls in, leaves you stumbling around for a while, and then dissipates with a little light. Forget about Jordan, Conlean, and continue with your artistry."

With a sinking feeling in the pit of his stomach, Conlean shook his head resolutely. "I'm marrying Jordan, and I'll accept the consequences of my actions."

"Do you think if you marry her, I'll embrace you as the future Patriarch with open arms?" his father demanded, his voice rising. "Because I promise you, Conlean, if you don't drop this, I'll do everything in my power to block you from inheriting the Patriarchy upon my death ... including fathering another son with a new bride. A bride painted by Grand Artisan Tobias, perhaps."

"I don't want the Patriarchy," Conlean insisted, although inside, he knew that the power of the Patriarchy could bring him a lot closer to curing the plague. "I just want Jordan. To you, love means nothing. It used to mean nothing to me too. But since I've met Jordan, everything is different."

His father snorted.

"I've been lonely all my life." Conlean tried again, a touch of desperation in his voice. "But with Jordan, I don't feel lonely anymore. I feel hopeful. And I know I've just scratched the surface of what could exist between us."

"Son, you need a visit to the Counselor. He'll set you straight."

"The Counselor can't say anything to change my mind."

"Well, then, I guess we *do* have a problem." The Patriarch's voice was heavy. "What do you want from me, Conlean?"

"I want you to set Jordan's contract aside so I can buy it from you."

His father's eyebrows rose. "If I set her contract aside, it'll have to go up for auction. That's the rule. How do you know other men won't bid against you?"

"I'm sure they will," Conlean agreed. "However, I have a fairly sizable fortune. I'll spend it all if I have to."

"And if I refuse to set her contract aside? What then?"

"She'll invoke her right to put up her contract for auction."

"I won't be permitted to bid on it, of course." The Patriarch frowned. "You appear to have everything well thought out, Conlean. Do you have anything else you'd like to say before I make my decision?"

Conlean shook his head.

The Patriarch sat back against the cushions. "In that case, I tell you now that I've listened to all your arguments, and I've decided that I will not surrender my bride to you. She'll marry me, two days hence, at her presentation. I'll also send a footman to the Gallery demanding that you be relieved of her care. I do this as much for you as for myself."

The sinking feeling in the pit of Conlean's stomach worsened. "But—"

"If she invokes her right to break her contract," his father continued inexorably, "then you may, of course, bid on it. But if you do, you'll not set foot in any of my houses again, for any reason. Do you understand?"

Conlean bowed his head. "I'm sorry. I deeply regret hurting you this way."

Slowly his father rose from the couch. "Until her presentation, then."

Chapter Twenty-one

Jordan spent the next two days in a whirlwind of activity. Mr. Vogler the dressmaker stopped by her room several times and marched about, giving orders regarding her clothes and her personal care to the page who appeared at her bedside every morning. The page also walked with her on the grounds in the afternoon and schooled her on etiquette in the evening. The feeling that she was preparing for a beauty pageant continued to dog her.

Of Conlean, she saw nothing. He'd told her, of course, that she wouldn't be seeing him until her presentation, but she'd been hoping he might find the time to stop by and say hello, just for a moment. She missed him terribly, even though it had only been a day since she'd last seen him. Memories of the moments she'd spent with him constantly occupied her thoughts, and naturally she tortured herself with doubt . . . *had he changed his mind?*

Did he still love her?

Telling herself that she could trust Conlean, she followed Vogler and the page's directions and didn't complain once, not even in the hours directly before her presentation, when Vogler and his assistants came to dress her and had her standing for extended periods of time. They kept her from all the mirrors, refusing to allow her to see what they were up to, and when they finally stood her before the full-length oval mirror, she sucked in a breath at the sight of the beautiful, sophisticated woman staring back at her.

Now, as she faced Hawkwood, who'd come to collect her, she realized that her hands were shaking. Putting on a brave face, she took his arm and allowed him to escort her from the room.

"Are you ready for what you must do, Jordan?" Hawkwood asked, looking very dignified in a black velvet robe, his beard trimmed and his gray hair carefully combed.

"Let's talk about what I must do," she said. "I have to say that I wish to invoke my right to have my contract auctioned, right?"

"That's correct."

"How will I know when to say it?"

"You'll know. The Master of Ceremonies will ask if anyone has an objection to the fulfillment of the contract. After you invoke your right to auction, the bidding will begin."

She grimaced as they made their way down the stairs and into the central hall. "How many men will be bidding, do you think?"

"Plenty, I'm certain. But don't worry; Artisan Conlean has a sizable fortune."

"How is Conlean?" she asked anxiously. "I haven't seen him for two days."

"He's working very hard to make certain this evening's presentation goes as you both wish," Hawkwood replied, his face grim. "You do realize how much he's sacrificed in order to bid on your bridal contract?"

"I do, and I'm thankful for it." She lowered her voice to a whisper. "I'm hoping that after we're married, we can put our heads together and try to come up with a solution to the plague."

"That *is* the reason we brought you here." Hawkwood studied her with a piercing gaze. "The Artisan has damaged his relationship with his father by insisting on marrying you, so you must be prepared for the two men to be at odds this evening."

"Thanks for the warning," she managed, wilting beneath his stare.

They walked outside and started down a path that led toward one of the larger buildings near the perimeter of the grounds. Twilight had fallen, and opaque lanterns illuminated both the path and the front entrance of the building they were heading toward. In fact, the building at the end of the path blazed with light, and as she watched, a cart pulled up to its entrance to let out several women dressed in colorful fabrics and draped in jewels. Their spouses followed close behind.

"Is that where we're going?" she asked, indicating the lighted building.

"Yes. That's our reception hall, where all presentations are held."

"Who exactly comes to these presentations?"

"It depends on the groom. Usually, the artisan who

painted the portrait and the groom's family attend the presentation. Since this is the Patriarch's presentation, though, we'll be seeing all of the upper echelon of society, including the Patriarch's advisers. Most of the artisans in the Gallery are attending, too."

She swallowed. "Great. The entire kingdom is turning out to see me put up for auction."

"It won't be so bad. It certainly can't be worse than what you've already been through these past weeks."

They said no more until they reached the reception building and moved to a little waiting room stocked with all kinds of food and drink. Luxurious velvet pillows in rich colors lay strewn about the sofas and chairs, and a crystal chandelier alight with candles hung from the ceiling. Hawkwood chose a straight-backed chair and sat down, while Jordan selected a couch. She couldn't relax against the pillows, though. Instead, she perched on the edge of her seat and nervously smoothed her gown. Hawkwood urged her to eat, and she did manage to nibble on a cake until her queasy stomach insisted she put it down.

Somewhere, music began to play. She didn't recognize the song, but it had a formal air to it.

Moments later, a man stuck his head into the waiting room and informed them that the time had come. Hawkwood nodded and stood. "Take my arm, Jordan."

She did as he'd asked, leaning on him as much as she dared. "Will you walk with me?"

"Yes, I'm giving you away. Normally, the Artisan who painted the bride's portrait gives her away, but we've received a directive from the Patriarch that I'm to do so in your case."

"Giving me away?" She wrinkled her nose. "Sounds like I'm at a wedding ceremony from my own time."

"You will be married when you leave here tonight," Hawkwood agreed.

A sense of unreality washed over her. *Married!* No one had told her that this presentation was a marriage ceremony. She felt dizzy at the thought. Then, remembering she would need all her wits about her this evening, she told herself that she had better get it together and accept reality before she did something stupid.

She and Hawkwood approached a set of wooden doors. The music swelled from some unknown location above them. Two pages dressed in velvet finery swung the doors open to admit them to the presentation hall, and then she and the Grand Artisan were walking through the portal.

Ahead, a wooden platform lay in the middle of a room that reminded her of a high-class boxing ring. Velvet and mahogany seats rose up on all sides from the wooden platform, guaranteeing that many people could attend, and all would have an excellent view. The people sitting there halted their conversations and turned to look at her as she entered. The music urged her onward. Two men standing on the platform bowed in her direction, while Hawkwood marched her at a stately pace toward them. One man looked older and was dressed in finer clothes than anyone else in the building. His gaze fastened hungrily on her face.

The Patriarch, she thought. She could see Conlean's resemblance to him in the firm line of his jaw and his green eyes. He was a handsome man, his gray hair lending him an air of authority.

The other man wore a white and gold outfit that reminded her of the kind she'd once seen the Pope wearing on television. He was undoubtedly the Master of Ceremonies who would marry them.

Two small wooden stairs led up to the platform. She climbed them slowly, aware that the shoes on her feet had heels higher than any she'd worn in a while. She paused to glance around her.

In the first row of seats, all the men wore tailored black suits with red sashes.

Her gaze drifted to the man directly to her left.

Brown eyes, a smarmy smile . . .

Adviser Erickson!

She hesitated next to him, and then she smelled it: that same perfume she'd smelled before. She recognized the scent immediately, because it had been haunting her for days. The guard had smelled of it on the night someone broke into her room and rifled through her book about the plague.

The suspicion that Adviser Erickson had been directly involved in drugging her guard with a sleeping draught took hold in her.

She began to get a very bad feeling about the evening ahead.

Somehow she forced herself to move, returning his smile with a stiff nod before stepping onto the platform. She could sense the weight of a hundred gazes on her. Never before had she felt so exposed. She swept the audience with a glance and saw Grand Artisan Tobias in the second row, grinning at her like a madman. Shivering, she looked away. Just then, the music lowered in volume, and then both the Patriarch and the

Master of Ceremonies walked to her side and bowed. She curtsied as she'd been instructed, her gaze locking with the Patriarch's for a moment before sliding away.

A movement behind the Patriarch caught her attention. There, near the doorway, sat a man dressed in a black suit similar to the ones worn by the advisers, but without the red sash. He nodded at her, his green gaze like a beacon that cut through the darkness. Her heart leaping, she nodded back, noting that he no longer wore his Artisan's robes.

Gathering strength from Conlean's presence, she faced the Master of Ceremonies bravely, and placed her hand in the Patriarch's as the Master directed. Squeezing her hand, the Patriarch bent his head close to hers and murmured, "I wish, my dear, that I could have met you sooner. Much trouble would have been avoided. But we'll survive this and, after we're married, you'll forget about my son because you'll be occupied in bringing up the future Patriarch of Blackfell."

She swallowed. Clearly Conlean's father didn't intend to surrender without a fight. Her fear that the night would be a bad one intensified.

The Master of Ceremonies motioned with his left hand, and the music stopped altogether. With his right hand he picked up a large leather tome and began to read from it, his voice droning on about contracts and marriages and what could be expected from each party.

She swayed a little on her feet as he spoke. She was starting to feel very dizzy. She didn't know if the stress of the evening had caused it, or if the heat gathering in the room was getting to her. When the Master of Ceremonies paused, however, and asked if anyone in the room had an objection to the fulfillment of the contract, she nearly fainted.

She sensed more than saw Conlean's urgent gaze on her. His father was looking at her too, a pleased smile on his face. But her tongue refused to work, and the room had started to spin. She felt as if she'd gotten caught in a bad dream. In another second her chance to invoke her right to auction would pass, and then she would end up married to the wrong man . . .

"I would like to voice an objection," a male voice suddenly announced from the first row.

Everyone turned to look at the man who'd objected: Adviser Erickson.

She shot a glance at Conlean. He was frowning.

"Approach the stage, please," the Master of Ceremonies intoned.

Adviser Erickson wore a serious look as he climbed the two steps and then walked past her and the Patriarch to stand before the Master of Ceremonies. The Patriarch bent a furious glare on Erickson as he passed by.

The Master lifted an eyebrow. "What is the nature of your objection, Adviser?"

"I have a document I wish to show you," he said in ringing tones.

"What kind of document is it?"

"It is the acknowledgments page from a book that the bride herself authored."

Whispers rippled through the audience. Jordan felt her knees go weak. She almost stumbled.

The Master cleared his throat, then asked, "And why

does this page create a need for an objection to her contract?"

"The page contains a biography of Jordan Connor, and includes a statement that she is infertile." He paused and stared at the Patriarch. "Jordan Connor is incapable of having children."

Jordan pressed a hand against her heart. The room became gray around the edges. Erickson stepped forward and held her arm to steady her. His grasp felt possessive.

Simultaneously, a gasp rippled through the gathering, and suddenly, everyone was talking about the gravity of the crime, and how shocking that Jordan had signed the contract knowing she couldn't bear children, and how terrible that the Patriarch himself would have to suffer through this. The commentary grew so loud that the Master of Ceremonies had to shout to quiet everyone down.

Erickson leaned so close to her ear that she could feel his warm breath brush across her skin. "Are you all right, Jordan?"

"Yes. Let me go," she whispered faintly.

He complied, and the Master of Ceremonies begged everyone to be quiet.

"What kind of book, exactly, did my bride author?" The Patriarch demanded when silence reigned once more.

Jordan looked at Erickson. He was holding a virtual axe to her neck and he knew it. She waited for him to swing, and make her head roll.

But he didn't. Instead, he said, "Jordan is the author

of a book on caring for young children. It was called *And Baby Makes Three: Caring for Infants.*"

She swiveled to stare at him in shock. Why had he spared her?

As soon as she thought of the question, though, she knew the answer. Erickson supported the bride retrieval system and was probably even making money off it in some way. Just like Grand Artisan Tobias and everyone else with a vested interest in the Gallery and the bride retrieval system, he didn't want a cure, and didn't want anyone knowing that she might be able to find one.

The Patriarch took the page from Erickson and scanned it. "I need to have this acknowledgments page authenticated. Is a Librarian present tonight?"

A little man with glasses stood up and made his way to the stage. He took the page from the Patriarch and brought a little tool out of his jacket. He examined the page both with and without the tool, then returned it to the Patriarch. "It is authentic."

The Patriarch gave her a sad smile. "I'm afraid that Conlean is going to get his wish, Jordan." He turned to the Master of Ceremonies. "I object to the fulfillment of this contract. The bride in question has lied about her ability to bear me a son, the most basic requirement for any woman brought to Blackfell. I wish her contract to be put up for auction."

"Who will want her?" someone from the audience shouted.

"I do," Conlean yelled, his voice strong and true.

Another gasp went up from the audience.

"You cannot bid on your father's bride," Grand Artisan Tobias declared, standing up. "Artisans may not marry any woman they, themselves, have painted and retrieved. It's a conflict of interest and against the rules. If you persist in this disastrous course of action, I'll have no choice but to banish you from the Gallery. Are you renouncing your status as Artisan?"

"I am." Conlean left his seat and started down toward the stage.

Grand Artisan Tobias pointed a finger at Conlean. "Then as of now, you are officially banned from the Gallery and forbidden to practice artistry in the future. There are no exceptions."

"So noted," the Master of Ceremonies intoned. "Artisan Conlean will be permitted to buy this bride's contract at its original purchase price. All proceeds will go to the Patriarch."

"Wait a moment," Erickson said. "If the Patriarch is putting aside her contract, then it must go up for auction, no?"

The Master of Ceremonies eyed him closely. "She is infertile, Adviser, and is quite lucky to have even one man willing to buy her contract. I don't see the point of an auction."

Erickson slid a glance toward Jordan. Something wolfish glittered in his eyes. "I wish the opportunity to bid on her contract as well, and I raise my bid two parts over the original purchase price."

The audience, at this point, had gone completely silent.

Jordan shivered, recalling Conlean's story about Erickson's first wife, and how she'd disappeared without a trace. Did Erickson have the same kind of future planned for her? And who would really care if he did? Everyone but Conlean and Hawkwood considered her worthless, a burden with nothing to offer anyone. . . .

Conlean reached the stage and squared off in front of Erickson. "I raise my bid four parts over the original purchase price."

"Six parts."

"Eight parts." Conlean scowled.

Erickson wiped a bead of sweat that was running down his temple. "I raise my bid fifteen parts over the original purchase price."

Hushed whispers broke out across the audience. The Master of Ceremonies' eyebrows had nearly climbed into his forehead. He stepped forward. "Do you understand how much money your are bidding, Adviser? Don't forget, she can't bear you any children."

"Fifteen parts," Erickson insisted.

"I need a guarantor to support Adviser Erickson's bid to purchase this contract for fifteen times its original price."

Grand Artisan Tobias rose. "I guarantee the Adviser's bid."

Jordan stared at the two of them. Erickson and Tobias appeared to be as thick as thieves.

"All right, then, a bid of fifteen parts from Adviser Erickson. Artisan Conlean . . . that is, Conlean of Arador, do you have another bid?"

Conlean sent an agonized glance her way. "Sixteen parts."

The Master of Ceremonies shook his head. "I need a second to support Conlean of Arador's bid to purchase this contract at sixteen times its original price."

Hawkwood stepped forward. "I support his bid."

Goggle-eyed, the Master swiveled to Erickson. "Adviser? Another bid?"

The Adviser smiled slowly. "Twenty parts."

The audience gasped, then grew so silent that the room nearly echoed with it.

Grand Artisan Tobias stood up. "I support his bid."

"Twenty parts. I don't think I've ever heard of a bride going for this kind of money," the Master uttered. "Conlean of Arador, would you like to increase your bid?"

Grimacing, Conlean opened his mouth, then closed it again. His eyes appeared dark, tortured.

The Patriarch stepped between the two bidders and faced Erickson. "My son doesn't have the necessary funds to purchase this contract and he knows it. The bidding is over. Her contract is sold to Adviser Erickson. May he enjoy her in good health."

Jordan swayed. Her knees gave way and she started to collapse. Erickson quickly stepped forward to grab her elbow and keep her upright, claiming her in that one simple gesture.

A second later Conlean stalked toward Erickson. "Get your hands off her. I won't let you add another victim to your list." He grabbed at Erickson, clearly planning to break the Adviser's hold on her arm, but then the Patriarch and Hawkwood were between the two men, with Hawkwood restraining Conlean and whispering urgently in his ear.

When Conlean appeared to have calmed down some, Hawkwood grabbed him by the arm and half-dragged him away. Conlean resisted long enough to send one burning glance toward Erickson before Hawkwood managed to hustle him out of the room.

"Due to the extraordinary nature of this presentation," Erickson told the Master of Ceremonies, his attention still on Conlean, "I would like to take my bride back to my house and complete the ceremony there, in the morning. With your permission, of course."

The Master of Ceremonies nodded. "An understandable request, granted. Just remember, you aren't truly married until the ceremony is completed."

Nausea gathered in Jordan's stomach. She thought she might be sick.

The Adviser tightened his grip on her arm. "You're mine now, Jordan," he whispered. "We're going to have a lot of fun together, you and I. You may not like it at first, but you'll grow to enjoy it."

Jordan collapsed completely.

Erickson scooped her up into his arms and hurried her outside to a waiting cart. He put her on the seat and jumped up next to her. She fell back against the cart, her mind spinning, her stomach churning. He spared her an annoyed glance before demanding that his driver take them to his estate immediately.

The waves of nausea caught up with Jordan as soon as the cart began to move. The perfume smell on Erickson that she had earlier recognized near her room now enfolded her like the stench of decay. She leaned over the side of the cart and was sick. Erickson swore when he saw what she was doing, and when she finished, he informed her that if he ever saw her vomiting again, he would lock her in her room for a year.

His threat cleared away the fog that had been gathering in her brain. Suddenly she needed answers. "Someone drugged my guard and broke into my room a while ago. That was you, wasn't it? I know it was you because I remember your aftershave, or cologne, or whatever it is that you wear."

"It isn't aftershave, but soap, made from night jasmine that the Counselor grows on his estate," he informed her. "The flower only blooms at night and supposedly has restorative powers. And as far as my being the one to break into your room, you're right. You see, I don't like to hire people to do my dirty work. I *like* dirty work, so I do it myself."

"How did you even know I had the book in my room?" They were traveling very quickly through the countryside, and Jordan held on to the sides of the cart to prevent herself from touching Erickson in even the slightest way.

Erickson sighed. "Rumors had begun to circulate about a woman who would be brought to Blackfell, one who could supposedly cure the plague. We wanted to make sure that this woman didn't do anything to disrupt our system of bride retrieval, so I went to your room to see if *you* were that woman. Sheer luck led me to stumble across the book you'd been reading, and I stole the acknowledgments page. We needed evidence against you that the Patriarch would accept, in order to prevent your marriage to him."

She hadn't even realized that the page was missing. "Who's *we?*" she asked.

He shrugged. "The Counselor, Grand Artisan Tobias, and I are all working hard to make sure the Gallery and our system of bride retrieval stays in place."

"You must make quite a profit from it." She suddenly felt very tired. "You know that curing the plague would be the best outcome for the people of Blackfell, and yet you choose to perpetuate a system that makes men suffer simply because that system turns a pretty profit. You disgust me, Erickson."

"Good. That will make training you more enjoyable."

She shuddered. "Why didn't you tell everyone that I had authored a book on the plague, and not a book on infant care?"

"We didn't want anyone thinking even for a moment that a cure could be found. As you pointed out, more than a few people want a cure, and if we revealed your knowledge on the subject, the demand for a cure could turn a few rabble-rousers into revolutionaries with an entire kingdom behind them."

"You're talking about the FFA," she said.

Their cart turned onto a gravel drive. In the distance, a mansion loomed on the horizon, the lights in its windows casting a sickly yellow glow that did little to penetrate the night.

"We're home, and I'm tired," Erickson said with a yawn. "We'll finish the ceremony tomorrow, and then we'll begin."

Begin what? she wondered.

The cart rolled to a stop outside the front door. Erickson jumped out and muttered to a footman on his way inside, "Get her out of the cart and upstairs to my first wife's bedroom."

The footman silently helped her down and slung a lap blanket over her shoulders when he saw she was shivering, but the blanket did little to banish the fear that had chilled her blood.

Chapter Twenty-two

Conlean paced in Hawkwood's apartment like a man possessed. The Grand Artisan stood nearby, trying to soothe him and insisting that all might not yet be lost, but Conlean didn't hear him. He wasn't about to listen to platitudes at that moment. He knew only one thing: that Adviser Erickson, suspected of killing his first wife, had just purchased Jordan's contract and had walked off with the one person Conlean held more dear than his own life.

He had to think. He had to come up with some way to save her, fast. And yet, only the idea that he shouldn't have taken her from her own time in the first place kept running through his head.

"I shouldn't have brought her here," he said aloud.

"You can't blame yourself." Hawkwood tried to shove a glass of amber into his hand, but Conlean wanted nothing to do with drink. "We couldn't have known this would happen. And our cause was good. We need a revolution, Conlean. You know that. Unfortunately the FFA isn't strong enough to force a change, and too many Advisers who profit from the bride retrieval system are fighting hard to keep it in place. We had to do something to help—"

"The FFA," Conlean said softly. "Families for All."

Hawkwood eyed him quizzically. "Yes, the FFA."

"That's who I need." A plan was forming in Conlean's mind. "The FFA."

"What?"

"I'm going to the FFA," he announced abruptly. "Tonight. Now. They're holding a meeting at an old warehouse on the docks. I'm going to find that meeting place and enlist their aid."

"How did you know about their meeting?"

"My father is planning a surprise raid on the warehouse. He's hoping to catch and imprison a few of the members."

Hawkwood's face paled. "Assuming that you arrive at the meeting before your father's guards, what do you plan on asking them to do for you?"

"They're going to help me kidnap Jordan. And this time I'm not going to lose her."

"Conlean, if you do this, you'll be treading on the ground of complete and overt treason. No one will be able to help you if you're caught, and if you're lucky, your father will imprison you. If Tobias has his way, you'll be executed. At least now, although you may not be in your father's good graces, you still have many privileges that place you in a position to help our cause—"

"I don't give a tinker's damn about the cause. I'm going to rescue Jordan, and I'm leaving now."

"Well, in that case, I think I can help you out," Hawkwood murmured. "I know the exact location of the FFA's meeting. It's in the warehouse on Sonobe Street. Do you know which one that is?"

Conlean stared at him. "Are you a member of the FFA, Grand Artisan?"

The older man smiled grimly. "Let's just say I'm a . . . consultant to the group. If you leave now, you just might get there before your father's guards do."

Aware that he might not see Hawkwood again, Conlean paused long enough to shake the older man's hand; then he was running for the stable, with Hawkwood's "Good luck, Artisan," echoing in his head. In less than ten minutes he had selected and saddled the fastest mount the Gallery possessed and was tearing down the path for Sonobe Street and the men who could help him. He only hoped he reached them in time.

The full moon lit the landscape almost as well as a lantern and helped speed him along as he reached the main thoroughfare leading into the city. Aware that more than a few travelers were shouting at him as he passed by at a breakneck pace, kicking up dust, he galloped across the bridge over the rice fields and pelted down along the docks until he came to Sonobe Street. There, he stopped and dismounted, tying his horse to a post before walking over to the warehouse.

The building appeared dark and dilapidated. Conlean approached the closest door and tried the knob. It turned easily, but as he tried to open the door, it swung crazily on one hinge. Inside, broken pieces of glass and rotting timbers lay in heaps that spoke of years of neglect. He began to wonder if the FFA's meeting place had been changed.

And yet, a slice of orange light coming from beneath another door gave him hope. He approached the door and discovered this one was far from dilapidated. Quite solid-looking, it didn't open when he turned the knob. He rattled the door on its hinges and quickly realized that he wouldn't get in unless someone opened it for him.

So he knocked.

"Name, please." The voice came from the other side of the door.

"Conlean of Arador."

"One moment."

"Wait," he hissed. "Go and tell whoever's in charge that the Patriarch's guards are on their way right now to raid this warehouse. You have to leave if you want to escape prison."

"One moment." The voice seemed unperturbed.

Nearly a minute passed before another voice spoke to him from behind the door, this one deeper, with a note of authority in it. "Why are you giving us this information?"

"I need your help," Conlean answered. "I need it very badly, and I need it now. I offer the information in exchange."

"How do we know you're not trying to lure us out into the open, where your father's guards can capture or imprison us?"

"Send one person out," Conlean suggested. "Look

around. Check my story. But do it quickly. We may not have much time."

"You had better not be lying to me, Son of Arador," the deep voice said, and then the door opened just enough to let a man out, then closed again.

Conlean faced the owner of the deep voice. The other man appeared to be about his own age, but stood six inches taller, with well-defined muscles and scars that suggested tough battles he had fought . . . and won. Some strong emotion—anger, maybe—had drawn deep lines in the man's face. Still, his blue eyes were clear and honest-looking.

"Rourke, Son of Colinswood," Conlean said matter-of-factly, abruptly recognizing the man as a youth who had once studied with him at the Gallery, before he disappeared one night, never to be found again. They'd all assumed he'd met with foul play.

"Son of Arador." The other man assessed Conlean closely. "You're carrying no weapons?"

"No."

"Come with me."

Together, Conlean and Rourke walked through the warehouse until they reached the point where Conlean had entered. On silent feet and with catlike grace, Rourke scanned the rest of the warehouse and the street outside, until, evidently satisfied, he turned back to Conlean and studied him again.

"I can see you've brought no one with you, so I know that I can trust you that far. Still, how did you find out about the raid this evening?"

"My father mentioned it during a conversation," Conlean replied.

"And why are you telling me this, Artisan?"

"I'm telling you this because you and the FFA are the only ones who can help me, and I need to keep you out of prison until you do."

The other man hesitated a split second before asking, "Exactly what kind of help do you need?"

"I want you to help me kidnap another man's wife."

Rourke grew very still, and then let out a small sigh. "You want us to help you kidnap a woman."

"I've heard you're very good at it—" Conlean murmured, stopping in mid-sentence when a movement down the street caught his attention. He saw the flash of a silver gun barrel in the moonlight and turned to Rourke. "I think we have a problem."

Rourke followed Conlean's gaze and abruptly hunkered down. "Time to leave. Follow me."

He started off in a direction away from the door with the orange glow.

Conlean stayed close to the other man. "What about the rest of the FFA? Aren't they still downstairs?"

"They're already gone. They left through one of the secret tunnels beneath the city as soon as you mentioned the word *raid*."

"Why didn't you leave with them?"

"Because I wanted to hear what you had to say, and I knew you were sympathetic to our cause. Hawkwood has mentioned you before."

Impressed, Conlean followed Rourke out of the building. Leaving the warehouse and the Imperial guards behind, they hurried through the streets until they reached a small apartment building in one of the poorer sections of the city.

"I thought you were dead," Conlean said. "No one's seen you or mentioned your name since you left the Gallery."

"I found better things to do with my time," Rourke offered in an offhand way. "I've maintained my connection with Hawkwood, though."

"How long have you been a member of the FFA?"

"For many years now." Rourke didn't elaborate. Instead he brought Conlean through a bug-infested hallway that stood in direct contrast with the much cleaner apartment they entered.

Inside the apartment, three men awaited, all of them as worn and determined-looking as Rourke. They all deferred to Rourke, making it clear they thought of him as their leader, and gathered around the table where he sat down.

"I'd trust these three men with my life," Rourke said, and then introduced the men one by one. Conlean reciprocated by introducing himself and explaining the plan he and Hawkwood had hatched to bring Jordan to Blackfell, so she might cure the plague. To his surprise, he discovered that Rourke and his men already knew many of the plan's details. They hadn't yet heard about Erickson, though, and how the Adviser had stolen Jordan right out from under his nose.

"So you want us to go and kidnap her from Erickson," Rourke said, summing it all up.

"We have to do it now, before Erickson harms her in some way," he agreed. "Since you know about Hawkwood's plan, you know how important Jordan is to our cause. She might possibly find a cure to the plague, but she won't be able to investigate it as long as she's Erickson's wife. Once we free her, she and I will go into hiding, and work on the cure in secret. Will you help me?"

Rourke looked at his men and, clearly noting their nearly imperceptible nods, he agreed. "We leave now."

Finalizing their plan and riding to Erickson's estate took only a few hours, but every moment that passed was an agonizing one for Conlean. He kept imagining Erickson's hands on Jordan, marring her soft creamy flesh, frightening her, making her cry. Or worse. When the time came to slip into the house itself as they'd planned, he nearly slumped with relief.

Their features hidden by bandannas tied around their heads, Rourke and his men immediately moved to subdue the strongest members of the household and corral them in Erickson's study. Erickson, for his part, was discovered in his bed and promptly hog-tied, while Conlean ran from room to room, searching for Jordan. When he finally found her, she was in a giant four-poster bed, sleeping, her face swollen from crying.

He immediately put his arms around her and held her close. "Jordan," he whispered, "tell me that he didn't hurt you. Because if he did, I'll have to kill him." This he said with absolute certainty, for he knew that if Erickson had harmed one hair on her head, he wouldn't be able to stop the bloodlust that would surely spread through him.

Clearly startled, she opened her eyes and sucked in a deep breath of air, but when her eyes focused on him, the air went out of her and she melted in his arms. "Oh, Conlean. Thank God you came. I thought I'd never see you again. I wanted to die . . ."

"Shh. I'm here. Did he hurt you?"

A tear slipped down her face. "No. He said that to-morrow—"

"Don't say any more," he begged.

"You don't understand," she whispered. "We didn't complete the ceremony. He and I still aren't officially married. We were going to finish it tomorrow."

Pure joy spread though him. "Guess what? I'm kid-napping you again, Jordan. And I want you to be my bride. Will you marry me?"

"I'd marry you this very moment if I could," she murmured, her breath warm against his cheek.

Smiling widely, he wrapped a blanket around her, scooped her up in his arms, and carried her out of the mansion. Rourke and his men followed once they saw that Conlean had left with Jordan, and soon they were all hurtling down the road in a closed carriage.

Conlean focused on Rourke. "How long do you think we have before Erickson frees himself and comes after us?"

"In my experience, we have maybe half an hour," Rourke said. "That'll be enough, though. He doesn't know which way we've gone and will need some time to get help from the Patriarch. In the meanwhile, we'll hide you both at a few different farmhouses until we find a safe place for you to stay permanently."

Jordan snuggled against him. They were huddled be-neath a blanket in one corner of the cart. She was wear-ing a flimsy nightgown, so her warmth easily seeped through her clothes to heat him and give him one of the more painful erections he'd had in her presence. "Who are these men?" she whispered.

Conlean kissed her ear. "They're with the FFA. We can trust them."

"If you trust them, I do too." She smiled shyly at Rourke. "Thank you for helping me. You probably saved my life."

"Most of the women we kidnap say that," he informed her with a pirate's grin. "Now I just have to get you married to the Son of Arador and my work will be done."

"I hope we can marry at our first stop." She clasped Conlean's hand tightly.

Rourke's grin widened. "We've a preacher first on our schedule."

"A preacher?" Conlean didn't know what he meant.

"It's an old way of marrying. The preacher unites you both before God. It may not be legal in the eyes of the Master of Ceremonies, but it's legal in the countryside, where I come from."

"A preacher it is," Conlean said, holding her close.

"We're going to stop in a while and change horses," Rourke informed him. "If you want to take your lady into the inn while we make the change, you're welcome to. There'll be some hot food there for all of us too."

"That sounds wonderful," Jordan said, and Conlean had to agree.

A jovial atmosphere lingered inside the cart all the way to the inn, the men's attitude reminding Conlean of thieves who were gloating over their spoils. Amused, he said little, preferring to rest his chin against Jordan's head and draw her scent deeply into his lungs.

Upon arriving at the inn, they all jumped out of the cart. Rourke and his men walked the cart toward the stable behind the inn while Conlean carried Jordan's blanket-wrapped form into the main dining room.

"Ah, the poor girl," a woman—the innkeeper—exclaimed when she saw Jordan. "Rourke sent me a message saying you'd be coming, so I took it upon myself to get her some clothes. They're upstairs in the first room on the left, along with some hot food. Go on up. Call me if you need anything."

Muttering his thanks, Conlean went to the room indicated by the landlady and laid Jordan down on the bed. Before she could sit up to put on her new clothes, he pressed her back against the mattress and kissed her thoroughly. "You don't know what I've been through these last few hours," he whispered huskily. "I thought I'd lost you. And I was determined to do whatever it took to get you back."

"I know what you've been through, Conlean, because I've been through the same. I couldn't imagine a life with Erickson, couldn't bear even a day without you. Thank God you came for me."

"Oh, Jordan." He kissed her again, the kiss deepening into something hotter, more demanding, until a knock at the door interrupted them.

"Ignore it," Jordan advised, entwining her arms around his neck.

"What if it's Rourke, who's come to tell us that Erickson is in hot pursuit and closing in on this establishment?"

"I guess we have to answer, then."

The knock sounded again.

"I guess we do," Conlean admitted, and turned the knob.

Rourke's tall form filled the doorway.

"We have to go," he informed them.

"Now?" Jordan asked.

"Now. We don't want you to be recaptured. You have five minutes at most. I'll see you downstairs." With that, Rourke left them.

Conlean packed some of the food on the table so they could have it later, while they were on the move. Jordan, for her part, began to get dressed. Once Conlean had finished packing, he stopped to watch her, and he counted his blessings as she drew a silky gown over her head and settled it down along her curves. For the first time in his solitary life, he felt at peace, for he knew that wherever he went, and whatever he did, he would have the one person he loved most in this lonely world at his side.

Epilogue

Jordan stood up from the stool she'd been sitting on and stretched her back. It felt cramped, and a quick glance at the clock confirmed that she'd been studying viral specimens for almost two hours now. At some point during the last several months of work, she and Conlean had managed to acquire an old electron microscope and get it working with the help of a gas-powered generator. This discovery alone had increased the pace of their work threefold, and every day they came closer and closer to understanding the mechanisms of the plague.

A cure still eluded them, however.

She walked over to Baudrons, who lay immobile near the furnace, and drew her hand across the cat's silky white fur, which felt as if it could ignite at any moment, it was so hot. "You're going to catch fire, Baudrons," she murmured. "How about I move you to the chair?" She started to pick up the cat, but when Baudrons mewed softly, she shrugged. "Have it your way. I'll keep a glass of water handy to put you out, if need be."

Baudrons lifted one eyelid, glanced at her without much interest, and then went back to sleep. The cat had come to stay with them a few months earlier, brought by Hawkwood, who'd come on one of his secret visits to supply them with Prima Materia and see how they were progressing. According to Hawkwood, the cat had lost her desire to do anything but mew once Conlean had left, and Hawkwood felt certain she was grieving.

Jordan could understand that feeling exactly, because if she ever lost Conlean, her life would be over as well.

As if thinking about him had conjured him up, Conlean walked into the studio and moved to Jordan's side. He pressed a soft kiss against the top of her head. "How is it going?"

"Not well," she admitted, putting an arm around his waist as he drew her into his arms. "From what I can tell, the virus seems to have mutated from the form it took when I originally worked on it. I can't be certain of the differences between the old and the new form, though, without a specimen of the old. Knowing those differences could help. A lot. At least I would know where to focus first in figuring out a cure."

He kissed her lightly on the lips. "Time for a break?"

"No, it's time to start thinking. What are we going to do?"

He placed a row of kisses along her jawline. "I know what I want to do."

She punched him playfully on the arm. "Be serious. We've reached a plateau as far as the research is concerned and can't go any farther until we make some changes."

"What sort of changes?" another male voice asked.

Rourke walked into their studio. He'd been staying with them for the last few months, keeping them supplied with the materials they needed while they focused on finding a cure for the plague. But Jordan could tell that his self-imposed position of supplier was starting to wear on him. Rourke was the kind of man who needed action. Unlike she and Conlean, he wasn't suited to hanging around a studio, mixing concoctions of Prima Materia and isolating plague viruses from blood.

"We need some of the plague that was in existence in my time," Jordan said, and then went on to share with him all the details that had led her to this conclusion.

Rourke nodded attentively, and when she'd finished, he shrugged. "We need someone to go back to your time, then, Jordan, and get these plague samples for you. The person who goes can also negotiate with this Rinehart character, the one who published your notes, and maybe persuade him not to pursue your research."

"Yes, I agree with both suggestions, but whom do we send?" she asked aloud, not really expecting an answer.

"I'll go," Rourke said.

Both she and Conlean stared at the other man.

Conlean's brow furrowed. "I don't know, Rourke. You're needed here, and a mission like that is very dangerous. You might not come back."

"I think this is important enough for me to risk it," Rourke said, with just enough of an edge to his voice to tell Jordan that the man wouldn't allow anyone to tell him that he couldn't go. "I'll find Conlean's mother when I get there. Marni will help me."

"There's also my sister Alexis," Jordan said. "Although we weren't close, she's my only relative and would have access to everything I owned in my own time. She'd be a good starting point for you, as well."

"Wait just a minute," Conlean said. "You think you know enough about artistry to do this, but your talent is undeveloped. You ran away from the Gallery before you'd retrieved your first bride. Do you realize that you stand a very good chance of losing yourself in between time?"

"Give me a canvas and some brushes," was the only reply Rourke had for them. "I need to start practicing my artistry."

"And you also understand that if you go back to Jordan's time, the portal will close and you won't be coming back?"

Rourke shrugged. "I've done everything I can here. We're not making any progress against the plague. Going back in time is the only option left."

"If the General Assembly discovers that you've gone back in time without their consent, they will send someone after you," Conlean pointed out. "And the Seeker they send won't stop until you're dead."

Rourke shrugged again. "So, what else is new?"

Jordan studied him with both fondness and worry. "Rourke, we should think this over—"

"Tell me what your sister Alexis looks like," he said, cutting her off. "Tell me what she looks like, and I'll start painting her portrait."